CAUGHT

Light flickered, spent cannon shells arced; then Digger's left leg jerked. It somersaulted foot over knee further into the alley, bouncing off one building, crushing a Dumpster. Digger's next step, which would have been with that leg, jammed the severed knee joint into the ground. It punched through the ferrocrete and stuck fast, slinging the 'Mech around to the right before the whole hip assembly shrieked and popped free.

That released Digger and let the 'Mech slam back-first into a building. It crumpled, but so did the thin armor on the engines. The impact crushed the engines, causing a minor explosion that kicked Digger up about a meter, then dropped it flat on its back. Sparks flew in the cockpit and equipment shorted. My head smashed back against the command couch and I sat there, stunned.

Soon enough Constabulary officers appeared on the cockpit canopy and looked down at me. They had guns.

I had nothing.

And the day had started with such promise.

MECHWARRIOR® DARK AGE

GHOST WAR

A BATTLETECH® NOVEL

Michael A. Stackpole

A ROC BOOK

ROC
Published by New American Library, a division of
Penguin Putnam Inc., 375 Hudson Street,
New York, New York 10014, U.S.A.
Penguin Books Ltd, 80 Strand,
London W2CR 0RL, England
Penguin Books Australia Ltd, Ringwood,
Victoria, Australia
Penguin Books Canada Ltd, 10 Alcorn Avenue,
Toronto, Ontario, Canada M4V 3B2
Penguin Books (N.Z.) Ltd, 182–190 Wairau Road,
Auckland 10, New Zealand

Penguin Books Ltd, Registered Offices:
Harmondsworth, Middlesex, England

First published by Roc, an imprint of New American Library,
a division of Penguin Putnam Inc.

First Printing, December 2002
10 9 8 7 6 5 4

Cover design by Ray Lundgren

 REGISTERED TRADEMARK—MARCA REGISTRADA

Printed in the United States of America

PUBLISHER'S NOTE
This is a work of fiction. Names, characters, places, and incidents either are
the product of the author's imagination or are used fictitiously, and any
resemblance to actual persons, living or dead, business establishments,
events, or locales is entirely coincidental.

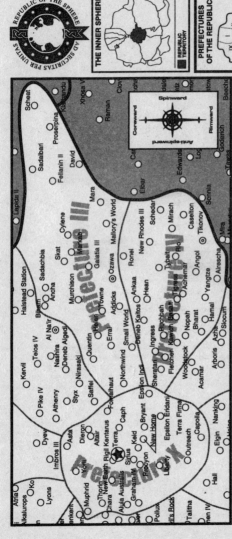

REPUBLIC OF THE SPHERE

THE INNER SPHERE

REPUBLIC TERRITORY

PREFECTURES OF THE REPUBLIC

I II III IV V VI VII VIII IX X

REPUBLIC OF THE SPHERE
PREFECTURES III, IV AND X

Spinward

Coreward

Anti-spinward

Rimward

Maximum Jump approx 30 LY. For nav purposes use 9 PARSECS (29.34 LY)

40 PARSECS OR 130.4 LIGHT YEARS

8 PARSECS

Prefecture III

Prefecture IV

Prefecture X

Scheat
Kusandu
Xhosa V
Clov
Proserpina
Raman
Lapida II
Sadalbari
David
Fellanin II
Mara
Cylene
Skat
Sadachbia
Ancha
Murchison
Helen
Galatia III
Mallory's World
Eibar
Edwards
Halstead Station
Bham
Towne
Ozawa
New Rhodes III
Schedar
Mirach
Ronel
Quentin
Al Na'ir
Denb Algedi
Errai
Small World
Addicks
Ankaa
Hean
Tybalt
Caselton
Rio
Somla
Kervil
Telos IV
Nashira
Northwind
Deneb Kaitos
Ingress
Richbah
Besant
Tigress
Angol
Achernal
Mira
Pike IV
Atheny
Saffel
Styx
Nirasaki
Fomalhaut
Sheratan
Fletcher
Kawich
Nopah
Bharat
Hamal
Yangtze
Airescha
Slocum
Tikonov
Imbros III
Dyev
Asta
Diergn
Altair
Bryant
Caph
Epsilon Indi
Epsilon Eridani
Woodstock
Acamar
Azha
Arboris
New Home
Terra
Rigel Kentarus
Keid
New Earth
Sirius
Procyon
Terra Firma
Capolla
Elgin
Nanking
Afra
Nkalurops
Lyons
Ko
Muphrid
Thorin
Chara
Graham IV
Alula Australis
Pollux
Lipton
Outreach
Hall
Talitha
Beecho
Godcritch
Tawas

Wise men think twice before they act once.
                                        —Ancient Terran proverb

Leary's Eyrie
Joppa, Helen
Prefecture III, Republic of the Sphere
13 November 3132

I once heard someone complain that the two most abundant things in the universe were hydrogen and stupidity, but she declined to say which led the way. I figure that in the random distribution of things throughout the universe, hydrogen probably has the edge, but in Leary's Eyrie stupidity was being stockpiled at an alarming rate. This wasn't unusual or even rare, but the pressure of it seemed to dull even smart folks and fray nerves.

I'd come to the Eyrie hoping for a Tri-Vid beer ad. Not for a specific advert, mind you, but the sort of situation they depict: warm night, hot woman, cold beer, sweat—on the beer bottle and otherwise. I wanted the full-on fantasy that had inspired generations of men to swill the liquid that gave them the bellies they sucked in when such a woman appeared in their midst. I knew it was a fantasy, but that was all we had out here in the hinterland of Helen.

Of course, I wasn't looking much like a fantasy. Or an ad, unless it was one of those late-night ads for a product that is guaranteed to make you feel younger, look younger and turbo-charge the parts you'd need working if the beer-ad fantasy came through. The crew and I had just come off the line after eighteen hours straight, and I'd not been near a bed for about double that time and a razor triple it. I did have a clean shirt on, but the jeans and work boots could have starred in their own ads for miracle cleaning products.

Or public service spots about toxic waste and hazmat dumping.

We'd been up in the forest, harvesting old growth, and having to pour on the diesel to clear a swath before noon. The local courts had issued a restraining order pending the review of some endangered species protection action filed by the People and Divergent Species Union. PADSU was the political arm of the militant Gaia Guerrilla Front, which viewed the use of any tool against the earth or anything on it as an assault that needed avenging. While they preached a sort of Luddite, return-to-nature-and-embrace-peace philosophy, they were pretty good at wielding high explosives and other weapons in attacking the forestry and mining industries on Helen.

Rusty, over by the pool table, sucked beer from a bottle. "What do you mean you don't believe PADSU and the GGF are behind the collapse of the communications grid? Good Lord, Pep, it's obvious. They hate technology, and that was huge technology. It goes down, they crawl out of the woodwork and begin really going to town on us. One and one is two."

Pep, who earned her nickname by being small and quick, pointed her pool cue at him as if it were a rapier. "Problem is, you ain't got one to add to one. The grid goes down, The Republic gets divided into its various worlds. No news flows, so The Republic can't react. Folks get fearful, opportunists take over and groups like the GGF pop up. PADSU's been around forever, always protesting and things, but peacefully. Now that the Knights of The Republic can't figure out where to tromp with big BattleMech feet, the GGF forms up and starts getting nasty."

"Not like the old days. They'd never have done that in the old days." Keira-san glanced over from the table where he sat watching a Tri-Vid program. It was a rerun of some 'Mech battle on Solaris. Looked like turn-of-the-century stuff to me, with some kid who was supposed to be the next Kai Allard-Liao—which every fighter there wanted to be, of course, and every fighter there got billed as until the next Kai-wannabe flamed his butt. And in the nine years since Kai Allard-Liao died fighting for The Republic in the Capellan Confederation, every titleholder dedicated his title to Kai's memory—though not one of them got out into the real universe and put his butt on the line fighting for something other than a market share of audience.

Pep brought her cue around in a slash that passed bare centimeters over Keira-san's brush-cut scalp. "What do you know of the old days? Ain't a one of us here wasn't born in The Republic era. Devlin Stone helped put down the Word of Blake attacks, then disarmed folks and established peace. In the old days, as you put it, the local lordlings would have been out in their own personal BattleMechs, shooting up the peasants, then claiming they were putting down a rebellion. Check any history of the time before and after Stone, and you'll see how good The Republic Peace has been for everyone. And will continue to be once Com-Star gets planets talking to each other again."

Keira-san slumped down in his chair and focused his attention on a fight he'd seen dozens of times before. The biggest tragedy of his life had been the lack of new Solaris fights since the grid's collapse. The finer points of how a lack of communication between planets was creating pressures that were allowing society to melt down were lost on him.

That wasn't really his fault, though, since Keira-san had been born on Helen and raised here as a part of a minority community from the Combine. He'd never played well with others, whereas elsewhere on Helen, old and new communities had really banded together under the leadership of The Republic. All the old tensions that used to pit the successor states one against the other had vanished. Everyone *was* living happily ever after.

The Republic had used a carrot-and-stick approach to make that union work. People who worked to bring divergent communities together were rewarded with land grants and community investments. People who worked against that sort of thing were punished, either through neglect or being forcibly relocated to other worlds within The Republic, and never got the incentives that made others happy to move. Those who liked The Republic's way of doing things found it to be "progressive" and "inspiring," whereas the victims found it to be "repressive" and "conspiratorial." Regardless, it worked.

Then two things happened. Nearly three years ago Devlin Stone stepped down as Exarch of The Republic. This shook the confidence of the people who had grown up equating peace and prosperity with his rule. While Damien Redburn, his hand-picked successor as Exarch, had been doing a good job and confidence had begun to rise, the collapse of the Hyperpulse Generator grid really knifed The Republic in the gut.

"I'm telling you, it was PADSU who did it!" Rusty punctuated his remark by plunking his empty bottle on the bar. "They didn't want anyone seeing what was going on here, so no one could react to it. It makes perfect sense."

Hector sent the nine ball crashing into the corner pocket. "Game, Pep, you owe me twenty Rep credits."

"Double or nothing."

Hector gave her a broad smile. "Going for forty stones? You're on. Brave girl."

Boris, who in physical bulk makes up for what he lacks in wit, raised a hand large enough to palm a rack of balls. "I had next game."

"You have next set. Rack 'em, Pep." Hector glanced at Rusty. "The filings in your lubricant there, Rusty, is that PADSU is local. You've heard the rumors coming in from JumpShip traffic. The grid is down everywhere."

Rusty sniffed. "Not *everywhere*."

"Yeah, okay, so your mama did send you birthday greetings, but the last leg was made on a JumpShip coming in from Towne." Hector shook his head, then looked up at me with dark brown eyes. "Sam, explain it to him, will you?"

"Uh huh, like I understand it." I sipped more beer, and abruptly decided that talking was better than swilling that crap. "Okay, here's the deal the way I heard it. Someone coordinated a lot of strikes on a lot of worlds, taking out the HPGs. No one talks to anyone. No one knows who is doing what to whom, or who did the attack. It wasn't PADSU's doing, but Rusty could be half right."

"I could?" He sat up straighter. "Yeah, see there. You tell 'em, Sam."

Pep concentrated on racking the balls so she wouldn't bust out laughing. I gnawed the inside of a cheek so I'd not join her. "Well, it could be, Rusty, that the GGF is part of whoever took the grid down. They weren't around before the grid went down. They might have arrived, made a deal with PADSU to help them out, creating discord here so something else could happen."

"Nothing is going to happen now, though, Donelly." The bartender, Max Leary, replaced Rusty's beer with another sweaty bottle. "News came up from Overton. The DropShip that burned in last night had a Republic Knight on it. Looks like the piece will be here keeping the peace."

"Piece?" I shot the bald man a hooded glance. I knew he'd used the term *piece* to rile Pep, since she'd rejected more advances from him than I had fingers and toes to count—and that was just this afternoon. Of course, with her being so small and him being so, well, *round*, they would never hook up. Save for the lack of gun turrets and his wearing lumberjack castoff clothing, Leary could have been mistaken for a Union-class DropShip.

Pep ignored Leary, so the bartender growled at me. "Yeah, some beauty-queen Knight was the main cargo."

"You catch a name?"

"Why, you looking to ask her on a date or something?"

I nodded solemnly. "That's right. I am in powerful need of female companionship."

I'd said that with a smile and braced myself for the barbs that would be flying in my direction, but then a funny thing happened. Actually, it was a coincidental thing, which really led to an eruption of stupidity.

In through the door came two women. Gorgeous women, beer-ad gorgeous they were, and one was even clad in the sort of baby-doll T-shirt and short shorts that's the style in beer ads. Young enough to look innocent, old enough to know how to use that look of innocence, with blond hair and a dazzling smile, she paused inside the door and looked at all of us.

She had luscious azure eyes.

By the way, my using the word *azure*, that's how you know this is literature. If it wasn't, I'd have just said blue. Sapphire could have worked, too, or lapis lazuli, but she had that sort of softness that doesn't make you think of minerals.

But I digress, which is another literary thing to do, just in case you were keeping score.

Her companion seemed a bit older and harder, so I could use minerals to describe her, except she had nothing rocky about her. I could have called her hair rusty red, but that would be confusing, and her eyes weren't dark enough for emeralds, and there are so many shades of jade that just saying jade wouldn't really tell you what color they were. Nice green eyes, though, very much alive and wary, taking us all in for more reasons than her companion did. She moved fluidly, stepping from behind her friend quickly, freeing her to act if she needed to. Her red hair had been gathered back into a braid and I noticed it had been tucked down into the collar of her shirt.

This is where the whole explosion of stupidity thing began to boil over. They were both PADSU—if the coeds-on-a-hike attire hadn't told us that, the little info-disks the blonde held in her left hand did. And while the blonde might be here to enlighten us, Red was clearly prepared to fight, and starting a fight with lumberjacks is just dumb. You might beat them up, but at least one of them will hunt you down and his ForestryMech will saw your house into a duplex.

Leary knew what was coming. He started to put the good liquor under the bar. Both bottles.

I turned on my stool and slid from it. "Excuse me, Miss."

The blonde, who had been halfway to Rusty, reading him rightly as the most susceptible to PADSU's message, stopped and gave me the sort of smile that would have had me investing in a brewery a keg at a time were a brand name plastered over her chest. "Do you want to help us save the Mottled Lemur?"

"Well, not exactly."

"Oh, you should." She spoke in one of those little-girl pouty voices and, just for a moment, I felt my resolve weakening. "There are only fifteen thousand mating pairs left on Helen. Their natural habitat has been greatly reduced through logging and mining operations that have despoiled hectare upon hectare of pristine nature. Hundreds of thousands of divergent species of plants and animals have perished."

I held a hand up. "And bugs. People always forget the bugs."

The blonde blinked and hesitated for a moment. "Yes, and insects, too."

"Arachnids." Pep smiled and chalked her cue. "And bacteria. No one ever remembers them."

I nodded. "I seriously lament the death of slime molds. No one can remember if they are plants or animals, so I think they should be mourned twice."

Blondie stared at me, her face slackening. Her lower lip began to sneak out in a pout and her shoulders sagged just a little. In a heartbeat I knew the lower lip was going to quiver and tears would gather in those azure eyes. "This is very serious. We're trying to save lives."

"I know, darlin', so am I. I'm trying to save yours." I reached out and took hold of her left arm with my right hand. "We're not the audience you're looking for."

"Get your hand off her."

I glanced past Blondie at Red. "You don't want to be making an idle threat in here."

Red had three choices. She could talk and just delay making a choice between the other two. She could back down and they would leave. Or, like every other woman who dyed her hair Natasha Kerensky-red and thought she was tough, she could act.

She picked number three, which did have the desired effect of making me take my hand off Blondie's arm. As Red took a step forward, planted her left foot and snapped her right leg around in a kick—rather quickly, too, I'll give her that—I, too, stepped forward. I caught her thigh in my ribs and locked my left arm down on it. I sank my fingers stiffly into her hamstring, which added a gasp to her snarl of frustration.

Then I crashed my right fist down into her face. Twice. I think it was the second punch that broke her nose. I *know* it was the first that broke her jaw. Then I pitched her off into a table, from which she rebounded heavily and hit the floor hard but limp.

I turned to look at Blondie. Color had drained from her face, or had been washed from it with the tears. "Oh, my God."

"Rusty, help this young lady get her friend into their hovercar and down to the trauma center in Kokushima."

Rusty drained his beer, then stood, straightened his plaid flannel shirt and smiled. His smile wasn't as dazzling as Blondie's, but she had more and whiter teeth than he did. Still, she reciprocated and he helped her drag a moaning Red from the bar.

One would think, of course, Leary's Eyrie had been home to enough stupidity for one night, but this would be because one was not taking into consideration Boris. Boris was frustrated because he was just sitting around waiting, which runs contrary to his self-image as a man of action. His job driving a ConstructionMech adapted to clearing underbrush runs contrary there, too, but Boris lives in his own little world, which, unfortunately, allows him to emerge into mine.

"You didn't ought to have did that, Sam."

"I shouldn't have did, er, done, what, Boris?"

Boris carefully set his cue down and waded across the bar floor toward me. His shadow fell over me and I actually felt a chill. Leary might have been a DropShip, but Boris was a planet. "You hit a woman."

"And?"

"That wasn't very nice."

"Uh huh. You missed that she tried to kick me, right?"

Boris shook his head, which, in a way, amazed me. He looked so like a granite statue, with strong features and black hair that never seemed to shift out of place, that half the time I didn't think he could move. Fact was, that hair came out of his neurohelmet that way, which just is not natural.

"I saw that, but that was no excuse. You hit her *twice*."

I nodded and sighed. "And how would you have handled it?"

Boris moved far faster than I'd ever expected him to, which meant he was really steaming. He grabbed me by the shoulders and spun me around, then dropped his arms around me in a bear hug. He squeezed tight and lifted me from the ground.

I struggled for a second, then shrieked and went limp. A quick jolt ran through him, then his grip slackened for a moment. He leaned forward to put me on my feet again, but my knees buckled, so he grabbed me to hold me upright.

I pushed off the ground with my feet and smashed the back of my head into his face. Something snapped and a warm fluid gush ran down through my scalp. Boris' hands left my body to go to his face, which is why, when I snapped my right heel up between his legs and into his loose flesh, there was nothing to protect his beer-buying brains. His previous howl of pain rose into the inaudible range, then he toppled back with the slow grace of the tall trees we cut, and shook the ground about as hard when he landed.

Hector, our foreman, looked over at me and shook his head. "I wish you hadn't done that, Sam."

"He'll be fine by morning, Hector. You won't lose him for work."

"I don't care about that." Hector jerked his head toward Pep. "He had next game. His paycheck was gonna be mine."

"Glad to know you have our best interests at heart, Hector."

"He does, Sam, unlike you." Keira-san shifted in his chair and gave me a venomous glance. "You just messed up someone from PADSU. The GGF is working the area. You just issued them an open invite to make our lives miserable."

"I hadn't thought of that, Keira-san." I smiled. "Oh, well, working beats unemployment. Leary, another beer, for tomorrow I may die."

2

*When you cannot clothe yourself in a lion's skin,
put on that of the fox.*

—Spanish proverb

ARU Lot 47-6
Joppa, Helen
Prefecture III, Republic of the Sphere
14 November 3132

I didn't wake up dead, which was all to the good, nor did I feel that bad. I had a couple of swollen knuckles on my right hand, and a bump on the back of my head, but I wasn't in jail and didn't need stitches, so I figured I was way ahead of other mornings. I crawled out of my rack and pulled myself into crusty jeans and my work boots, then stumbled to the head to divest myself of my beer inventory and, to use the literary term, attend to my other ablutions.

I found a mug, knocked dirt out of it, and poured myself a cup of something hot, black and strong. Since I found no metal parts I decided I'd gotten coffee this time, not solvent, though it would have been easy to be wrong. Still, it burned down into my belly and opened my eyes. Being as how it was still before dawn, that was only a marginal benefit.

When we'd gotten back from Leary's, Hector had gotten a notice that said the judge had given us a twenty-four-hour extension before the restraining order went into effect. I'm sure PADSU would say he'd been bought off, but I doubted it. The lumber company did everything on the cheap, and if he couldn't be bought off for a metric ton of sawdust mulch, they weren't going to pay. Closer to the mark was the fact that the Mottled Lemur wasn't actually native to Helen and, for centuries, had been the object of summer festivals devoted to killing the little things before they could descend like locusts on a farmer's fields. And they were stupid, too—cleaning their mortal remains out of the guts of an AgroMech after harvest is seriously bothersome, I've been assured.

So we thought of the lemurs as varmints and PADSU thought of them as "cute." Cute becomes something of a trump card, but I guess the judge wasn't of a mind to be trumped, giving us another day to decorate the forest with sawdust. Not the greatest of jobs, but it had me driving a 'Mech, so I was not of a mind to complain.

I wandered out to the hangar and mounted the ladder to the cockpit of the ForestryMech I'd been assigned. It still had that ugly, factory shade of yellow paint on it, but had been scraped down to bare metal in a number of places. Aside from Alpine Resources Unlimited decals on it, the only decoration was a finely scripted name, "Maria," above the cockpit. The story goes that one of the other pilots named it after his wife. That sounds romantic until you learn that it was the shrieking of the chainsaw that most reminded him of her.

I secured the hatch behind me and settled into the command couch. My coffee mug went into the holder beside the right joystick, freeing my hands to pull on and snap closed the cooling vest. It was bulkier than others I've worn—"Cost cutting begins with YOU," being one of ARU's more endearing motivational mottoes—but it did the job when I plugged it in. It had a ballistic cloth cover that wouldn't stop a bullet, but might soak off a few splinters.

Reaching up and back, I pulled down the neurohelmet and settled it on my head. It, too, was bulky and heavy, but the extra padding in the cooling vest helped there. I made sure the brainwave pickups were seated in the right places and snug, since the last thing I wanted was having the machine lose track of my sense of balance when things got rough.

Punching a few buttons, I brought the secondary systems on-line, then waited to initiate the engine start. The computer flashed me a check code, which I replied to, then a mechanical voice asked for my personal activation code. I always opt for a voiceprint check as opposed to something keyed in, so I said, "There once was a fair lady Knight, whose smile was so very tight . . ."

I won't continue because I suppose you've heard it before. So had the computer, so the huge engines began their popping, gasping and smoky journey to life. Maria shook like a house on a fault line, but no coffee sloshed from my mug. Across the command console all the systems came live and were green.

Up against a real BattleMech, a ForestryMech like Maria wouldn't seem to be much of a threat. The left arm ends in a grabbing claw, which could crush light armor or snap off some small weapons. The chainsaw that is the right hand can do some serious grinding, and the pruning laser mounted above it might melt some ferro-ceramics, but it was a jury-rigged laser rifle and so would probably only bubble paint. I'm not saying Maria could put a BattleMech down, but anything that came to tangle with her would have scars to show it had been in a fight.

And if you don't believe me, there are plenty of tree stumps in the forest that would say otherwise.

I stepped on up and out, guiding Maria past Black Betty, the ConstructionMech Boris drove. I keyed my radio and greeted him, but it looked like he wasn't talking to me. Or, it could have been that his broken nose was making him talk funny enough he couldn't get his 'Mech started. I laughed at that idea, then began the trudge up to the worksite.

Pep raced by in her hovercar, hauling a butt-cart full of trimmers. They are the folks who swarm over the trees we fell, trimming off branches and affixing the chains we use to lift the logs into another cart for Pep to drag back to the loading station. They're actually the ones who are in the most danger from GGF attacks. Hitting an iron spike driven into the trunk of a tree won't even nick Maria's chainsaw, but it will destroy one of the handhelds these folks use. That leaves a lot of chain shrapnel flying about which could, as moms everywhere warn, poke an eye out.

The base of our work area was about three kilometers up the mountain, though taking the road we'd carved out made the trip a bit longer than that, what with all the switchbacks and everything. The road was actually looking pretty beaten up, with 'Mech tracks frozen in mud like fossilized dinosaur footprints. The piled mud squished down pretty easily under Maria's heavy tread, but it was as difficult for her to make headway as it would have been for me to go mucking about through a swamp. Maria was using my sense of balance to control the gyros and keep her upright, and I was fighting the controls with every step, sloshing coffee all the way.

I finally reached the clearing and saw Hector over at the trailer he used for his command post. I keyed the radio. "The road sucks, Hector. If Rusty told you he graded it, he's lying something serious."

"Good morning to you, too, Sam." Hector's tone was a bit testy, but I could see a smile on his face, so I just listened. "Rusty's driving Black Betty today. Boris is down in Kokushima getting his nose set."

"He should have them make it smaller. That way the next time he sneezes his brain won't fall out."

"What brain?"

"Good point. So, where is it you want me waging war on trees this fine morning?"

He punched a couple of buttons on a datapad and beamed the coordinates to me. "Gonna have you plunge in, cut a swath due west, then down to the south, isolating a patch for us to clean up later."

"Great. Trailblazing. Thanks."

He shrugged. "Orders come from above my pay grade."

"What did our masters say about the chances of GGF taking out their own restraining order?"

"Same as always: no damage to personnel or equipment." Hector scratched at his cheek. "You thinking on

what Keira-san said last night about GGF doing some pay-
back for you decking that girl?"

"Maybe. Keira-san isn't right often, but when he is . . ."
I shrugged. Maria didn't. I raised the chainsaw up and then
brought it down again. "Those of us about to die salute
you."

"Go and die if you want to, Sam, just don't dent the
metal."

"You're all heart, Hector."

"You know better than that: I'm management."

I laughed and started Maria trudging off to the place
where we were supposed to start working. As the sun came
up I was figuring it was going to be a pretty uneventful
day. Despite PADSU's rhetoric, the forest we were cutting
in had been harvested fifty years earlier, so this wasn't old-
growth forest in any true sense. ARU might well have been
cheap in terms of the equipment they bought, but Pep spent
as much time hauling reseeders and seedlings up the mountain as she did dragging logs back down, and nary a splinter
went unused. Unlike most corporations, ARU did better
than abide by The Republic's rather stringent land-use
regulations.

I got to where I was meant to be and sized up the job.
It was pretty much notch and cut. When looking at a ForestryMech a lot of folks think we hold on to the tree with
the grabber and cut it, sort of the way one might trim a
sunflower. The problem is that the trees can mass more
than my 'Mech, and even when that's not the case, a falling
tree will rip the claw right off. The claw's useful for lifting
and shifting or leverage, but not much more than that.

The chainsaw does make pretty quick work of harvesting
trees, however. I notched on the east side, then cut from
the west, which dropped the trees to the east as pretty as
you please. Kind of mindless work, but you get into a
rhythm and pretty soon you've cut a swath twenty-five meters wide and a hundred meters deep, with a river of trees
pointing back the way you came.

Pretty soon, in this case, meant nine in the morning. My
stomach, having once more survived ARU coffee, was rum-
bling. I turned the 'Mech back around toward the base
camp and radioed in. "Hector, you sending me out some

trimmers, or do I have to come back there and get my own breakfast?"

"Sam, just hang there. The mud is slowing everything down. Rusty couldn't get Betty rolling, so he's grading the road now. Pep's stuck behind him. Be about an hour."

I frowned on behalf of my stomach, which couldn't. "Geez, Hector, I thought our mid-morning repasts truly meant something to you."

"You only love me for the sweet rolls. I'll have Pep bring you extra."

"Deal. I'm so easy." I turned Maria back around to continue my cutting, and that's when I caught the glimpse of the guy. He had just flitted behind a tree and had been coming at my six. Someone had been reading old Gray Death Legion adventures, because he was hauling one huge old satchel charge and I was pretty sure he'd planned to sneak up on me and tag Maria's heel as I trudged off to breakfast.

I pointed the chainsaw toward the tree he'd used for shelter, then flicked on the external sound gear. Before I could say anything to him, voices boomed, this time coming from the north. Men in black combat fatigues, carrying submachine guns and looking very lethal, moved forward toward my quarry.

"Halt! This is Commander Reis of the Overton Constabulary's Civil Defense Reaction Force! Don't make us do something we don't want to do."

I really do require another digression here. Commander Reis thinks he's the next coming of Morgan Hasek-Davion and might be, save that he's too short, too fat, too arrogant, too ignorant and, despite his girth, utterly gutless. The people in his CDRF were dedicated, but were trained on a shoestring budget while being given all sorts of gadgets and other stuff they never really learned how to use. The CDRF were all heart and brave, but in combat that means you don't really know when you are outgunned and need to retreat.

The situation was pretty simple. The GGF had come to blow up a 'Mech. They knew that the 'Mech might not be crippled by their attack and that the pilot, being me, might take it poorly that I had been attacked. For that reason they'd brought their commando troops up on a couple of hovertrucks that were mounted with heavy machine guns. Reis' warning alerted the gunners. Had he said nothing, his people might have been able to take the bomber quietly.

The GGF gunners opened up. I could only see little flickers of light deeper in the woods, then watched bullets track up and through one CDRF trooper. She spun down into rusty pine needles that stuck to her bloody uniform. The other CDRF folks dove to dirt, but one more got tagged before the whole of the squad took cover in a bowl-shaped depression.

The machine guns let up and the CDRF thought that was their chance to counterattack. They didn't realize why the gunners had stopped shooting, but I did. As the bomber came out from behind the tree to loft his satchel charge into their haven, I crisped him with the laser. The charge still flew, but not very far. When it hit the ground it exploded, killing the first of the CDRF guys who had come up over the berm, and stunning the rest of them.

I charged Maria forward and the gunners started shooting at me. Unless they were going to keep a constant stream up against the cockpit, I didn't really think they could stop me. I knew they'd figure that out after a moment's reflection, and they'd also realize that I couldn't get to them without a lot of time-consuming cutting.

They weren't wrong, but neither were they completely right. I got to the tree that had sheltered their smoking friend, notched and dropped it, but this time sent it crashing west.

There's a reason logging is a dangerous operation. Trees are big and heavy, and even though a branch seems pretty light, when it's falling fast and connected to a tree, getting hit with it is like being swatted by a broom driven by a hurricane. In addition, when trees are dropped hastily, they tend to collide with other trees in a chain reaction that can make a terrible tangle of things. Cracking trees, splinters flying everywhere, needles, dust, dirt; it can be an unholy mess.

One you'd not want to be caught in, especially if your only shelter is a hovertruck. The tree I chopped caromed into another one and another, dropping even more heavy lumber. One tree smashed a hovertruck flat. The other hovertruck backed out of a lot of branches and jolted away without even checking on survivors.

The whole thing took a minute, maybe two, and would have been over save for one little detail. When his people had been pinned down, Reis ordered his command vehicle into the fray. His driver was coming on hard, so when a tree dropped across his path, he juiced the hover-louvers to get maximum lift. That turned out to be about two centimeters short, so the hovercar skipped off the log like a rock on a lake, then drilled the rootball of another tumbled giant. Reis catapulted from the back seat and somersaulted unceremoniously into a lot of tigerberry bushes—which, contrary to common opinion, are not named for the striped berries, but for the two-inch thorns on the branches.

Hector's voice boomed in my ears. "Sam, you okay? Heard an explosion. What's going on?"

I pinched my right thigh. It hurt. "I thought it was a nightmare, Hector, but I don't seem to be waking up. Tell Rusty to hurry on grading the road and send Pep back for the evac cart. And forget the sweet rolls. I'm not hungry anymore."

$$\equiv \quad 3 \quad \equiv$$

Don't make yourself a mouse, or the cat will eat you.

—Federated Suns proverb

ARU Lot 47-6
Joppa, Helen
Prefecture III, Republic of the Sphere
14 November 3132

I set about, as quickly as I could, trying to clear away as much brush and material as possible so rescue teams could get to the CDRF folks and the GGF terrorists. Off the latter they'd only be getting DNA samples, since the tree mushed the hovertruck into half-pipe and made the occupants rather oozy. The guy with the satchel charge had been reduced to vapor and scattered limbs.

Reis picked his way out of the bushes and pretty much looked as if he'd been through a wood-chipper. He was livid, of course, and started yelling at me about destroying evidence. I just flicked the external pick-ups off and kept clearing stuff so that when Pep got there with some med-techs, they were able to pull the wounded out.

Alas, they didn't take Reis with them. When Hector got

there, Reis gave him two ears-full, and was looking for a bucket for when that ran out. Hector listened and calmed him—or so I guessed from the body language—but glared at me hot enough to melt armor. I was getting the impression it would be a long time before I ever got sweet rolls again.

It was mid-afternoon before I got called off the line. Hector had me park Maria at the command center and Pep gave me a ride down to our housing. She gave me a sidelong glance with those blue eyes. "You are in serious trouble, Sam. Reis says you're one of them and that you dropped trees to stop his pursuit."

"You think that's true, Pep?" I let my anger flow full force into my voice.

"Hey, Sam, I'm a friend of yours, remember?"

"Then mind your own damned business."

She gave me a harder look. "You telling me it's true?"

"Leave it."

Pep stopped the hovercar and punched my shoulder. "You know, I used to think you were different. I thought this tough-guy act was just that, an act. I know it is. You didn't need to do anything there, but you did, and now you won't tell me about it? What's going on?"

My nostrils flared. "What's going on is that you don't know me, Pep. I've been here, what, ten weeks? Sure, we've palled around, had some good times, but what you're seeing as an act isn't. I really just want to be left alone, and I thought I had that here, and now this. It's a disaster."

She hesitated. "What's going on, Sam? You can tell me. Are you in trouble with the law and think Reis will find out or something?"

"Just leave it at 'or something,' okay?" I softened my voice a bit. "What I did last night got this going and people got hurt. Just walk away."

Pep nodded and, hurt, started the hovercar again. We rode the rest of the way down the mountain in silence. She dropped me off then headed back up. By the time I got to my billet I was told I had to report to the Constabulary headquarters in Overton as soon as I took a shower and cleaned up.

I lingered in the shower. I washed off a lot of grime and wished the water could wash away the image I had of that CDRF trooper rolling through the pine needles. I knew she was dead the second she started to spin. The medtechs confirmed it, but when an antivehicle weapon is used on a human, the human usually comes up worse for the experience.

Eventually the hot water ran out, so I dried off, found clean jeans, and would have used the shirt from the night before, but Boris had gone and bled on it. I had another clean shirt, one I saved for special occasions, and I didn't want to use it, but I really didn't have any choice. I looked pretty good in it, but decided not to shave just so Reis wouldn't think I was going to show him respect.

In retrospect, not looking my best was a mistake. By the time I'd finished with my shower, Reis had dispatched a Constabulary vehicle to fetch me. Riding in the back, I looked like a felon nabbed for something horrible. I could see it in the eyes of others at the yard and even in Pep's eyes. That hurt, but there was little I could do.

The driver didn't talk, which was fine with me. In a little over an hour we arrived in Overton, which is the largest city in the district—known as the "Gem of the South" in all those adverts trying to get people to come visit the sort of pristine forests I was cutting down. Overton isn't built up too much—I don't know what name it had when it started as a Combine town—and aside from the stone-and-steel central corridor, most of the town is low and built in harmony with the hills and valleys that make up the city.

The Constabulary headquarters is a big blocky building convenient to the spaceport. I was led up the steps and immediately taken in a lift to the fourth floor. The driver passed me off to someone else who, apparently, was deaf. She never heard my request for water. She took me to an interrogation room and sat me down. For just a second or two she considered restraining me but thought better of it.

As interrogation rooms went, this one was pretty good. It had a strong central light that allowed the walls to remain in shadow. Over on the far wall they had a one-way mirror, but I just sat in the hard metal chair in the center of the room. I could have gone over to the mirror and inspected myself, but that would make them think I was bone stupid. *That* assumption on their parts might be amusing, but would make the whole ordeal that much more unpleasant.

The door banged open behind me, and Reis strode in as if he were Devlin Stone himself. He carried a lot of weight that made his jodhpurs and two-tone shirt look even more ridiculous than the thorn-torn fatigues I'd last seen hanging in tatters from his body. I could see the shape of countless bandages beneath the clothes, but he bore two scratches bravely on his face. I'm fairly certain he would dismiss them as nothing in some media conference, and the local media would laud his bravery.

He gave me about as steely a stare as his piggy eyes could manage. "You clearly thought you could fool me, didn't you? Make it look like you were helping, but you let them get away. You stopped my troops from catching your confederates."

I frowned. "That's the way it's going to go in your memoirs?"

"Yes, Sam Donelly, *if that is your real name*." He loaded that last with a lot of gravity, as if the only way I'd save myself was to confess, since clearly he already knew everything. "You're not going to get away with this."

"Get away with what?" I snarled at him, sitting forward in my chair rather abruptly. "I was out there, someone was going to bomb my 'Mech, and you walk and talk your people into an ambush. I did what I could to stop your people from getting hurt and, in the process, killed more terrorists than your whole operation did."

Reis snorted and began to pace back and forth before the mirror, so I knew he was doing it for an audience. "We're checking everything, Donelly, *everything*. We know already that you had congress with PADSU members last night."

"I decked one."

"And don't think your history of violence has gone unnoticed. You also attacked a coworker last night and he required hospitalization." He clasped his hands at the small of his back—it was a bit of a struggle, but he did it. "You are of bad character, Donelly, and we don't tolerate people like you in this district."

"Yeah, that's why we like it here. No competition." I spitted him with a harsh stare of my own. "You know what I don't like about you? You're incompetent, don't want to believe it, and just charismatic enough to make good men and women believe what you say about yourself. You got your people killed out there, and you're going to pin it on me."

"Oh, so that's what this was about then, is it?" Reis began to chuckle, sending a wobble from navel to jowls and back. "This is a GGF conspiracy to discredit me and get me removed. Well, it won't work, mister, not a bit of it!"

His face had gotten purple as he worked himself up, and spittle flecked white at the corners of his mouth. His right hand had appeared so he could jab a finger at me. I was fairly well convinced the next jab would be with a fistful of fingers and though I had made fun of him, I had no doubt that a clout from him would rattle my teeth something fierce.

Which is when *she* appeared.

I heard the door open and Reis' face went from fury to beneficence in a nanosecond. He straightened up and smiled. "My lady, I thought . . ."

She spoke before I could see her, since Commander Bloat was blocking the mirror, but that voice came cool and soothing in contrast to his rasping rage. "Your technique is illuminative, Commander, and I merely thought I might reciprocate by demonstrating some of the interrogation techniques we use on Terra."

Yes, the word *Terra* did send ice water trickling through my guts. The only folks who come from Terra to a backwater like Helen are Republic folks, which meant this was The Republic Knight Leary had been talking about. Her intervention here meant things were serious—as in well above Reis' pay grade.

She walked past me on the left and casually dropped a bottle of cold water into my lap. I'd not expected that and had to scramble to catch it before it hit the floor. I did, then pressed it to the back of my neck as I looked up at her. It was a long way to look, but well worth the effort.

You've already gotten she was tall, and you can add slender to that. Great shoulders, too, tapering down into a narrow waist, a gentle flare of hips and seriously long legs that weren't hurt by her wearing knee-high riding boots. She wore them much better than Reis. The rest of her outfit, from black leather skirt to dark blue blouse and black blazer, looked sharp enough to distance her light-years from the reality that was Helen.

She had a creamy complexion, which combined with her straight black hair and emerald eyes to make one believe in the supernatural. She moved easily, almost casually, but I could read purpose in her steps. The way she'd dropped the bottle had been simple, but I knew it was a test.

I smiled. "I wanted water. How'd you know?"

She smiled and parts of me started to melt. "I know your type, Mr. Donelly."

"You can call me Sam."

"Well, Mr. Donelly, I am Janella Lakewood."

Reis cut her off. "That's *Lady* Janella Lakewood. She's a Republic Knight."

"Really?" I gave him a wry smile. "There once was a fair Lady Knight . . ."

The Constabulary commander's cuff snapped my head around. "How dare you speak to her like that?"

Lakewood held a hand up. "Commander, please. Mr. Donelly never would have finished that limerick, would you, Mr. Donelly?"

"Whose smile was so very tight . . ."

The second cuff hit my cheek hard enough that I cut the inside of my mouth and was bleeding. I spat on the floor. "You want to hear more? I've worked up some variations."

Lakewood raised her chin and those green eyes bored right through me. "Perhaps I misjudged you, Mr. Donelly."

"You don't know my type after all, then?"

"Oh, I know it, and know it very well. Yours is the type that comes to a bad ending, very bad." She let her voice get all husky and, if not for the tone, I could have listened to her for hours. "You're on the brink of making a decision, Mr. Donelly. On one hand you can help us here and we will help you. On the other, you will make enemies and we will be forced to destroy you."

Reis slammed a fist into his meaty hand to emphasize that point.

I probed my cheek with my tongue. "Reis has got it all wrong. I have nothing to do with the GGF or PADSU."

She shook her head. "Last night PADSU confederates of yours entered a bar where they intended to pass you information in the form of an info-disk, but you contrived an altercation to get them out of there."

"That's *his* story, but that's not the truth."

"Then why don't you give me a truth that makes sense?"

I blinked at her. " 'Makes sense?' You mean you buy Reis' story that I was helping the GGF up there on the mountain?"

"It reads well, Mr. Donelly. You're in league with them. You incapacitate another of your coworkers so jobs shift around guaranteeing you'll be alone. GGF comes and blows up your 'Mech, hampering ARU efforts to log. You continue to feed GGF info, and no one would believe they had you on the inside since you assaulted that one member. How much are they paying you?"

"Don't you know? GGF is doing it for the Mottled Lemur. Liberation for our furry little brothers." I raised the bottle of water in a salute and snatched my hand back down before Reis could take a swipe at it. I snorted and a couple of things suddenly made sense to me. "Oh, that's rich. You're incredible, the both of you."

She shook her head. "Please, Mr. Donely, enlighten me."

My eyes narrowed. "You have the spies going the wrong way, m'lady. If it weren't for inside information, there's no way Commander Credulity here could have had his people in place to pick off the GGF. And, furthermore, since my assignment was new this morning, and the extension of the deadline for the restraining order was new, oh, yeah, that's great. The constabulary's insider tips Reis to my fight with a PADSU member and GGF vowing revenge. Reis calls the judge, gets the deadline extended, then someone, probably you, m'lady, since Reis doesn't have the juice to do it, calls someone at ARU and gets them to hang me out there with a work assignment. You used me as *bait!*"

Reis began to chuckle in that sort of superior way that told me I was right, but Lakewood cut him off before he could lord all the details over me. "Interesting speculation, Mr. Donelly. You think well on your feet. Well enough to manufacture a dozen different explanations for how things went down. The fact remains that people died and your efforts prevented Commander Reis from apprehending suspects. Moreover, you entered a crime scene and destroyed evidence."

I pressed the bottle to my cheek. "Destroyed enough evidence that you can't charge me with anything, right?"

She hesitated for just long enough to tell me I'd called her bluff.

Reis, undaunted by the obvious, snarled. "Oh, we have more than enough to put you away for a long time, Donelly, and in a hole so deep you'll only see the sun at high noon." He'd have continued, but someone knocked at the door and he went to answer it.

I looked up at her. "You want to try to push it, or just retreat now and avoid looking stupid?"

"Believe it or not, Mr. Donelly, I'd like to help you."

"Geez, that has to be the first time that's ever been said to *bait*."

A hint of sympathy entered her voice. "Mr. Donelly, if you cooperate, things can go well for you. . . ."

"Yeah? Got another hit team you want me to go trolling for? To Hell with you and Lord Leviathan there. Charge me with a crime or let me go home."

Reis began to chuckle again. Think of that superior laugh with another track of malevolence laid in counterpoint to it. It sounded like an asthmatic frog in heat.

"Oh, you're free to go, Donelly, but don't go far."

"I'll just be going back to work."

"No, you won't." Reis came back into my sight holding a little noteputer. "It's a message for you from ARU headquarters. Your taking that 'Mech into that fight goes against company policy. You scanned the file and signed off on it. You're fired."

A chill tightened my skin. "You did this, didn't you, you bastard! You made me bait. Things went bad and you try to make me a scapegoat, and you get me fired. You're one sick man, Reis."

"Yeah, maybe I am, but at least I have a job."

I shot to my feet, sending the chair skittering back. I cocked my left fist to punch his flat face out the back of his bald skull, but Lakewood grabbed my wrist.

"Are you sure you want to do that?"

"I'm sure, yes, I do." I did, but as she released my wrist, I lowered my fist. "But I won't. I won't give him the satisfaction."

Her emerald gaze flicked toward Reis and back again. She lowered her voice. "I'm sorry he did that."

"Yeah, really?" I snorted. "As long as you're going to play his game, you're a liar. As they say, m'lady, jackals run with jackals. If I were you, this isn't the company I'd want to be keeping."

"Words you should live by, Mr. Donelly. Don't do anything stupid."

"Like you think I can do anything but." I tossed her back the water. "Thanks, but no thanks. I don't want you to think you've done me any favors."

4

A donkey that travels abroad, will not return a horse.

—Hebrew saying

Overton
Joppa, Helen
Prefecture III, Republic of the Sphere
14 November 3132

When moving between the stars, you have to take a DropShip up to a JumpShip, and that JumpShip then rips a hole in reality and crosses up to thirty light-years in the blink of an eye. In that moment, since the Kearny-Fuchida jump drive is playing with all sorts of quantum mechanical things, human perception can go all weird. When I've jumped, for that nanosecond, I feel like the whole universe has opened up for me, revealing all its secrets and its immeasurable possibilities.

When I snap back into reality, trapped again in my body, I feel the lack. I feel as if all the doors that I viewed as opened have shut again. It's almost suffocating to go from omniscience to ignorance in a flash.

Well, walking out of the Constabulary headquarters, I

felt like that, but worse. Reis getting me fired, I'd not expected that. I knew he was trying to turn the pressure up on me to get me to confess to my involvement with GGF. In his worldview, since he could do no wrong, his mistake was my fault. He had just enough cunning to paint a picture that Lakewood could buy into, so I was stuck and stuck hard.

I started wandering down the street and passed by a ComStar office. ARU had my universal linknumber. They'd wire my severance, if there was any, to it, and forward any messages there, too. Having a ULN was really useful when the commo-net was truly universal. With the HPGs going down it still functioned planetwide and, as with Rusty's birthday greeting, offworld messages did get through, but slowly and unreliably.

I opted not to go in and see if ARU had sent money already. If I had it I'd spend it, and since I really was thirsty, I didn't want to drink it all up. I didn't figure it would be much of a stake, but I'd have to work with it. If I couldn't, if I weren't able to maintain a job, Reis would come after me, nab me on vagrancy charges and get me expelled from The Republic, and then where would I be?

A couple generations back I'd have headed for Outreach and tried to hook up with some mercenary company. I was good with 'Mechs and in my grandfather's time there was always enough work for a pilot with some skill, some luck, and enough neurons to form a synapse. I could have gotten work, maybe not with Wolf's Dragoons or the Kell Hounds, but some smaller company or some minor noble who wanted his own security force would have snapped me up in a heartbeat.

Devlin Stone and his reforms changed all that. Back in the dawn of time, when the Word of Blake launched their jihad on civilization, they did a lot of damage and took over some worlds. Devlin Stone was a guy they tossed into a reeducation camp, but he did the reeducating. He escaped, and with the help of confederates liberated the camp, then the world, then the worlds around it, creating the Kittery Prefecture, which was a prototype for The Republic.

Stone realized fairly quickly that when unscrupulous people pilot BattleMechs, violence is just going to break out.

After all, if someone has a hammer, all problems look like nails, and when your hammer is a BattleMech, you can do some serious pounding on that nail—be it another BattleMech or some tiny village.

He embarked on a two-step process for changing society. First, he restricted those who could use hammers. In some cases they gave their hammers up voluntarily, and in other cases they were *convinced* this was a good idea. A lot of blood got spilled, but a lot less has been spilled since then, so that was a good thing.

The second step was to institute programs that helped folks see that not all problems were nails and, furthermore, that there were other tools that could solve those problems. Since Stone had the only hammers and no one wanted him to see them as a nail, they started making use of his other tools and we flowed into this Golden Age of peace that worked for everyone.

At least, that's what the school files would tell you. As with generalizations, things fray around the edges. I wandered into a worn and grubby section of Overton. If it had seen a golden age, it was the old days when Hanse Davion sat on the throne of the Federated Suns. The whole area just had the stink of rotting garbage and overheated engines.

I knew I'd found an area where I could lose myself. I trolled through the streets, looking down alleys for just the sort of sinkhole that could swallow me up and found it half hidden behind a Dumpster. I threaded my way around the rusting metal box and down some steps. The neon sign over the door was supposed to read "Banzai," but the way things had burned out all I saw was "Banal."

Perfect.

I shoved the door open and stepped into the dark bar. The miasma of rotting veggies made it into the place, but the reek of human vomit overpowered it rather sharply. A couple of steps in from the door I picked up the stronger perfume of stale beer and the sharper scent of whatever burning herbs the two guys in the back corner were sucking out of a hookah.

Those two were clearly the cream of the crop for clientele. Most of the other folks huddled over drinks at their tables. They looked like ticks sucking supper from some dog, all bloated and disgusting. Save the guys in the corner, and the bleached blonde working the tables, I had to be the youngest person in there by twenty years.

I slid onto a stool at the bar. I had plenty of choices and picked a place with two empty stools between me and an old souse nursing a beer. He watched me sit down, sprinkled a little salt into his beer to bring the head up, then gave me a nod.

I returned it automatically, which I knew was a mistake. The bartender had been keeping well away from him at a time when he should have been pushing more suds, which meant he didn't want to deal with the guy. My nod was a nice little acknowledgment of his existence, so sooner or later I knew I'd be listening to his life story.

I glanced at the bartender. "I'll have what he's having."

"You can't. We've had a new delivery since then."

"Just draw it wet, will you?" I fished in my pocket for a couple of five-stone coins, got a knight and an exarch in change. I left the exarch for the bartender, then drank. The beer was surprisingly good, which meant I was doomed.

It is a fact of life that the better the beer, the greater the idiot sitting near you.

"Young fella like you shouldn't be in a place like this."

I gave the old man a sidelong glance. "You checking IDs, gramps?"

"There was a time you wouldn't have taken that tone with me, you pup. Better days." He raised his glass and drank a little, but not much. As he drank I saw a tattoo on the inside of his right forearm.

I put another five-stone coin on the bar, then pointed to the old man. "Give him one from this week's batch."

"I don't need your charity." He said it sharply, hoping his vehemence could cover his desire.

"Not charity, grandfather, gratitude." I nodded at him. "That tattoo for real?"

The man snorted. "If it weren't, do you think I'd show it? You know the stories. It would be long gone."

I nodded. Though it was faded, I easily recognized the insignia for Stone's Lament, one of the core regiments that fought with Stone to liberate worlds from tyrants. Of the hammers Stone wielded, Lament was the one he gave the truly tough jobs.

As will always happen, there are those mountebanks who will claim to have been part of something they were not. More than once I'd heard of Lament vets seeking out those who claimed to have been part of Lament and had the tattoo to prove it. Those folks underwent retro-voluntary laser dermabrasion to erase those tattoos—usually in a medical facility since the field operation, using a laser pistol, usually removed a bit more than just the pigment.

"Where did you see action?"

The man sucked the foam off his new beer then licked his mustache away. "You name it. I joined up in '93 and went through all the campaigns. Capellan was the hardest. Those Warrior Houses weren't surrendering a centimeter until they were drowning in blood. They killed Allard-Liao and one of Victor's sons, you know. I fought with Burton. I wouldn't be sitting here if he hadn't saved my ass."

The bartender rolled his eyes, so I could tell a story was going to be coming if I didn't do something. "What are you doing here, then? I thought Republic vets got taken care of. Half a dozen of the Knights have to be Lament alums."

The bartender shook his head and went over to stand near a patron who'd passed out at the bar. Lament looked at me with bloodshot blue eyes. "They forgot me. After the peace I got out, came home here, had some trouble adjusting, got in trouble with the law, did some time. The screws didn't like me, so they sent in paperwork saying I'd died in the hole. I've tried complaining, but no one listens. Be easier to come back from the dead than to file all the forms to show I'm not dead."

I frowned. "But there's a DNA registry, right?"

He laughed. "Sent a sample. Got a letter back confirming I was dead."

"You look pretty much alive to me." I extended a hand toward him. "I'm Sam Donelly."

"Andy Harness. Folks call me Croaker. That's what I was in the Lament. Obliged for the beer." He drank again. "Being dead's my excuse for being in here. What's yours?"

"Like you, I'm dead." I snorted and sipped more beer. "Until an hour ago I worked for ARU harvesting trees up by Kokushima. GGF ambushed some Constabulary folks up there, killed a few, and some damned Republic Knight

has decided I'm working with the GGF. She got ARU to
fire my butt and since they were housing me, I've got nothing. ARU isn't going to give me a recommendation, so no
one on this rock will hire me, and I can't afford passage
away. They've dug me a nice little grave and are shoveling
dirt on me as fast as they can."

My voice rose as I spoke, but only the bartender seemed
to take notice. I could tell from the expression on his face
I was going to be strictly cash-and-carry, and he'd be biting
the coins to see if they were real.

Despite how he'd been treated, Andy was still a Republic
man. "Well, now, if a Knight thinks that there's a problem,
he must have a reason."

"It's a *she* and she's listening to that moron Reis. That
bloated slug . . ." I grabbed Andy's saltshaker. "I've half
a mind to head back there and just pour this on him and
watch him shrivel. Better yet, I can run back to ARU,
sneak in, take my 'Mech and show him why a house divided
against itself cannot stand."

Andy laughed at that idea. "He was the assistant warden
when I was let go. He's the one who did me, so I'll help
you."

"I'm telling you, Andy, he jobbed you and he jobbed
me, and the worst of it is that The Republic believes him.
You know, if Stone were still around, he'd come down and
kick that jerk in the butt, and hard, too, but where are
things now, right? Why doesn't The Republic wake up?
That Knight is here backing Reis when he's a little toy
dictator. She ought to be taking him apart and you know
what? If she doesn't, I'm gonna. He's ruined my life, you
know, so I don't see why he should be sitting fat, dumb
and happy. For a stone I'd . . ."

Andy held a hand up. "Easy there, Sam. Reis is dumb,
but in the hole I learned he has spies everywhere. You
don't want to be attracting attention, especially *his*
attention."

I nodded and drank. "You're probably right."

"Oh, I know I am." Andy frowned. "So you don't have
no place to stay, right?"

I opened my arms. "This is it, Andy, everything I got."

"Okay, we gotta get you a place to stay. There's a mission over on Akuma that should have space. They have

food, too. Not much, not very good, but it will fill a belly. You can get some rack time there, too. You'll have to listen to some preaching after supper, but it usually ain't too bad."

"I can handle that." I gave him a smile. "For a dead guy, you're pretty nice. If Reis has spies all over, though, aren't you running a risk? He's got it in for me, and I'm sure he'd love to have you be collateral damage."

Andy heaved himself up from the bar and slid from his stool. He shook his fists out, not with the awkward motions of a drunk, but the fluid force of someone who once could have whipped everyone in the bar before the head had settled on his beer. Though white hair, gin-blossoms and a keg of paunch cloaked it, I could see the old MechWarrior in him.

"Son, all I been through, I've never been afraid of Ichabod Reis. He's a conniver and he has a special hate for MechWarriors because he couldn't never get accepted into any training program. When I was with Lament, I'da thought nothing more of him than things I scraped off my boots. Now just my being alive must rankle him, and that's good enough." His eyes sparked for a second. "At least, good enough until we saw his house in half."

5

It's easy to cut to pieces a dead elephant, but no one dares to attack a live one.

—Yoruba saying

Overton
Joppa, Helen
Prefecture III, Republic of the Sphere
20 November 3132

Andy took me under his wing and over the next week I learned quite a bit. Given that he was dead as far as The Republic was concerned, he did pretty well without any official status. When we didn't make it to the mission in time for food, he knew which restaurants had picky eaters. Sure, the food was all jumbled together, but it all mixes in your stomach anyway.

There's always a need for day labor. Sure, ConstructionMechs might be the things that put buildings together, but they're notoriously bad at getting into small spaces and are really too big to be pushing a broom and hauling junk. When we worked on trash details we'd get first pick of the scrap, which we could then sell to dealers for a couple of knights. It wasn't much, but without food and housing expenses, we didn't need that much.

Banal was only one of a couple of dives that Andy frequented. Most were pretty close to a mission or where the day labor trucks would drop us back. We'd get paid in cash, of course, and kick some back to the driver so he'd let us onto the crew the next day. The rest of the money didn't stick with us for very long, but we didn't go to bed thirsty, so it was counted as a good day.

On the rounds I learned a lot about Reis that made my experience with him seem benign. He'd always been bad, but really had let his power blossom in the south when Helen got cut out of the net. The arrival of a Knight-Errant must have filled him with dread until he managed to seduce her into thinking he was the second coming of Devlin Stone. With Lakewood backing him, no one could oppose him.

Except for the Gaia Guerrilla Front. After the incident on the mountain they laid low for a bit. Reis was at his pompous best during the funerals for the constables he'd lost on his raid. He delivered a eulogy that would have made a rock cry and then sign up to join the CDRF to avenge fallen comrades. Even the barflies watching the funerals on the Tri-Vid were thinking Reis was doing a good job until they were pointedly reminded that he'd already done a job on them.

That wishy-washiness really brought the worst out in me. I was good and vocal about what I'd do with him. My plans had progressed well beyond sawing his house in half. In bragging about my plans I showed a little bit more in the way of technical expertise in some areas than I should have, but I was hoping word would get back to Reis and he'd start sleeping with one eye open.

As it turned out, I should have been the one who avoided sleep. My seventh night in the shelter I was awakened by having a rough canvas hood pulled down over my head. I heard Andy wake up, ask what was happening, and get a punch for his trouble. My covers were ripped away, I was rolled over and placed in cuffs, then dragged from the mission.

About the only words I heard my captors speak were a stern warning to someone. "If you know what's good for you, you'll forget this ever happened."

I got stuffed into the trunk of a hovercar and it took off. I tried to memorize the route, but we sped up, slowed down, circled left and right, so I had no clue as to how far we'd gone or where. After ten minutes I surrendered and pretty much decided that I wasn't going to be killed immediately. Given that they'd pulled me from a mission in the slums of Overton, if they wanted me dead, they'd have just blasted coherent light through my skull and left me in the gutter.

Since I wasn't dead, I had to assume I had information my captors wanted. It was pretty obvious that no one was going to be paying a ransom for me, after all. I could only think of three people who would think I had something valuable between my ears. Lady Lakewood wouldn't have used a midnight snatch. Reis would, but he'd have made it a public event.

That left the Gaia Guerrilla Front. It made perfect sense for them to tag me. As the saying goes, the enemy of my enemy is my friend, and I'd made it pretty well known that I considered Reis just this side of Stefan Amaris in terms of evil. I'd also turned out to be pretty lethal when it came to dealing with their ambush.

That thought caused me to pause. It could be they wanted me alive for some sort of sham trial, *then* they would execute me. Then again, I was nobody. If they wanted to attract attention to their cause by trying me for crimes against nature and their organization, they'd have been better served to kill me first, publicly, and then send out a media release explaining why I was a target.

The hovercar stopped and I heard the clanking of a panel door being cranked down. The trunk popped open and I was yanked out, my shins scraping over the lip of the trunk. I cried out and caught a cuff for my trouble. It wasn't a Reis-quality cuff, but hurt enough to make me quiet down.

They sat me in a chair, then pulled the hood off. A bright light blinded me. I shied away, then sucked in as much good air as I could. Good, in this regard, has to be qualified, since we were in a large warehouse that had been built to house 'Mechs, but clearly had been unused for a long time. Roof leaks had left pools of standing water ringed by rusty shores.

Once my eyes adjusted I looked about. Five people stood

around me and right off I noticed a bad sign. None of them wore masks which, in a kidnapping situation, is not good. It means your captors don't care if you can identify them, and the easiest way for them to make sure of that would be to kill you.

I did recognize one immediately. Red stood there, absolutely boiling. She still had two black eyes and her jaw had been wired shut. She folded her hands beneath her breasts and tapped a toe. I was fairly certain she was eyeing me with the intent of planting that toe where it would do a lot of damage, and I did not like that prospect at all.

The other four were unremarkable save that they looked pretty fit and tanned. I guessed they spent a lot of time in the outdoors, which would fit with devotees to the GGF philosophy of loving the earth and hating the metal maggots that chewed into it or cut the trees down. A couple of them watched me very closely, which suggested some military experience, but I didn't see anything like a convenient tattoo to give me a clue as to where they might have gotten it.

What I did note is that the four of them had on jackets with CDRF insignia. I had no doubt that the story of my snatching would make it through the Overton slums quickly, building more fear and resentment against Reis. No mention of it would appear in any public media, but the honest folks in Overton would have a hard time believing anything bad about Reis anyway.

Another man entered the warehouse from a small office. He kept to the shadows mostly, though light did glint from glasses. I wasn't sure if he needed them to see, or thought they would serve as a disguise, but it didn't matter. I couldn't see enough of his face to recognize him later anyway.

He spoke and his words buzzed through a voice-modifier worn at his throat. "Good evening, Mr. Donelly. So glad you chose to join us."

"I'm usually a wallflower, but your people were convincing." I sniffed and tried to wipe my nose on my right shoulder. "So, is this the meeting of the Ichabod Reis Appreciation Society?"

"Please, Mr. Donelly, do not insult my intelligence. I have not insulted yours. Letitia here you recognize, of course. She has volunteered to kill you if necessary. You know who we are."

I nodded. "I do, and your girl there knows I don't care about the Mottled Lemur or anything else. I was working for ARU because it was a paycheck. I don't care about politics or anything, just getting by."

The leader wore black, so his long-fingered hands showed up as white spiders as he pressed them fingertip to fingertip by his breastbone. "You again misspeak, Mr. Donelly. You *do* care about some things. You care about seeing Ichabod Reis get his due, correct?"

I frowned. "Okay, maybe, yeah."

"Splendid. And you care about money, clearly."

"Who doesn't?"

"A point that could be argued, but I have neither the time nor the inclination." The hands spread apart. "My associates and I take action because of our deep commitment to the preservation of the environment. We believe deeply in the sanctity of life, in all its forms."

The image of the constable rolling through the pine needles flashed into my brain. "The firefight on the mountain was holy hell."

"Unfortunate, yes, and unintentional. The hovercars were to cover our retreat once your 'Mech had been disabled. It was a debacle to which you contributed, though I bear you no malice for the casualties incurred. You were merely reacting in self-defense, as you did with Letitia. Had the strike team been acting as per orders, they would have been away before your attack would have proven effective."

I nodded. "These are the survivors of that cell?"

"Oh, very good, Mr. Donelly, you know about cell systems, do you?"

"I've read Word of Blake histories. Every one of them tends to go on and on about how elaborate their system was. Couple of the books might as well be texts for revolution."

"Indeed, and thus does a society that values freedom of information sow the seeds of its own downfall."

"To be supplanted by a system that doesn't value personal freedoms?"

"Hardly, Mr. Donelly, we would seek to expand them beyond their current humanocentric confines." The fingers interlaced. "Has it ever struck you as odd that in the centuries humans have been expanding into the stars we have never found another sentient race?"

"The universe is big and old. No aliens, so what?"

"You see, even *you* fall prey to the subtle lures of nomenclature. Why would they be aliens? If we came to a world and found them here, wouldn't we be the aliens? We would, but everything is defined in terms of humans. The fact is that we probably have encountered dozens of intelligent races, like the Mottled Lemur, but because they did not measure up on a scale created by men who sought to distance themselves from their biological roots, these creatures are dismissed as raw materials awaiting exploitation."

I could see this conversation going off in a number of different directions. The fact that Letitia and others were nodding as he spoke told me they were sold. I almost started a counterargument, just to mess with minds, but since she was willing to scrag me and my hands were still in cuffs, I put that plan on hold.

"Okay, I see where you're going with that, which is great, but I'm paycheck-ocentric and I was getting a feeling that my commitment to piling up stones in my account was something you were willing to trust."

"Were it not combined with your pathological hatred for Reis, I would not. The simple fact of the matter, however, is that your loathing of that toad and your unique skills make you an asset worth recruiting. If we can come to a suitable agreement on pay . . ."

"Save it, 'cause I'm not that stupid. I don't agree to work with you, I'll be planted where I'll fertilize a new crop of trees. My skills, that you know of, are driving a 'Mech, and that comes with a price. I'll let you buy me on a per job basis, assuming you have a 'Mech for me to drive. A 'Mech that will do the job."

"We are making arrangements for getting a 'Mech that will be up to this operation. I will pay you five thousand stones, as ComStar bills, Republic scrip, your choice. I will deposit it with ComStar for you. It will be quite clean."

I nodded and gave him my universal linknumber. He'd send it into my account and once the job was complete he'd give me a password that would allow me to unlock the funds. He could cheat me out of the money by refusing to give me the password, but ComStar wouldn't give it back to him without an arbitration hearing, and I was pretty sure he'd want to avoid something like that.

"That ought to work. I do need to know one more thing, though, before I can begin to feel comfortable."

"And that is?"

"Who was your spotter?"

The hands were back fingertip to fingertip. "Someone outside this cell, therefore you may not know their identity."

I shook my head. "You tell me, or she can just kill me. I didn't spot him, and if I didn't spot him, I need to figure out why. I've not made that big a mistake in a long time, and I don't plan on making it again. I need to know what I missed."

The leader remained silent and his hands motionless for a minute, then he rubbed his hands together. "Very well. It was your boon companion."

"Andy?"

"The very same."

I shook my head again. "That's the last time you're going to lie to me. If Andy was your man, you'd not be needing me. He has my skills, my hatred of Reis, and has already been on the dark side of the law. Last chance."

"Forgive me, it was a test."

"Did I pass?"

"You did. The bartender, the short one, at the Scrapyard, has been keeping an eye open for someone with certain skills. Andy had been considered but old Laments do not revolutionaries make."

"They've already done it once."

"Quite true, Mr. Donelly. Letitia will be your contact and will see to your needs." One hand pointed to the office where the leader had been waiting. "We have a billet for you here. Then, tomorrow, you will be briefed on preliminary activities leading up to our operation. Is that satisfactory?"

I doubted that having a woman whose jaw and nose I'd broken taking care of me would be anything but hellish, but I nodded. "Long live the Mottled Lemur."

"Indeed, Mr. Donelly. Chances are very good they will outlive all of us."

6

*The cat and dog may kiss, but are none the better
friends.*

        —Federated Suns saying

**Overton
Joppa, Helen
Prefecture III, Republic of the Sphere
21 November 3132**

The office to which Letitia led me might have been described as cozy. A desk had been shoved against the wall
and stocked with a variety of drinks—meaning fruit juices,
sparkling waters and natural spring water—and snacks, all
of which had no taint of meat, no salt, no fat and, save for
the dried fruit, no real flavor. The fact that it was all the
sort of stuff that would grant one a much longer life struck
me as a bit ironic, but also hopeful.

A rusty iron cot had been set up in the far corner and
had a ratty old mattress unrolled on it. Sheets, blanket and
pillows were piled on the lumpy, gray-striped surface. I
took a look at it, then turned my back and waggled my
fingers at my captor. "Undo these and I can make my bed."

She snorted and I figured she'd be grinding her teeth,

but that would have hurt a lot. Letitia unlocked the cuffs and had them tucked away by the time I turned around, rubbing my wrists. I gave her a quick nod as she backed away and perched herself on the corner of the desk. It seemed pretty plain to me that she wanted nothing better than an excuse to kick my butt, so I said nothing to her and instead turned to making the bed.

The sheets were clean and had even been ironed. I somehow imagined Blondie having done that job, and had that impression before I found a long, blond hair on the pillowcase. She'd struck me as the sort who would do anything for a friend, be it human or a tree-dwelling varmint. I smoothed out the sheets, then lifted the folded blanket and turned to face Letitia.

"Assuming you're going to keep an eye on me, and assuming you're going to use that chair over there, do you want this to keep you warm?"

She gave me a hard stare which, had it been composed of microwaves, would have roasted my heart in a beat or two.

I shrugged and tossed the blanket on the seat of the leather office chair. "It's there if you need it." I shucked my jeans—I'd worn them to bed at the mission because they'd have been stolen if I hadn't—and slipped into the bed. Stretching out I could feel my spine cracking all the way up, so I started breathing deliberately to relax myself and quickly slipped off to sleep.

While a case could be made for the stupidity of falling asleep in an enemy's lair while being watched by someone holding a grudge, the simple fact was that I fell asleep easily. There had been ample opportunities to kill me earlier, and lulling me into a false sense of security before acing me made no sense at all. Whatever the Gaia-guy wanted with me was anyone's guess, and I was pretty sure there were wheels within wheels. As long as I didn't get pinched between them, I was happy.

I woke up fairly early and made enough groaning and stretching sounds for Letitia to come alert before I did. She crawled out from beneath the blanket very slowly and washed a pill down with water sucked through a straw. I figured the pill for a painkiller and also assumed she was using a fraction of the prescribed dosage so she'd not drift into some narcotic nirvana. While I admired her guts at doing that, I was pretty sure that the drugs would dull her edge enough that I could take her if I needed to.

I decided to wake up slowly. When I finally reached for my jeans, I found they were gone. On a nearby chair I found a new set of clothes, including a nice pair of khaki work pants, a button-down shirt and fresh underclothes. I could have concluded that to have things in my size there they had been watching me for a while, but I'm pretty much a pure medium, so outfitting me from some all-night department store wouldn't be that much trouble.

That, and the shoes they got me were a half size too big.

With my eyes barely open, I shuffled to the desk and appropriated a carton of fruit juice. I fumbled with it, growled, then opened it and drained it. Setting it down, I let one eye open fully. "Coffee?"

Her glare suggested I might as well have asked for lemur blood.

I came round and stepped up to her fast, far faster than she expected me to, and yet again faster than she could react to. "Okay, Letitia, you and I need to come to an understanding. You don't like me, and I get that loud and clear. You don't like me because I busted your jaw and your nose, but that's personal, you and me. You'd have that under control, too, I know, except for the other thing."

She took a half step back and I didn't pursue. "The other thing is this, sister: you're angry with yourself for the people who died on that mountain. Because I busted you up, you weren't there. You weren't in command, so people got stupid and got dead. I was the one who killed them, sure, so you hate me for that, and that's fine. You can't be putting on me your anger at yourself, though. You know it isn't right and it's the sort of thing a sniveler like Reis would do."

Letitia planted a hand on my chest and shoved me back. She mumbled something at me that I didn't quite catch, which is fine, since it was hardly ladylike language. If I related it verbatim this chronicle would plunge from the exalted realm of literature and I would be accused of pandering to the prurient interests of the lowbrow masses.

I could have done a variety of things, from grab that hand, twist it around and drive her to the floor, to use it to drag her forward and plant a kiss on her. The latter would certainly have been pandering, and would have even been an assault, given the state of her jaw. As it was I opted for the easiest of choices and let her turn away to sulk in silence.

That suited me fine because I wanted some time to think, too. My interview with Reis had revealed the presence of a Constabulary agent within the GGF. This was something that Letitia would know all or nothing about. She would know all about it if she were the mole, and nothing if she wasn't. The case for her being the mole was good, since a quick report to Reis about the altercation at the Eyrie would get things going to leave me hanging out there as bait. My assaulting one of his officers would make me a perfect target, though, as much as I wanted to hate him for hating me, I'd made myself the perfect target anyway. Reis would have found me convenient no matter what.

If Letitia was the mole, her anger at me could be born out of the deaths of the CDRF folks. Had she not been sidelined by the broken jaw, she could have been at the ambush and prevented anyone getting killed. While she probably was happy at the death of the GGFers who got smooshed, the loss of comrades would have hurt. Even so, she'd have to see pretty quickly that there had been nothing I did, save decking her, that contributed to their deaths in any way.

There was a further problem, however, with the way the ambush had gone down. Reis sets me up to be bait after he learns of the fight. GGF learns I'll be out there and decides to move against me, which is also communicated to Reis. Reis plans his ambush and brings in a handful of people and one small hovercar. The GGF, on the other hand, was packing explosives, had two hovertrucks and some heavy weaponry. The GGF, it could easily be concluded, had known he was going to be there and had gone gunning for him.

The only conclusion to be drawn from those facts was that the GGF had someone inside the CDRF. The easiest link to make, and again Letitia could fill the bill, was that Reis' agent was really a double agent. Presumably that double agent would only report to Gaia-guy. No one inside the cell would know who she was. Letitia, if she was Reis' agent, wouldn't have been told of the counteroperation prep since she wouldn't be involved and everything could have devolved into a complete massacre of the CDRF troops had I not intervened.

There was a slender possibility that Reis' agent had been killed when I dropped a tree on the hovercar. This would, in some ways, explain his anger with me. Despite my dislike for Reis, I didn't dislike his people, and the idea that I might have killed one of them made me uneasy. Still, the way the hovercars opened up on the CDRF troopers suggested Reis' agent was either a double agent and did nothing to stop the attack, or wasn't present at all. I was okay with either of those cases.

So, what it all boiled down to were these things. First, cop or crook, Letitia had ample reason to hate me. I had to assume that if she had a chance, she would hurt me. Second, anything we planned would be leaked to Reis. Third, anything leaked to Reis would be leaked back to Gaia-guy.

I tried to look at things from Gaia-guy's point of view. He knew this cell was contaminated with a Constabulary agent, so it was expendable, unless the agent was a double, in which case it could be trusted. Because he knew this cell was compromised, any plans he made would require two phases. The first was the overt operation, against which Reis would be expected to move. The second would be a reaction operation designed to punish Reis for going after the first op. Properly set up, the secondary operation would seem to have been bad luck on the CDRF's part, and would allow Reis to point out how diabolical his enemy was.

I had to assume that whatever we were going to be doing, then, would be the primary op. If that was it, we were being used as bait. Gaia-guy's CDRF source wouldn't be one of us, so we could be wiped out and it would be cool: more martyrs for the cause.

If, on the other hand, we were part of the secondary op, we could only be employed that way if Gaia-guy thought we were completely secure. This idea pleased me because it meant we'd be getting the resources needed to do our job, and that would greatly shrink the chances of my ending up as the autopsy du jour at the coroner's office.

This led to a further thought that bothered me a bit. Gaia-guy had offered me five K stones for an op. That's not the kind of money you make strumming a *bazuki* on a street corner for tips. I'd only been on Helen four months and never during that time had I seen PADSU hold a bake sale, much less some thousand-stone-a-plate dinner with the glamorati all sparkling on in for the cause. My fee and Gaia-guy's promise to make arrangements for getting me a ride suggested someone had deep pockets. I was fairly certain that it wasn't Gaia-guy himself. I was also pretty sure his talk of doing it for the lemurs was nonsense, too. While I didn't know much about him, his fingernails had been freshly manicured and the chronometer lurking up his left sleeve would have paid my fee several times over.

So, it was pretty much at that point that I realized I'd landed on both feet deep in a minefield I'd not known existed. Getting out with all my ancillary bits intact was not going to be easy. I shrugged. If this whole thing was going to kill me, at least I'd be wearing clean underwear.

I asked Letitia about a shower. She pointed me out the door and to a corner with drains set in the floor. A hose had been rigged, but no shower curtain or anything, so I just stripped down and washed myself. I used my old shirt to dry myself off, then pulled on fresh underdrawers and returned to my prison.

The tags had been cut from the underwear and all the other clothes. That surprised me a bit because it was more professional than I'd have expected GGF to be. The lack of tags would make more work for local law enforcement in tracing GGF's steps. I could have read a lot into that, but decided Gaia-guy just wanted to impress his people with his experience. It was a good way to build their confidence in him, which meant he was not a long-term acquaintance.

I smiled and thought back to the bar before the fight. Perhaps GGF had only arrived after the net collapsed. Gaia-guy had been brought in to organize it, but by whom? The why—power—was obvious, though from whom it would be taken and to whom it would be given were less so. As things geared up, we'd see how it would go and I was itching to figure out who signed Gaia-guy's pay vouchers.

One of the kidnappers from the night before appeared in the office doorway. He tossed me a coat that I caught easily. "Oh, leather. Are we allowed to wear it?"

He hesitated for a moment. "Well, yeah, it's a disguise, isn't it?"

I nodded. "Good point." I shrugged the jacket on, then slipped a bottle of water into one pocket. I followed the man to a door in the side of the building and out into an alley. It had a corrugated tin fence on the street end, so we headed back to a connecting alley, then slipped through a gate into a playground attached to a block of low-rent housing. Over in the parking lot he indicated a late-model Gaijin hovercar and pointed me to the driver's side.

"You want me to drive?"

"Just do what I tell you and we're going to be fine."

I slid in behind the wheel and punched in the ignition code he gave me. The engine purred to life on the first go. I keyed in the sequence requesting performance statistics and they popped up onto the auxiliary monitor, showing that while the outside of the car wasn't much, the propulsion system had been tweaked to perfection and beyond. "This monster will move."

"Yeah, well, with any luck we won't need any of it. Nice and calm, drive."

I brought the hovercar up on a cushion of air and we were off. He had me do some lazy circuits while he watched the rearview to pick up anyone tailing us. He didn't see anything, and started giving me directions that headed us back into the heart of Overton. I began to get a little antsy as we drew closer to the Constabulary headquarters. That seemed to amuse my compatriot.

"Relax," he said. "We're just going to pick up where the other team left off."

"And what will we be doing?" As I asked that, the Castel Del Reis came into view.

He smiled. "Waiting and watching. Park anywhere along here and look sharp. We're at the enemy's gate and we're going to bring it crashing down."

7

The fish sees the bait, not the hook.
— Capellan Confederation saying

Overton
Joppa, Helen
Prefecture III, Republic of the Sphere
21 November 3132

My tall, rangy companion said his name was Ray, and whether that was a *nom de guerre* or not I didn't know and didn't care. His brown eyes appeared real, his blond hair colored. He moved pretty easily and looked about warily. I couldn't tell if he was carrying a weapon, but if he was it was small, like a hold-out laser.

I parked on the street, which was a lucky break, and we sauntered on down to a small bistro with a sidewalk annex from which we could watch the Constabulary building easily enough. He sat facing it while I was positioned at an angle where the building was to my left and I could see our hovercar off to the right. He had a little noteputer on which he appeared to be reading the news, but his thumb kept flicking every time someone walked in or out of the building.

He didn't say much to me. In ordering his espresso, in fact, he said more to the waitress than he said to me. This left me alone with thoughts and my own observations.

Ray had mentioned that we were taking over for another team, but I didn't see him signal anyone else that we were on station, nor did I see anyone else head out. I certainly didn't see any of my other captors, so if there was another team, it was from a different cell. I'd already concluded that to make any plan work, Gaia-guy was going to require at least one more cell.

Bringing me this close to the Constabulary headquarters was not a very smart move because it was possible Reis might wander by and spot me. Then again, I pretty much doubted Reis would expect to see me in the shadow of his domain. Even if he did, what could conceivably go wrong? He gives me a rough time? Even if I told him everything, there was very little I could tell him. The place I'd been kept had probably already been abandoned, and Ray would have us heading back to some other location when our shift was over.

I ordered caffeine hot and tall, and relaxed as I sipped it. Likewise, other folks seemed to be enjoying the seasonably warm start to Helen's autumn, and not a few hearty souls had already been shopping for the holidays. Within their conversations, however, I could pick up hints of the anxieties that had been running rampant in the underclass. Recent events had more profound effect on the society's professionals, and while they might be stronger, the pressures would eventually make them snap as well.

The collapse of ComStar's communication network was the equivalent of a massive earthquake. Everyone knows the earth is not supposed to move, so when you're in an earthquake, it's bizarre. In its aftermath nothing you took for granted can be trusted. The sun has always risen the next day, but would it tomorrow? Maybe not.

ComStar had always allowed folks to communicate between planets. That ease of communication was what held society together because it created demand and inspired people. Once a news report came in about the latest fashions on New Avalon or Tharkad, the desire for those things grew. Industries would hustle to supply that demand, and satisfied customers do a contented populace make. As long as everyone thinks they are at parity with their peers throughout the universe, they are pleased.

The media also managed to inspire both positively and negatively. In instituting Stone's reforms, David Lear had clearly seen that information was the key to everything. When news stories came through that praised and valued the folk arts of a particular minority, or praised the efforts of a local group to deal with post-pollution cleanup, people were inspired to emulate or repeat that behavior. When stories came through decrying an injustice, others rallied around that cause. Republic officials harnessed that momentum, provided programs and resources to see that things could be accomplished, and successful efforts in turn generated more stories that inspired.

I know that could be read very cynically, primarily because it does involve the manipulation of the populace. That manipulation, however, was not the sort of ham-handed coercion Reis practiced. Taking action in those causes made citizens feel good about themselves. Those who were already Republic citizens were inspired to continue good works, and those who were not threw themselves into such causes to earn their citizenship.

The bane of the Inner Sphere had long been national rivalries, and they burned hottest on border worlds. Stone knew that the most contested worlds were the places from which all future conflicts would arise, which is why the worlds he built into his Republic are some of the most battle-scarred and storied in the tale of humanity. If he could bring peace to these worlds, he reasoned, so it could spread to the rest of the Inner Sphere.

For two generations he had succeeded. His retirement had caused some trouble, but things had been peaceful until the HPGs got hit. That was a fairly nasty blow because it left everyone in the dark, both about what was going on elsewhere, and about the identity of those who took the Hyperpulse Generators out.

Rusty—God love him because no one else will—immediately jumped to the conclusion that the GGF had hit the local HPG because they were his bogeyman of choice. If GGF had the ability to take down an HPG out there in space, they'd not have a guy pussyfooting around the woods trying to blow off one of Maria's legs. Still, his reaction wasn't completely illogical, and was actually benign compared to some of the others.

The Draconis Combine and Federated Suns had contested ownership of Helen down through the years. It had changed hands so often that coin collecting was a minor industry. Faces changed on the coins on a monthly basis in some years. At least once the switch happened so fast that scrip had Kurita faces and FedSuns' backs.

Listening to folks in the bistro, which sat in a largely FedSuns district, I could hear traces of us-and-them conversations. Simple things like, "Well, I heard *they* want to . . ." and "One time I dated one of *them* and . . ." The conversations went from benign to vehement and, most tellingly, would drop to whispers when some of the citizens of Asian descent passed by.

Absent any indication of who had taken down the HPGs, everyone was free to speculate. While the adults of today might have grown up in an era of peace where they played nicely with people of diverse backgrounds, they still had parents and grandparents who had been in the old wars, or had heard the old stories from their sires, and passed them on with the transparent frame of "In my day . . ."

Even without the efforts of a group like the GGF, society was going to be shaking itself apart.

"Look alive, Sparky."

I glanced at Ray. "What?"

He nodded toward the Constabulary building. "Let her go past, then trail her. I'll get the hovercar. Keep her in sight, but don't let her see you."

"*She* is your target?" Lady Lakewood had begun to descend the steps.

"She's a bonus. Keep her in sight."

I nodded and rose from my seat, then hopped the little railing that separated the bistro from the sidewalk. I slipped into the pedestrian stream easily enough and managed to keep an eye on her. It helped that she was tall, and helped even more that a few folks who recognized her bowed in deference.

I followed from the other side of the street, which is a pretty good position to be in. Even so, I knew the chances of keeping her in sight and remaining unobserved were minimal. A solid tailing job like this would take a dozen people all connected by radio, so teams could switch off and cover a variety of routes she could be taking. If she ducked into a store, then went out through the rear of the building, she was gone.

That assumed two things, however. The first was that she noticed she was being tailed. The second was that she wanted to elude pursuit. Unfortunately for me, she *did* notice, and she had no intention of fleeing.

What had escaped Ray's notice was that, as a Knight of The Republic, Lady Janella Lakewood had her own security detail. This detail consisted of two rather large individuals, one male and one female. They wore sour expressions, as if they'd applied to join Stone's Lament and had been turned down. They came up from behind me before I noticed and each grabbed my upper arms and quick-marched me into an alleyway. There I was thrust face-first against the wall and patted down by the woman while the man spoke into a personal communications device.

The frisking wasn't as bad as it could have been. The hands landed in all the right places and she wasn't bashful, but the pressure was all wrong. If she'd been any more thorough I could have skipped my next physical, which was good since I'd need that time to be picking brick grains out of my left cheek.

When they finally spun me around, there stood Lady Lakewood. "Been following me, have you?"

"In your dreams."

"Not even a daydream, Mr. Donelly." She crossed her arms and peered down at me with a gaze that was pure malachite fire. "Been hearing some interesting things about you. You've been making threats against Commander Reis."

"Drunk talk, and you know it. I should be filing charges against him, a lawsuit and everything. He's as rotten as a month-old corpse." I shifted my shoulders indignantly, which brought her guard dogs back to alert. "So, maybe I was coming by the Constabulary to see him and tell him off, you know, and then I saw you. I thought I might tell you something, but thought better of it—then Jack and Jill here had me dancing cheek to cheek with this wall."

"What is it you were going to tell me, Mr. Donelly?"

"That I've been asking around, and Reis is rotten. What

he did to me he's done to other people." I snorted. "Back when The Republic was something, he'd have been stopped."

Her chin came up. "Can you prove anything?"

"Data files and the like? The people down here don't have such things, but that doesn't mean they don't know the truth. You could start with when he was a warden with the local penitentiary and work from there. He's dirty, you'll see."

"Just as I thought. You have nothing." She shook her head. "Let me give you something to think about, Mr. Donelly. You are in way over your head if you think you can hurt Commander Reis with unsubstantiated innuendo. This is especially true when you have established yourself as a liar."

"I'm not a liar."

Lakewood glanced at Jack. "The subject was observed at the Marketplace Bistro two hours and seventeen minutes ago. Upon your ladyship's emergence from the Constabulary building he began to follow. On your order we apprehended him."

I slumped back against the wall. "Okay, I was watching for you. Reis took my job. I thought I could appeal to you for some help. I have nothing."

Jill chimed in. "Clothes are new, but there are no labels inside the jacket."

"Nothing, Mr. Donelly? Are you sure you are not lying now?"

"You know what? The hell with you and The Republic. I'm an innocent guy who got in the middle of something that turned out bad for constables commanded by an idiot. He ruins me. You ruin me. Once I get passage off this rock, I'm long gone from The Republic. I'm going, I'm going . . . I'm going to the Capellan Confederation where there's still some freedom left."

Lakewood smiled, and I would have liked that smile under other circumstances. "Commendable histrionics, Mr. Donelly, but I've learned something in my tenure as a Knight of The Republic. The truly innocent protest neither so vehemently nor so eloquently. You've gotten yourself into something and you are afraid. Well, you should be.

You should come to me and confess all before it is too late."

"Oh, you'll hear from me in the future, you can bet on that." I brushed a hand over my cheek, wiping brick crumbs away. "Now, you gonna trump up other charges, or am I free to go?"

Lakewood stepped aside and waved me toward the sidewalk. "This *is* The Republic, Mr. Donelly. You are quite free."

I squared my shoulders and mustered as much dignity as I could as I wandered from the alley. It did not help that one of my too-big shoes came off at the heel. I glanced down and noticed that Jill must have untied it when she was giving me the once-over. I refrained from turning back and snapping off some witty remark in her direction and kept walking.

I went to the next intersection and crossed over, then walked down the street. Eventually Ray pulled up in the hovercar and opened the passenger door for me. In a completely foul mood I slipped in beside him and strapped myself in.

"Tell me what happened."

"Not here. Make sure we are clean, then stop somewhere we can get a drink. I need a drink." I flipped down the solar-visor and used the vanity mirror to check the damage to my cheek. "Damned Reptiles."

Ray chuckled, circled the hovercar a couple of times, then headed for some beer-skellar. He parked down the street from it and glanced at me. "Will this do?"

"Yeah, fine."

The close confines of a hovercar make some acts difficult. Having my way with Jill, for example, would have been impossible. Likewise, throwing a punch is tough, but I found it very easy to drive my left elbow into Ray's face. His head snapped back, then rebounded off the head restraint. I slipped my left hand out, grabbed the back of his skull and smashed his face into the steering wheel. Twisting in my seat, I unbuckled his restraints, then reached across and opened his door. I shoved him out.

I got out of my side before he'd done much more than get his hands under him. I kicked his door shut, or as shut as I could given that his chest stood between it and closed. He shouted weakly, then moaned as I dragged him from the vehicle and pitched him into a trash midden. He was bleeding from the nose and had his arms hugging bruised ribs.

I grabbed a handful of blond hair and cranked his head back. "You get one chance to answer this question right, or I leave you here with a crushed windpipe. Was it your idea to use me as bait to bring Lakewood's bodyguards into the open, or were you under orders?"

A bloody bubble formed under his right nostril, then popped. "Orders. Mr. Handy."

"Mr. Handy?"

"The boss, what we call him."

I pulled the bottle of water from my pocket, drank a bit then poured the rest down over his face to wash away the blood. "Okay, you're going to call Mr. Handy. I expect him to be at our rendezvous by the time we get there. Reis used me as bait once, and now so has Handy. The next person who does that gets very dead. You can tell him, I'm not bait, I'm the hook, and he wants me attached to his line if it's Reis he's going to catch."

8

> *Though the enemy be only like an ant, regard him
> like an elephant.*
>
> —African saying

Overton
Joppa, Helen
Prefecture III, Republic of the Sphere
21 November 3132

Ray managed to snivel directions to our new rendezvous point and I drove. We got there quickly enough and it didn't surprise me to see Letitia already there. Her furious glare didn't surprise me either. I put it down to her being angry that I'd not busted Ray's jaw, but she calmed down when he clutched his ribs and moaned about them being broken.

I glanced at her. "You'll want to call Mr. Handy and get him here, or get me to where I can talk to him. We need to have a serious talk. *Now!*"

Letitia hesitated. She didn't like the idea of taking orders from me, but Ray eased himself down into a chair and waved her away. With her face set in a steely mask of resentment, she stepped into the kitchen to make the call.

We'd taken a safe house in the older suburbs of Overton. It was the kind of neighborhood where it took a year before you got to know your neighbors, and few were the neighbors who lasted that long. We could nod politely, exchange greetings, but beyond that we didn't want to know each other or be known.

I stayed with Ray and didn't explore the house. From the looks of it, and others in the neighborhood, they'd been first-generation tract homes created just after the establishment of The Republic. Others had been expanded, with second floors added, or window treatments and lots of landscaping, but our home was still the basic low box. Thirty years earlier the neighborhood would have been open and friendly, but now, after its golden age had declined, the houses and owners had aged and old suspicions returned. It could be best thought of as a place where folks once grew up and moved away from. If The Republic lasted, decay and gentrification would follow in natural sequence. If not, the neighborhood was doomed.

Letitia returned. "He'll be coming. A couple of hours."

I nodded. It was good that she had his direct line, whether it was connected to a mobile device or some location. That went a long way toward ruling her out as the CDRF mole. If she were, the CDRF would have been able to swoop down on him and there would be no reason why Reis wouldn't have hauled his butt in after losing officers. Destroying GGF fast after that debacle would make his popularity skyrocket.

Letitia did what she could for Ray while we waited. That consisted mostly of sticking rolled-up gauze pads in his nose, getting him some analgesic tabs—though none of her high-speed stuff—and wrapping his ribs. When she removed his shirt to do that I could see the mottled purple lines where the door and the car frame had smashed him. I didn't see enough swelling to make me think I'd broken ribs, but they were bruised enough to hurt for a long time.

It's kind of funny how time passes in a situation like that. The two of them were radiating pure hatred for me. Not only did they resent my having hurt them, but they resented my presence. They didn't want to leave me alone, but they also didn't like having me there and able to listen to what they might be saying back and forth to each other. Watching them interact, I didn't think there was anything going on between them, but they'd clearly been friends and united by the loss of their other comrades—another discomfort they could lay at my feet.

So time dragged on slowly. I really didn't care that they didn't like me. I actually enjoyed the fact that they feared me. That's the funny thing about intellectual folks—and it's only the educated who can get behind causes like endangered species. While they might be willing to embrace violence to further their cause, it's always some imaginary, ennobled form of violence. It's clean, the one-punch knockout, where you ask the other guy to say "uncle" and then you accept he'll act according to his word.

I didn't play by those rules and that really got under their skins. With Letitia, one punch would have been enough—heck, just trapping her leg and tossing her back into a table would have been enough. With Ray, the elbow made sense, but driving his head into the steering wheel, that was over the top. And kicking the door into him, well, that was just fighting dirty.

With their attitude toward violence, how could they justify shooting constables? It was easy. First, the shots were at range and they couldn't see the aftermath. Second, they were defending a comrade. Self-defense layered nobility on their act while overlooking the fact that had they not been engaged in criminal activity, there would never had been a need for self-defense.

Eventually Handy arrived. He made no attempt to disguise himself. He still wore black and was cadaverously slender, with a pasty-pale complexion that suggested he was a vampire who had not fed in a long time. He did wear glasses that darkened in the sunlight, and left a gray haze over his eyes indoors. He'd shaved his head, confirming for me once again that there is nothing uglier than a white man with a bare scalp.

He surveyed the damage to Ray, then looked at me. His expression hovered between peevish resentment and amusement. "Well, Mr. Donelly, you have been busy."

"I have." I stayed slouched in the overstuffed chair I'd appropriated. "The two of them, out. This is just you and me talking."

Letitia was prepared to take issue with my orders, but

Handy waved her away. "Ray will be more comfortable lying down. We will not be that long. There will be no need for Letitia to safeguard me, will there?"

"Nope."

Letitia guided Ray from the room and down the hallway to the bedrooms. Handy slipped onto the couch where Ray had been and flicked a bloody tissue into a wastebasket. "Was that really necessary?"

"You tell me." I narrowed my brown eyes. "Bunch of choices here: you dangled me like bait in front of a Republic Knight, or Ray is the mole the CDRF has in this cell. Could be both, or could be that Ray is just a moron. You want to sort them out for me?"

"Fascinating." His face betrayed little of his reaction. "I asked Ray to take you on the scouting mission. I might have suggested that you might be spotted, in which case he should be cautious and observe all he could. Ray is not an intellectual giant, but deliberately sacrificing you to the other side was not my intent, nor was it suggested to him."

I nodded slowly. "But you didn't mind that the CDRF thinks I'm still a factor in play. They spot me, talk to me, and now have to devote resources to figuring out what I'm up to. I'm disinformation."

"That is but one of your purposes, Mr. Donelly. Lying low here, you will cause a bit of a stir within the CDRF. While you are out of their sight, you can be trained for our new mission."

I gave Handy a hard stare. "I know you're not stupid, so I know you know this cell has been compromised. There is a mole, and I think Ray was it. Blondie, the PADSU girl, lets Letitia's friends know she's hurt, or Letitia reports to you directly. You plan a quick op, Ray tells Reis, and your forces are lucky enough to ambush his people."

Handy smiled. "It's better to be lucky than good."

"Given a choice, that's what I'd pick every time." I shifted in my chair and leaned forward. "What I'm thinking this all means, though, is that whatever you have planned, you're going to use this cell as bait for some trap you're springing on Reis. While I like the idea of trapping him, I don't like the idea of being what he sinks his teeth into so you can bite him in the butt. I'm not the sort of resource you should be tossing away."

"I can assure you . . ."

"No, I want to assure myself. You tell me what we're doing and I'll decide if I'm in. If I can make it better, we'll both win."

Once again Handy steepled his fingers. He rested his chin on his thumbs, then pressed his lips to his index fingers. His eyes all but closed as he thought. I waited quietly, not fidgeting at all. He was going to decide to trust me or not, and any sign of nerves on my part would kill any chance of his taking me into his confidence.

Finally he opened his eyes. "Five days from now is Overton's Founders Day. They have a huge celebration, replete with parades. This year's Grand Marshal is Ichabod Reis. He will be on a reviewing stand with dignitaries, perhaps even Lady Lakewood. A significant portion of the Constabulary will be in the parade, or lining the route."

I nodded. "Lots of crowds. If you take that reviewing stand out, you stand to hurt a lot of innocents."

"Which is exactly why we won't. I had intended to use your cell to lead a raid which would draw the Constabulary off to the north while we hit other targets. You would point out that you're now depleted, so you could barely muster much of an attack."

"Something like that, but . . ." I gave him a sly smile. "We might be able to hit a small target and do significant damage that would be maximized in terms of negative publicity for the good commander."

Handy canted his head to the right. "Do go on."

"Based on the offer you made me, I guess we have a 'Mech. I know we have a hovertruck and a heavy machine gun. As the constables start to react, we hit a precinct house. We open it up, bust up a bunch of their vehicles, perhaps crack open their armory and steal weapons. Depending upon how much damage we do, we strike fear into the hearts of those who were covered by that station, and we earn the gratitude of those who feel oppressed by Reis. We will be taking the war to him."

His brow wrinkled. "I could shift resources to let that happen. It would put another cell at the most risk, but it is possible he has another agent in the organization. Moreover, if I pull Ray from your group and use him to coordinate the other cell's activities, we have Reis in position to pounce on them. Then we pounce."

"Good, I'll set it up. I'll need to know a sector of the city I can hit and remain outside your other operations. I think Overton is broken down into a dozen precincts, so pick one and I'll drill it—provided I have the equipment I need, that is."

He nodded. "The equipment you described before is what you will have."

"And Letitia will be my communications link with you?"

"If that is satisfactory."

"It'll work." I gave him a quick smile. "And I'll want a bonus if this comes off."

"Of course you will." His fingertips played one against the other. "I shall double your fee and cut you in for ten percent of the value of equipment recovered."

I thought about it for a moment, then nodded. "Done. You'll also give me a red frequency that you'll monitor during the operation. If things go badly, you'll know instantly."

Handy smiled. "It is so good doing business with a professional."

"I'll monitor that frequency, too, so I expect warnings to flow both ways."

"Of course." Handy stood and picked invisible lint from his coat. "I shall send for Ray, then have you all shifted to another site. There will be five of you: Letitia, your other three kidnappers and yourself. I will let them know you are in charge of this operation, and that should be good enough. Please do not incapacitate any more of my people."

"They're *my* people now." I rose from my chair, but didn't offer him my hand. "I'll take very good care of them."

True to his word, he took Ray with him. About an hour after that Letitia fielded a call and we headed back into the city and into a warehouse district. We moved into a loft conversion that was actually quite posh. I got the impression that someone who sympathized with PADSU was lending it out, doubtless getting some warm squishy feeling inside over being so bold as to harbor those who would defy the law. The food storage unit was packed with gourmet cheeses, designer waters and other exotic foods. I had little doubt that the week's grocery bill would have fed some hinterland village for the better part of a month.

The other three members of my team arrived within two hours. Jiro, the smallest of them, and the only one to show any Asian blood from the Combine side of things, brought a datafile that contained map coordinates and a holographic breakdown of the precinct house we were supposed to hit.

Steve, a blond with blue eyes who bore a faint resemblance to Ray, helped me study the thing and he seemed pretty sharp. He was all over the data indicating shift changes. He pointed out that all the vehicles were parked beneath the building, so if we hit the west side, where the in/out ramps were located, we could completely destroy their ability to respond. "It's a stupid coney has only one way in and out of its house."

The third guy went by the *nom de guerre* of Falcon. While tall and big, he wasn't the most handsome of men and I had the feeling he'd primarily joined things to meet women. He kept making plays for Letitia. If she'd hit me with the glare she gave him, I'd be the one whose jaw was wired shut. He told me he "crewed the heavy weapon." I guess that was meant to assure me he was a professional.

The best information I had, however, was that the 'Mech I'd be driving was a MiningMech. It was close enough to Maria that I knew what I was getting into. The main difference was that instead of a chainsaw it had a digger arm meant to do to rock what the chainsaw did to trees. For burrowing into the precinct house, which was ferrocrete slabs with some molded decorations, it would be perfect.

We spent two days poring over the plans and patterns until we had the plan down solidly. During that time I got a good feel for the team and knew they'd be able to pull the job off without a hitch. I'd rip open the armory, Falcon would keep the constables back, and the others would load weaponry into my 'Mech's bucket-loader attachment. We'd be in and out fast and victorious.

The only bad part about the planning was that the pure food got to me. After forty-eight hours of eating things that, in theory, had been grown organically but never showed a speck of dirt, I'd had it. I needed something, be it greasy or loaded with caffeine or sugar or *anything*. I declared we were going out and wrote down the names of five restaurants on a scrap of paper.

"We're not compromising this op, so we're picking where we're going at random. Jiro, pick a number between one and five."

"Two."

"Steve, between one and five, not two."

"Three."

"Okay." I crossed one, four and five off my list and looked at Falcon. "Up to you, big guy. Three or two?"

He glanced at Letitia, but she was no help. "Two."

"Two it is." I smiled, already feeling caffeine jolting through my system. "Javapulse Generators here we come."

Letitia snarled through clenched teeth. "That's owned by Jerome Redhawk. He's a Republic Knight. We can't go there."

I frowned. "He's an industrialist, knighted because he gave a lot of money to The Republic. If you think every one of the places his corporations own are Republic spy centers, we're in serious trouble. The realtors handling the other two lofts here are one of his companies."

That set her back for a second and I pressed my attack. "Besides, it's like wearing leather. Who would expect us to go there?"

She sniffed. "I'm not going."

"You're not staying alone."

Falcon immediately volunteered to stay with her, and Steve decided he wanted to double-check some numbers, so Jiro and I took orders and headed out. We resolved to do a quick recon on our target before hitting the coffee place. The both of us grinned as we headed out.

We didn't want any surprises.

9

One must plow with the horse one has.

—Steiner saying

Overton
Joppa, Helen
Prefecture III, Republic of the Sphere
23 November 3132

Jiro was not very talkative, and I think this was natural to him, not some sort of act. I let him drive and gave directions while watching our backtrail. We were clean, so we proceeded on, but not taking any direct route. We weren't exactly traveling aimlessly, either, since our path ran across the parade route a couple of times, and we could see where the Constabulary had already begun to position ferrocrete barriers, and where grandstands had been built along the way.

Our precinct house, the ninth, held no real surprises. Three stories tall—roughly a third again as tall as the 'Mech I'd be driving—with narrow windows and some statues of Justice by the front door, it sat in a regentrified area with little shops and restaurants clustered about. It was located close to the starting point of the parade, and by the time our op took place, the parade would be an hour and ten blocks distant.

So would the crowds.

As we were looking around, I did have to assess the chances that Handy was still using us as the bait operation. I couldn't wholly discount it, but it seemed unlikely. We were more of a "salt in the open wound" affair. Reis would be embarrassed by the success of the primary operation, and our strike would just deepen his difficulties. Given that I only had four clowns to help me, being outside the center ring of the circus struck me as being just fine.

Jiro and I found parking near the Javapulse Generator shop—one of them, I should say, since they are more common than mildew in showers. We wandered in, waited in line and listened to folks order drinks as if the names were magic formulae used to conjure the things. The drinks were sized as *giant*, *titanic* and *Leviathan*, and if it grew anywhere within the prefecture you could get it added to it. Jiro, the quiet one, ordered something so quickly I couldn't follow it, but the server punched buttons on his noteputer and some machine spit out a frothy, bile-colored drink billowing with a frosty vapor.

I ordered for everyone else, then myself. "I'll have coffee, black, Leviathan, I guess. Oh, and three sugars."

The server looked over toward Jiro. "The service station is over there. We have a variety of sweeteners."

"All I want is sugar, raw, not exotic, not processed, not flavored." I gave her a smile and fished Republic scrip from my pocket. "You can't just punch that in?"

"Sir, we let people sweeten their own drinks." The sour expression she gave me suggested the possible reason for this. "Will there be anything else?"

It's at that point that one usually has to make a decision: will dealing with this person make my life more miserable, or her life more miserable? I saw it as a draw, but ordered a bunch of baked goods to go. While it was a zero-zero thing for her and me, I knew Letitia would consider the stuff as evil as a rare steak, and that was one in the win column for me.

The server bagged the order and gave me change, including a beat up five-stone coin that I bit just to see if it was real. Jiro caught that and smiled. I shrugged. "The place *is* owned by a Knight, after all."

The machine spit out my drinks and we hauled them to the hovercar. We managed not to spill and, luckily, our backtrail was clean. That meant we didn't have to try any tricks that might have caused spillage and certainly would have made the drinks cold.

Letitia's reaction was as predicted, but Falcon scarfed down the food I'd brought for her. I'm sure he saw that as the equivalent of tossing himself on a grenade for her. She seemed less than impressed. I did note, however, that she drank the herbal *tisane* I'd gotten her.

Our field trip let us refine a couple other points in the plan, but we were good to go from that point forward. Letitia reported same to our master. We worked through our plans for the next two days and then, on the eve of Founders Day, we made our final move. It took us three blocks away, to another warehouse just that much closer to our target, and waiting therein was a wonderful surprise.

The biggest problem with 'Mechs of any variety is that they are *huge*. Not only are they tall, but they are heavy. Your average roadway is not built to withstand a lot of 'Mech traffic. Even just wandering along, a 'Mech can compress the ground enough to snap water mains and crack storm sewers, which is why they tend to be restricted to certain routes in the cities.

The second biggest problem is that there is no hiding them. MiningMechs, for example, come from the factory in a bright yellow or brick red, depending on manufacturer preferences, and despite being humanoid, are odd enough looking to attract a lot of notice. While folks are used to seeing them around construction sites or in industrial parks, it would easily be possible for folks to go days if not weeks without ever seeing a single one anyplace other than on a Tri-Vid broadcast.

On a parade day like Founders Day, however, 'Mechs abounded. My MiningMech had seen better days. It had languished in a warehouse, then been recently fixed up, splashed with bright paint and hung with bunting and metallic garlands that made it look like it was ready for a night out on the town. Whoever had decorated it had even run holiday lights around the legs and torso and plugged them into the auxiliary power sources at the heels.

I smiled. "Hiding in plain sight, I love it."

The hovertruck had been decorated also, with hand-painted wooden signs proclaiming it to be a float created by the United Farmers for Good Food. More bunting and garlands softened the vehicle's outline. Golden flowers strung in a wire mesh and lots of green streamers transformed the heavy machine gun into a large ear of corn, which prompted Falcon to note proudly, "It'll be popcorn tomorrow."

Had I not told Handy I'd leave the help alone, I'd have dropped him for that one.

Everyone was a bit giddy that night, but we retired to our pallets and tried to sleep. Letitia ended up writing a letter to someone—by hand, on paper. She entrusted it to me, since I'd not be in the vehicle. Steve checked things one more time, and Falcon ate through his nerves. Jiro meditated and, as a consequence, appeared the most energetic the next morning.

I mounted up in the 'Mech we'd all nicknamed Digger—hardly original, but decidedly functional. On the secondary monitor I brought up the local Tri-Vid feed with some of the glamorati doing play-by-play on the parade. Once we saw Reis in his open hovercar reach the intersection of Grand and Independence, we started to move. By the time we got into position, he'd be in the grandstands watching folks troop past.

The hovertruck cut a course parallel to mine, on a road that I couldn't take. Digger moved out fairly quickly and Letitia held the hovertruck back to keep me in sight on cross streets. I took a 'Mech route, which worked out very well, since the pressure sensors under the roadbed would switch traffic signals to give me a straight shot through the town. On occasion, when a 'Mech moves through a city like that, some hotshot in a small sports-hover will dart around and take advantage of the clear sailing. All it takes, though, is one careless kick and the sports-hover will do a tumble and roll that is far from pretty and hurts a lot.

The entrance to the garage was on the south side of the precinct building and I was coming in from the north. I cut along a side street going south, leaving half-meter-deep tracks in the roadbed. Digger handled easily enough that I made both turns without much effort. As I mashed my thumb down on the righthand joystick, the digging claws started their rotation with a loud whine that devolved into a wonderful grinding noise.

One stroke and the ferrocrete sidewalk came up in chunks that bounced into the street. The claws trenched the roadbed a meter deep with ease and the debris was sufficient to cut off traffic from the east. Nothing was going into or out of that garage.

The hovertruck pulled up on my left as I brought the digging claws up and stabbed them at the precinct house. I started burrowing in at the southeast corner and cutting west, looking to open up the evidence room and the armory. Once I had the building open, I'd lift Steve and Jiro in, they'd load, and we'd go.

Unfortunately, that was when things started to go bad.

The digging claws jammed and froze before I'd done much more than cat-scratch the building's ferrocrete. I keyed the radio to the tactical frequency I shared with the hovercar. "I have a fault, might have to restart the software."

Letitia remained calm. "Claws look clear from outside."

"Roger, give me a second here." I raised the grinding arm and smacked it down on the sidewalk, hoping to unfreeze it. I felt the jolt on up into the cockpit and it did the trick. The digging claws started again, but I wasn't ready for it. The claws slashed deep through the sidewalk and yanked Digger forward and to the right. They slashed through a water main, sending a geyser into the air, which washed over my 'Mech and shorted out the auxiliary power unit, since it had the lights plugged into it and was exposed.

"What are you doing, Donelly?"

"No names, idiot!" I stopped the digging and yanked the blade free. I twisted around to look at the hovertruck just in time to see Falcon angle the corncob up and rake the second-story windows with bullets. They shattered glass and spanged off ferrocrete. I didn't see him hit anyone, but other windows burst outward and we all started taking fire from within the building.

And a lot more fire than we should have been taking.

"Move it! Go, run! This op is busted. They were waiting for us!" I raised the digging arm and used it to shield the hovertruck, but saw Jiro blasted off the back of it. He rolled for a bit, leaking a lot. More bullets chewed up the road near him and his body jerked with impacts.

Letitia whipped the hovertruck around and jumped the far sidewalk to work around the debris I'd tossed up. As she sped east, two Constabulary vehicles tried to cut her off, but she nosed the truck right between the two of them, sending them spinning off into a couple of boutiques. The hovertruck slew around through a 360, but she got it back under control. Somewhere in there she lost Falcon. I didn't see a body, but there was a smashed glass window in a china shop where he could have been flung.

Constabulary vehicles began to close in on me. CDRF officers hung from every running board and out every window, peppering Digger with submachine-gun fire, which the 'Mech didn't even feel. I stabbed the digging blade down at the geyser and redirected a flood toward the nearest hovercar. The water knocked it askew and I started moving west. A quick cut north would bring me to the 'Mech route and I'd be able to move faster, just because the roadbed wouldn't give.

It was really the only escape route I had.

And Lady Janella Lakewood managed to figure that out. Moving in from the west, she brought a *Centurion* into the intersection. As BattleMechs go, it's a fine-looking machine. Humanoid in configuration, it has a huge cannon for a right hand, and a missile-launching rack built into the left breast. It sports a laser in the torso and moves fairly quickly. It outmassed my MiningMech, and definitely outgunned it.

I flicked my radio over to the emergency frequency. "Op Nine was blown, team broken. Get going."

I got nothing back from Handy, but I really didn't expect to. A light began to blink on my console, so I punched it, which flicked me over to a frequency Lakewood was using. "Got something to say?"

"Had intercepts not told me who you were, the insolence would have. Give it up, Mr. Donelly."

Had it not been for the condescension in her voice, I

might have just shut Digger down, but I couldn't. Without replying I cut west. Now, if you'd been reading closely, you'd be wondering why I would go west when there wasn't a roadway there. It was precisely because there was no roadway there that I chose to go that way. While there wasn't a road, there was a wide alley used for deliveries and I started charging down it as fast as Digger could go.

It really must have been quite a sight. The 'Mech's shoulders scraped sparks from the buildings on both sides. Metal fire escapes screamed as Digger ripped them free, and clotheslines added more fluttering decorations to my 'Mech. In one of those very weird slice-of-life moments, I saw a man in his underwear, the T-shirt creeping up over his belly, watching his Tri-Vid set as I raced past and carried away his wooden balcony.

He never even batted an eye.

While the dash into the alley surprised Lakewood, it doomed me. The 'Mech's holographic display managed to condense 360 degrees into about 160, which showed a narrow alley behind me, and a *Centurion* turning to stab its autocannon muzzle at my back. Hemmed in as I was by buildings, I could do nothing but watch.

Light flickered, spent cannon shells arced; then Digger's left leg jerked. It somersaulted foot over knee further into the alley, bouncing off one building, crushing a Dumpster, then wedging tight. Digger's next step, which would have been with that leg, jammed the severed knee joint into the ground. It punched through the ferrocrete and stuck fast, slinging the 'Mech around to the right before the whole hip assembly shrieked and popped free.

That released Digger and let the 'Mech slam back-first into a building. It crumpled, but so did the thin armor on the engines. The impact crushed the engines, causing a minor explosion that kicked Digger up about a meter, then dropped it flat on its back. Sparks flew in the cockpit and equipment shorted. My head smashed back against the command couch and I sat there, stunned.

Soon enough Constabulary officers appeared on the cockpit canopy and looked down at me. They had guns.

I had nothing.

And the day had started with such promise.

10

> *The fox's cunning avails him little when the tigress unsheathes her claws.*
>
> —*The Book of Liao Wisdom*

Overton
Joppa, Helen
Prefecture III, Republic of the Sphere
23 November 3132

Up to this point I had hopes I could leave one detail out of this narrative, but I really can't. In order to appear festive and suitable for parade duty, I had worn a clown costume over my cooling vest. Consider it: white, puffy, big cuffs, lots of big, bright polka dots. You can see why I didn't want to mention it, but since it was the object of much mirth among my captors, omitting it would leave much unexplained.

Luckily, because I had a neurohelmet, no outrageous wig or makeup was needed—unlike Falcon and Jiro. I didn't see Falcon come in, but the way folks were coming to the interrogation room from outside, I gathered he'd been captured and was singing like something less raptorish than his name.

Reis and Lakewood handled my interrogation, and their contrasting costumes almost made my attire seem appropriate. Reis was in full Commander regalia, which was something less ornate than anything worn at Devlin Stone's final address to the Knights. That's taken all together, mind you. He had more medals on than the average fish has scales, and they were brighter than a school of fancy guppies.

Heck, his uniform was more clownish than mine.

Lakewood, on the other hand, looked stunning. She'd come from the *Centurion*'s cockpit, and so still had on skin-tight black leggings that ran from the tops of her knee-high boots to her bare midriff. She'd shucked her cooling vest, so she only had a bandeau top on. Over that she'd pulled a black silk robe cut to the tops of her hips and tied with a red sash. Her dark hair had been pulled back into a braid tied with a matching red ribbon.

She'd have been the picture of beauty were it not for the fire in her eyes.

Both of them, despite their anger, did look better than I did. My clown suit had been ripped open so I could be stripped out of my cooling vest. The constables had shoved my arms back through the sleeves—the left one, anyway. My right hand tore through the shoulder seam, so I had a flaccid arm hanging there. My inability to dress with their help had been taken as a sign of resistance, so I got slapped around a bit and my left eye was beginning to swell shut.

Reis' outrage towered. "Did you honestly think your pathetic plan would succeed?"

I gave him half a glare. "I do know my rights. I don't have to answer your questions."

The little man backhanded me solidly, snapping my head around so that I looked at Lady Lakewood. The anger in her eyes intensified. Before she could say anything, however, Reis hissed in my ear. "What rights? Because of your action, martial law was declared. You are an enemy combatant and subject to the Uniform Code of Civil Defense Justice."

I resisted the desire to jerk my head to the right and bash it into his face. Instead I looked up at her. "What is he talking about?"

"Local constitutions allow for the exercise of power in

the event of a civil defense emergency. This includes the suspension of certain civil rights." An edge crept into her voice. "I would remind you, however, Commander Reis, that since I apprehended the suspect, he is a *Republic* prisoner. This interrogation is a courtesy before I take him away."

"Republic prisoner? Take me away?"

A smile slithered on to her lips. "Just because the communications grid is down, Mr. Donelly, don't imagine we are not able to collect information about you from other worlds. You were lucky that when you left Acamar your trail grew cold. Your luck, however, has run out."

I looked at Reis. "You can't let her take me."

The CDRF leader planted his fists on his hips and began strutting. He'd picked out the note of fear in my voice and was on it like a vulture on carrion. "I can't? Oh, Mr. Donelly, I am powerless to stop her unless"—he let that word hang for a moment longer than he really needed to—"unless you can supply me the name of your boss."

I had to think quickly because I was in serious trouble. I didn't have that much to give him: Mr. Handy and a description. A wig, some contacts, a bottle of insta-tan and a raid on a thrift store for clothes and Handy would be someone else entirely. I could supply some addresses, but those places would be clean or would provide no evidence that would touch Handy.

Things got trickier than that, of course, with Falcon confessing to everything from lustful thoughts about his third grade teacher on up. He'd been with GGF longer than I had, but I'd been put in charge of our operation. From his point of view—one Reis would quickly come to share—I'd been brought in to purge that cell and then take it over for a strike pinpointed at the Constabulary. While I had been given a position of responsibility, I didn't have the background information I should have had.

I was really given little choice in what I could do.

I looked up at him and nodded eagerly. "He was called Mr. Handy. I don't know who he was really. I didn't have a way to get in contact with him. Letitia, she was driving the hovertruck, she was my liaison with him. Classic cell system. All the groups in on the other attacks were from other cells."

A feral grin drew the corners of his mouth back like opera curtains. "*Other* attacks?"

My stomach clenched. "Yes, yes, there were to be other attacks, while you were at the parade stand."

"And what were these other attacks supposed to be?"

My mind was reeling. "I don't know. Cell system. I was isolated and insulated."

"And you expect me to believe this?" Reis barked harshly. "You're a fool, Donelly. This is how things went down: you were the GGF's inside man at ARU. You showed up a month before they did, after all, so you fed them information and they went to war on the company. You intended to do more damage, but I out-foxed you on the mountain. You went underground, arranged for this little outing, never figuring we'd be there waiting for you."

"But . . . but . . ." I frowned, which hurt a lot. If Ray and Letitia hadn't been the inside agent, then who? Jiro? Going out for coffee that day was the only time we were out of sight of each other. It was possible some covert signaling could have been done, but, if so, I missed it. But then Jiro got killed in the raid, and Reis would have been beating on me because Jiro had been one of his people.

"So, was I the only person in GGF who wasn't on your payroll?"

"Maybe. I don't employ idiots."

I shook my head because a lot of things were not making sense. "Mr. Handy exists. Go ask Falcon. At Handy's request he helped kidnap me from the Akuma Street mission."

"We'll see if that name comes up. So far our sources make you the leader of the group, Donelly."

"That's not right." I glanced at Lakewood. "Your security people spotted me at that bistro. They had to have seen the man I was with. They have holos of him. He was in the group, too. Find him and he'll tell you about Handy."

Lakewood shook her head. "We found the body of a male answering that description early this morning. He had been beaten, but those were old wounds. He'd also been shot in the back of the head."

A chill sank into my bones. The last person I'd seen him with had been Handy, which meant Handy had drilled him. If there were no other ops and no other cells, then Handy meant to betray us from the start. He takes Ray away, has him report to CDRF about our raid and say he's getting more info on other operations, then is killed.

Reis' voice became very cold. "There, yes, you've established you knew him. You found out he was my man inside the GGF, so you killed him."

"But, if he was your man, then you would have reports about Mr. Handy."

Lakewood raised a hand to silence Reis. "If you don't mind, Commander." She grabbed a handful of my hair and cranked my head back. "It breaks down simply like this. Prior to your joining the group overtly, all of your orders were communicated through Letitia. Mr. Handy is a sobriquet applied to a figure who appeared to give orders but, as nearly as the constable could document, only provided money and equipment. It appears that *you* have been covertly communicating with the GGF from the ARU facility—we have the communications logs to show access from the numbers. You ran the operation from there, used your materiel supplier, or one of his agents, as your front, and stepped in when the commander here eliminated your base of operations. Your setup was good for as long as it lasted, Mr. Donelly, but it slowly collapsed in on itself."

I opened my mouth for a moment, then closed it. I'd been led into a box and just proceeded to close things up behind myself. The circumstantial evidence could make me into the group's leader, while the physical evidence showed quite a trail of damage that could be laid right at my doorstep. Handy had sacrificed me, which would allow him to disappear. Reis could claim he'd broken the back of GGF, be hailed as a hero, and then Handy would use his other cells to do something else and crush Reis. My cell really had been the bait for a trap but, instead of springing it shut on Reis right then and there, they wanted to let hubris lead him on, then drop him the way Lakewood dropped Digger.

I glanced down at my gaudy knees. "You didn't get the hovertruck?"

"Abandoned, but your people won't get far." Reis resumed his swaggering, then waved a hand dismissively. "He's yours, take him. Get him out of here."

"*What?*" I tried to shoot up out of my chair, but Lakewood got a hand on my shoulder and drove me back down into it. "We had a deal, Reis."

"You didn't give me any useful information, and you never would."

"But you need me. You need a show trial, so you need me."

He snorted. "Nonsense. I let Lady Lakewood haul you off and point out that you were a notorious terrorist who had escaped authorities on Acamar, but couldn't get away from me. I cry loud and long about wanting to have tried you myself, and I vow to get you back here once Acamar is done with you, and I save myself a whole lot of budget problems. Trials are expensive, but media conferences are not."

"I'm not going back to Acamar!" I shifted my shoulder from beneath her hand. "I have rights. I demand them. I want an extradition hearing!"

Reis chuckled. "You're a Republic prisoner. I have no jurisdiction."

"Look, you strutting ape, you've overstepped your bounds so many times, you might as well go one more. Hold me here."

His eyes bulged and his face got purple. "Oh, I am so tempted, but the Universal Code gives me supreme discretion in such cases. And I decide to deny any request for extradition proceedings. He's yours, my lady, to do with as you will."

"You are most kind, Commander. I shall not forget this."

The man smiled broadly. "Please remember me to your superiors."

Reis swept from the room and Lakewood's guards, Jack and Jill, came in through the open doorway. Jack hauled me to my feet and checked the restraints on my wrists. Jill bent and shackled my ankles with a meter of stout chain. Maria's chainsaw might have gotten through it, but it would have taken more time than normally imagined.

Lakewood did do me one favor and waited until Reis had called the media together for a briefing before hustling me into the basement garage and into a hovercar. Jill drove. Jack sat beside me with his meaty right hand on the back of my neck. I rode the center of the seat while Lady Lakewood squeezed herself into the corner. I could feel her eyes on me and caught the little shakes of her head.

Republic identification let us into the spaceport and past security to the Leopard-class DropShip *Valiant*. Being one of the smaller DropShip designs, it had an aerodynamic shape and could carry four BattleMechs. Through the ports into the cargo hold I could see two: what I took to be a *Centurion* and a *Black Hawk*.

Jack helped me from the vehicle, then picked me up off the ground and marched me up the loading ramp. Jill drove the vehicle up another ramp and into the cargo bay. I expected Jack to hustle me through narrow corridors to a tiny cabin and shackle me to the wall, but instead he took me to a fairly large conference room and sat me down in a relatively comfortable chair.

He took up a position next to the hatchway, with his back to the bulkhead. He was just where I could only catch a hint of him without turning my head to the right, which I had no intention of doing. He wanted to make me look, and I refused. Because of my swollen left eye, though, I didn't see Lakewood until she appeared past my left, and I jolted, rattling my chains.

Jack laughed.

Lakewood sat on the edge of a rectangular table back against the bulkhead opposite the door. She looked past me. "You can go now, thank you, Sergeant Gaskin."

"As you wish, my lady. He may be restrained, but he is still dangerous."

She nodded slowly. "I will be careful."

I snorted. "So will I. Not a word about Acamar. I don't care what you do."

"I've heard that before." The door shut behind Jack and she levered herself off the table. "I think, however, I have the key that might unlock your tongue."

And with that she took my face in her hands and planted on me the third-best kiss I've ever had.

11

*A sense of duty is moral glue, constantly subject
to stress.*

—William Safire

Outbound, Republic DropShip **Valiant**
Helen
Prefecture III, Republic of the Sphere
23 November 3132

That kiss would have been solidly at number two, and
might have rivaled even number one, save that my face was
still tender from the beating I'd taken. Moreover, still being
shackled prevented me from slipping my arms around her
and hugging her tightly. Despite those handicaps, it was
still a seriously great kiss, and since she'd already planted
the gold and silver kisses on me, this one taking the bronze
was not a bad thing at all.

I licked my lips as she pulled back, tasting her and smiling. "It's been so long, I'd begun thinking you were a fantasy spun out of Tri-Vids and dreams."

She towered over me and traced a finger over my left
cheek. "I've missed you terribly, Mason. Four months and
no word."

I stared up. "You didn't get the messages I sent?"

She shook her head and stepped back. "Not a one. I did get reports that money was moving into and out of your account, so we knew you were here, but nothing else."

I sighed. Because I'd come to Helen as a drifter, I couldn't be sending high-priority, high-cost messages to a Knight of The Republic without attracting a lot of attention. I did send lower-priority messages designed to go through a cutout who would relay them on to others, and eventually they'd get to Janella—or at least that was the plan. I'd sent one a week, but with the collapse of the grid, what little traffic was getting out had to be the high-price stuff.

"So, if none of my messages to you got out, then none of my reports did, either. Why are you here, then?"

She arched an eyebrow at me. "I believe you meant to phrase that: 'Thank goodness you interpreted my silence as a cry for help and came to see what you could do to rescue me.'"

"Ah, yes, sorry. Been here . . . *I've* been here on Helen a long time, talking to lumberjacks and Greens far too long." I frowned. "Are you going to leave me bound up like this? Your man Jack has a touch of the sadist in the way he tightened these cuffs."

"Jack?"

"Gaskin, you called him."

"Oh." Janella smiled playfully, then crossed behind me and unlocked the cuffs.

I rubbed my wrists. "And the shackles?"

"Maybe I don't want you running off."

"Not me. No place to go on this ship, and no desire to run."

"Good answer." She knelt before me and released my feet, then placed her hands on my knees and stood. "We have a lot of work to do."

I smiled. Janella was always work before pleasure, which might sound less than desirable after four months apart from each other. The simple fact was, however, that since we were back together, things were back to normal as far as she was concerned. We'd work, then we'd celebrate, but in the meanwhile, we'd enjoy anticipating the celebration.

I stood and stretched, then enfolded her in the hug I'd

wanted since I saw her in Overton. She felt terribly good in my embrace. Just having her weight against me and feeling her arms sliding over my shoulders burned off the time we'd been away from each other. I nuzzled her neck and smiled. "By the way," I whispered, "thank you for rescuing me."

"My distinct pleasure." She kissed my left cheek softly, then slipped from my arms. "We'll collaborate on a single case summary, then do our own reports to supplement it?"

"Exactly what I was thinking." I jerked a thumb at the hatchway. "What's the status on your bodyguards, Jack and Jill?"

"Sergeants William Gaskin and Amanda Poole. Both are seconded from Lament for temporary duty. They're cleared to know, but there has been no need." Janella shrugged. "It's your call."

"They know you came to get me, though. Having my BattleMech in the cargo hold likely tipped them off."

"Both could pilot it, so it was assumed they were my backup. They know The Republic has an interest in you, and we'll have to let them know you're working for us. How much more than that you want to tell them is up to you."

I nodded. Lady Janella Lakewood is a Knight of The Republic and serves as a Knight-Errant—traveling to worlds, unraveling problems, acting somewhere between a diplomat and a tactical reaction force. She grew up a noble and went to the Murchison Academy, where she got her military and 'Mech training. Then, instead of taking a position in Stone's Pride—another unit akin to Lament—she went to law school and became learned in the ways of the law.

Knights-Errant fell into one of four classes of Republic Knights. The Knights had been born back when Stone created The Republic and, initially, consisted of his closest advisors and best military leaders. Many of them were later elevated to the rank of Paladin, advising him and, now, advising the Exarch. Only eighteen of the Knights made it to that rank, and upon their shoulders rested the fate of The Republic.

Knights were not drawn from the military alone—Janella's father, for one, was knighted for his work in the sciences. While Stone realized the people of the Inner Sphere were primed to accept as leaders those who were loaded with martial skills, he wanted to use the Knights to do more as he reformed society. David Lear, his closest advisor and chief planner, helped establish as Knights a group of individuals whose example would inspire those who had no martial skills or inclinations. Because Stone's reforms included the nearly wholesale decommissioning of privately held BattleMechs, the chances for advancement through the military were severely limited. As other opportunities for glory opened up with Knighthoods awarded for economic, scientific, artistic and humanitarian efforts, the best and brightest found new outlets for achievement.

The other group of Knights is the Ghost Knights. We don't exist in any documents or on any organizational charts, but rumors abound about us and all the things we do. The tales would suggest there are just legions of us, but I don't think so—though it could be that I don't really have a clue as to how many of my brethren there truly are. Like Knights-Errant, we get covertly thrust into situations to look for resolutions, and to implement them if we can do so within our mission parameters. So, while people assume Ghost Knights are real, exactly who we are and how we get chosen is kept very secret. Janella's guards didn't need to know I was a Ghost Knight, so coming up with a story that would function but keep them in the dark on that point would work.

It's not as if I don't actually exist. Mason Dunne has his own little spot in the Table of Organization for The Republic. I'm a researcher in an obscure forestry office in the Interior Secretariat. I'm seldom seen and often forgotten, but if a Paladin or Knight calls me in for a consultation, being closeted with a researcher like me attracts no attention.

I crossed to a bulkhead cabinet, opened it and got myself a bottle of water. "We don't need to tell them anything right now," I told her. "I think I'm a bit paranoid because the other attacks didn't happen, and that's got me really twisted around. You picked me up because of the Javapulse run, right?"

She nodded. "You got the tracker with your order, so

we were on you. We pulled the security Tri-Vid and identified your companion. What's interesting is that I worked
out where and when you were going to hit your target, but
I never got a chance to tell that to Reis. Instead, he told
me what you would be doing."

"But the only way he could know that is if Handy sold
me to him."

"Not necessarily. Your communications woman could
have done the selling. One time you were thinking she was
talking to Handy, she could have given the whole plan to
Reis. You *did* leave her alone when you went to
Javapulse."

"True." That particular Javapulse location actually *was*
a contact point for Republic agents. While what I ordered
was fairly common, the microphone in the register picked
up and identified my voice. The data was logged and provided some basic information that Janella was able to use—
my asking for three sugars, for example, meant things
would be happening in three days. The register also spit
out a specific five-stone coin that had been fitted with a
tracking device. Once we left the store, Janella knew every
place I went.

She tapped a finger against her lips. "It's also possible
that Constable Rivers—your late friend from the bistro—
discovered more information than Handy wanted him to
know. He passed some or all of it along to Reis, and was
killed for his trouble. Handy then could have aborted the
other ops and given you up as expendable."

"Possible. Could be he figured out who was backing
Handy, which is why he had to be executed. And it could
be that Handy's boss ordered things curtailed to let Reis
puff himself up, to cut him down later."

"Provided there actually *are* other cells to the GGF."

"Yeah." I opened the water and drained half the bottle.
"Four months on Helen and all I have to show for it is a
handful of dead terrorists and constables, and a lot of property damage done to a precinct headquarters. The Republic
will pay for the repairs, I am assuming."

"Yes, but it won't come out of your salary." Janella
smiled easily. "The ninth precinct house was scheduled for
demolition anyway. Reis showed me plans for a Justice Pal-

ace that he wanted to build on that site. If you'd taken the building apart you would have saved taxpayers a lot of money."

I pressed the cool bottle to the back of my neck. "Someday this will all sort itself out. I'm just afraid it will be when I'm reading Mr. Handy's memoirs."

"Before then, my dear, I'm certain."

A warning tone sounded through the ship, indicating that we had been cleared to leave Helen. Janella and I crossed to the exterior bulkhead and strapped ourselves into couches. I offered her some of my water as the *Valiant* started to roll down the runway. She drank and passed it back, then held my hand as we took off.

We both watched the world shrink behind us, then I gave her hand a squeeze. "Did you have to convince someone to come after me, or were you sent?"

She turned and a huge grin blossomed on her face. "Mason Dunne, is that a hint of ego? Did you want to know if The Republic couldn't get along without you in such dark times?"

"Well, um"—I frowned heavily, hoping that would hold the blush down—"it would be nice to think that some folks thought I might be useful."

"Actually, my love, it was assumed you were able to take care of yourself. The few news items coming out of Helen were heavily influenced by Commander Reis' publicity machine. That made it look as if the GGF was strong enough to take the whole government down. People did some checking and realized that not only had we not heard from you, but the contingency support material that you should have been able to draw upon hadn't made it either."

"So you flew to the rescue?"

"I wanted to be here about three minutes after you left Terra." She leaned over and kissed me softly. "Then, after the grid went down, I wanted to come to Helen immediately. Circumstances wouldn't allow that, however, so I stayed on Terra and did all I could to avert the crisis."

"How bad is it? The reports here have alternated between it being the end of the universe and a minor hiccup. To hear folks tell it, all the Houses have been swept away, the Clans are gone and if someone like Hanse Davion were alive today, he'd recognize nothing of the Inner Sphere he knew a century ago."

She sighed heavily and I caught a strong dose of frustration in her voice. Janella did not do frustration well. Being as smart as she was, she could figure a lot of things out when she had all the facts. That particular sigh meant she didn't have but a fraction of the data she wanted, which told me more than four months of news media on Helen.

"That bad, huh?"

She nodded. "The strikes that took out the HPGs were very well coordinated. Not only were they systematic and timed tightly, but they had sufficient force to overwhelm local security—when it existed. Moreover, they targeted key components on the devices that took them down or used computer viruses so the arrays can't communicate with ground stations. In theory the tactics would allow for bringing them back up fairly quickly since they weren't destroyed outright. They won't have to be replaced, but repaired, and there is the big problem."

"I don't follow. If it was so precise a series of strikes, why aren't repairs being made?"

"It's a matter of supply. The HPGs really are a marvel of technology and were built to last. When they were designed they had some basic, highly durable components that have functioned for centuries without failure. The smaller things, like circuitry and memory, were added in a modular fashion, assuming that as technology progressed, new, better and faster parts would be put into them. The problem was, of course, that the Succession Wars stopped progress and degraded the industrial capacity needed to manufacture HPGs and new parts quickly. With damage to eighty percent of the alpha circuit, a lot of parts are needed."

I nodded. Centuries ago, the Inner Sphere had melted down in a civil war that threatened to blast humanity back to the Transistor Age. High-tech industries failed or were converted to the production of BattleMechs. The ability to produce JumpShips and, apparently, the parts that went into HPGs, had been severely limited—right at a time when we could use both.

"So, if there were a supply of these parts, we could have things up and working?"

"Right after the software was fixed, yes, but there isn't a supply of parts. People aren't even sure if some of the power couplings and radiation conversion units can be manufactured. In theory we have the technical information about how they were made, but the factories that can do the work need extensive retooling for production."

I shivered. "We can't talk, we won't be able to talk, save through messages hauled by JumpShips and relayed. What news, then?"

Janella shook her head as her smile died. "It's not good, Mason, not good at all. Republic programs encouraged co-operation. They rewarded it and punished examples of old hatreds. With no communications, the carrot-and-stick approach no longer works. People are beginning to gather power to themselves. Minorities who think they were suppressed are reacting. What you found on Helen is hardly an isolated incident."

"The Republic is coming apart?"

She gave me a frank stare with her green eyes. "Lover, I've been gone from Terra for three weeks. We're bound for Terra now. Until we get there, we won't know if there's still a Republic or not."

$$\equiv 12 \equiv$$

*New nobility is but the act of power, but ancient
nobility is the act of time.*

—Francis Bacon

Inbound, Republic DropShip Valiant
Terra
Prefecture X, Republic of the Sphere
8 December 3132

It is a bit of an irony to think of any transport that can
fling you thirty light-years in the blink of an eye as *slow*,
but when you aren't where you want to be, any delay seems
enormous. It took us three days to get to the nadir jump
point and find transport. From there we jumped to Northwind and were lucky enough to immediately transfer to a
JumpShip bound for Caph. After only a small delay we
headed on to Terra, and had another week to transit from
jump point to world.

We did make good use of that time, and even got a lot
of work done. Helen kept shooting us data right up to the
point we left the system. Handy and Letitia had escaped
capture. My last compatriot, Steve, had been snapped up
two days after we left, but was useless in helping bring in

his comrades. Reis made it very apparent that while he would continue looking for Handy, he considered him a minor functionary and certainly not worth the man-hours needed to find him. I was the key man, Reis knew it, and was happy to be rid of me.

There were two reasons for that. The first was that at a trial I could trot out my story and some journalist would start digging. I was certain there were things Reis' people wouldn't uncover that would have embarrassed him and, possibly, got me acquitted. That would be a major problem for him, so having me gone and convicted in the court of public opinion was just fine.

Second, and more importantly, Reis' responsibilities had been expanded more broadly. The southern continent of Joppa wasn't still under martial law, but all news suggested a "state of emergency" existed. Most civil rights had been returned and, not surprisingly, public opinion agreed to surrender little bits of them so they could feel safe. A number of events that I thought of as benign were canceled. That worried me, because Reis was just the sort to grab for as much authority as he could and would surrender it very slowly.

The only heartening news out of Helen was that there had been no more attacks. That was something. Given that The Republic was slowly coming apart at the seams, peace couldn't be overrated, but the lack of resolution for the whole situation left me uneasy.

We solved the problem of the security folks by letting them know that I was Mason Dunne, Republic functionary whom Lady Lakewood knew. After I had first been brought into Overton, she recognized me and quickly recruited me to investigate the GGF. Since, as our story went, I'd been there investigating the lumber industry, I was already a trained investigator, so the shift was not wholly implausible. The two of them accepted the tale, which is *not* the same as believing it, but they didn't push the story so the cracks would become too obvious.

By the time we arrived at Terra our reports had been completed and we sent them on ahead of our arrival. Janella looked for incoming information about another assignment, but we got nothing more than hearty thanks and assurances that once we were planetside we'd have plenty to do. We were urged to relax, which isn't easy to do on a small DropShip with nothing but survival rations, recycled water and bunks that make curbstones both broad and soft by comparison.

It's also tough to relax when returning to Terra. It's weird because I was born elsewhere and was close to being an adult when I made my first journey there. Terra is the cradle of humanity—everyone knows that, no matter how far away their world is located. Men have lived, thrived and prospered on worlds that are incredibly diverse, but we were only bred to survive on one: Terra. Until you arrive there, you don't how special a world it is.

I watched the white-streaked blue ball grow larger through view ports and couldn't help smiling as we went into a braking orbit, then began our descent. I really did feel like I was arriving home, and it was because of more than my residence being there. The air smelled sweeter, the trees looked natural to the eye, the water tasted better and the animals had subtle little aspects from our shared evolution that meant they didn't feel alien even though I'd not seen them before.

The pilot brought *Valiant* down as smooth as Janella's cheek and rolled us up to the main Republic spaceport terminal in Albuquerque. By the time he cracked the hatches and the loading ramps had slid down, a shuttle arrived to gather the four of us and run us across the terminal to the maglev lightning train. Janella and I took the rear compartment of the single car while Jack and Jill went forward and strapped in. The train headed north, and fifteen minutes later we were in Santa Fe, at the Knights' Hall.

The fact that we landed in Albuquerque didn't surprise me, but once again suggested things were worse than I'd ever let myself imagine. The Republic had facilities all over the planet and most often I used the Knights' Hall in Zurich as my base of operations. The Santa Fe facility had everything needed to deal with knightly affairs, but moving the martial part of the Knights out of Zurich meant a decentralization which suggested The Republic wanted to make its key personnel hard to hit.

In Santa Fe we were met by three individuals. The first paid great deference to Janella and conducted her off to the rooms that had been prepared for her. A military officer took her bodyguards off, while a clerk was there for me. He was a skinny kid with big eyes and a goofy grin that made me think of him as the younger brother I never had.

"I was sent to get you, *Mr. Dunne*. This way, please."

His emphasis on my name made me suspect something was going on, but he didn't feel inclined to let me know what it was. I shrugged, then worked my shoulders around to loosen them up. I followed him through the twists and turns of the sprawling complex. Its corridors featured golden wood walls and large windows that looked out over the countryside. The facility had been constructed to run with the natural landscape and blend with it, so it shot amoeboid pseudopods around hills and down into valleys linking various buildings.

He was taking me off to one of the newer wings. I knew the chambers there were not as sumptuous as the ones Janella would be given, but blue blood hath its privileges. I did recall, rather fondly, the huge bathtub she had last time we were here and decided I was willing to settle for one half that size in my room.

The clerk brought me to my door and handed me a passkey. Without so much as an "I'll get your luggage," he turned on his heel and left. I caught the strains of some tune being hummed, which again struck me as odd, but taking odd as it comes is part of my job.

I opened the door and had to smile. I glanced quickly down the hallway to see if I could spot the clerk, but the last of him vanished around a corner. I think he'd been watching for my reaction and, given the job he'd done, I hope he caught it.

The rooms I'd been given matched my Zurich apartment down to everything but the small triangle of dust on the bottom shelf beside the fireplace. The furnishings looked identical, and the dark green of the living room walls contrasted perfectly with the dark wood of the shelving. I couldn't tell if the framed holograph over the fireplace was a copy or my original, or if the keepsakes on the shelves and mantel had been duplicated or transported, but all of them were right where I'd last seen them.

Without looking right, toward the bedroom door, or left to the kitchen, I knew everything would be perfect. That someone had gone to all that trouble meant a lot. I knew I'd have to find that clerk and thank him. In fact, I was tempted to run down the passage and find him, but one anomalous detail stopped me.

I dropped to one knee and bowed my head. "My lord, I am at your service."

The man sitting in the chair beside the fireplace lifted a cut glass half full of amber liquid. "And I am at yours. You've always had good taste in whisky. Get up off your knee, boy. I'd rise to greet you, but I like where I am right now."

I rose as commanded and couldn't help but smile. Victor Steiner-Davion wasn't a big man—in fact, he was quite small, but the force of his personality filled the room. When my gaze met his steady gray eyes I could see life burning fiercely in them. His white hair and beard were trimmed and the hand holding the glass was rock steady. He looked much as I remembered him—as I had always seen him.

Then I noticed the cane beside the chair. He'd used it after having his right hip replaced several years earlier. He'd worked hard at rehab and had given the cane up in time for his hundredth birthday, so going back to it wasn't a good sign. I noticed the slight sag of his shoulders and the deepening of the lines around his eyes.

He was beginning to look his age.

Victor Steiner-Davion is someone people either love or hate, and many love to hate him. Right before I went off on the Helen assignment, I read Gus Michaels' biography of him, *Victor Ian Steiner-Davion: A Life*. The book was pretty good and painted a strong picture of the man who was born to the throne of the most powerful of the Successor States and had it all crumble around him. Attacked from without by the Clans, betrayed by his family, he watched the nation his father had built through war and alliances just erode. He survived the murder of his first and greatest lover, Omi Kurita, the death of his son, Burton, and the death of his second love, Isis Marik.

I'd first met him shortly after her passing, while I was still pretty much a kid, but I had no clue about the weight of tragedy on his shoulders. I knew who he was, of course; I mean, I knew the name. To me he was just an old geezer, and it wasn't until he fished an old coin from his pocket and let me examine its profile and his that I believed. He'd still been strong then and, until I saw him now, I'd thought he would continue on forever.

He nodded to the chair on the other side of the fireplace. Another tumbler of whisky waited there on a side table. "Please, make yourself at home."

I smiled at the joke, and he smiled too, which made me feel better. I sat and raised the glass. "To your health."

"What of it there is left." We drank, then he leaned heavily on the leather chair's arm. "I'm a sight, I know it. You cover it no better than anyone else. They all think I'm going to flop down dead at any moment. I won't, I promise you."

"I'd like you to keep that promise, my lord."

"I will." His eyes twinkled. "I read your report on the Helen situation. Why is it you feel compelled to make your reports read like potboilers?"

I blushed. "All that dry 'the subject did this and that' is boring. It doesn't get across what I experience out there. I get sent out to infiltrate and work from within, and that's not clinical or surgical. It's messy. I'm pretty sure Hector and Pep are feeling bad about trusting me."

"You're probably correct." He sighed. "I excised the last bit from the report before I sent it to Zurich. Once you left CDRF custody your report ends."

"Yes, my lord."

Victor sipped a bit more of the Irish whisky, smiled, then regarded me again. "I know you well enough to know you don't like how the Helen situation resolved itself. I refused Lady Lakewood's first few entreaties to bring you back, but I need you here, for as long as I can have you. You were being wasted on Helen.

"I don't know how much Janella was able to tell you, since there are things we didn't know when we sent her out, and there is a lot of intelligence we're not broadcasting in any way. It would be devastating. The damage that could be done by panic alone would be irreparable. We actually think that's what the enemy wants."

I nodded. "No clue as to who it is?"

"Unfortunately, no. One of the leading theories is it's the Word of Blake trying to strike again, but Stone pretty much wiped them out. We know there are a few pockets in what was the Free Worlds League, but those who've taken Blakism to heart won't cause much trouble for a while. They've devolved their own societies so they're barely above the Stone Age. They're searching for a new form of technology that will be liberating and uplifting, but they spend most of their time fighting disease and insects that devour their crops."

I drank a bit and let the whisky slowly trickle fire down my throat. "If not them, then who? The peace was good for everyone. I do know that the Capellan Confederation's leader always spouts revolutionary rhetoric, but he's been all growl and no fang."

Victor's eyes hardened. "Daoshen Liao is not someone to be underestimated at any cost. He is undoubtedly smarter than his father was, is tainted by his aunt's madness, and negotiated a settlement with Stone that allowed him to preserve his dignity and an illusion of power. The problem is that Daoshen is very much an illusionist and has done much over the last twenty years to create this aura of invincibility. Reports from the CapCon are very rare, but it looks as if the grid's collapse has given him a chance to crack down on enemies and tighten his grip on power."

The old man shook his head. "That being said, however, none of the Successor States, to our knowledge, possessed the troops and ships needed to stage the raids that took the grid down. Worse yet, having hit, they have pulled back. I think they anticipated old hatreds coming to the fore again, and are willing to let us tear ourselves apart, so they can just sweep in and take over."

I set my glass down as my guts knotted up. "Then what I saw on Helen was pretty mild?"

"Like a match to a supernova, Mason." Victor tossed off the last of his whisky. "The Inner Sphere is smoldering and unless we can put out the hot spots right now, it will reach a flashpoint and everything will be lost."

13

It is to be all made of faith and service . . .
It is to be all made of fantasy.

—Shakespeare

Knights' Hall, Santa Fe
North America, Terra
Prefecture X, Republic of the Sphere
8 December 3132

I got up from my chair and found the whisky bottle where I normally kept it, then returned and refilled his glass.

He smiled up at me. "My doctors would tell me this isn't good for me, but I've outlived a number of them. My cousin Morgan used to take a dram of scotch before he'd go to sleep."

I glanced at my chronometer. "It's not quite that late, my lord."

"I've not been sleeping much anyway." He sighed heavily and I could see the weight of events settle on him. I had no doubt that dealing with the communication grid's collapse had exhausted everyone, but Victor appeared to be *wearied* by it. In his lifetime he had seen what had been believed to be an endless cycle of war and peace, then the cycle was broken. Stone's reformation ushered in an unparalleled era of peace and it might well have appeared to him that, unlike his peers, he might die peacefully.

Weary though he may have been, Victor Steiner-Davion possessed a keen intellect and hunger for knowledge. Michaels, in his biography, suggested that Victor's greatest strength had been his ability to learn. When responsibility was thrust upon him he had been trained to be a soldier, but he managed to learn to be a politician and a ruler and a diplomat. His enemies never recognized that, given enough time, he would learn enough to be able to defeat them; yet he had done so time and time again.

He sat me down and began to ask me many questions about my time on Helen. While the whole problem of who had been behind Handy and why did dominate the conversation, he also zeroed in on how the people were dealing with the stresses tearing at The Republic. "Do you think, Mason, were power brokers to leave things alone, that the people would be content to do so as well?"

I had to think about that for a moment or two, and took the time to refill my glass as I did so. Setting the bottle down, I turned my back to the small bar and leaned there, watching him. "Well, my lord, the common folks are concerned about keeping a roof over their heads, food in their bellies and some basic creature comforts. As long as they don't have any evidence that someone else is trying to do them out of something they think they've earned, they tend to make do. When it appears they're losing something they've been counting on, or that has been promised to them, that's when they grumble and protest. The crew I worked with was happy with hard work, good beer, Tri-Vid fights and fun. When PADSU started to threaten those things, they began to react.

"It's the way it is with dogs, I think. A dog's head comes up and his hackles rise before he growls. And he growls before he snarls and snarls before he bites. Without someone agitating out there, we're at hackle stage. Get folks stirred up and you have growls and snarls."

Victor accepted that and we spoke more about what I'd heard concerning power factions in Prefecture III which, on a world like Helen, was less than might have been hoped. Katana Tormark's resignation as the military leader of the Prefecture had caused a stir, but most folks liked her replacement, Tara Campbell of Northwind. I'd seen no evidence of anyone like Tormark or Jacob Bannson trying to curry favor or garner power though, as Victor aptly pointed out, either could have been Handy's paymaster.

"If I'd thought it was Bannson, I would have asked for more money. He can afford it."

Victor smiled at that remark, then bade me accompany him back to his chambers in the Hall. I offered him my arm, not because he needed it, but out of friendship, and he accepted it. We walked along slowly and he leaned both on my arm and the cane, though not as heavily as I might have expected.

We reached his chambers easily enough and discovered a dinner already waiting for us. The old man had glanced up at me with a twinkle in his eyes. "I know how you detest DropShip rations and, unfortunately, your Lady Lakewood will be dining with Consuela Dagmar and my granddaughter, Nessa, as she is debriefed on the situation on Helen. I hope you do not mind my ambushing you this way."

"My lord, I am honored."

"But if I had invited you, you would have begged off."

"Only to see what had been stocked in the storage unit in my chambers."

Victor laughed. "It was all the food you had in Zurich, still frozen."

"Ugh."

"Well, I never go into battle without a reserve, and knowing it would be inedible was another inducement for you to join me."

"Again, my lord, I am honored." As I was bidden, I sat at his right hand and we ate happily. At least, I know I was happy. I assumed, based on his smiles and laughter, that he enjoyed things as well.

While there is quite a bit of interaction between Knights of various ranks, and friendships do grow and fade, the kindly interest Victor had taken in me was a bit out of the ordinary. I'm not certain why it was that he took me under his wing, for he recruited me, engineered my education, and guided me to my present role as a Ghost Knight.

Janella has advanced two theories, each of which supports the other. The first is that Victor had lost his son, Burton, and then Isis Marik in relatively short order. The burden of his own mortality had to be upon him, for Kai Allard-Liao and Hohiro Kurita, both powerful contemporaries and close friends, had since passed, leaving him very much alone. Janella thought, in learning about me, Victor had found someone who could be shaped into one more good thing he had done for the universe. I became his hobby.

The problem with that idea was simply that Victor really had no time for hobbies. His duties as a Paladin kept him very busy. His stature within the Inner Sphere meant that he could intervene in situations and calm them almost by just showing up. In his years he had learned so much about what motivated people that he could pick out their weaknesses and desires, then play one off against the other to resolve difficulties.

Her second theory was that I reminded him of someone he'd known. We both rejected the idea that I reminded him of himself, since our backgrounds and natures were completely different. From time to time we searched for candidates who would fill the bill, and found the search fruitless until Janella heard a story about Phelan Kell and his being expelled from the Nagelring on Tharkad. What he'd done to get kicked out was similar to what I'd done to earn Victor's attention—though Phelan was dealing with ice and I was dealing with fire.

Phelan had gone on to become a member of the Clans and to lead the Wolf Clan into exile on Arc-Royal. There had been tension between the two of them that was later healed as they joined forces to end the Clan war once and for all time. The idea that Victor might have seen me as someone who could hare off as Phelan had, and that he had acted to channel me into more constructive pursuits did bear weight.

And I was lucky that true affection grew up between us.

At meal's end, Victor led me from the dining room to a small study. There, servants brought both of us snifters with generous dollops of brandy. He relaxed in his favorite chair—a big, overstuffed leather one which the chairs I had aspired to be—and slowly began speaking. Those gray eyes didn't so much focus distantly as they slowed a bit and let some of their wariness drain away.

"It has been difficult, Mason, to watch this attack on The Republic and not know who is behind it or why. If we could identify them, we could rally the people behind a battle to destroy them. The problem is, just as your friends on Helen came to assume, everyone chooses their own bogeyman to blame for the problems. We can't fight shadows, and we have been given less than shadows."

"And it hurts to watch Stone's work teeter on the brink of destruction." Victor swirled the dark liquid in his snifter, then breathed its vapors in. "Have I ever told you about when I first met Devlin Stone?"

"No, my lord. I've read of it in biographies."

Still staring into the depths of his drink, he smiled. "None of them have gotten it right. I was on Tukkayid, as the Precentor Martial. I was doing all I could to oppose the Word of Blake, but then, as now, things were fragmented and difficult to coordinate. Not only were we getting too much data, but half of it was rubbish. At home Jade was all of three and a half years old, and the twins barely a year. It was chaotic all around.

"Kai's son, David, had vanished when the Word of Blake attacks took place in '67, and the first word we'd had of him came in late '71. I thought it was more Blakist disinformation, because it said David was among a group of warriors who had liberated the world of Kittery from Blakist forces. I passed the information on to Kai reluctantly, but as more word came from that area, more reports mentioned David. They concentrated on this man named Devlin Stone, but ComStar had no records of him at all and, at that time, if ComStar had no records . . ."

"You didn't exist."

"Exactly. Well, early in '73 we got more news of Stone. It appears he liberated a bunch of worlds around Kittery and set up a 'prefecture.' You have to know I immediately thought this man must be some sort of a bandit-king looking to create his own house, but then Kai told me he'd heard from David and that David was extolling Stone's virtues. I got passed some information about the Kittery

Prefecture, all of which looked very good—and I thought it had to be propaganda."

Victor drank a bit of his brandy, then his eyes flashed at me. "The histories you've read glorify Stone, but we had none of that back then. All we had was the raw data about a man who had laid claim to worlds and forged them into a self-supporting unit. He was doing things no government had been able to match. He stepped on toes when he did it, but it was working.

"Through David, Kai arranged for Stone to meet with me. Stone thought traveling to Tukkayid would be a waste of time, but David prevailed upon him and in October of '73 we met. He was a big man, with dark hair and dark eyes—you've met him, but you were looking at him through the eyes of someone who knew what he had done. I was looking at raw potential and knew what he had been forced to do in winning his successes. I was looking at a very dangerous man."

I shivered. "I'd not thought of it that way."

"Not many do. Having a kindly profile on coins tends to hide the nature of the subject. Stone was respectful, I'll give him that, and sat down and told me what he was doing. There was no bragging on what had already been done, and no bragging on what would be done. He was straight and direct with me.

"Mason, down through the years I'd met all sorts and, with few exceptions, these people either wanted me to accept them as a peer right away, or they wanted to curry favor. Both wanted some portion of the power they thought I had, some for good, some for ill, but both groups treated me as a well of power, and most wanted me to give them a bucket to haul some away.

"Stone wasn't like that. He just told me what he was doing. He didn't want my approval or help. He just wanted me to be informed so I could decide whether I was going to stop him, or if I was going to get out of his way. And I did think about both of those options, for his reforms were rooted in breaking down and rebuilding some core facets of the way society had functioned for centuries. It was less that he wanted to dip from the well of political power than that he wanted to dig down, find the spring feeding the well, and open that up into a river that would sweep the old order away."

Victor's eyes hardened for a moment. "That was a scary thought, and I would have moved to oppose him save that he clearly valued David Lear as a counselor *and* the changes he was making were changes that needed to be made. Moreover, given the damage the Word of Blake had done, unless there was restructuring, society was going to collapse. There was no chance to return to the way things had been before the attack."

I smiled and swirled my brandy around, inhaling the rich aroma. "You threw in with him."

"I did. Some of the histories will have it that I was the first person to bare a sword, lay it at his feet and swear fealty to him. That's not true, for The Republic was a dream at that point, and the swords I was entitled to wear would be laid at the feet of no man. I did, however, introduce him and his programs to some of the leaders of the Successor States—to Hohiro, and to Peter and Yvonne. I introduced him to Morgan Kell and, through Phelan and Hohiro, Stone met with the leadership of the Clans as well. He made his case to all of them. Those who felt they could lend him support in one form or another did so, myself included, and the Reformation began."

I nodded. "I read one history that suggested you intended to use him as a puppet and take control of the Reformation. I know that's not true, but when you met him, did you think he would succeed?"

"It was hard to look in those dark eyes, Mason, and not read success there. The people fighting against the Word of Blake forces were fighting for freedom, while the leadership of those worlds wanted a return to antebellum society. Stone's leadership showed that power truly flowed from the people. Nobles who forgot or fought that notion went away, because the more people saw what Stone accomplished, the more they turned to him. In many ways, it was the culling of the weak, which made society that much stronger in its wake. Stating things so easily in evolutionary terms can be harsh because those who were stripped of power or killed were humans, but they had abrogated their responsibility to the people they led. Society could not have survived had they been left in place."

"And you will not survive, grandfather, without some sleep." Nessa Davion, Burton's youngest daughter and Victor's aide, entered the study and gave me a smile. "Good to see you, Mason. I don't see any bruises from the trouble on Helen."

I returned the slender woman's smile. Her white-blond hair had been plaited into a thick ribbon with a pale blue thread running through it. That blue matched the hue of her eyes which, in contrast to her grandfather's eyes, were flecked with gray highlights. I'd known her for years and thought of her as a cousin.

"They didn't do that much damage, Nessa."

"Not what Janella suggested."

"It's because she wasn't in a position to smack them back for me." I finished my brandy and set the snifter down. "My lord, it *is* late. I should be retiring."

Victor glanced at his granddaughter, then nodded. "You'll find you have plenty of work tomorrow, Mason, so perhaps a good night's sleep is in order. Thank you for keeping me company."

"The pleasure was all mine, my lord."

"I'll see him out, grandfather, you just wait right there."

Victor rolled his eyes. "She fusses a great deal."

"You are a great deal to fuss about," Nessa quipped. She took my arm and guided me to the door. "How does he look to you?"

The worry in her voice demanded the truth. "Like events are nibbling away at him. He still looks good, and his mind is as sharp as ever."

She nodded. "It takes its toll, but seeing you was good for him. Thank you."

"No thanks necessary." I patted her arm and kissed her on the cheek. "Given how things might break down, I wouldn't wonder if he outlives us all."

"He thinks that, too, sometimes." Nessa gave me a grim smile. "I think that's what worries him most of all."

14

O God! I could be bounded in a nut-shell, and
count myself a king of infinite space, were it not
that I have bad dreams.

—Shakespeare (*Hamlet*)

Knights' Hall, Santa Fe
North America, Terra
Prefecture X, Republic of the Sphere
9 December 3132

I hate dreams. I am lucky in that I don't remember too
many of them, but my dreams know that. They seem to be
content to labor in obscurity. They lull me into this false
sense of security then just dump the mother lode of anxiety
dreams on me. I thrash the night away and wake up hag-
gard and worn.

This particular dream was just nasty. I was back in
school, not even ten years old, looking at a big holographic
projection of the Inner Sphere, only it wasn't the map I
was used to seeing. When I'd grown up, Stone's Republic
of the Sphere formed the hub of humanity's interstellar
empire. All the other nations were spokes—some fat, some
thin, some barely there—or were patches on the rim. As

far as the Federated Suns were concerned, The Republic was an ally, and since we were pretty sure Stone was originally from the Suns, we could lay claim to everything he did.

That map wasn't there anymore, not really. Instead it was an older map, the sort my grandfather had known. All of the Successor States were much bigger and their borders all converged in and around Terra. Along those borders wars had been waged for centuries. That had been part of Stone's wisdom, for he laid claim to worlds that had been sore spots for generations. Not only did his reforms take away the means of making war on a grand scale but, in many cases, it took away the reasons for it as well.

I could still see the ghost of The Republic superimposed over the old map, but throughout its confines and down along the borders I could see little flames burning on various worlds. The Federated Suns' border with the Capellan Confederation was a line of fire. The Draconis March likewise burned, but the greatest concentration of fire was within the worlds that had once been in The Republic. Forces from outside were tearing into it, and forces from within were trying to burst back out.

I heard a voice—all stern and booming. "Thus is the lot of Mankind forever. War flows with our blood and can only be quenched by drinking the blood of others."

It went on to say some other things but, being a dream, they wandered into insensibility. Some of them likely could be judged to have been prophetic—foreshadowing, if you will—but I didn't see it at the time. If my subconscious wants to tell me something important, I'd prefer a direct message, not something I need to puzzle out.

The message of the voice was pretty clear. Stone's dream was dying. There would be warfare and a lot of people would die. The fact that BattleMechs remained in the hands of a select few did little to reassure me. Digger and Maria were more than capable of destroying a lot of real estate and the people living in it, and having a militia mount machine guns on or further modify such a 'Mech was easily done. Mankind is frightfully inventive when coming up with the means for killing someone.

I didn't wake with a start, but instead slowly emerged

from the dream. That's the worst, as far as I am concerned, because reality melds with the dream's fantasy. It didn't help at all that thunder crashed outside, and brilliant argent light limned my curtains.

I scrubbed a hand down over my face and understood Victor's weariness. The shutting down of the communications grid was akin to a huge thunderstorm that touched off countless little fires. Before they could be put out, they had to be identified, analyzed and remedies had to be sought. That all took time, and the problem was that time only served to let the fires grow further and hotter. On top of that, we didn't know if the storm would be back or where it might strike next, so while we were fighting the little fires, it would do maximum damage.

In short, we had to do *everything* and prepare for yet more things of a nature and timing unknown to us.

I dragged myself from bed and considered, just for a moment, pouring myself more whisky. The drink would have been bracing, and I would have stopped at just one. The difficulty was that I wouldn't have wanted to stop there, and getting drunk would have just increased the frustration I already felt simmering in my chest.

I opted instead for two handfuls of a sugary breakfast cereal, milk to wash it down, and a hot shower. The cereal's crunch did help wake me up, and the shower got me straightened out enough that I could manage to shave without slitting my own throat. There's something about drawing cold steel over your flesh that promotes clarity of mind.

I dressed in gray slacks and jacket over a white shirt and the black throat ribbon that functioned as staff drone dress. Clipping identification to me, I left my chambers and headed toward the central building of Knights' Hall. The interactive message center built into the door of my food storage unit had displayed a notation indicating that I was expected to meet with Knight Consuela Dagmar by nine, and I arrived with five minutes to spare.

We met in a small conference room that had been outfitted with black leather couches thick enough to cushion a 'Mech's drop from the ionosphere. They'd been arranged in a square, with a holoprojection table in the center. It had dark wood panels rimming it and a black glass plate that protected the projection equipment. Back behind the couch where I would sit, a sideboard lay against the wall stocked with water, juices and a variety of healthy foodstuffs like fruit, nuts and seeds.

Janella and Nessa—who was there to act as Victor's eyes and ears—had already arrived in the room and sat whispering with each other from contiguous corner spots on two couches. A drone in gray like me—save his ribbon was purple and fixed at the crossing point with a silver stud—gave me the eye as I entered. He puttered around with the foodstuffs, then bowed to the doorway as the Countess entered.

"All is in readiness, my lady."

She smiled and nodded to him. "Very good, Wroxley. If I need something else, I will call."

"I await your command, my lady." With that the older man bowed sharply, letting a strand of his comb-over flop down, and departed.

The door hissed shut behind him and Consuela Dagmar smiled at me. "It is good to see you again, Mason. You are looking much better than I'd been given to expect."

I shot a glance at Janella. "They only used fists, not chainsaws."

"But they were *big* fists, my love." She gave me a smile. "Luckily you heal quickly."

I gave her a wink, which coaxed a blush onto her cheeks, then returned my attention to the Knight. Though in her seventies, she looked not a day over fifty. She wore her black hair short, still, after the fashion of many a MechWarrior, and her dark eyes remained alive. In many ways she reminded me of Pep—rather, Pep had reminded me of her, younger and quite feisty. Consuela had plenty of fire yet, but through the years she had learned to temper and direct it.

She waved me to a seat on the same couch as Janella, then she took a place opposite us. She wore a cream-colored jacket and skirt over dark brown boots, with a royal blue blouse beneath. The outfit complimented her olive skin, a fact made apparent as she smoothed the skirt, then leaned forward.

"First, I've read the reports from Helen and, while I agree that the resolution was less than satisfactory, it was probably the best we could have gotten from the situation.

Had Handy not sold you out, I suspect you would have risen in the organization and might have eventually pierced the veil surrounding those behind him. So you know, a Republic magistrate on Acamar quashed the warrant for Sam Donelly's arrest, noting evidence had been gathered illegally. He was released from Republic custody on Epsilon Indi. There he has gone to ground since prosecutors on Acamar are still seeking him for questioning."

I nodded. "Thank you, my lady. I don't know if I'll ever need Sam again, but he was useful."

"We'll keep him alive for a while. All his datafiles are in place, and with all the confusion right now, creating a new identity and getting the data spread out far enough would be a problem we just don't need to address."

"Yes, my lady."

Consuela reached beneath the edge of the table and hit a hidden button. A small blue cube sprang to life, hovering above the table. Darker blue letters burned on the sides of the box as if projected from within—and looking through the side I could see the words in reverse on the side opposite me. The cube slowly rotated clockwise as the Countess from Lambrecht began to speak.

"The current crisis presents us with a series of problems on three levels: strategic, operational and tactical. I have further divided them into two camps, which I have labeled Lions and Jackals. The lions are those who managed to take the grid down, while the jackals are feeding on the resulting confusion. And, yes, to answer the first obvious question, the lions could be masquerading as jackals.

"Of the lions we know very little. On 7 August of this year they hit HPGs on ComStar's alpha circuit. Over the past four months we have collected a lot of information about their methods and they vary from using aerospace fighters to strafe or having a zero-g assault team hit a site, to using missiles and other DropShip weapons to do the damage. In some cases the ships were coming up from planets. In one case, and we have confirmation of this, a JumpShip released a DropShip, jumped out, released a second, then jumped again and released a third, hitting three stations."

My eyes narrowed and somehow I managed to keep my jaw from hitting the floor. A JumpShip could easily travel between worlds, but it required time to recharge between jumps, and that recharging took anywhere from days to over a week, depending on the nature of the sun it was using to recharge. It was possible to use onboard generators to hot load an engine, but that increased the chances of damaging the Kearny-Fuchida drives. Damage them and the ship would go nowhere or, worse, would go somewhere and never be seen again.

To do what had been described meant the ship was carrying a Lithium Ion battery. That wasn't unheard of, but it was rare. The presence of such a ship meant whoever the lions were, they had serious resources at their disposal. That ship should have also made it easier to track them because of its uniqueness.

I glanced up from the box. "There was no tracing that ship."

"None. We had positive identification of it, or of the ship it was supposed to be. Registry was old Free Worlds League and it's been plying a simple trade route. Interviews with DropShip captains who jumped with it indicate nothing out of order. Rates were normal. There was nothing to mark it as unusual, though no one seems to remember interacting much with the crew. In fact, the only odd thing there is that descriptions of the JumpShip's commander vary, as if members of the crew took turns commanding."

I nodded. "And, as a trade ship, it's in a perfect position to gather intelligence. Agents can send messages, or ship cargo up. Local authorities are concerned with things that enter their gravity well, not lurk in high space."

Janella shifted on the couch. "Hitting all of the alpha circuit in one fell swoop, though, that requires an incredible amount of coordination. There are a lot of stations to hit."

Consuela nodded. "As reports filter back in, the depth of planning is astounding. Attacks were matched to the amount of security available in each system. Data from the Capellan Confederation is sketchy at best, but there it seems a lot of stand-off weaponry was used, and a few attacks were made by agents who had been part of the Capellan military. In one case, ComStar was conducting a VIP tour of the HPG when one of the VIP's entourage produced a laser and did the damage. All of this was clearly years in the planning stages. They picked their targets and struck hard."

I sucked on my lower lip for a moment. "What about the beta circuit? Did they get hit at the same time?"

"A few sites did, yes, but most of them were taken down over the next week or two. The HPG network is vast, and the operators at the secondary stations were not unused to having the alpha stations go down from time to time. They would routinely save traffic and either dump it to JumpShips heading to the appropriate location, or would just wait until the alpha stations started sending them data again. It is believed that, in a number of spots, ComStar gave data to the lions, then had their stations hit. We have no idea what sort of data they got and what they are going to do with it, but that is a whole other level of concern.

"Some stations did get warned and defended themselves. Others have made crude repairs, but eighty percent of the grid is, for all intents and purposes, down and unreliable. JumpShips are relaying as much data as they can, but having to wait weeks for data that used to make it in hours or days is disrupting the whole of the Inner Sphere."

Nessa sighed heavily. "The strikes have taken out key components that can be repaired or have corrupted software that can be recoded. It will just take time—a lot of it. We hoped whoever did this might just offer to repair the damage and extort money for the privilege, but aside from a few instances of price gouging or swindles to get people to invest in replacement parts, there is nothing on that front."

"So they just hit and vanished." I swiped my hand over my mouth. "This leaves us with nothing for the lions. No motive or easily understandable opportunity, and means that really don't tell us much other than that they're willing to wait a long time to put their plan into effect. The trouble with that is that since they've been thinking about this for a long time, and they're obviously patient, we don't have much of a chance of anticipating them."

Consuela nodded. "That's it in a nutshell."

I winced. "Small nutshell, and not much to rattle around in it. That is not good."

"No, it's not." Consuela's shoulders slumped just a hair. "And when you look at the jackals, things are not much better."

15

Power corrupts, but absolute power is kind of neat.
—Ancient Terran slogan

Knights' Hall, Santa Fe
North America, Terra
Prefecture X, Republic of the Sphere
9 December 3132

Just her having chosen the word *jackal* to describe people made me shiver. *Jackals, eaters of the dead.* A quick glance at Nessa revealed a glower. Janella's expression suggested that her thoughts paralleled mine.

Consuela hit another button and the box blossomed into a spherical map of Prefecture III. "One of the reasons that it was fortunate that you were on Helen when all this started is that you were able to provide some perspective on where and how forces are gathering. The players we have identified are still drawing forces to themselves and trying to position themselves to advance their causes. Movements such as the one you infiltrated might be part of a larger plan but, for the moment, no one is making any grand moves. They are still feeling things out."

The world of Proserpina glowed in the hologram. Nessa

hunched forward, resting her elbows on her knees. "Proserpina is the current home of Katana Tormark. Until late last year she was the military leader for Prefecture III and was based on Ozawa."

I nodded. "I remember her story. She was offered a chance to be a Knight-Errant and turned it down."

"What you may not know is that she has very strong ties to the Combine—not its current leadership, but to the traditions. She is a psychological refugee." Nessa glanced at Consuela and got a nod before continuing. "She was undoubtedly qualified to become a Knight, as her service to The Republic had long showed, but certain people felt that if she became a Knight it would bind her more tightly to The Republic. Her refusal and resignation are in keeping with her strict code of ethics, but she is also not someone who is going to sit back idly as things fall apart."

"What are you afraid she is going to do?"

Consuela shook her head. "Right now she is on Proserpina and has gathered a cadre around her called Dragon's Fury. She seems to be consolidating power, securing supply, maintaining order, and it is this last point that becomes a problem with all those who are seeking power. If they are able to maintain order while things descend into chaos, people will view them as saviors. They will support them and cede them more and more power until there will be no chance to get it back."

I nodded. I'd seen that subjugation of personal rights on Helen as people traded peace for security. "And if she is maintaining order, it is very difficult for The Republic to come in and depose her. Her cadre is made up of Mech-Warriors she has commanded in the past?"

Nessa straightened up. "Her cadet corps at the Northwind Military Academy used the name Dragon's Fury. Given the number of defections from her old corps, she has probably surrounded herself with warriors she hand-picked and trained herself. Regardless, it looks as though Tara Campbell has managed to keep quite a few in the fold. Most of those who have gone over are ethnically Combine, and there is some evidence that she has rejected adventurers."

I glanced at Consuela. "And we have no one among her people?"

The Countess shook her head. "I don't know and, even if I did, I might not be able to tell you."

"Fair enough." Tormark was going to be tough to deal with. I'd never met her, but I'd been present at a Kendo tournament and watched her fight in exhibition. She's a tall woman of African and Asian ancestry, and was devastating in her display of sword skills. Victor Steiner-Davion had commented later that she was one of the best he'd ever seen, and expanded that to include her skills in a BattleMech. Just the tone of his voice made me happy she was on our side.

But, that was *then.*

The map swirled down into a pinpoint, then expanded back out to represent Prefecture IV. There several worlds glowed. I gasped. "There's already fighting on all those worlds?"

Janella laid a hand on my left forearm. "Those worlds are all places where Jacob Bannson has homes."

"Very good, Janella." Consuela gave her a generous smile. "Jacob Bannson, the richest man in The Republic, and a man who is bitter about the fact that he's not been ennobled because of it."

Janella smiled. "Bannson is also rather angry that Republic economic policy has severely limited his ability to expand his holdings—at least, has limited it in terms of speed if not actual scope."

Bannson was a household name in The Republic, both because of his incredible wealth and the army of publicists he maintained to remind us he existed. If there was anyone who could have laid his hands on the resources to be the lion king, it would have been him. That said, however, his business empire had to have been hurt very badly by the grid's collapse. For someone who was as controlling as he was, the idea that his companies might have to run themselves without the benefit of his wisdom would have been anathema. I doubted he had any contingency plans that provided for decentralized control. If he'd been the lion king, he would have alternate communications channels operational.

"Bannson is an interesting case." Nessa lifted a panel on the table's edge and typed on the keyboard she'd revealed. The holographic image of a short, stocky man with bright red hair and a bristly beard flashed to life above the map. Even in holo his green eyes glowed with intense hatred—there was no other way to describe it and I was fairly certain it was not some programmer's joke that he appeared this way.

Janella shivered. "I met him *once*."

In her tone I caught a lot of meaning. Bannson was known to be a womanizer, so I assumed he'd made suggestions that Janella had rejected rather forcefully. This gave me ample reason to hate him.

Nessa glanced at Janella and nodded. "Yes, I have, too, but on more than one occasion. His act is no better for repetition. Worst of all, he affects to forget he ever met you before, unless he wants to impress you with the fact that you were unforgettable."

Consuela cleared her throat. "His personal dealings are reflected in business and, by extension, in his political meddling. If ARU were not partially owned by him, I might have pointed to Bannson as the person funding the GGF. It would not be the first time when labor trouble or other such things have weakened a firm enough that Bannson has been able to swoop in and snap it up at a bargain price."

"Stocks and deeds are fine, but what will they count for when Tormark decides she wants to dispossess him?" I narrowed my eyes. "Or are we assuming that she wants to consolidate power in Prefecture III and he'll be content with Prefecture IV?"

"Right now it does look as if their areas of interest do not overlap too much, which is a blessing." The Countess crossed her legs. "As it is, Bannson has spent a great deal of money hiring up MechWarriors. There are those who are quite legitimate and who are, for whatever reason, blind to his machinations. He has also been buying the services of the less scrupulous. There is some worry that a couple of his factories have been building a few more BattleMechs that he has licenses for, so he could have a fully armed force ready to deploy already—and will claim he is just protecting his holdings in this time of uncertainty."

I nodded. Since Stone's reforms had been instituted, the manufacture of BattleMechs and munitions had been placed under strict regulation. While Bannson had the capacity to produce lots of them, without government contracts or the allowance to sell the 'Mechs outside The Republic, he could be fined for creating too many. Stockpiling them in a time of uncertainty made sense, and if The Republic could not sanction him for producing too much, he would emerge as a very strong player on the military scene.

"That would be Bannson all right—show up as a knight in shining armor and tell everyone how he's already saved them. Thing of it is, of course, that a lot of folks that I befriended on Helen do think Bannson is pretty special; for them, he does have a certain charisma. They see him as someone akin to Robin Hood, defying the establishment as he proves you can start with nothing and become something. It's a seductive message. Someone like Sam would buy into it wholesale, and Bannson might just make it come true for a bunch of folks."

I tapped a finger against my chin. "Bannson's another reason you've kept Sam alive, isn't he? You're hoping Bannson or his agents will hire Sam."

Consuela nodded. "I hope your being used as bait in this regard will not be a problem."

I smiled and was reminded of the old joke: Strategic is when you get reports about fighting; operational is when you hear shots fired; and tactical is when you're taking fire. "This is strategic bait, so I'm okay. You're thinking that there will come a time when he decides that hostile takeovers are just more convenient than bribery?"

Nessa snorted. "Bannson is the sort of cold-blooded bastard who would look at it in terms of a balance sheet. If it would cost him 100,000,000 stones in bribes and economic incentives to gain control of a world, versus 70,000,000 to invade and repair, he'll go for the latter, damn the cost in lives."

Janella shook her head. "He doesn't think of them as lives. He refers to them as actuarial risk units. Deaths are not tragedies, but exposures to lawsuits. Wiping out a village of farmers can be calculated in terms of settlements and factored into the equation about how he should take a place. It's the cost of doing business."

"I can see why he was never made a noble," I said. "Countess, I could see Katana Tormark being persuaded to be reasonable by an appeal to honor and tradition, and that might limit what she chooses to do, but I don't imagine any brake of that sort on Bannson. If he is going to be stopped, he'll have to be killed."

She looked at me with an unwavering, dark-eyed stare. "No one has authorized the murder of a citizen, and certainly not one who would be seen as a martyr." Her comment left me no doubt the concept had been discussed but rejected with good reason.

That actually heartened me a lot because I'd been afraid that the madness that seemed to be spreading through The Republic might actually have seeped into the government. If Bannson or Tormark or any of a number of other people were challenging the power structure, the authorization of extreme measures to be taken in such desperate times would have been easy. There were those who would argue that eliminating those challengers would certainly slow, if not stop outright, the dissolution of The Republic. They would go further and suggest that the swift dealing of justice to these people would also deter others from following in their footsteps.

A few would even suggest that this is the course of action that Stone would have taken, but I didn't agree with that. Stone had certainly crushed his share of enemies, but they had known he was coming and had opportunity to reform their ways before he imposed reformation on them. A shot in the dark did not seem like the sort of thing he would have condoned.

I was also dubious of the deterrence argument because, for each person who would decide he wanted to live more than he wanted to rule, there would be two others who would make alternate decisions. One would decide that she could do it better and avoid the mistakes that got her predecessor killed. The other would decide that such an arbitrary abuse of power needed to be opposed, and would rally forces to depose the government that sanctioned the execution of one of its own citizens.

In my advancing the question, Consuela read exactly what I was asking: if Bannson hired me, would I be ordered to kill him? As a Ghost Knight I got all manner of training, and most of it with a wide variety of weapons. I learned them inside and out, both so I could use them and so I could learn to defend myself against them. I could never beat Katana Tormark in a swordfight, but then I knew the best defense against someone with that sort of skill is a 12.5mm sniper rifle at one klick.

It also wasn't a question of whether or not I'd refuse the order to kill him. As a Ghost Knight I'd been trained to use my discretion to deal with problems. Assassination might be authorized, but that didn't mean I had to kill him. If there was another way to neutralize him, I would be free to use it. The problem with Bannson, however, was that the man was a shameless boor who was too rich to buy, too bitter to pacify with a title, and beyond blackmailing over indiscretions.

In fact, if Bannson knew his murder was being discussed, he'd rejoice and start buying advertising to let everyone know he was under a death threat.

Chewing my lower lip, I scooted forward onto the edge of the couch. "I take it these two are emblematic of a number of other jackals. Right now they are functioning on operational and tactical levels—though we have rumors of skirmishing on Ankaa and New Rhodes III. Once they have consolidated their power bases you think they will go strategic and formally carve out their own little empires."

"Exactly. We still have many loyal people. Tara Campbell on Northwind is gathering the Highlanders. Helen, Towne, Murchison and Galatia III could become a diamond of worlds where the Highlanders and Dragon's Fury decide the fate of Prefecture III. Bannson has his enemies and the Prefect of Prefecture IV, Aaron Sandoval, is likely to resist him strongly."

I nodded. Learning more about the whole situation did help clarify a lot of things, but brought with it more dread. Before I was just afraid, but now I had really good reasons to be afraid. People who had the skills, will and resources were ready to divide The Republic. Other people were willing to oppose them and, regardless of who won, the damage that would be done to their forces and to The Republic itself would weaken it to the point that when the lions did return, they would scatter the jackals and gorge themselves on the kill.

I could also see why the leadership was in a quandary about what to do. The Republic had maintained order and guided progress through economic stimulus and education.

Those who opposed The Republic could not participate in the prosperity, and those who made The Republic better were vastly rewarded with money and honors.

That method of ruling required the free and swift flow of information. By cutting that off, the lions had severed the links between worlds. Those who had power locally now assumed more and sought to guarantee it. I was certain some of those people were quite altruistic, but others, like Bannson, clearly were not. Anyone who assumed power and had a distrust of or hatred for The Republic would not return that power without a fight.

But The Republic had never fought against its own citizens. To do so now would be to unite locals against The Republic. Moreover, landing a force to stop Bannson before he'd done anything would weaken Republic forces. That, clearly, was what the lions wanted. The Republic then, mindful that the lions lurked out there, had to keep one eye on them and one eye on the jackals. As a result, of course, The Republic would get gnawed.

Whether or not it was gnawed to death was really the question.

I looked up at Consuela again. "My lady, what is it you desire from us?"

"We need fresh eyes." She smiled with a hint of relief. "We have been here in the maelstrom and there are certain assumptions from which we've been operating. We don't know if they are right or not. The two of you, having been away, have a new perspective. Assume nothing, challenge everything and, with luck, you'll see what we have not."

Janella nodded. "And if we're not lucky?"

The Countess sighed. "Then the blind shall continue to lead the blind, and into perdition we will go."

16

The two divinest things this world has got:
A lovely woman in a rural spot!

—Leigh Hunt

White Sands Training Ground
North America, Terra
Prefecture X, Republic of the Sphere
10 December 3132

I drove Ghost to the right, cutting the 'Mech through the contrails of Janella's long-range missiles. The smoke blinded me for a half second—at least on the vislight level as I looked out through the *Mad Cat III*'s cockpit. The holographic display was on magres, so the smoke didn't show up, and I got to follow her missiles as they slammed into the target.

A dozen and a half of the missiles actually hit, some of them slamming into the steel girder construct housing the data-display sensor. It was projecting into our sensors the image of a *Centurion*. As the missiles hit the datafield, they detonated, blasting armor from the BattleMech's image. Sheets of the previously pristine ferro-ceramic armor glittered down in a rain of shards.

My right hand coaxed the red crosshairs on the holographic display over the *Centurion*'s outline. The dot at the center pulsed gold, so I hit the trigger. Ghost rocked back a bit as forty LRMs launched from the shoulder missile racks. I let the 'Mech hunch down on its birdlike legs, splaying the arms wide for balance.

As the 'Mech came back up and continued to the right, dozens of new explosions wracked the simulated *Centurion*. The right arm went whirling off to vanish in a haze of data dissolution. The left leg buckled at the knee and some of the hatch covers over its missile launcher went sailing off like playing cards tossed into a gale.

Janella punched Andrea, her *Tundra Wolf*, forward. Unlike my 'Mech, the *Tundra Wolf* is humanoid in configuration, though it has no hands. She thrust the right arm forward and four ruby beams of light stabbed out. They clawed through the 'Mech's left knee, severing it completely. The shin fell left, the knee slammed into the ground and the *Centurion* plowed turf face-first.

"Nice shooting!"

Her voice came back a bit tight, but happy. "Thanks. On the right, coming up. *Catapult*."

"I've got it." I planted the 'Mech's right foot, digging the clawed toes into the ground, and pivoted. As I brought the 'Mech around, the *Catapult* resolved itself on my holodisplay. It looked a lot like my *Mad Cat III*, save it lacked the arms. The forward-thrust cockpit did have two underslung autocannons, and they fired. A second later the shoulder-mounted LRM launchers blossomed fire and smoke.

While the *Catapult* was merely a figment of the range-control computer, it was able to project data into my 'Mech and it did so with a vengeance. A glance at my secondary monitor showed armor evaporating over Ghost's chest and right leg, expanding a hole opened by an earlier tangle with a *Panther*. The autocannon slugs pounded my right arm and one of my small lasers winked out of existence.

Worse than all that damage was the computer kicking the gyros out of phase. This left me in a metal machine the size of a small building, moving about thirty kilometers per hour, suddenly out of control. It wasn't as if I were on ice, but as if I'd been smacked with a twenty-five-ton sledgehammer. Ghost staggered back and sank lower, then the left foot clawed the ground and got a hold, which stopped me from going over backward.

Janella's 'Mech sailed right through the space I'd occupied and cut loose with another salvo of LRMs. They streaked in, some corkscrewing down, and pulverized the *Catapult*'s cockpit. Ferro-titanium supports shattered, the cockpit canopy disintegrated—save for one rounded sheet that popped out intact—and fire shredded the interior. The crumpled nose came up, then the 'Mech fell over backward, with the cockpit burning like the mouth of a volcano.

Ghost came back up and I surveyed the damage. The 'Mech had weathered the attacks pretty well, with only minor reductions in speed. My targeting capability had been slightly degraded, and I'd lost that one laser, but otherwise the machine was in very good shape.

The rangemaster's voice broke into the radio channel. "I've got all the data I need right now. You two want to call it quits here, or head into the Valley of Death? Holding others off the range won't be that difficult."

I shook my head as sweat stung my eyes. "Not today, but soon."

Janella had turned Andrea to face me. Her 'Mech had been painted gray, with blue highlights on legs and arms. It didn't have the fierce designs some other MechWarriors favored, instead retaining the subtle tones that had belonged to the machine since a Wolf Clan warrior had brought it into Republic service nearly fifty years earlier.

"I'm done, too, thanks. We're coming back in." Her voice revealed a bit more weariness when she flicked over to the tactical sideband we'd been sharing. "It was good to get this workout, but I wasn't focusing."

Damn, woman, if you can shoot like that when you're not focusing . . . I nodded. "Well, when they have your stats from this run worked up, I think you'll find you blasted the hell out of everything here. Going back to your taking down my 'Mech on Helen, you have a nice string going."

"Dusting that 'Mech on Helen was just varminting."

"Ouch."

"Sorry, my dear, but it's true. You were running down an alley, couldn't maneuver. Had you been standing still you'd not have been a much easier shot."

"Given the way I was shooting here, even facing you down I'd not have been much of a challenge."

She laughed, and it was good to hear those rich tones enter her voice. "Mason, you're in a brand-new 'Mech. You're the first pilot, and this is a new design and that was your shakeout run. We've run this course before and you might not have been hitting as you have in the past, but you handled that beast very well. It's quite mobile and does have power."

She was right. The *Mad Cat III*—which some wags had designated Miffed Kitty—was a variant on the very successful *Mad Cat* design from the Clans. Being lighter than its predecessor, it ran faster, which I favored. It did lack some of the punch of the *Mad Cat II*, but I've long been of the school that suggests being able to move and avoid damage is preferable to taking a beating to administer one.

Janella's Andrea ran seventy-five tons, which brought the *Tundra Wolf* up into the heavy class, but the way she could make it move you'd have thought it was an under-armored light 'Mech. Her ability to shoot and judicious use of long-range weaponry meant that she picked her enemies to pieces before they closed. By the time they got to her—*if* they got to her—their armor was so ragged that a well-placed shot could cripple them.

"I will admit, my lady, I do like this 'Mech a lot. Next time you come save me, bring it instead of that *Black Hawk*. And bring Andrea."

She sighed. "I wanted to bring Andrea to Helen, but we had no reports of heavy weaponry being deployed. The *Centurion* was not a bad little machine. Against AgroMechs you don't need much more."

"Provided they don't start arming them."

"Good point, though the modifications needed to get them combat operational will be expensive."

I didn't reply to that comment because I knew where it would take us. On the train down from Santa Fe we'd gone over some of the material we'd been briefed on the previous day. Neither of us had slept well thinking about it all and the commoline between her billet and mine was fairly active, even though we'd agreed to sleep apart so we'd not be keeping each other awake.

Consuela or Victor, in their wisdom, had scheduled us

for a run at White Sands. Because I am a Ghost Knight and keeping my identity a secret is important, I was sent down under an alias, with records that made it look as if I was Janella's bodyguard. Since she is a Knight, they restricted the range, making it our private playground until whenever we were done. Anyone wondering why would assume it was at her request, and I'd go unnoticed, which is exactly what everyone wanted.

While allowances are made for Knights off on missions, I was actually two months overdue for my performance evaluation. Janella was more up-to-date, but was close enough to her due date to let her make the run when I did. I also suspected that some folks wanted to see how I would do in the new 'Mech, especially after the way I lost my last one.

The run was good for more than clerical reasons. White Sands is beautiful in a Spartan sort of way, but then I find deserts fascinating because they are so unlike the forests in which I grew up. The place was completely steeped in history, too, with the first nuclear bomb having been tested at Alamogordo, and I was pretty certain that placing a testing range for BattleMechs here had not been accidental.

And I knew the creation of the Boneyard definitely had not been.

I liked to think Stone had ordered it into existence, but I also saw the hand of David Lear in its creation. To the west of the testing center, between it and the San Andres Mountains, a cemetery for broken 'Mechs had been created. They came in every configuration and color scheme, from every House, Clan and mercenary unit I'd ever heard of. Legless 'Mechs rested on their sides or backs. Others stood there with broken arms resting at their feet. On more than one occasion the 'Mech's battered head lay on the ground or sat askew atop pitted and chipped shoulders.

Stalking past it I always felt a chill running down my spine. Here, in this place, the most devastating weapon known to mankind had been created. In the shadow of where it had been detonated waited these battered engines of war. Just as mankind had realized using nuclear weapons was folly, so perhaps would we someday learn to eliminate the need for BattleMechs.

When I'd first come here an old MechWarrior guiding

me out to the range taught me a rhyme whose authorship was lost in antiquity. "As you are, so once were we. As we are now, you shall someday be." Every one of those 'Mechs had been piloted into combat by someone just like me. They'd had the myth of their invincibility proven a lie one day. Some of them lived to profit from the experience, but many more paid a fearsome price for it.

Looking at them now I realized I still clung to the idea that I was not going down. That was ridiculous, after all, since I'd been shot out of my last two 'Mechs—Maria being an exception. Digger's going down had been a wild ride, but little more. The other 'Mech, well . . . I squinted but couldn't quite see its twisted carcass amid those roasting in the sunlight.

We guided our 'Mechs into the hangar and crawled out of the cockpits. A tech came over to me with a noteputer and had me sign off on various forms. She smiled at me and I wondered if the clerk who'd fixed my room in Santa Fe was a cousin of hers. "We'll be getting the name painted on her soon, sir. You sure you want Ghost?"

I nodded. "That's it."

She frowned for a moment. "Not a good omen. Why would you want it?"

I shrugged, peeling off my cooling vest in the same motion. "Prince Victor Steiner-Davion's unit in the Clan war was called the Revenants. Revenants are Ghosts. Maybe some day I'll be good enough to have been a Revenant."

"You pilots." She shook her head, but her broad smile didn't die. "You want it, it's done. I'll even make sure they do a good job with the painting."

"Thanks." I gave her a nod, then cut along the catwalk to Janella. She finished signing off on her forms and beamed a smile at me. "My score puts me in the ninety-eighth percentile for those tested this year."

"Good. My score indicated I have a future in a service industry where if I do anything more than shoot someone a nasty glance I'm overmatched." I traced a finger along her jaw, then leaned in and kissed her.

She smiled. "Now *that* was directly on target."

"It was a ranging shot. Should I fire for effect?"

Janella blushed, then hooked her arm in mine. "First, my

dear, we are going to get a lot of water to rehydrate, and some food. Then we are going to shower."

"But the showering facilities here are segregated, my dear."

"Pity, true."

"And if we do that, by the time we're done . . ."

She smiled. "Yes, the train back to Santa Fe will be here. And we'll have to think of something to do to occupy our time heading back home. This shouldn't be a problem unless you don't think you can hit a moving target."

"Only one way to find out." I covered her hand with mine and squeezed. "And if I can't, I'll just have to practice."

"Indeed, Mason." Her eyes flashed. "Good thing it's a long ride."

As rides go, it wasn't long enough. Janella and I managed to find an unoccupied cabin in first class and locked it using certain override codes I knew. Laboring in obscurity as a Ghost Knight is not always fun, but it does occasionally have its perks.

Our arrival back in Santa Fe had been anticipated. Inside the station we docked our noteputers and got complete updates of news and our schedules. We could have done this at White Sands or even on the train, but having the information would have been a distraction and, as I have learned, when practicing to perfect skills, eliminating distraction is vital. *Focus. It's all about focus.*

Luckily, our superiors did not want us to report for more briefings. I wasn't certain if this was because they wanted to give us time off, or if they were just too busy sorting wheat from chaff so that we went unnoticed for the moment. Whichever, I was pleased since it looked as if Janella and I would be able to have a quiet dinner together.

She glanced over at me from her noteputer. "You remember that dinner?"

"My mouth is watering already."

She gave me a quick smile, but it shrank pretty fast. "My parents came in from Zurich. The good news is that they want us both to join them. Kind of a preholiday dinner."

The bad news was self-evident, and pretty much ran

along the same lines: they wanted us to join them. Her father, Thomas, is a Knight and, while not a warrior, his simply requesting we join him and his wife for dinner would have been enough to get our schedules cleared. Andrea, her mother, was a world-class jurist and I liked the both of them. They were very nice people and clearly were proud of their daughter.

But, they were parents and clearly thought that she, a noble from Fletcher, could do better than some guy who inventoried pine needles for a living. To make matters worse, while her father was happy that I had a job and seemed to enjoy my work, her mother was pretty sure something else was going on. She had a prosecutor's nose for deception and clearly knew I was hiding something. Janella did a wonderful job of deflecting her mother, but Andrea still came after me—much in the way her namesake 'Mech relentlessly drove in on targets.

The problem was that despite his being a Knight and their both being proud and honored Republic citizens, neither one of them was cleared to know who I was or what I did. Heck, not even all the Paladins knew the identities of the Ghost Knights. Each might know one or two, and a few a handful, but the secret of our identities were held more tightly than licenses to pilot 'Mechs.

"Command performance, lover?" I put on my best I-can't-think-of-anything-I'd-rather-be-doing face. "This time I *am* going to pay for dinner, and I'll order a good wine, too—a pre-Christmas present."

She kissed me on the cheek. "That will be perfect, yes, my dear. But, don't worry, I will make it up to you."

I smiled. "As long as you're with me as you were today on the training ground, there's nothing that will daunt me."

TECHNICAL READOUT

3130

INTRODUCTION

Technical Readout: 3130 is the latest in a series of reference books describing the equipment and materials of war in common use in the Inner Sphere; wherever possible, a full range of technical and historical data has been provided. Though IndustrialMechs are not normally machines of war, history has taught us that they can be quickly and easily pressed into service when the need arises. As such, the most common IndustrialMechs are included herein.

Commissioned by the Exarch himself, this volume is for use by the Republic Army, as well as the Knights of the Sphere. Even in a time of peace, familiarizing oneself with the potential weapons of war is a must for any soldier of the Republic.

I am honored that the Exarch commissioned me to oversee the research and writing of this document. I hope that it will serve its function well.

— Jacob Tolsum
Republic Military Historian
19 December 3129

Mason,
These pages are from the latest TRO I could find. Everything correct? Hope you can read my scribbles.

— Janella
5 June, 3132

FORESTRYMECH

(Modified)

Mass: 25 tons
Chassis: Duratron Light
Power Plant: 125 I.C.E.
Cruising Speed: 57 kph
Maximum Speed: 89 kph
Jump Jets: None
Armor: StrongArm

~~**Equipment:**~~ *Armament*
1 EarthWerks "Shredder"
Industrial Chain-Saw

~~1 Class IV Heavy-Duty~~
~~Utility Claw~~

1 Mydron LB 5-X Autocannon
(for example)

Commentary:

Variously known as WorkMechs, UtilityMechs or IndustrialMechs, these workhorses have been on the job for more than seven hundred years. Including AgroMechs, Construction-Mechs, MiningMechs and ForestryMechs, this class of 'Mech has been plowing fields, harvesting crops, digging mines, logging and constructing buildings at a speed that has allowed the colonization of literally thousands of star systems in the last millennium. Furthermore, the BattleMech — the most fearsome weapon of war ever devised — was based on such designs.

The latest model in a long line, the Earthwerks Ltd. Forestry-Mech is the cutting edge of logging technology; Earthwerks is currently one of the largest suppliers of such IndustrialMechs in the Inner Sphere. With its clawed right arm, it can uproot even very large trees; the mounted chain on its left side saw can cut through almost any known material.

Cuts through armor fast!

Internal combustion engine prevents use of energy weapons

ForestryMech

Some
modified
with ballistic
weapons

AGROMECH

Mass: 35 tons
Chassis: IM Heavy
Power Plant: 140 I.C.E.
Cruising Speed: 43 kph
Maximum Speed: 65 kph
Jump Jets: None
Armor: StrongArm II

~~**Equipment:**~~ *Armament*
1 Archenar Series 3
Industrial Rotary Saw

~~1 Class III Heavy-Duty~~
~~Utility Claw~~

1 Armstrong Autocannon

Commentary:

An IndustrialMech — like the ForestryMech, ConstructionMech, MiningMech and even the rare AquaMech — this newest series comes from the production lines of Achernar IndustrialMechs. Originally Achernar BattleMechs, this company produced some of the finest BattleMech designs in the Inner Sphere, such as the Enforcer, Osiris and Argus. With the formation of The Republic and the planet Achernar's inclusion, however, the company quickly saw the writing on the wall and retooled their line to produce IndustrialMechs.

This latest model of AgroMech includes twin combines with a lift hoist for added utility. It mounts significantly more armor than almost any other AgroMech model, which means it can be employed on even the harshest planets. Because of its utility and ruggedness, the Achernar AgroMech has become the best selling AgroMech in the Inner Sphere in just a handful of years.

AgroMech

Most common variant features autocannon jury-rigged to right shoulder

LEGIONNAIRE

Mass: 50 tons
Chassis: 2A Type 15 Endo Steel
Power Plant: 350 Magna XL
Cruising Speed: 56 kph
Maximum Speed: 98 kph
Jump Jets: None
Armor: StarGuard II

Armament:

1 Mydron Model RC Rotary
Autocannon 5

more like 76 Kph

clocked at 119 kph last encounter - fast!

Commentary:

The Legionnaire was one of the final new designs to be mass produced by the Achernar BattleMechs factory of the Federated Suns, before the plant was scaled back following the end of the war against the Word of Blake and the formation of the Republic of the Sphere. Nevertheless, the Legionnaire is a powerful design that combines exceptional speed and firepower into a potent package.

With a top speed of a hundred kilometers an hour, the fifty ton Legionnaire is one of the fastest medium 'Mechs in existence and can keep up with the majority of light 'Mechs. This speed allows the pilot of a Legionnaire to quickly bring to bear its only armament, a Mydron Model RC Rotary Autocannon 5. With its horrific rate of fire slaved to an advanced targeting system, the 'Mech's autocannon has the ability to deal extensive, accurate firepower. If need be, the Legionnaire can then quickly slip away before the target can return effective counterfire.

Critics of the design note the autocannon's lethality, but cite the fact that it is the only weapon system the 'Mech mounts. Nevertheless, the Legionnaire has proven itself in numerous battles, most notably the third battle of New Avalon during the World of Blake Jihad.

07MW-1223-11B

Legionnaire

Scott Tracyk of Davion Guards seen piloting this model

M1 MARKSMAN TANK

Mass: 95 tons
Movement Type: Tracked
Power Plant: 285 Pitban
Cruising Speed: 32 kph
Maximum Speed: 45 kph *(conservative... clocked at 55 in the field)*
Armor: Protec 12
   Ferro-Fibrous *(high-end protection for such a workhorse)*

Armament:
1 Lord's Thunder Gauss Rifle
2 Guided Technologies 2nd Generation SRM4s
2 Ayukawa "Slapper" SRM 6-packs
2 Shigunga Medium-Range-Missile Ten-pack
4 Bulldog Miniguns

Commentary:

The M1 Marksman Tank, like the Demon Medium Tank, was contracted by The Republic and designated as such to tie in with the original Marksman first produced in 2702 for the original Star League. However, unlike the Demon, which many pilots consider to be an inferior design, the M1 is far more powerful. Though the original Marksman actually mounted an artillery weapon, the current design is a more traditional tank. At thirty tons heavier than the original, however, it has an arsenal of weaponry that few other modern tanks can match.

It needs that defensive capability. Its treads make the M1 mobile and stable over almost any kind of terrain, but its weight makes it a slow mover and an attractive target on the field of battle. With its next-generation armor as a last resort, the M1 is well defended against all comers.

This model made its first appearance in combat in 3083 during the Capellan Confederation Resistance Skirmishes, just two years after Devlin Stone declared the formation of the Republic (suggesting that its development and production were made a priority). The devastating firepower provided by the M1 made a huge difference to the Republic's strategy and in the end was considered instrumental in the final outcome.

07MW-1223-11B

M1 Marksman Tank

Used by Katana Tormark's troops – who's her source?

CLAN BATTLE ARMOR

Mass: 1 ton
Chassis: Medium Humanoid
Power Plant: 285 Pitban
Ground Speed: 11 kph
Jump Jets: Standard Jump Pack
Armor: Standard Clan

Armament:

1 Short Range Missile 2-pack
(detachable)
Mounts 1 of the following:
  1 Heavy Flamer
  1 Support Laser
  1 Support Machine Gun

Commentary:

MechWarriors of the Inner Sphere were baffled when they first encountered Clan Elemental troops wearing battle armor in 3050. Awestruck, Inner Sphere MechWarriors watched as battle-armored Elementals withstood machine gun fire and even direct laser hits from BattleMech weapons, bounded about the battle field and swarmed enemy 'Mechs, and even fired support-sized missiles. The armies of the Successor States had never seen anything like these battle-armored troops. Indeed, the capabilities of the Clan battle armor were so far beyond any Inner Sphere infantry-armor technology at the time, it is hardly surprising that some Inner Sphere MechWarriors believed the Clan Elementals were some type of alien life form.

All battle armor suits, including the Elemental, are powered by myomer musculature controlled by the wearer's own movements. They're also all atmospherically sealed, with self-contained life-support systems that allow them to function underwater or in a vacuum. Built-in sensors also provide short-range tactical communications (easily tied into long-range systems) and weapon heads-up display — that each tie into a suit's weaponry — and monitor the condition of the pilot, automatically activating medipacks if the circumstances warrant it. Many suits, including the Elemental, also contain integral jump jets that drastically improve their mobility.

One final feature of the Clan-produced Elemental battle armor — something that the Inner Sphere has yet to replicate — is an automatic, self-sealing mechanism that seals all breaches in the trooper's armor; it is a jelly-like substance, unique to the Clans, known as HarJel. This feature allows this type of battle armor to continue far beyond the capabilities of those fielded by the Inner Sphere.

*...and battlefield presence!
Deadly in formation*

Clan Battle Armor

Typical design in widespread use

Flamer-equipped model is most common and effective

Walks Again

MechWarrior
DARK AGE

A MechWarrior: Dark Age Ghost War Exclusive!
Get your...

"Janella Lakewood", Tundra Wolf 'Mech
Unique, Limited Edition Figure – Available only while Supplies Last

Get your own "Tundra Wolf" BattleMech miniature, piloted by the elite
MechWarrior Janella Lakewood. This unique, limited edition game piece
is from the run-away hit collectable miniatures game, MechWarrior: Dark
Age. The Jannella Lakewood 'Mech is only available through this exclusive
offer and not part of the standard figure set. Don't miss your chance to get
this rare figure! Order one today!

The Tundra Wolf BattleMech miniature stands approximately 2 3/4" tall.

Name: | | | | | | | | | | | | | | Date Of Birth: | | | | | | | |

Shipping Address: | | | | | | | | | | | | | Apt. #: | | |
(Will only ship to billing address on credit card.)

City: | | | | | | | | | | State/Province: | | | | |

Zip/Postal Code: | | | | | Day Phone: (| |) | | |

E-Mail Address: | | | | | | | | | | | | | | | | | | | | | |

Do you wish to be added to our mailing list? ☐ Yes ☐ No

☐ VISA ☐ MC Credit Card # | | | | | | | | | | | | | |

Exp. Date: | | / | |

X _____
Card Holders Signature

Ordering Information:	PRICE	QTY* (LIMIT 2)	TOTAL*
U.S. Address: Each Figure with Shipping & Handling	$5.00		
Canadian Addresses (Credit Card Only): Each Figure with Shipping & Handling	$6.00		
Outside US & Canada (Credit Card Only): Each Figure with Shipping & Handling	$10.00		

* Total = Price x Quantity. Limit two (2) per order.

Send this Order Form with Payment and Original Cash Register receipt to:

Janella Lakewood 'Mech Special Offer
WizKids, LLC
12145 Centron Place
Cincinnati, OH 45246

WizKids™

Cut along dotted line

17

> *Logical consequences are the scarecrows of fools*
> *and the beacons of wise men.*
>
> —T. H. Huxley

Knights' Hall, Santa Fe
North America, Terra
Prefecture X, Republic of the Sphere
10 December 3132

Dinner went as well as could be expected. Janella's mother did make a couple of runs at me, but they were halfhearted. I actually welcomed them because her fire returned when she started on me, but quickly petered out. When she got going I recognized her, but otherwise Janella's parents were strangers.

On Helen I'd been able to see the effect of the grid's collapse on everyday folks. While it had an impact, folks didn't spend a lot of time pondering the larger consequences of it. They looked at how it would affect their lives right then, right there, and didn't waste the brain sweat on looking beyond because they had no way of calculating the consequences that far out.

Thomas and Andrea Lakewood did and had. For Thomas

it meant interminable delays in important experimental data. He worked on projects where multiple labs were running parallel or complementary experiments, and lessons learned in one place would immediately be applied elsewhere. Any slowdown in that sort of information exchange wasted hundreds of man-hours and thousands of stones. The delays literally would cost lives as people waited for medicines and improved food crops.

Andrea seemed to feel the impact more keenly. Being a lawyer she liked order, and the grid's collapse was a mortal blow to order. While she did not see an anarchist lurking in every shadow, she reacted sharply to Janella's recital of her recent trip to Helen. My role there was left out, but it would not have mattered as Andrea burrowed in on Reis and GGF, balancing their roles, their actions and the subsequent changes in the power flows on Helen. As dangerous as GGF might have been, she saw Reis' gathering power as more so, and clearly feared this would be happening over and over again throughout The Republic and beyond.

I don't mean to suggest her parents were panicking, for they were not. They were just smart enough and had enough education to permit them to think several steps down the line. If people as intelligent as they were could see doom in the offing and, more importantly, didn't see any immediate solutions, the future was not very bright at all.

Eventually conversation spiraled down into comments about the food and remembrances of meals we'd had elsewhere. It might just be my opinion, but beyond the obligatory questions about how your food tastes, or the near orgasmic moaning that accompanies dessert, dinner is not the place to discuss meals eaten elsewhere. That's only one step above discussing the weather, and when you have nothing better to discuss than the weather, you just have nothing to discuss. There is no conversation, the meal is dead, and everyone should just go home.

We did rise above weather when, over coffee, Andrea declared she thought it was nice I could travel to Santa Fe while Janella was there. "When next she is given a mission, you'll have to come see us. You still live in Zurich, don't you, Mason?"

"I'm here for a while, Judge. Meetings, consulting."

"On what?"

Janella smiled. "He's had a meeting with Victor Steiner-Davion."

"Oh, really, Mason? Helping him with his gardening, are you?" She phrased it sweetly, as if showing me the rose's blossom would make me forget there were thorns lurking there.

"Yes, Judge, helping with his roses. Tough to grow here." I got up, excusing myself and found the restaurant's manager. I covered the bill, then snagged two roses from a woman who had a basketful. I returned to the table and gave one each to the ladies—red for Janella and white for her mother. I had nothing special in mind concerning the colors, but I let her mom chew on the possible meanings for a bit.

Thomas beetled his white brows. "Now, if they will just bring us the check."

"I've taken care of it." I held hands up to quell protests. "No, the last few times we've had dinner, you've paid. My turn is long overdue."

"Nonsense. This was expensive." Andrea gave me a kindly smile. "We know The Republic doesn't pay . . ."

"Mother!"

"Dear, it is just a fact of life. Now, Mason, we insist."

"Appeal denied." I rapped my knuckles on the table. "I appreciate it, but I needed to do this."

A glance passed between husband and wife, and Andrea relented. "Well, at least come back to our place and have more coffee."

"Andrea, I think we've taken enough of their time."

Janella nodded. "There are briefings in the morning."

I smiled. "And aphids. Can't get after them quickly enough."

Thomas' hand swallowed mine. "Good to see you again, Mason. Thanks for dinner, and that was an excellent wine. Next time, though, there will be no slipping off to pay the bill."

I shook his hand solemnly. "Just beat me to it."

He laughed and lowered his voice. "You know, we'll both be behind them."

"Uh huh." I smiled as mother and daughter hugged, then I gave Andrea a hug. "Thank you for the invitation. I appreciate you letting me intrude on your time with your daughter."

Andrea held on a bit longer than was necessary. "Our pleasure, Mason. We almost think of you as family."

We left the restaurant and walked quietly with them through the streets of Santa Fe. We reached Knights' Hall quickly enough and refused another invitation to join Janella's parents for coffee. As we made our way through the various corridors, Janella hugged my arm and laid her head on my shoulder.

"You do know I will have a talk with my mother, right?"

"No reason, she's just being a mom. It'll be interesting when she meets my mom."

A little shiver ran through Janella. "I don't know that I'm ready for meeting her myself."

"My mom will love you."

"You've said that. You've also said that she's had umpty-eleven kids and works as a wildlife-management specialist in the forest preserve your father ran. She's going to take one look at me and decide I'm soft."

"Your being soft isn't bad, you know, because it's all in the right places."

"Such a sweet talker. You think that's going to get you somewhere?"

I smiled. "Well, *that* and the fact I let you eat half my dessert."

She licked her lips. "Ah, yes, gallantry under fire. That does indeed deserve a reward, and I think I know just what it shall be."

I awoke the next morning feeling well rewarded if not fully rested. We skipped breakfast, save for some coffee that brewed while we were in the shower. We swung by Janella's place to get her a change of clothes, then both reported to the briefing room we'd spent so long in two days earlier. Nessa and Consuela were both back, and I saw evidence of Wroxley's handiwork as well.

A fifth person joined us for the meeting and I immediately bowed low and respectfully to him. "*Konichi-wa, Kurita Kitsune-sama.*"

The man returned my bow, with the overhead light shining from his shaved head. The traditional Japanese garb he wore bespoke his Combine origins more than the slight almond shape of his eyes. That Asian shaping was easy to miss, since the eyes were a brilliant gray that reminded me very sharply of Victor's eyes.

Which was only natural, since Kitsune Kurita was Victor's son by Omi Kurita. Kitsune had been born while Victor was off on the Clan homeworld, and his birth was hidden from his father when Victor returned. While a lot of people believe Victor knew of him, the two of them never met until Kitsune, being elevated to the rank of Knight of the Republic, asked for the honor being bestowed on him to be given by "one without whom I would be nothing." Devlin Stone and the others gathered thought he was referring to one of his uncles, either Hohiro or Minoru Kurita, but instead he addressed Victor. "*Father*, it is from your hand that I would receive this honor."

This revelation caused quite a bit of a stir in the Draconis March of the Federated Suns, where propagandists turned Omi into a succubus who had seduced Victor for nefarious purposes. The upset was even greater in the Draconis Combine, however, as certain reactionary elements had been looking to champion Kitsune as a rival to the current Coordinator, Hohiro. Once they realized that Victor's blood ran in his veins, the divisive talk stopped and, rumor had it, two minor lords committed *seppuku* out of mortification because they had championed a Davion to replace a Kurita.

Straightening up, Kitsune extended a hand to me. "It is good to see you again, Mason. Your scores from yesterday are promising."

"Promising more work, yes."

He smiled, then bowed to Janella and shook her hand, too. "And your scores are promises fulfilled."

"You honor me, my lord."

We sat again, with Kitsune sharing the couch with his niece. Consuela let us get settled, then began. "There has been nothing truly significant that's developed over the last twenty-four hours. Stone's wisdom in limiting access to BattleMechs is proving itself to be providential. The scramble to consolidate those resources is one that is hard to hide. We're taking steps to secure the supply of ordnance, but 'Mechs going on a rampage can cause a lot of damage regardless. Luckily most of the industrial conversions we've heard about do not have sufficient power to use heavy energy weapons."

I nodded. BattleMechs have a fusion reactor as their heart and it puts out a lot of energy. Not only does the 'Mech rely on it for powering the myomer muscles that give it the ability to move, but it also fuels the energy weapons. Lasers, particle projector cannons and Gauss rifles could suck a small city dry of power, and the diesel engines of 'Mechs like Digger and Maria just can't generate that much juice. While Maria's small pruning laser was enough to kill that one terrorist, aside from bubbling up paint on a BattleMech, it wasn't going to be much of a threat.

Janella leaned forward. "You've clearly anticipated moves to establish supply lines. Security has been increased at storehouses. I assume you're covering production facilities as well."

The Countess shifted her shoulders uneasily. "We are doing our best, but the lack of data is hampering us. For all we know, we are sending requests to garrison units that have already decided to take power by themselves. Industrialists may have already thrown in with one power broker or another, and plant security forces may have decided to hijack the factories themselves. If a factory puts out two 'Mechs a week, they could have two companies of fully armed 'Mechs ready to go. Given what they would be arrayed to fight, that's a formidable force."

"It is indeed, Countess." Kitsune's voice came softly, making me lean in to hear him. "And this problem extends beyond The Republic itself. In instituting his reforms, *Stone-sama* always had Republic forces ready to deploy against those who opposed him. Their power was seen in the Free Worlds League and the Capellan Confederation, and it was enough, at the time, to cow forces in the Combine and Federated Suns. There is a difference, however, between feeling the lash and watching someone else get whipped. Those who only watched are now thinking the lash will never fall on them.

"As you know, the reformation of the Combine was declared early on, but forces resisted for the better part of another decade. BattleMechs were decommissioned, but in the Combine this did not have exactly the same meaning as it did elsewhere. To have a 'Mech destroyed would have been akin to asking a samurai to break his swords. A family's pledge to retire a 'Mech was accepted and, for the most part, those pledges have been honored out of respect for Stone and The Republic."

I rubbed a hand over my forehead. "With Stone gone and The Republic seeming to lose its grip, people are looking to get those 'Mechs back in working order. I don't doubt museums throughout the Inner Sphere are being scoured for 'Mechs. Do we have any idea how many could be out there?"

Nessa shook her head and tapped a request for data into the keyboard. The holoprojector flashed up a cube that just bled numbers. "Exhaustive studies have been done concerning industrial capacity, demand for parts, munitions consumption rates, regimental muster sheets, everything. For centuries 'Mechs have been scrapped, salvaged, purchased new, stolen, shipped covertly to rebels, you name it. The gap between those we know are in service and being produced, and those that were decommissioned, destroyed and otherwise neutralized could be anywhere from a few hundred to thousands, even tens of thousands. And that's just for the Inner Sphere records we can get our hands on. Clan figures are sketchy at best and if someone were to find some ancient Star League cache of equipment, all bets would be off."

Consuela spread her hands. "So, not only do we have internal disputes here that could tear The Republic apart, but those who had been laying low for fear The Republic would land on them could be rearming themselves. For all we know, there could be dozens of skirmishes taking place right now."

I shook my head. "It's insane, though. If everyone just remained calm and at peace, no one would get hurt."

Janella shot me a sidelong glance. "We're talking about human beings, Mason, not angels."

I winced. "True."

Kitsune held a hand up. "But we are not talking about devils, either. Many people are just preparing to defend themselves, if it comes to that. It would be a pity were there devils among them who would exploit this drive for self-preservation. It is upon them we must focus."

"So the trick is to identify them and then deal with them." I sighed. "And we just have to hope that they won't have sufficient momentum in their movement that nothing can stop them. If things go too far, the blazes that get touched off will just sweep through the Inner Sphere."

Nessa sat back, her shoulders slumping. "Two to three potential devils per world, thousands of worlds, well, if that's the task, we have lots of job security."

"Yeah, until one of those devils shows up here on Terra and tells us our services are no longer required." I stood and stretched. "I expect, if that happens, the severance package we'll be given will include severing our heads from our bodies."

Janella looked up. "Ever the optimist."

"It could be worse."

The Countess raised an eyebrow. "Yes? How?"

My mouth gaped, but no words emerged. The problem wasn't that I couldn't answer her question, but that I had too many answers that would suffice.

18

The first casualty when war comes is the truth.
—Hiram Johnson

Knights' Hall, Santa Fe
North America, Terra
Prefecture X, Republic of the Sphere
7 January 3133

Over the next month things settled into a pattern, though not quite a routine—with a break for the holidays that made the workload bearable. We sifted through reports, which were digests of news reports coming in from everywhere. When an item seemed interesting or important, we'd call up the actual story and all relevant facts surrounding it. We'd pore over that material and prepare our own digests of it all.

Now, with the grid down, the assumption would be that the amount of data we had to go through would be limited. This was true on one level, since it was a fraction of what would have been available to us were the grid working. The problem was that when the grid was working, we would get reports from Republic personnel on the ground, who would already be able to sort fact from fiction, and provide background and nuance to what news there was.

Those reports were not getting through in a timely or reliable basis—for all intents and purposes they did not exist. Instead, what we got was a wealth of material that was similar to the tailings from a mine: there might be some valuable trace elements in there, but getting them out was tough, expensive and time-consuming.

JumpShips were moving information between worlds on a spotty and indirect basis. While they sat at a recharge point, they'd also pull wideband scans of all communications media from the system—they sucked in Tri-Vid channels the way some folks gorge on spaghetti. They pulled in everything, duplicated it, traded it with other ships and distributed it. In a week-long recharging stay they'd pick up an average of 20,000 channel hours per world, so by the time ships got to Terra, they'd be dumping off hundreds of man-years of things to be reviewed. While computers could scan the data and screen for keywords, developing the lexicon took time, and when something significant showed up in one report, new keywords would be added, so more scanning would have to be done.

In some ways a hunt like that was exhilarating. It felt to me as if I was out on some savanna somewhere, crouched down, staring at the tracks of jackals, seeking beneath their steps for the spoor of lions. There were times I was certain I'd seen it, too, and would follow that trail until I had to admit I had nothing. Then I'd go back over the jackal tracks and prepare a report on what was happening there.

All too often those reports amounted to a big fat zero as well.

The core problem was, of course, that we had no way of verifying the information we were looking at. In the most simple terms, how could we evaluate Tri-Vid news reports coming out of Helen that were based on media releases by Commander Reis? Even if the facts were accurate, even if we eliminated all the guesses, the spin put on the facts would lead us to one conclusion or another.

And trying to evaluate the things that weren't said made it just that much tougher. Were we not getting tales of abuses of citizens' rights from Helen because Reis had repressed those reports, were there simply no abuses or were we not getting reports because no one had been scanning that week? Were polling numbers that we were seeing accurate, or had they been manufactured to cloak a multitude of sins?

Victor's sister Katrina had used the manipulation of such data to steal the Federated Suns away from him while he was off fighting the Clans. Victor had left his realm in the hands of his youngest sister, Yvonne. Katrina started changing polling numbers and reports such that, by the time reports arrived on New Avalon, Yvonne believed the people thought she was the incarnation of Satan. She asked Katrina for help, then abdicated in her favor, leaving Victor homeless when he returned in glory from quelling the greatest threat mankind had ever known.

Though we found no lions, jackals did abound in a variety of guises. There were some, like Bannson and Tormark, who were clearly making strong moves, but they were equally subtle. They skirted the edge of treason. We could project countless cases where efforts may have strayed over that line, but we also assumed that the big jackals were smart enough to insulate themselves from true trouble. Mr. Handy had been a layer of protection for whoever was directing the GGF efforts, and someone like Bannson had to have multiple such cutouts.

Other jackals were bolder and more direct. Some were from noble families whose patriarchs had ceded power to The Republic, and the children resented their reduction in status. To be kind to some, they saw the ebbing of The Republic's influence as a call to again shoulder the responsibility their families had long borne. Others saw The Republic as an aberration that extorted their rightful power from them, and they meant to take it back. They brought local militia troops under their direct control and declared martial law. By hinting at enemies without and within, they were able to rally majorities behind them.

This spawned countermovements, of course, of self-described Republicans, or others harkening back to ethnic and nationalistic ties. Someone of Kurita descent on a majority Davion-populated world could easily gather Combine families to them. By defining themselves as Combine loyalists they could also appeal to Tormark for support, or even go to forces inside the Draconis Combine itself. That wasn't happening with Combine loyalists alone. All of the nations had their claimants.

We did get reports of open combat, but in some ways I found those reassuring. They were little skirmishes that defined boundaries. They clearly were the precursors of other fights to come, but they bled off pressure and let things quiet down for a bit, even though the desire for revenge would grow and spawn new rounds of combat.

I knew it was time for me to walk away from analysis when I was worrying more about places that only reported peace than places where shots had been fired. Those peaceful worlds defied the madness breaking out around them. While I could have hoped that sanity prevailed somewhere in the Inner Sphere, I saw darker forces at work. Could it be that those worlds have been completely pacified by the lions? If our only window into them was through news reports flowing out, and those reports only told of sweetness and light, how would we know? The lions could be hiding in plain sight, waiting until we had mauled ourselves, before emerging from their peaceful dens.

Worst of all was the fact that even the best sorting, sifting and analysis could not change the fact that all the data was *old*. The Republic could not function with ancient news. If a reply to a request for help took two months to come back, it was far too long, and the crisis that spawned the request could have easily consumed the world from which it originated during the lag.

And, of course, tomorrow could bring in missing data from a world that would force reevaluation of everything, plunking us back at square one. We'd start over, but always had to be mindful of the fact that we remained in the dark about most of The Republic and even larger chunks of the Inner Sphere beyond our borders. Once I was operating in that mode, that had me swapping black for white on a regular basis, I'd find something else to do for a while. Running down to White Sands and working more with Ghost had a lot of appeal. Watching things blow up is cathartic. I could easily imagine that all the enemy 'Mechs were lions and pride-busting left me exhausted and smiling. My scores shot up significantly when one of the techs dressed the enemy 'Mechs in tawny and brown, with little lion-rampant devices on their chests.

Janella and I were able to slip away to a beach on the Baja coast for two days. It was supposed to be three, but we returned early, recharged and sunburned, to dive back in. I also spent an afternoon with Victor, helping him tend to the roses growing in the small courtyard off his lodgings. This turned out to be fortunate because Andrea asked if she could see the roses and I got to give her a brief tour. Victor, as gracious as ever, praised my help with the flowers, which confused Andrea and did little to quell suspicions.

Toward the end of that month the pressure just kept building. With each and every report, the clouds gathering on the horizon became thicker and darker. There was no denying that a nasty storm was coming and a lot of lightning would be cast around.

" 'The fateful lightning of His terrible swift sword.' " Victor's voice sank to a cold tone. "There is a theory that suggests mankind cannot resist war because we forget pain so easily. It's a survival trait. What woman who endured hours of labor would agree to bear another child if she could remember every moment of pain? What person would risk being trampled or stuck through with horns to bring down a buffalo if he'd survived that sort of wounding before?"

I waved bandaged fingers. "What gardener would tend roses?"

Victor smiled at my jest, but from the other end of the table, Nessa gestured at him with her fork. "That theory dismisses the fact that we're thinking creatures. We can weigh the risks of pain and injury against gain. We can also empathize with others and feel their pain. This is the basis of altruism and even heroic sacrifice in emergencies and war."

The old man nodded. "There is no denying that, Nessa, but two factors in that serve to reinforce the theory. The first is that because we forget pain, it is never weighed heavily enough when being slotted into that risk/gain equation. This is especially true when it might be someone else's pain. I would go so far as to say that those who empathize with the injuries of others disregard risk/gain equations, and almost fly in the face of overwhelming odds precisely because they believe that behavior is required of them."

Nessa nodded, lowering her fork to spear some lettuce. "We could argue some of that, but I'd end up agreeing. What was your second point?"

"I would challenge your assertion that we are really thinking creatures."

That brought my head up. "Okay, my not using gloves to help with the roses is probably not going to work in my favor when I defend mankind's sapience, but all of us here, at this table, in this place, we're thinking in high gear."

"Your hands aside, Mason, you are slipping past my point. Yes, those of us gathered here are thinking, and thinking hard and long about events, but we have the *luxury* of being able to do that. We also have the basis of experience that allows us to do that. While we can hope we are wise, most of mankind is barely sentient. When you look at Maslow's Hierarchy of Human Needs, it is concerned mostly with food, shelter and reproduction. These are all the biological urges and while some abstraction might occur—like having to work a job to secure food and shelter—they really don't rise much above the levels of creatures who are just out satisfying those basic, biological needs."

Janella arched an eyebrow. "You're not trying to say that humans are cattle, are you, my lord?"

"Not at all. Sheep is a preferable comparison because it allows for the existence of shepherds and wolves." Resting his elbows on the table, Victor pressed his hands together, fingertip to fingertip. I could see the delight dancing in his gray eyes, just like the reflected light from the candles on the table. "When you think about it, experience almost divides humanity along species lines. Just the four of us here at the table, we have traveled to how many worlds. Hundreds? Thousands? We've traveled further in light-years over a single year than some people will travel in kilometers in their entire lives. Some worlds are fabled places to people, and I've shed blood on those worlds. We have, by dint of our experience, a perspective on events that far too few people possess."

Nessa nodded. "This is why we are the shepherds."

Her grandfather frowned. "But why are we not the wolves? Those out there who will take advantage of the chaos have the same experience we do. Why aren't they making the same decisions we are? Why would they risk war with each other while we have a threat hovering out there?"

"Perhaps they have made the same decision." Janella toyed with the stem of her wineglass. "Those we call wolves probably see themselves as shepherds. They define their flock as different than we do, and they are gathering their forces to protect their constituency. Perhaps they see their rivals as the wolves behind the grid's collapse. They view our inaction and warnings of a foe unseen as our folly, and they move to secure things for their people."

"A very good point, my lady." Victor gave her a half-smile. "Several, in fact, which just makes everything that much more complicated."

I shook my head. "I can't believe someone like Jacob Bannson would ever think of himself as a shepherd. He sees himself as a wolf, as the Big, Bad Wolf, and he's out for sheep and piggies and any shepherds that get in his way."

My comment came out a little more vehemently than I might have liked, and the surprise on Victor's face made this quite apparent. "It would seem, Mason, you have taken a specific dislike to Mr. Bannson."

"Yes, my lord." I raised my napkin to my lips and wiped my mouth. "The more I read, well, I can understand the motivations of the jackals out there—wolves in the current analogy. Take Katana Tormark, for example. She's steeped in the Combine's warrior tradition, and her sense of tradition is urging her to do what she's doing."

"To the best of your knowledge, Mason." Nessa jabbed a hunk of romaine with her fork. "We don't truly know what she is thinking or dreaming."

"Sure, that's true, and I might not be looking deeply enough in her case, but with Bannson, there's no looking deep. He's as shallow as a pie plate to my mind. Greed is driving him, pure and simple. He likes money, he wants more, and he also wants to punish The Republic for not praising what a great human being he is."

Janella kept her voice soft. "I doubt making him a Knight would convert him to the cause."

"No, it wouldn't, not at all, because he'd want to be a Paladin, and then the Exarch. Bannson wants to be at the top of the food chain, not because that's the top, but because he can then start nibbling away at the links below him." I frowned. "Look, I can understand greed, but he's so open about it. If greed is what's motivating Tormark, or Aaron Sandoval or anyone else, fine, but at least they dress it up in tradition."

Nessa smiled. "Bannson would say he's a traditionalist, too. He's not out for greed, but for prosperity. You even said, Mason, that plenty of folks see him as a champion for the little guy, and someone who wants them to succeed. Perhaps you've misread him."

I shook my head. "Okay, score one for the Devil's advocate, but we can be realistic about this, too. Bannson is only out for himself and while I think it's great that those who run in his pack will get eaten up by him, I fear for all the little-guy sheep they'll tear apart while on their rampage."

Victor pushed his salad plate away from the edge of the table. "I don't disagree with your fears, Mason, but I wonder what we can do about it. There are too few shepherds."

"But we can make more shepherds. Looking over the reports, there are folks out there who really are pleading for peace and reason. We have to use our resources to help promote them and their ideas. If we protect the peacemakers, if we hold them up as examples, we will get others to think along those lines. If people equate peace with stability, we kill two birds with one stone."

"A laudable plan, but the wolves will still prey upon them."

"Yes, my lord, which means we need to add one more creature to the menagerie of wolves and sheep: the wolfhound. While the shepherd may be stuck waiting and watching for whoever took the grid down, we have to stop the wolves somehow."

The old man's eyes narrowed. "Assassination?"

"Tyrannicide? That would be one way." I glanced at Nessa. "It comes back to where we started here: making sure that pain gets properly factored into any risk/gain analysis. Wolfhounds would have to start working on the weakest individuals in the wolf packs. Subordinates whose activities cross the line would have to be punished swiftly. The wolves will have to see that they're not going to win in a walk. Not only will it make them think twice, but in culling their packs of the weak and defective, it will make them more efficient and tougher."

Janella frowned. "And that would be good exactly how?"

"When whoever took the grid down makes their next move, the wolves will have the strength to resist."

Nessa pursed her lips. "And if that blow never falls?"

"Then really healthy and efficient wolf packs will tear each other apart."

"An interesting theory, Mason." Victor gave me a smile. "But, if there are too few shepherds, I fear wolfhounds are in even shorter supply."

Victor's majordomo entered the dining room and whispered in his lord's ear. Victor nodded, considered for a moment, then looked around the table. "Thank you, Pebworth. I think we are ready for dessert and brandy."

"Yes, my lord."

The old man looked at me and I saw a gleam in his eyes. "He gave me a message. It's for you, Mason. It came from Basalt."

I blinked. "Basalt? I don't know anyone there."

"No, I suppose you don't." His smile grew sly. "It seems Sam Donelly does, however. It appears your Mr. Handy wants to offer you a job."

19

> *The greatest obstacle to discovery is not ignorance—it is the illusion of knowledge.*
> —Daniel J. Boorstin

Knights' Hall
North America, Terra
Prefecture X, Republic of the Sphere
8 January 3133

The message was necessarily vague, but rather expressive.

Sam,

Sorry to hear about your in-law trouble with Helen. I thought things would turn out differently there, but nightfall changed plans. I am pleased you are without entanglements. I am interested in resuming our partnership, with a significantly higher level of participation for you. Contact me as soon as possible. I have made good your loss and advanced passage.

Handy
Basalt 12 December 3132

Janella looked up from reading the text. "You already know he's untrustworthy. It has to be a trap."

"Oh, without a doubt, if he can sell me out as he did on Helen, he will. Then again, this message did come with a deposit of the five thousand stones he owed me *and* enough for passage from Epsilon Indi to Basalt. He must have sent it by courier to any number of worlds, and on Epsilon Indi our folks picked it up and routed it here by Black Box."

Janella nodded. "That does not make it any less a trap."

"True, but at least he has no suspicions about who I am. He thinks I'm really on Indi."

Black Box communications technology was old stuff, and much less efficient than the HPGs. They couldn't transmit much more than the message I'd gotten, but they had proved useful for Hanse Davion in circumventing a ComStar Interdiction last century. The Republic used the technology as a backup for Ghost Knight communications—slower being better than nothing—and the people maintaining Sam's cover on Epsilon Indi used it to get the message to where it belonged.

I furrowed my brows. "What's important here is this: we left Helen on the twenty-third of November. We can assume he left roughly the same time. He sent that message from Basalt only twenty-one days after leaving Helen. Three weeks of transit works, if he's moving fast or lucky in catching rides. The money he's sent for me to get there from Indi will get me there fast, so someone backing him has deep pockets."

She gave me a knowing look. "More people than Jacob Bannson have deep pockets, Mason."

"True. We're also looking at an organization here. It's a safe bet that news of a small-time felon from Acamar being released from Republic custody on Epsilon Indi was not a hot-flash news item on Basalt. Handy had someone seeking information on me. I'd go so far as to suggest that he was looking for data on a variety of people he could use on Basalt, and I was just one of them. If he's hiring talent that is 'Mech-capable, fairly serious stuff is going down."

"I'm still not seeing Bannson's hand in this, nor the hand of anyone else, for that matter."

"Okay, here's the trick: Handy's message suggests that your arrival—his 'nightfall'—prompted the change of plans.

If he were going to fade because you'd arrived, he'd have done so *when* you arrived. He waited a week. I think he sent a message to his off-world boss asking for advice and it took that long to get the message back."

She shook her head, then got up from the conference room couch and crossed to the refreshment station to get herself a bottle of water. She tossed me one, too. "Or his local boss took a while to decide what to do."

"And, in the meantime, Handy gets an offer to head to Basalt?" I opened the bottle and drank, then put it down and clapped my hands. "Wait, that's it! What if Handy has two bosses? What if local talent hires him, but he's taking orders from others who want to pit little jackals against each other?"

Janella sat back down and looked at me with disgust. "Mason, if you have to start your statement with 'what if,' it's a fantasy, not a theory. You're arguing from facts not in evidence. All we know is that your pal wants to know if you want a job. We can presume he wants you to engage in illegal activity and that your ability to pilot a 'Mech is important in this enterprise. Anything beyond that is purely speculative and we don't have even circumstantial evidence to support it. We don't even have a good idea of why Basalt is the target here."

Janella was absolutely right about that. She grew up on Fletcher, which was a short jump from her home, but she'd never been there. The same could be said for the majority of the population of the Inner Sphere. Though the world was located in what had once been a slender finger of the Federated Suns, with both the Capellan Confederation and Draconis Combine in easy striking range of it, Basalt endured nothing more serious than the occasional raid down through its history. While the population was racially diverse, it had been politically stable for centuries.

The Germayne family had ruled it since the early days of the Federated Suns and the world had prospered. The people had been fiercely loyal to House Davion, and staunch allies of the Draconis March's Sandoval family. Basalt stood ready to act as a bulwark against advances by the Combine, but they really were never called upon for more than sending troops, which they did enthusiastically.

Count Achilles Germayne had accompanied Victor

Steiner-Davion to the Clan homeworld of Strana Mechty. While he had not been instrumental in the Clans' defeat, he did fight honorably beneath Victor's banner, and even agreed to lay down his arms when Victor called his army to do that. Later he brought a company to help Victor in the civil war against Katrina. Once that was won, he returned to Basalt. During the dark times of the Blakist uprising, he married and his wife bore him two sons, Hector and Ivan. When Stone began his reforms and Victor supported him, Achilles Germayne declared Basalt to be for Stone.

His eldest son, Hector, became the planet's ruler upon his father's death. Both he and his brother had two children, a son and a daughter each. Ivan died fifteen years ago in a hovercar accident and Hector took his nephew and niece into his care. While the Germayne family was hardly the wealthiest on the planet, all of them seemed more committed to public service than making money.

The Republic files, both old and the sketchy new ones, reported little else of interest about the world. By all accounts it was a beautiful place, with lots of rain forests and natural resources. The climate featured terrific lightning storms. The planet boasted mostly light industry that served the local needs and, in that way, it was lucky since it was actually self-sufficient.

A number of reports and articles, including some written back before I was born, predicted that Basalt would be the next "in" spot for tourism—citing the vast rain forests and diversity of plant and animal life as the main attractions. The follow-ups to those articles still touted the unspoiled nature of the world, but at the same time chronicled the collapse of deals designed to make luxury resort projects a viable concern there.

The only other item that really caught my attention was a profile from a business journal that covered Aldrington Emblyn. He'd come to Basalt to manage one of those failed resort projects, but had stayed on and had become "Basalt's own Jacob Bannson." I'm sure that was meant as a compliment. The man, in twenty short years, had amassed quite a fortune and had been linked in the news with the most beautiful of women in Basalt's upper crust. There were even rumors of his planning to marry Sarah Germayne, Hector's niece, but those stopped appearing a year ago.

After doing the basic research, I still couldn't figure out why Basalt was the target, and I said as much in the briefing Janella and I gave Consuela and Kitsune. "It makes no sense. Basalt isn't even a convenient jump point. Winning Basalt will gain no one anything."

Kitsune half-closed his eyes. "Perhaps, Mason, Basalt is not a prize to be fitted into some grander scheme, but simply is a prize for itself. Basalt, as you have noted, plays little part in the affairs of the Inner Sphere. Perhaps this is yet true. The forces on Basalt may be content with winning Basalt for itself. After all, Helen was no more special and you have not fit it into a larger plot."

My mouth gaped open for a moment, then snapped shut. "Yes, my lord, you raise an excellent point. Handy's presence there may be no more significant than his reprising his role on Helen."

Consuela regarded me with dark eyes. "You resist this notion."

"Only because Handy is so much of a blank. He was clearly employed as an agent provocateur, but by whom and for what purpose we don't know. For him to be employed there and then so quickly engaged on Basalt does suggest that he has a reputation, and it must be a good one since no one is going to hire him based on the events on Helen."

"I concur, that is a problem. Moreover, a variety of Paladins have expressed concern that an individual like this is operating within The Republic. The last thing the current situation needs is agitation." She closed her eyes for a moment or two, then set her shoulders. "We're going to ask you if you would be willing to go to Basalt."

I frowned. "My duty is to obey your orders, my lady."

Consuela raised a hand. "Mason, this is not an ordinary mission. Usually you are called upon to go into the field, investigate, infiltrate, slip away and report. Most people think the Ghost Knights are called that because no one knows who they are. You know that we want them to be phantoms.

"Circumstances have changed. We are sending you into a situation where we know your contact is untrustworthy and is willing to have you apprehended or killed. He may be hiring you precisely because you are expendable. Your supposition that you are but one of many people with your talents is a good one, which means you will be in dangerous company. We can assume that, whomever is on the other side, they are equally skilled."

"My lady, I do know my way around a battlefield."

"I've seen your scores, Mason, and were we sending you into combat with Janella here by your side, or a Lament lance, I would have little worry about your ability to survive and even conquer. The fact is, you will be going in without any support. We'll be setting you alone among wolves."

Her choice of words let me know that one of the Paladins she'd been talking with had been Victor. I grinned. "This is a chance for me to try out my wolfhound idea."

Consuela nodded solemnly. "Then you will do it?"

"I'm leaning that way. I need to know the parameters of my activity. If you're right and there is combat, how far shall I go? You know there is no such thing as shooting to wound. What if I have to engage loyalist forces in combat?"

Kitsune knitted his fingers together. "You will have to defend yourself. You have no choice. You know what the limits are."

"What about activity outside a 'Mech? There's likely a host of felonies I'll have to commit. I'd keep mayhem to a minimum, but I may be required to do some fairly nasty stuff."

"That came up in my discussions. The Republic will indemnify the injured parties. Just try to make things a little less spectacular than last time."

I winced. "How far can I go, and what is sanctioned?"

Consuela leaned forward and started ticking points off on her fingers. "First, you are to learn what is taking place on Basalt and Handy's role in it. You are to intervene as best you can to maintain The Republic's stability. Second, you are to discern the players in whatever is happening, including Handy's superiors. If it is possible, we would like evidence collected that would be sufficient for prosecution in our highest courts. If we can make an example of people on a world like Basalt, it might well give others pause."

"And if they are beyond prosecution?"

"How so?"

"If they have destroyed the evidence or if witnesses are slain so they are insulated from any and all charges?" I looked Consuela straight in the eye. "What if someone's continued existence is a direct threat to The Republic's stability, and the only way to stop them is to kill them?"

"We would prefer other problem-solving methods that could be reversed."

"If I have other options, I'll exercise them." I chewed my lower lip for a second. Through my mind's eye ran the holographs of Aldrington Emblyn and the various Germaynes. I had no desire to kill or cause the death of any of them, but if they were the ones injecting poison into The Republic and I couldn't convince them to stop, I would be left with little choice.

Kitsune regarded me carefully. "You will accept this mission, then?"

"I have to. It took me four months on Helen to get close to Handy. If you were to assign this to any of the other phantoms it would take at least that long to get to him. A lot of blood could flow in that time, and that's just unacceptable." I gave them both a grim smile. "It's time for this wolfhound to get out and begin some pest control. I want the job and I'll do it very well."

20

The ultimate result of shielding men from the effects
of folly, is to fill the world with fools.
—Herbert Spencer

Inbound, DropShip **Somerset**
Basalt
Prefecture IV, Republic of the Sphere
29 January 3133

Arrangements were made for me to leave Terra immediately. I'd go to Epsilon Indi, then on to Fletcher and finally to Basalt. I sent a message ahead indicating I'd go from Epsilon Eridani to Ingress and then Basalt. I pegged my arrival on that later course as being the third of February. That put me on the ground four days before Handy was expecting me, which is exactly what I wanted.

We doubted my message, which would originate from Epsilon Eridani, would get there much before I did. I wasn't certain if The Republic would have someone traveling on the ships I said I was going to take to look out for any agents Handy might have in place on the journey in. It wouldn't have been a bad thing, and would have put at least one more Republic official on the ground where I could get some help if I needed it.

And I was pretty sure I was going to need it at some point or other. Whether this was a wolf pack or a lion's den, things would definitely get messy. Having backup would be useful, and I was given a variety of locations for dead-drops and names of contacts I could use if need arose.

The toughest thing about the journey was that Janella's parents chose to head back home to Fletcher on the same DropShip. They were utterly unaware of my journey and apparently had made a spur-of-the-moment decision to leave Terra. "I'm not sure what more good I can do on Fletcher," Thomas Lakewood had said, "but as long as I'm a Knight of The Republic, I should be doing something."

Dodging them was not as difficult as might be imagined. I let my beard grow, which changed the line of my jaw and filled my face out. I also cut my hair shorter and colored it. If blonds do have more fun, you couldn't tell by the trip I made, but, then again, that shade of yellow is seldom seen in nature so most folks didn't look at it or beyond it for long. When going undercover I usually avoid dyeing my hair, since dye jobs have to be maintained and that looks suspicious. Handy would know exactly why I was dyeing it, though, so he'd accept it.

From Terra out to Fletcher I flew on the *Munson*, then transferred to the *Somerset* for the run to Basalt. On the *Munson* I kept to steerage, didn't make many friends and skinned enough folks playing poker that I soon didn't get invited to games. That worked fine for me, as I spent the time downloading books from the ship's meager library and boning up on Basalt history.

My arrival on the planet proved uneventful and, using my poker winnings, I took a room at the Grand Germayne Hotel. I liked the place a lot, even if it was on the shabbier side of elegant: carpets just a bit too worn, Tri-Vid sets small and outdated, the menu the sort of thing that would have made my grandparents think they were eating all that cutting-edge cuisine enjoyed by the royals on New Avalon. The hotel's chief claim to fame was that Duke Aaron Sandoval had once stayed there, and it was pretty easy to imagine I was seeing the same wallpaper in the halls that he'd seen.

Once I'd gotten settled in, I ventured out into the downtown of Manville, the capital city. It had been built on a series of nine hills at the confluence of three rivers that joined on their ways north. The downtown occupied the area just south of the convergence and had been built up into a lush riparian park with bridges over the rivers and cable cars running from one hill to another.

On this particular world, the native plants tended toward shades of blue instead of green, and while quite edible by humans and our herd animals, provided an exotic air to a world, especially for me so recently come from Terra. When disembarking I'd heard someone else remark that the plants made the world look as if the Tri-Vid needed adjustment. It could have been the result of the time I'd spent tending roses, but I actually appreciated the subtle shapes and colors that let these plants thrive here.

The color of the plants was not the only thing that struck me as unusual. Perhaps it was because I'd been on Terra of late, and at a Republic facility to boot, but the signs of stress on the society surprised me. Basalt, in theory, had been stable for a long time, but the signs of division were easy to spot. Ethnic Capellans and Kuritans tended to glance down and move out of my way as I walked through a largely Davion section of the city. In some shop windows I could see faint hints of Japanese lettering that had been hastily scraped away. In other places I saw hand-lettered signs reading "Loyal to Basalt," accompanied by iconic pictures of Achilles Germayne shaking hands with Victor Steiner-Davion.

This shocked me. I did see a few boarded-up shops, but no signs of overt violence. Some Asian shopkeepers did hang in the doorways of their stores, glancing hopefully in my direction, but dejectedly dropping their heads as I made no move to enter their establishments. I might have, but the venomous glances given to them by other Anglos like me suggested patronizing those establishments would be outside the norm. Since my job was to fit in, I avoided attracting attention and went about my business quietly.

I had not traveled to Basalt with much in the way of clothes for two reasons. First, Sam didn't leave Helen with much. Moreover, my job was to fit in with society here at least until I met Handy. Since fashion varies world to world, had I decked myself out in what was the very latest on Epsilon Eridani, for example, I'd look like a clown on Basalt. The last time I'd looked like a clown, things had not gone well, so I was determined to avoid repeating that experience.

I hit several department stores and didn't buy the latest and greatest, but instead went to the clearance racks and picked out those clothes that were the least ugly. I mean, some of those clothes never should have been stocked in the first place, so it is little wonder they never sold. The normal stuff, though, made it to the clearance rack because it was a season behind. Okay, a season old on Basalt was an antique on other high-fashion worlds, but by purchasing slightly dated clothes here, I'd look as if I'd been around for a while. I'd fit in easily, and that was what I wanted.

I made one exception to this rule and went to a high-end store where I got scanned for a suit. I added to it all the appropriate things from head to toe, skin out. If I needed to move into some upper-crust circles, I wanted the right uniform there, too. This made the clerk very happy and I agreed to return the next day to get the altered clothes.

My last stop was to a styling salon, when I got my hair, as the personal-care consultant put it, "color corrected," to a shade that wouldn't make people's eyes bleed. I also got my beard trimmed down into a barely there line of stubble that was supposed to be all the rage on Basalt. It didn't do that much for me one way or another, but it looked easy to maintain, so that worked in my favor.

Coiffed and accoutered, I returned to the Grand Germayne and my room. A lot of the spycraft I'd been taught focused on noticing the little things, as they might give one an edge in any situation. I had, in fact, seen two people in the lobby I thought might be house detectives, or local police, but both were plainclothed and didn't pay any attention to me. I'd also been trained to do something like close my door on a thread, which would invariably fall out when someone opened my door, thereby warning me someone had been through the room.

This is good in theory, save for three things. In general, household staff will be in and out of hotel rooms on a nearly random basis, whether delivering things or lifting things. They won't look for, notice or replace an errant thread. Spies, on the other hand, will look for those things and will make sure they're back in place so there will be no warning at all.

The third thing was what confronted me. My door was standing wide open. There wasn't a housekeeping cart in sight, which did send up little alarm signals for me. It seemed pretty obvious that whoever had opened my room had no desire to hide this fact, which meant this visit was benign or the individual was beyond being disciplined.

In this case, it was both.

As I came through the door and the narrow hallway with the bathroom to the left, the first I saw of him was his legs. They were long and thick, which was in keeping with the rest of him. I'd seen hams smaller than his upper arms. He rose from the chair and it groaned in relief. He towered over me by a good eighteen centimeters and likely was carrying twice my weight. Looking at him I wondered if he weren't a Clan Elemental, bred for size and strength, shucked out of his powered armor.

His voice came deep and powerful, despite the long trip the words had to make to escape his chest. "Drop the packages, turn around, hands against the wall. You've done this before."

I tossed the bags onto the bed and, apparently, this was not exactly in keeping with his instructions, or I wasn't complying with the rest of them fast enough. He reached me very quickly, grabbed me up under the armpits, spun me around like a child, then gave me a little toss against the wall. I'd have rebounded from it and landed on the bed, but a big hand in the middle of my back jammed me against the wallpaper which, this close up, appeared to have weathered long years of service rather well.

He patted me down very professionally, checking all those places where a holdout blaster or a titanium throwing dart might be hidden. Once he'd finished, his left hand snaked up and grabbed me by the scruff of my neck and pitched me backward onto the bed. My landing scattered bags. I lay there looking up at this giant with his balled fists planted on his hips.

"I am Colonel Nicodemus Niemeyer. I command the Capital District's Public Safety Department. We are not the Constabulary. My people answer to me and I answer to Count Hector. He likes my work. A lot. We deal with the problems they are not equipped to handle."

I raised my hands. "I believe . . ."

". . . I have you mistaken for someone else?" The man's

deep blue eyes became angry slits, and the thick white mustache he wore quivered. "Though you are here, I shall assume you are not a fool, and you will do me the same courtesy. ComStar may not be functioning well, but I review with interest criminal cases. We are very diligent here in logging the names and identification numbers of those who cause trouble. You, Sam Donelly, are such a person. What is the purpose of your visit to Basalt?"

Lowering my hands, I slid myself back on the bed and leaned against the headboard. "You don't want me to take you for a fool, then live up to your end of the bargain. This is The Republic. I don't have to answer that question or any other without advice of counsel. That said, I'm here to enjoy Basalt's scenic beauty."

"Then you will be remembering the key rules to your wilderness adventure. Leave everything as you found it. Don't disturb the native life. Stay on the paths and don't go wandering because it could be dangerous out there."

I listened to his words and watched him standing there, and I found it easy to imagine Commander Reis adopting the same pose and saying the same things. The main difference was that with Reis it would have been posturing, backed by empty threats. Niemeyer was what Reis would have aspired to be, but never could become without a steel spine insert and a gallon of neurons being poured into his skull.

I wanted to like the man, but until I knew the political lay of the land, he was one of those dangers waiting for me in the wilderness.

"I'll do my best to remember that."

"Good. Now, this is the part of the conversation we've never had. I know why you're here. I know why all of you are here, and I won't have it on my planet. If trouble erupts and I know you did it, I'm not going to worry about proof beyond a reasonable doubt. If I bring you in and book you on charges, I face hours of paperwork, months in court, and I hate that. If I burn the back of your skull off with a laser and leave you out there for the nibblers, I file one missing persons report and I'm done. I already have yours filled out, in fact."

"Oh, transmit the file to my ex-wife. She'll be a big fan of your work."

His expression soured and the white brush-cut hair on

his head actually seemed to bristle. "You've been down this road before, Donelly, and you've danced around disaster somehow, but your luck runs out here. I'm going to be especially watchful of you because you're smarter than the others."

"Smart enough to stay out of trouble, Colonel."

"You better be, Donelly. I've got enough trouble dealing with problems *native* to my world here. The last thing I need is more mercenary thugs making life here difficult. I've not always subscribed to the idea that the only good mercenary was a dead one, but the concept is growing on me."

"I'll be no trouble at all, Colonel."

"Next time, try it with more feeling, moron." He snorted. "You're not as smart as you think you are. You'll fall."

"You'll be there to catch me?"

"I'll be there to make sure you don't get back up." His expression tightened. "Basalt is a peaceful world. It has been that way, off and on, for centuries. Even during the civil war we kept things quiet. Reforms were painless and we've done well. I'm not letting that change now. And you tell your boss that he can think himself immune to my touch, but he's not."

I almost tossed off another denial, but nodded instead. "If the opportunity arises, I'll pass your message along. I won't be bringing you a reply."

He considered for a moment, then nodded. "You can just go home, you know. You can head back out on the *Somerset*. I'll get money to cover your passage."

"Offers like that will gut your tourist trade."

"I don't want my world gutted."

"You've made that clear." I rose from the bed. "I appreciate your stopping by. Don't hesitate to come again. I look forward to seeing you."

"Yeah, sure. You won't like it when you don't see me, Donelly. Staying, you're being stupid." He started for the door, then looked back over his shoulder at me. "Don't go all the way to idiocy, because it's a fatal disease around here."

21

An ally has to be watched just like an enemy.
—Leon Trotsky

Manville, Capital District
Basalt
Prefecture IV, Republic of the Sphere
29 January 3133

Niemeyer's visit, though brief, was enough to focus me on an important part of my job, and the reason I'd arrived early. I needed to scan the local political situation to see if I could figure out what the teams were and where Handy was going to have me work. Niemeyer was clearly one faction, though exactly how strong and how aligned I had yet to figure out. Clearly if he were warning folks off and even offering to pay them to leave, he hadn't yet made the transition to outlaw that his threats suggested. While I had no doubt he could murder me and leave me in the wilderness for the nibblers to get, telling me he would do it and actually doing it were worlds apart.

Nibblers were, in some ways, the antithesis of Niemeyer, because their bite was definitely worse than their bark. The little predators were native to Basalt, ran up to sixty centimeters in length and fifteen kilos in weight. Thoroughly disagreeable creatures, they would hunt and scavenge anything, consuming its bone, sinew, hair and meat. It was highly recommended that folks should not go camping alone in Basalt's parks because if you happened to die in your sleep, or fall down and get injured, the only traces of you that would ever be found would be badly dented metal like belt buckles and jewelry.

A smaller species of the creatures had entered the cities, occupying the same ecological niche as rats on other worlds. As a result, animals that were considered pets on Basalt tended to be medium to large dogs with a history of ratting. Someone once had the plan of introducing large snakes to Basalt to clear off the nibblers, but the beasts got to gathering at the point where the snakes were released into the forests. They just loved that wriggle-steak.

In fact, the only thing that kept them in check is that they were as cannibalistic as they were territorial. I definitely had the feeling that Niemeyer saw me as a nibbler, along with the *others* he'd alluded to. The analogy seemed rather apt and when I got back to Terra I was going to convince Consuela to change from jackals to nibblers as her totem creature for troublemakers.

In one more way the idea of our being nibblers was appropriate because, twenty years ago, the locals made an effort to soften the image of nibblers. Cuddly plush toys were created in their image. A local author started a series of children's books featuring one as the hero. The "Nifty the Nibbler" character had even starred in a series of Tri-Vid shows I remember seeing as a kid—not that I knew what he was or where he was from.

I suspected that any effort made by those folks in Handy's employ and our opposition would similarly be dressed up and softened to make it more palatable to the citizenry. In essence, we would be two groups of nibblers fighting for territory, with each side trying to take on the role of Nifty and painting the other side as his evil cousin, Naughty.

Regardless, nibblers we would be, and hiding our nature would be difficult. In fact, Niemeyer's comments to me suggested he knew a lot about us. I had to assume nothing much had happened yet, but that talent had been gathering rather noticeably and no one had taken the good Colonel up on his offer to send us home.

I waited for a half hour after Niemeyer left before I headed out again. I spent the time clipping tags and labels from my clothes, then dressed in things that would sink me into anonymity in the crowds. I walked out of the hotel and watched for any tails, but saw nothing. I flagged down a hovercab, or tried to. The first two were driven by Dracs and refused to pick me up. Finally a Capellan who was adventurous or just really hungry stopped. I climbed in, then asked the driver to take me to a place where the liquor wouldn't kill me, but some of the patrons might. He started to laugh, then caught my look in the rearview and just started driving.

He took me north along the east side of the river. Manville had grown up around the downtown. The river became navigable to the north of the city, so the docks, warehouses and industrial sectors had sprung up there. To the south, where the three rivers allowed for a lot more in the way of waterfront property, the suburbs had grown. The hilltops became the Olympian domains of the rich like Emblyn. The Germayne palace covered a hill to the southeast and shone like a fairy-tale castle when the clouds broke and a lance of sunshine pierced it.

The driver began talking cautiously as he drove into a commercial area in the industrial district. It seemed pretty clear to me that thirty years ago some regentrification had been tried here, with factories being converted into lofts and other things to attract the rich, but they had wandered elsewhere, letting the area begin to slide back down into decay.

I had him drop me a block south of a place called the Cracked Egg. We drove past it once and then circled the block. He picked up speed as we went by it, which I took as good omen. The fact that the place's sign showed an ovoid *Union*-class DropShip that had been ripped open by savage fire told me this was the sort of dive I was seeking.

He grumbled about the lack of a tip, but I snarled at him. His comment in Chinese pertained to my ancestry and doesn't bear repeating here. He sped off angrily and I gestured eloquently and obscenely in his direction.

He turned the corner and I turned my attention to the bar. I watched the Egg for a little while and didn't see too much traffic going in or out. I did notice some activity at a fourth-floor window in the building across the street and down one. I figured it was Niemeyer's Public Safety Department hard at work. My wandering into the Egg so quickly after he spoke to me would likely engender a return visit to my room, so I'd have to be careful.

I walked down the block and into the tavern. The door opened into a small corridor made of corrugated steel that forced you to turn left, walk three paces, then turn right again. I was fairly certain that on that short walk before the second turn I got scanned for weapons. I didn't see anyone in position to stop me if I did have them. My eyes had not yet adjusted enough to the darkness for me to glance up and see if there were walls that would slip down and trap someone coming in with heavy gear, but that wouldn't have surprised me.

The Egg looked as if it had once been a department store as it was deeper than it was wide and a lot taller than it needed to be. Thick pillars held the ceiling up. It had four bars, the largest being along the first quarter of the left wall. In the right corner, halfway down the right wall, and then a bit further down on the left were the others. That last one serviced the tables where folks were playing cards. Back in the far right corner a Tri-Vid projection system had been set up and was playing old music Tri-Vids. The one they had on showed little Becky Shaw gyrating. Apparently they didn't know she'd gone and grown up and had been repackaged as Rebecca! when her career was relaunched.

I stood in the opening and felt more thoroughly scanned by eyes than I'd been when dropping into a hot zone. There were probably a hundred people in the Egg, excluding staff, and easily half had a feral sense to them. They were sizing me up as trouble, as a possible ally, and most certainly as a potential kill.

I let them have a good look, then walked to the bar. A bartender came over to me and glanced a question. I pointed to a neon sign. "That sign true? I'll have one."

The heavyset guy wearing a sleeveless shirt to my left hunched his shoulders and chuckled into his beer. "The only way there'd be Timbiqui Dark in the place is if you drink it someplace else and pee it out here."

I looked at him. "Do you realize you have more hair on your shoulders than you do on your head?"

He had so much beer in him, or so little sense, that it took him a moment to realize I'd meant that as an insult. As he began to get up I found it easy to imagine him being Boris' little, dumber brother—an assessment I did mean as an insult. His left hand tightened on the barrel of his mug. He intended to splash the beer in my face, crash the glass against my forehead, then pound glass splinters into my skull with his fists.

Everyone does need a hobby and, from a glance at his scarred knuckles, I gathered he rather enjoyed his.

A hand landed on his right shoulder. "At ease, Sergeant."

He moved up for another second, then turned to look at the speaker with confusion knotting his brow. "Did you hear what he said?"

"He asked for a beer." The dark-haired woman moved to slide between me and Boris Junior, but she had to wait for me to take my right foot off the back leg of his bar stool to do so. When I did, she bellied up to the bar and rapped her knuckles on it. "Tina, two bottles of Diamond Negro."

I looked up and saw no sign for it. "Never heard of it."

"Basalt brand, not quite up to Timbiqui, but good. They brew it up in Contressa, where Broad River meets the ocean. I have it brought in."

I reached into my pocket for money, but my benefactor shook her head. "My treat."

"I owe you for saving my life." The man behind her snorted as he parsed the sentence.

"If lives being saved is the criterion, Mustang should be buying for both of us, for a *long* time." Her brown eyes glittered with red-and-yellow highlights from the sign. "You'd have tipped his stool back, then what, stomped on his groin and his throat?"

"One or the other. I'm new here and don't know him that well."

"If you did, it would have been both. Repeatedly." The beers arrived and she slid one to me. We raised them and clinked them together. "I'm Alba Dolehide."

"Sam Donelly." I drank and the beer was good, *very* good, but I found myself distracted by the tattoo on her right forearm. It was the Lament insignia.

She lowered her bottle and smiled. "So, what is a MechWarrior like you doing in a scrapyard like this?"

"Could be a long story. Do you want to sit?"

"Sure." She started off through the crowd and I found myself distracted again, but not just by her body. She moved so well, so supple and lithe was she, that parts of me were inclined to aching. Her long black hair had been loosely knotted with a red bandana and swayed back and forth from shoulder blade to shoulder blade. She wore her sleeveless gray shirt snug where it should have been snug, and that applied to her cargo pants as well.

What distracted me more than her walk was the way the others looked at her. Whereas I'd been regarded with cold hostility when I came in, my being in her company offered me a dispensation. Some folks even gave me a nod, about as close to a welcome as I'd get before I'd bled alongside them, and maybe not even then.

Alba reached a table that, while she was still incoming, had been fully populated. By the time I got to it, an ashtray leaking smoke and several condensation rings were the only evidence that anyone had been there. She drew a chair back against a wall and I came around to her left. My back remained a bit open, but if anyone in here wanted me dead, they weren't going to worry about angling to shoot me in the back.

She sipped her beer. "You were going to tell me why you're here."

"Same reason as you are, I suspect. Victories are bought with blood or gold. Our blood, their gold."

Alba nodded easily, both in agreement with what I'd said, and acknowledging that she'd heard that sort of reasoning before. "Gold is to be had here, but I thought this was going to be a private little affair. Someone else sent for you because I know I didn't, which means you're not on my team. As the saying goes, you're either with us or against us."

"There's another saying: 'The enemy of my enemy is my friend.' "

She regarded me carefully with sloe eyes. "You have enemies?"

"A guy named Baxter Hsu. There was some trouble on Acamar and he set me up to take a fall for him. I was told he was heading here, to Basalt, so I came after him."

She shook her head. "Name's not coming up in my directory, Sam. He's not one of mine."

I glanced around the room. "I notice no Dracs or Caps. Personal preference or . . . ?"

"My employers' preference." She shrugged. "Pity, since they are good fighters, but the crew here will do fine."

"They look hard enough." I scanned the room again. "You're right. He's not here, at least, not *here*."

"Describe him."

"Average everything, black hair, brown, almond eyes, yellow skin. A bit more cunning than I expected, but I think someone was pulling his strings."

"Could be one of millions here." She regarded me quizzically. "You gonna climb those strings and go after the puppeteer?"

I drank, savoring the heavy taste of the hops. "Not unless he knots those strings on me. Now, if Bax isn't one of yours, who would he be working for?"

"Someone else. Take your pick." Alba shrugged her shoulders. "Warriors are being collected here like coins."

"Who's got the biggest collection?"

She smiled. "You follow the analogy. Good. Most of the folks here think analogies are why you sneeze during pollen season."

"Flattery. I like it." I gave her a nod. "And a nice deflection of my question."

"If you're as smart as I think you are, you can answer the question all by yourself."

I thought for a moment. "Emblyn, of course, can afford as much muscle as he wants. But the biggest collection isn't always the best."

Alba smiled in spite of herself. "Wise words. The best collection here might not be paid quite as much as the largest, but there will be a lot of slugs and plugged coins that won't ever spend their gold."

"Just leak their blood."

"Exactly."

"What does the best pay?"

She shook her head. "You're still an unknown quantity, Donelly. I will take some time to check you out. You'll be talking to others, I'm sure, so you'll know the going rates and see what you can negotiate. I'd expect nothing less."

"And I'd do nothing less." I finished my beer and set the bottle down. "Thank you. I'm staying at the Grand Germayne. If they don't have this in the bar, I'll ask them to order it. I'll buy when we speak again."

"I hope we can reach agreement." She nodded as I rose. "I'd rather it be your gold than your blood."

•

22

If you listen to what people say, you will fish rabbits in the ocean and hunt fish in the forest.
—Bulgarian saying

Manville, Capital District
Basalt
Prefecture IV, Republic of the Sphere
29 January 3133

My previous comments about the tradecraft of leaving threads in doors and the like, and the futility of doing that because the others in the craft know to look for such things, came around full circle as I returned to my room in the Grand Germayne. When I'd left my room, instead of trapping a thread between door and jamb, I just left one on the floor close to where it might have fallen were the door opened. The careful sneak subsequently entering my room would notice it and would likely believe that housekeeping or someone else had opened the door, knocking the thread loose. They then had to decide if they would leave it there—which they would if they wanted to get in and get out, since I would blame housekeeping for the intrusion—or replace it.

The thread had been trapped just below knee height, which is the recommended area, since no one ever looks there. The only reason for putting the thread back was because they wanted me to think things were normal in my room. They wanted to surprise me and, while I was getting used to the idea that I might as well not even have a door on my room, surprises I could do without.

Being unarmed at the moment, the dodge of pretending to be room service, or a valet, really wasn't going to work. Instead of opening the door, I backtracked to the lifts and used the house comlink to call my room. I let it ring four times and got no answer. I called again, waited for four rings, and hung up. I did that three more times and finally got an answer.

It was a female voice that sounded vaguely familiar. "Hello?"

"It's me, Sam. You'll be a long time waiting for me to join you."

My comment met with momentary silence, then she growled. "Gypsy sent me to fetch you."

"Gypsy?"

"You know him. He's quite handy."

I nodded and her voice clicked into place. I'd not recognized it because she was speaking without her jaw wired shut. "Ms. Elle, so glad you escaped Aunt Helen."

"We shouldn't talk over this line."

"Fine, meet me in the lobby and we'll go for a walk." I hung up the phone, punched the button for a lift to head down, then opted for the stairs. I descended quickly and reached the lobby, but didn't find her there. This I took as a good sign, as it meant she'd not rushed out to try to find me, which would have been stupid. She'd taken her time, looked around, made sure I wasn't going to ambush her, then headed out.

She was easy to recognize with that shock of red hair. It had been cut shorter, darkened a bit and styled nicely. Her clothes, unlike mine, were not dated and she wore them very well. Heads turned, and as she found me and smiled, men young and old glared pure hatred at me. They all wanted me dead so they could console her at my loss.

"Shall we talk of old times, my dear . . . ?"

"Elle will do fine. Gypsy was surprised to learn you arrived early." She steered me out a side entrance of the hotel, and we started walking south through a district that was full of galleries, antique stores, smart little bistros and the ubiquitous Javapulse Generators. "We got your message and were preparing for you to arrive next week."

"I know. That's what I wanted you to think."

She nodded. "Gypsy figured that out. He assumed you were still wary about the way things ended with dear Aunt Helen."

I patted her hand. "And did he think it was okay for you to let me know you've got someone working spaceport security who reported my arrival?"

A little jolt ran through her, but she covered her reaction with a dazzling smile. She leaned in and whispered in my ear. "We'll keep that between us, shall we, Sam?" I couldn't see her expression as she whispered, of course, but the look on the face of a couple walking toward us suggested they would have been grossly surprised by the benign nature of her murmur.

I faced her, our lips centimeters apart—close enough that I could feel her breath on them. "Your secret is safe with me."

We stayed that way for a second or two longer than we probably should have, then she turned away and guided me toward a JPG shop. We ordered and then took our drinks to a small table on the sidewalk. Both of us turned our chairs so our backs were to the building, giving us a full view of the street.

I noticed nothing of merit, but I kept watching as I spoke. "How did you leave it with Aunt Helen?"

"Things were very tricky. I was thinking I might never get out of there. You know how she is. I fantasized about shaving my head and disguising myself as a Buddhist Monk, but saffron robes are so not my color. Still I would have done anything to escape and finally I did."

Glancing over, I measured her hair with my eye. It was a couple of months' growth, so it seemed conceivable that she might have made it out that way. "And Gypsy?"

"I think he wanted to tell you himself. It's a surprise."

"He's like that, isn't he?" I sipped my coffee-flavored

chocolate beverage. "He's not worried that I would be holding a grudge, is he? He paid me what is due me. I do understand how the business can run."

Elle rested a hand on my arm and gave it a little squeeze. "Ah, but you're a professional, and so many others are not. Gypsy believed this and that is why he sent for you. He liked your arriving early. He said it showed you had even more intelligence than he'd given you credit for."

"Good." I smiled and groaned inwardly. The last thing you want someone who is into conspiracies and making odd things happen thinking about you is that you're smart. That makes him think you're a player and a plotter. The problem was that there was no way to reverse that assessment. The damage had been done and there was really only one way to repair it. Because Gypsy now would believe I was someone he couldn't trust, I had to make myself into someone he found it *vital* to trust.

We chatted about my escape and what I'd been doing as we finished our drinks, and then she hailed a hovercab. We got in and from the first it was apparent to me that the driver was in Gypsy's employ. Elle gave no directions and I was fairly certain she didn't know where we were going herself. This meant someone had been watching the JPG and, after we arrived, had brought the hovercab in on standby, with Gypsy telling the driver where we were supposed to go.

We headed north, but on the west side of the river this time, and to a small office complex with about half the units rented. Suite 301 still looked vacant. The name of the previous firm—a travel agency by the looks of the leftover graphic—had been scraped from the glass, and paper had been taped up over the windows. A sign read, "Coming soon, Basalt Astrology: By us, for where we are now."

Gypsy opened the door as we arrived. He'd changed a lot. His hair had grown out and had been colored jet-black. Either he'd gotten a lot of sun, or had spent a lot on a good skin darkener, for he had the healthy glow of someone who spent leisure time on the beach. In fact, had he been the poster child for the previous agency, I doubt it would have gone out of business. His clothing, I noted, was as nondescript as mine.

"Good to see you again, Sam."

"And you, Gypsy."

"Please, come in." He stepped aside from the door and let me through, then Elle followed and locked the door behind us. Gypsy took up the lead again and I trailed him down a corridor and to a conference room large enough to easily allow meetings of groups of eighteen or more booking expensive junkets to Solaris or some other hot spot.

And Solaris looked about right as a destination that would interest the crew gathered there. Not counting Elle and Gypsy, we were twenty, which was roughly enough people to command a pair of battalions with a couple left over. Men and women, they all looked hard and nasty—all-star survivors from every corner and culture of The Republic. A couple had replacement limbs and one a glowing red eye. I didn't see any Lament tattoos, but there were a scattering of mercenary designs on shoulders or necks, and more than enough scars to make a cosmetic surgeon drool.

Gypsy moved to the front of the room as I drew a chair back against the rear wall. "We're all here now. I apologize for calling this meeting so hastily, but our latest member arrived early and I wanted to get things started. Our situation here is relatively simple. We are here to affect a change in the leadership of this world. Revolution, reformation, conquest, call it what you will; we are the ones tasked with accomplishing it."

He smiled confidently as murmurs ran through the group. "You will be the commanders of our lances, companies and battalions. Major Catford will command our first battalion and Mr. Donelly will command the second."

This promotion surprised everyone save Gypsy and Elle. I was lucky that by being in the back of the room, I had a second to cover my shock before everyone else turned to look at me. I'd been scanned hard when I walked into the Egg, but the looks I was getting would have hard-boiled me by comparison.

The two looking the hardest at me were over on the right side of the room. One was Catford, of whom I'd heard. Back when Stone resigned and Damien Redburn had been appointed Exarch in his place, Catford had resigned his commission in a Republic Guards unit. On his native Epsilon Eridani he'd tried to raise a mercenary unit he called the Eridani Warhorses, recalling the glory days of the fabled Eridani Light Horse regiment. His efforts were frustrated when Prefect Sandoval refused to sign a company charter for him.

Since then I wasn't certain what the small, slender man had been doing. Had he waited two years he might have been able to follow in Tormark's footsteps and have a unit naturally rise around him. Since he was present on Basalt, I had to assume he'd fallen on hard times, or had been working as a consultant with those who anticipated the present times arriving in one form or another.

The other person stood a head taller than him and had her blond hair of a length that covered her shoulders and her neck. She'd probably have tucked it back on the left side to see me better, but I knew her ear had been reduced to a melted nubbin and the twisted mass of scars on her cheek and neck were enough to make even the most battle-hardened vet blanch. A piece of machinery replaced her left eye, and the stainless-steel socket in which it had been set covered her from temple to forehead, along her nose and molded to the top of her cheekbone.

Isabel Siwek didn't know me, but I knew her. She'd commanded a small militia unit on Acamar, in Prefecture V. She took her people out and put down a small protest by farmers, and put it down hard. She then burned four farms and a quarter of a small town, all the while claiming the farmers had done it to frame her. Janella had been sent in to oversee an investigation and Siwek refused to come in. Janella had been forced to bring her in and the resulting battle had left Siwek scarred and in a Republic prison.

How and why she was out, I didn't know. That had all happened four years ago. I'd known of Janella then, but wasn't dating her. When we started seeing each other, I did some background research, which is why I knew of Siwek.

Her reaction to the announcement suggested to me that she'd expected to command the second battalion. Moreover, her being seated near Catford had me thinking the two of them had already been talking together about how to run things. I could applaud their taking initiative, but given his ambition and her flexibility on ethical grounds, I was thinking having them together would not be the way to keep collateral damage to a minimum.

Gypsy waited for a moment until the tension in the room

was just shy of boiling over, then clapped his hands. "Mr. Donelly was instrumental to the successful conclusion of a recent operation, and showed great insight into these things. I am very pleased to have him with us, and I know he will be able to handle his responsibilities without question."

About a third of the people were willing to take Gypsy at his word, another third were waiting for me to prove it, and the rest of them wouldn't have deigned to follow me if I was Morgan Kell leading them in a raid on a nursery school. It could have been worse, as far as the numbers went, but was probably as bad as it could get otherwise. Those who resented my intrusion clearly were wondering who I was. Until they knew, and until Catford and Siwek could be put in their place, I was going to have trouble.

But, as every good wolfhound knows, you just start taking the pack apart one wolf at a time.

Our leader smiled. "Our goal is to destabilize the government so as to more easily effect a change. My associate and I have done the basic research on Basalt and have begun to outline a number of operations that will bring us . . . Yes, Major Catford?"

Catford rose and pulled the crimson beret from his head. "If you will permit me, Gypsy, I've been checking some things out myself, and I think there's some vulnerabilities here that we can exploit using some proven military strategies. With Captain Siwek and a few other company commanders, I have undertaken the development of operations protocols and plans that, when employed, will destroy the enemy's ability to strike at us. Once we have done that, effecting a regime change will be a simple matter of seeing to it that the current leadership relinquishes control, voluntarily or involuntarily.

"Our research has pointed out the triad keeping the current regime in power. The Public Safety Department is a paramilitary group that will be powerless to stop us. They are underequipped and trained for crowd control more than outright combat. The Basalt Militia has a few 'Mechs, and a fair selection of military vehicles, but all are outdated and underpowered. Moreover, their pilots are green and will be no real threat in combat.

"By far our greatest threat will be the group of mercenaries being gathered by our opposition. We have ascertained the location of their headquarters and are willing to initiate investigations to further track opposition forces. With a series of lightning strikes, we can eliminate this force. We anticipate that collateral civilian damage will be kept to acceptable levels and restricted to marginal underclass populations, so the potential elite backlash will be minimalized."

People listened intently, with heads nodding in agreement. Even Gypsy seemed to be open to this description, but not yet fully accepting of it. If this was the overture, I didn't want to be hearing the rest of the symphony. Catford was composing a bloody lament for Basalt, and goal one for my mission was to close that concert before it ever opened.

While I had hoped this would come later rather than sooner, circumstances were really directing me to act immediately. I let my chair rock forward and I stood. "If I'm not mistaken, Major, you're suggesting a direct military assault on a place like the Egg, to destroy the enemy's cadre of warriors?"

"That eventuality was covered in our ancillary operations to ensure complete neutralization of the enemy opfor."

"Ancillary?" I blinked. "You saw that as an afterthought? And your primary was, what, issuing a challenge to the enemy to go toe-to-toe in the northern flood plain?"

The sarcasm in my voice never even registered on him. "If you knew anything about 'Mech warfare, Mr. Donelly, or of Basalt, you'd know that the flood plain is hardly the optimal venue for combat."

"What I know about, Major Catford, is a lot more than just 'Mech warfare." I nodded toward Gypsy. "We're not here to kill 'Mechs and machines. We're here to kill a government, and I've had time and reason to think on that of late."

Gypsy smiled. "Would you care to share your insights with us, Sam?"

I thought for a moment, then nodded. "Sure. It's the only way to incite a reasonably stable and satisfied populace into wanting their government replaced. It will work. I call it Low-Intensity Terrorism. We do it right, and we might never need a 'Mech leaving a hangar."

23

I am as true as truth's simplicity,
And simpler than the infancy of truth.

—Shakespeare

Manville, Capital District
Basalt
Prefecture IV, Republic of the Sphere
29 January 3133

I'll give you the primer on Low-Intensity Terrorism pretty much as I gave it to them, and as you study the events on Basalt, you'll see the natural evolution of things. The one favor I'll do you is to leave their comments until the end. Most of the comments offered while I was talking were, funny or not, born of ignorance. The more I talked, the more people thought. It wasn't until the end that those who had made up their minds before I started, started in on me.

Traveling between planets takes a long time. Since I wasn't palling around with other people on the ship, I had a long time to think. What got me started was the effect of the grid's collapse on folks. It made them uncomfortable, skittish and nervous. Before that happened they'd have described themselves as happy. Twenty-four hours later—or whatever constituted a day on their world—they were antsy.

Several other things went into the mix. It's tough to peg when the first act of terrorism occurred. A case could be made for the plagues on Egypt. If we start it there, that's the only instance where the killing of people has actually succeeded in winning a social cause. Then again, killing one person in every family is a far greater impact than any other terrorist group has ever managed.

Killing people never does the job, especially in a modern society. All it succeeds in doing is drawing the opposition together. It makes the enemy appear to be homicidally insane. People know inherently that insane killers can't be trusted and that terrorism is extortion. There is nothing but the terrorists' good word to bind them to ceasing their activity once their goals are met. Like any blackmailers, they can keep modifying demands indefinitely.

And, face it, everyone knows there are those terrorists who just enjoy killing and wouldn't stop for anything.

A second aspect of modern society is something that Stone's reformation built upon: power comes from the people. A lot of people forget that because of the neo-feudal political system used to govern star-spanning empires. Stone did not, and his Republic thrived. Through service to The Republic people could earn citizenship. Their investment in The Republic was paid back, and they gave more of themselves to it.

The outright overthrow of a government assumed that the masses didn't exist. While many of them might not care who was sitting on a throne, their lack of connection with the government created an inherently unstable situation. Once someone with a bigger club came along, the old government was history and new faces appeared on the coins.

So, to overthrow a modern government and make it stick, you have to avoid killing too many people and you have to get the citizenry behind you. If the people are stable and relatively happy, as they are on Basalt, you have to manufacture dissatisfaction with the current government. You have to attack society at its weakest point, show the current rulers are out of touch, and point out that they are impotent and untrustworthy.

Hence my plan.

Where modern society is weakest, of course, is its insulation from reality. Basalt was fortunate in that the agro-industry and light consumer electronics, apparel, notions and appliances industries could supply the people of Basalt with everything they needed. Granted, it wasn't a grand life, but it was satisfying. Even so, Manville, like most large urban centers, was a week to ten days from starvation once trucks stopped bringing in supplies.

In short, if you asked the average Manvillian where food comes from, his reply would be "the market." Individuals like this are dependent on things like food preservation units, mass transportation and power. Everything that keeps them from grubbing in the dirt serves as a safety net that elevates them above being nibbler vittles.

Low-Intensity Terrorism, or LIT, attacks that safety net. Attacks in one area lead to attacks in others. Events begin to snowball because we provoke a particular reaction by the government. Having anticipated that reaction, we trump. People lose faith in the government and within months of a concerted effort, the tattered local regime will collapse.

The first LIT targets are nuisance strikes. In what little touring around Manville I'd done, I'd seen countless power substations, communications switching boxes, wireless communication towers, bridges and tunnels. As I explained the plan, I used power stations as an example, but each of these others works just as well. The first attack against a power substation denies power to a sector of the city.

It is important that this incident appears to be a property crime, and that no one gets hurt when the station is taken down. It's also important that just a single sector of the city loses power. LIT depends on citizens being aware of their neighbors' difficulties. In every strike we want people to be thinking, "I'm glad that's not happening to me."

Quickly enough, as attacks expand, they'll be thinking it *has* happened to them, and then they'll be wondering why the government didn't do anything to stop it from happening to them.

With that first attack no one takes credit. People will assume that it was an accident or act of mindless vandalism. The power company will be looking at repairs, however, that will cost a fair amount. They will not be pleased.

What's more, most people will feel the pain through a rise in rates—to cover the repairs or insurance premiums.

The second attack comes in two stages. The first is to hit another power station. Once repair crews have responded to that site and begin their work, a second attack hits the large repair-truck garage facility. These garages are all over the place, with utilities grouping their trucks for ease of fueling and repair.

Or, for our purposes, destruction.

Once this secondary strike goes off, people will be aware of a pattern forming. Moreover, they'll get the message that what have been temporary problems before are likely to be epidemic. There is no cure in sight since whoever is doing this has nailed the repair vehicles. In many ways we become the agents of entropy, just accelerating the normal decay of infrastructure.

How does the government react? They immediately posture about investigations and say they will make things more secure. The Constabulary is placed on high alert, which wears people out and drains the government's coffers. Its people are stretched thin. There is no way they can cover every conceivable target. When strikes continue, their promises are shown to be hollow and the government's credibility erodes.

As things progress from there, every move the government makes just digs them a deeper hole. We hit economic targets, slowing the economy and making powerful folks put pressure on government agencies to act. They enact more stringent security measures and perhaps even invoke martial law. Citizens are expecting them to be out looking for bad guys, but instead the security forces are keeping law-abiding folks off the streets with curfews or annoying them at checkpoints.

Resentment grows rather easily. A couple of strikes at government targets that should have been ultrasecure makes it apparent that no place is safe. It also paints the government as liars (now there is a tough job), so people are ready for a change.

At the end game, the government brings out its troops to go after the terrorists, and the terrorists fight back defensively. Before things get totally out of hand, however, a leader will step in to negotiate. If this person were seen as being competent, and had already exhibited charity and compassion during the crisis, he would be a natural choice to replace the government. It's suggested that he head up an interim government until things can be stabilized and, once he does that and the terrorists retreat, he's in for life.

As I made my presentation, the commentary dwindled. Those who didn't have the intellectual capacity to understand it all remained quiet. Those who did ended up smiling and nodding a lot. Several people made notes, and I could tell the lists of targets and methods of attack had just expanded. Gypsy's eyes had glazed over and Elle was looking as if she'd pretty much forgiven me for breaking her jaw.

Catford, while he had the smarts to understand what I said, didn't have the intellectual honesty to accept its veracity. "That is the most stupid plan I've ever heard in my whole entire life. It's based on things that are demonstrably untrue. Everyone knows power comes from the barrel of a gun. It has nothing to do with the masses."

The irony of his quoting millennia-old Communist truisms while denying revolution had anything to do with the masses struck only a few in the room. I frowned at him. "You hate this idea because you don't get to shoot anyone. You're a 'Mech commander, and this plan doesn't have a big role for 'Mechs."

"That's right, in part." He nodded solemnly, playing to the rest of the pilots in the room. "We were brought here to do a job, and that job is eliminate the talent the other side has hired. You want us to skulk and blow up things. That's not honorable. That's not the way of the warrior. You want me to commit . . . *unnatural acts*!"

He was making me wish he actually listened to himself, but I pretty much realized that even if he did, he'd hear nothing wrong. When your whole conception of yourself is that you're a hammer, that you've spent your life becoming the best hammer you can be, anything that isn't a nail is a very direct threat to you. But, you're a hammer, so all you can do to these threats is pound them.

It was at that point I knew Catford and Siwek would try to have me killed. They'd do it because my plan offended their honor. How fast they would kill me depended upon one factor: Gypsy.

In playing to the other pilots, the Major had failed to

play to Gypsy. Clearly Catford was seeing himself as the true leader of our little group, and Gypsy needed to straighten that misconception out immediately. If he didn't, Catford might just take the resources he'd been given and plunk his own skinny butt on the throne of Basalt. While power might not come from the barrel of a gun, having a 'Mech's big guns did make hanging on to it a lot easier.

"Major Catford, *any* dismissal of this plan would be premature. It does have merit and does not obviate your role at all. In fact, it elevates it to one of protector of the people. As you have noted, the other side has talent, and they will certainly deploy it to counter the threats we present. Your opposition to it will be seen as a stroke for freedom, which enhances your position and support."

Gypsy let Catford chew on that. Gypsy had already picked up on the key point in my plan, which Catford and the others had probably missed. They were all prepared to wipe the government away and impose someone else on the people. My plan focused on the people welcoming the new leader. Not only would this increase stability, but it would also play to the ego of whoever was bankrolling the effort. Yes, he wanted to be king, but how much better to have your adoring peasants beg you to walk all over them than to have to force them onto their bellies.

Catford was sharp enough to realize he'd overplayed his hand. "I still protest this idea as futile, but we shall always be in readiness to salvage the operation here. *Mister* Donelly will need us, I'm sure."

24

A battle sometimes decides everything; and sometimes the merest trifle decides a battle.

—Napoleon

Manville, Capital District
Basalt
Prefecture IV, Republic of the Sphere
29 January 3133

If I wanted to try a little more literary pretension I'd note that while we'd been in the meeting clouds had gathered like the furrows on Catford's brow. I could do that, or I could note that the gathering clouds mirrored my dark mood as I calculated how things were likely to go on Basalt. The simple fact is, however, that the clouds had gathered and had little more import than that.

One of the difficulties that Basalt had faced in trying to become known as a resort destination came from its climate. All of the advertisements described the world as "tropical," which is advertspeak for *humid*. This should have come as no surprise for anyone who wanted to venture here and explore rain forests, but oppressive stickiness tends to wear on tourists and eventually makes them irritable.

And judging by Catford's mood, he'd been here since before I was born.

Gypsy dismissed the meeting and people began to clump and drift. The largest clot formed around Catford. Given the way some of the others looked at that cadre and scowled, I gathered that he'd been handpicking people for his command and they were still looking to curry favor with him. A few other folks spoke with Gypsy, but no one came over to talk to me.

I guess that didn't surprise me too much since they were warriors and had come to Basalt to ply their trade. This didn't mean they couldn't appreciate what I had to offer in my plan, but they weren't going to commit to it until Gypsy required that of them. Given that they could make an enemy of Catford by being seen as my ally, I took no offense and headed out on my own.

On Basalt, gathering clouds presaged some fairly terrific lightning storms. They were actually spectacular enough to be a tourist attraction, save that they usually were coupled with driving rain. Aside from those who might be visiting from a desert world, rainstorms really were not high on the list of things most tourists want to do.

I caught a hovercab and took it back to the Grand Germayne before the storm broke. I figured that something or someone was waiting for me in my room, so I hit the hotel restaurant for some dinner while my visitor waited. I ordered a filet of *troses*, which was a troutlike fish the size of a tuna and very good. If packaging Basalt as a tropical paradise did not work, culinary vacations might be a viable alternative.

I couldn't finish my meal, so I had the leftovers packed up and carried them with me to my room. The thread was still on the ground, so I opened the door, flipped on the light and shut the door behind me. I found no one in the room and no evidence that anyone had been in since Elle departed, not even housekeeping.

My bed had been disturbed, with the covers thrown back, two pillows piled up and the clear impression of a body that had been reclining. Curious, I pressed my hand to the mattress, but it was plenty cold. I didn't find any short red hairs on the pillow, but I still assumed the outline would have fitted Elle. Why she would have waited for me in bed left me wondering, and none of the answers fit easily, save that she wanted me distracted and not thinking about things I ought to be considering.

My early suspicions that Elle had been Reis' man inside the GGF had been quashed. Reis had given Janella a complete rundown on his operation, and she wasn't one of his. Her escape and presence on Basalt with Gypsy suggested they worked as a team, and might well have worked together for a good long time.

On Helen she'd had a tough image going, but that had been shed here. I wasn't certain if that was because she knew it wouldn't work with me, and would be challenged by many others among the recruits Gypsy had gathered. The more I thought about it, the more it made sense because, while most warriors were more than willing to acknowledge the equality of women in combat, women who were not warriors—ditto men who were not—were just seen as lesser creatures and dismissed.

And since she wanted to be dismissed, she'd bear extra watching.

Sighing, and with a full belly, I locked the door, stripped off my clothes and slipped into bed. I stretched out, expanding the indentation Elle had left on the bed and fell quickly to sleep. The thunderstorm that raged outside bled a bit into my dreams, transforming natural phenomena into the unnatural sights and sounds of war and yet somehow I slept through it all.

The next morning dawned bright. With the storm's fury spent, the clouds had dissipated and the city awoke to crews cleaning up the damage rather efficiently. I washed up and headed out, watching them for a bit, then finding a little family diner where I sucked down enough grease and preservatives to lube a 'Mech and keep me in shape to be piloting until I was Victor's age. That thought actually brought a smile to my face, which the waitress returned along with more coffee and my bill.

I strolled around the city, making mental notes about more targets and found plenty of them. Because of the lightning storms, most power and communications lines had been buried, but junction boxes existed everywhere. Had I a pocket full of plastic explosive and detonators, I could have cut one half of Manville off from the other during a casual walk.

Looking around at the people out shopping and heading to and from work, I saw a lot of happy faces and heard a lot of laughter. These were good people. They probably worked hard, loved their friends and neighbors and were kind to animals. Their lives were pretty good.

And if my plan went into effect, that would change.

I knew my plan would work, and that made me very uneasy. I felt frustrated because I knew there was no way to defend against it. Actually, that's not true, there was: deny the enemy a reason to attack. If no one had any grievances, they wouldn't initiate terrorist activity. In our case, the grievance was one of a personal lust for power and money. While lots of folks want those things, few have enough in the way of resources to finance a revolution to acquire more.

Where a terrorist group was determined to act, Low-Intensity Terrorism had no defense. As the government moved to give itself more tools to root out the terrorists, they would be depriving the citizenry of more personal freedoms, which would breed more dissatisfaction. If someone like Niemeyer toed the line but didn't cross it, he'd have to be extremely lucky to stop the terrorists.

LIT also hit the government and corporate concerns hard where they could feel it: in the wallet. All too often people are classified as consumers or constituents and dismissed. C-bills and stones, on the other hand, show up on spreadsheets and determine stock prices and bonuses. Once those numbers start showing up in red, jobs are in jeopardy and action has to be taken. Corporations will stem losses as they must, ethically or not. While some might hire more security personnel to guard their assets, if we presented them with an economical plan where they could avoid that cost by buying themselves off our hit list, they'd choose our option.

I thought hard as I walked. LIT would bring the Germaynes down. It would take several months, but their government would fall apart, and Emblyn would be able to slide in to replace them. He'd be happy and, who knows, perhaps he'd even be good for Basalt. I could certainly hope that, because the Germaynes were history.

Of course, Emblyn's taking control was predicated on his being Gypsy's boss. I would have to confirm that. His taking over, however, wouldn't quite be in keeping with my directive to preserve stability, unless, of course, the Germaynes were inherently unstable. I'd have to check into that, too.

My stroll took me all over Manville. I ate lunch at a trendy little place on the ground floor of the city's tallest building. All around me people talked investments, stocks, money, politics and, of course, sex. People blurt out things in public places when they think they're in a private conversation, not aware that the person sitting in the booth behind them is actually closer to them than the person they are facing. It was the usual who was doing what with whom and her husband not knowing about it, and while I say it was the usual, and that I've heard it a million times before, it's just one of those things which ends up being fascinating.

Again, more of the cracks in the society made themselves apparent. Somehow it was more scandalous for a man to be going over to a Drac section of Manville to visit a house of ill repute, than his getting a "massage" at some cheap dive in a run-down Davion neighborhood down by the river. *Those* people were known to be dirty, after all, the whispered wisdom went, and *they* would couple with anything. The irony of one of the good folks being willing to lower himself was lost on these folks, but they fully succeeded in objectifying and dehumanizing people who, less than six months before, had been fellow citizens and friends.

Once I'd gotten my fill, I continued meandering. I stopped in at a file store and downloaded reading material into my noteputer. It was the usual tourist stuff: local atlas, highlights and hotspots, and other almanac-type data. To that I added an unauthorized Emblyn biography, the same for the Germaynes and a list of local charitable organizations and what they did.

By mid-afternoon I returned to the Grand Germayne and found I had a visitor, but not in my room this time. Elle emerged from the bar and smiled at me as I waited at the lift. I nodded. "I kept your place warm last night."

Her smile broadened. "If only I could have slipped away."

"Indeed, you wouldn't have had to wait in the bar."

Elle's smile slacked a notch. "Oh, I don't think Gypsy would have been welcome to wait with me."

"No, indeed." I glanced back at the bar. "Shall we?"

She didn't take my arm, but did rub against me, which I did find distracting, as I am sure she intended. We crossed the lobby to the bar, which was elegantly appointed in deep mahogany and brown leather. The rest of the hotel might have aged less well than I could have hoped in the past century, but the bar had just gotten darker and imbued with an ambience that I greatly enjoyed.

Gypsy, attired casually in a jacket and slacks of black, white shirt and black shoes, lifted a drink at the corner table in a salute. I let Elle precede me to the table and took pleasure in watching her walk in her dark green dress. The fabric had a bit of a satiny sheen to it, but was not garish. The gold-link belt matched her bracelet and earrings, and even hinted at the gold chain pattern on the heel of her shoes.

I sat facing Gypsy, with my back to the room. Elle sat between us, to my right, with her left knee pressed against mine. When the waitress came, I looked at the bar and didn't recognize any of the whiskies they offered, so I ordered a Diamond Negro.

Gypsy smiled. "You learn quickly."

"Pays to know the battlefield."

He nodded, sipping his drink which, as nearly as I could tell, was some mixed thing that wasn't fruity, but doubtless was sweet. Elle had a tall, slender glass with a lime wedge in it. It could have been nothing more than tonic water and I idly wondered if I'd taste any alcohol if I kissed her. The waitress finished pouring my beer into a frosted glass—an amenity the Egg did *not* offer—and retreated.

Gypsy brought his glass forward. "To Cleansing Storm."

I touched my glass to his and hers then drank. The beer did taste as good as I recalled and I flicked a drop from the corner of my mouth with a finger. "Cleansing Storm? Please don't tell me that's what Colonel Kitten wants to call some huge op."

Elle smiled and Gypsy rolled his eyes. "Oh, no, Cleansing Storm will likely make the Cat apoplectic, but this concerns me very little at the moment. Cleansing Storm will be the name of our organization. I have consulted with my superiors and we will get things *lit* in a big way here."

"Good, very good." I smiled broadly. "I have a key target in mind, but there's something very important I need to know first."

"And that would be?"

"Did you intend to use me as a stalking horse for the Cat, setting me up to be neutralized before he came after you, or is that just a happy coincidence?"

Gypsy's eyes widened. "It was your plan . . ."

I set my glass down carefully and slowly rotated it in my fingertips. "Gypsy, let's get one thing straight. You know I'm not stupid. LIT proves it. You'd given me command of a battalion *before* I offered my plan. Were you trying to get me killed?"

His dark eyes glittered for a moment, then he smiled slyly and sat back. "I am not stupid either. I watched the Cat and Isabel creating their own little coterie within my organization. To remove one or both would delay my plans from moving ahead. By interposing you, I gave them something else to think about. LIT is yet one more thing and they are under the impression it was because of LIT that I brought you in here. I was not looking to cause you trouble, primarily because I am mindful of how well you handled yourself on Helen. I don't see the two of them being obstacles for you."

"Obstacles, no, but trouble, yes." I drank more of my beer. "And when one of them is found floating north to Contressa on the Broad River, will this cause you a problem?"

"I would appreciate it not being a complete surprise."

"Noted." I licked my lips and felt Elle's pressure against my knee increase. "About my compensation."

He laughed. "I admire your restraint. The Cat has a most-favored agreement saying he makes a stone more than anyone else I've hired."

"That's fine, but there was that consulting fee you were going to pay me, and my signing bonus."

"Will thirty thousand do?"

"For starters. I like performance bonuses, too."

A frown began to corrugate Gypsy's forehead. "That could get expensive."

"Just grant me a percentage on the amounts we extort from corporations. This will please me. You'll have to check with your superiors, I imagine, and they will want to see the proof that the plan will work. I understand that."

"A reasonable man, very good." Gypsy nodded, then sat forward again, leaning his elbows on the table. "I have been thinking of possible venues for our emergence. Communications and power seem the most efficacious."

I shook my head. "Save them for later. I have a key one in mind. It will work perfectly, and at minimal risk to us."

"Really?"

I smiled, first at him, then at Elle. "Oh, yes. From the start of our campaign, the government will know it's in deep shit."

25

To that high Capital, where kingly Death
Keeps his pale court in beauty and decay,
He came.

—Percy Bysshe Shelley

Manville, Capital District
Basalt
Prefecture IV, Republic of the Sphere
4 February 3133

I explained my choice of target and watched Gypsy's expression move through shock and disgust to amusement and admiration. By the end of my discourse he looked almost giddy and the pressure of Elle's knee on mine had grown much greater. Gypsy was even willing to let me lay a bit of a trap for the Cat—more because it served his purposes than mine, but we both would be amused.

Though I made great protestations against it, with eye and touch and the mouthing of silent regrets, Gypsy whisked Elle away to attend to some details on my plan. She, for her part, made similar mouthings and gave me a very warm hug as we parted. The pressure from her knee transferred to other parts of her anatomy as applied against mine which, while quite thrilling, could have been preface to difficulties later.

It took several days to put things into place, since the plan was as dependent upon atmospherics and climate as anything else. In fact, the raid part of the mission looked ready to go off very well. The facility we needed to penetrate had incredibly lax security. As a stalking horse we called in and had delivered an order of pizza to the night crew, and the hovercar sped to the door with nothing more than a cursory glance.

Where Gypsy indulged me was at the next meeting of the staff, held in yet another location. He announced that we were going to begin with my plan, though trying to accelerate the timetable, since our master was a bit anxious about everything coming together as quickly as possible. Gypsy suggested that he would be double-tracking raids on my part with preparations for more solid military activity led by Catford. Then he invited me forward to explain my operation.

What I told them was that food and water were the most important things to a city the size of Manville. Using a holo-projection of the area, I showed how the mountains flowed down into the rivers, and how the rivers had carved the valley in which Manville sat, and how the rivers converged to form the Broad River, which flowed north to Contressa. I told them that the rivers supplied the water for the city, noted that several water purification and treatment plants had been built around the city, and pointed out that any disruption in water flow would cause a major problem in the city.

Up to this point I had made my presentation about as boring as humanly possible, which had Catford squirming. Once I saw I had him where I wanted him, all antsy and aching to do something, I shifted over into a much more enthusiastic mode of speech, and started things building.

"This operation will be one that requires extreme precision. It will be a commando operation, no doubt about it, undertaken under adverse circumstances. No two ways about it, the operation stinks, but once this first glorious blow is struck, the howls of anger and outrage will echo throughout the city. This attack could tumble the government all by itself, as a flood of resentment courses through every household. Because of the nature of the operation, we will have to choose the best we have to carry it out. Their victory shall be our victory, and the government will be sucked down the tubes as a result."

I accented the military words, like "attack" and "victory." Precision got emphasis, too. Catford, hearing that this one attack might decide it all, was inclined to scoff—based on his initial expression—but then he got to thinking. He didn't want to be shut out. Even worse than not having a 'Mech to pilot was having one and finding out your efforts would not be required.

He raised a hand. "You're describing the attack as a far more military operation than your initial discussions led us to believe were going to be coming off. Is that a fair characterization?"

I nodded. "Yes, this will require precision demolitions work. Some very good people are going to have to get their hands dirty."

He looked past me to Gypsy. "While I see the logic of this plan, and I agree that water is vital, I am wary of Mr. Donelly being able to carry off a military operation. I think it would be best if I were to lead the actual penetration of the facility and to oversee the tactical aspects of things. I have no fear of getting my hands dirty at all."

Gypsy frowned. "Are you certain, Major? This is Mr. Donelly's operation, and you would be usurping his power."

"No, no, not at all. He will be in command. I will just direct the military angle of things." He stood and looked around the room. "Siwek, Johnstone and Bridger, your companies have cross-trained personnel in them who can handle this. I would think a dozen to eighteen people would be right for what you have in mind, Mr. Donelly."

I nodded again, solemnly this time. "I'd thought of two dozen, but you would have a better idea about that than I would."

"Indeed, I would." The subordinates he'd mentioned by name nodded or raised hands to indicate they would go along with him. Catford moved to the front of the room and joined me beside the holodisplay. "Well, we have the people we need."

Gypsy shook his head. "I'm sorry, Sam, but he does have the experience that would give him an edge here."

"I know, and I just want this to work."

"It will." Catford grinned broadly and his lieutenants returned that smile with confidence. "So, which of these purification plants are we hitting?"

"We're not."

"What?" Catford looked at me angrily. "But after all you said . . ."

"Oh, water is very important, Major, in two ways. It comes *in* to the house and it goes *out*. Where it goes out, is where we go in."

Needless to say, Catford's face flushed—no pun intended—as the reality of what he'd volunteered for came to him. Others in the room were kind enough not to laugh, though smiles did occur when they recalled I said the job stunk. Catford, having claimed the glory of the assignment, and having avowed he didn't mind getting his hands dirty, was stuck.

He had to—no, I'll resist that pun—fish or cut bait and he decided to fish. This was good, because I really did need his people to carry the whole thing off.

Two days later, after a day and a half of torrential rains, we put the operation into effect. When Manville's downtown district had been created, the Broad River was channeled rather tightly within levees hidden by parks and walkways. Buried deep in the earth, paralleling the river, were massive storm sewers that handled all the runoff. According to the guidefiles I'd gotten at the store, and the wonderful tour of the storm sewers offered by Manville Public Service, during the storm season the sewers would actually carry more water than the river, and all of it had to flow to the water treatment plants before it could be allowed to run back into the river itself.

The water treatment plants had several holding basins to deal with this excess water. Massive pipes would channel it into these effluent lakes, where it would wait until it could be processed through the plants. Our operation demanded that the sluice gates that would pour the water back into the plant be blown open, and that the anti-reflux valves in the plant itself likewise be jammed open.

Catford and his commandos, working by the light of lightning, accomplished these goals at 2 A.M. on the sixth. What this resulted in was an incredible pressure wave where millions of metric tons of water flowed back into the city's sewer system. When you have ten-meter diameter pipes flowing at capacity, and their load is transferred to pipes running into homes—with their pipes being thirty centimeters in diameter—the result is rather spectacular.

Lucky homeowners on the west side of the city had old

pipes that burst somewhere in their yards. Water boiled and bubbled, churning turf and mud into a stinking swamp that, a year later, would actually result in a pretty good lawn. Apartment dwellers were similarly fortunate if the pipes burst in their building's basement.

But the unfortunate—and there were many of them according to news stories—were those people who had good pipes and, for whatever reason, happened to be enjoying a bath or a moment of solitude when the wave hit. Raw sewage geysered into homes, staining ceilings in cases where the flow was unimpeded. It filled tubs to overflowing, backed into dishwashers, dripped from sinks into kitchens, basements and vanities.

In a couple of places the larger street pipes burst, creating instant sinkholes that sucked down parked hovercars and left fetid lakes slowly creeping along the streets. In some places a drenched and irate citizenry raised the alarm immediately, while others were left to awaken to peculiar smells and woefully soggy carpeting.

And the toll on businesses, especially in the lowest areas of the city, was equally devastating. Schools were closed on the west side and Count Germayne appeared on Tri-Vid to ask that anyone who did not need to leave their homes just stay there while the city cleaned up. While his reasoning was sound, no one wanted to linger in a cesspit of a house, especially when anything that went into one sink just bubbled back up into a tub or the basement. The citizens started burning from the start, especially when the richer folks located in the hills were reported to have escaped disaster.

Aldrington Emblyn swung into action immediately, which was great. One of his subsidiary firms was a housecleaning concern that had grown out of the staff he had for his hotels. The company, NextToGodliness LLC, offered an immediate Good Neighbor discount of ninety percent, and hired people to expand the workforce. He also brought folks who had been flooded out of their homes into empty rooms in his hotels, which likewise endeared him to the populace.

The Germayne government countered by opening a variety of municipal garages and hangars where folks could camp out in donated blankets, sleeping bags and cots. Emblyn raised that bid by donating more blankets, pillows and spare beds. The Germaynes suffered an additional setback when vehicles they parked on the street to open a garage got swallowed up in a sewage swamp.

The local Tri-Vid media compounded our victory with their profiles that showed Germayne officials being inept. At first the disaster was explained away as a catastrophic failure of the restraining dikes. The rush of water just tore the blown gates away and erased all signs of our blasting. It wasn't until two days after the event that they found the doors and then started to claim it was a deliberate act of sabotage. Once they made that claim, all manner of hoots and tweets floated to the surface declaring that there had been a cover-up and that evidence had been faked, which covered our trail better than I could have hoped.

On the domestic front, Catford was left in a quandary. Everyone congratulated him for pulling the job off, and I gave him the lion's share of the credit. He knew he couldn't trust me, but I was quite sincere, so that confused him and, I'm sure, made him even more determined to get rid of me. He'd have to wait, though, until one of my plans failed.

Putting myself in Catford's shoes—soggy as they were—I figured out that if one of my plans did not fail on its own, he'd make sure to tank one. This meant I had to make sure he had enough to do that pleased him, that he stayed his hand. I also realized he'd now be trying to come up with operations that would continue doing what I was doing, so I'd have to be fighting him on that front. I was pretty sure I could stay out in front of him per se, but he had a brain trust to be bouncing things off and I didn't. Could be one of them would come up with a good idea and I'd have to scramble.

The success of the attack did win a lot of converts to LIT. Some were thoughtful in their analysis and insights, clearly cadging for future work, whereas others simply said, "That was good." Catford's attempts to paint me as someone stupid simply failed. I still didn't have the full confidence of those I had to work with, but they'd be willing to listen in the future, which was important. If I could offer them plans that would let them get paid without getting killed, they'd go along and I could minimize collateral damage.

Gypsy had been very generous in his praise for the effort, but on the seventh he surprised me by handing me a three-thousand-stone bonus in its C-bill equivalent. "Our master was pleased with your effort. He sent this money to you to express his pleasure."

I fanned the bills. "How much did you skim?"

He blinked, then smiled. "Twenty percent. I did sell him on the plan, after all."

"More like forty, I'm sure. Mine is the bigger piece though, so that's okay."

Gypsy smiled. "Ah, but there is more. He wants you to use that money to buy yourself suitable evening clothes. Two nights from now you'll be in Contressa at a little gala. The Emblyn Palace Contressa is opening its main facility and Mr. Emblyn is throwing a party for a thousand of his closest friends."

"And I'm numbered among them?"

"You are now."

"When do we leave?"

Gypsy shook his head. "Not *we*, just you."

I frowned. "You don't know me well enough to know I can deal with this sort of thing without causing trouble. I'm a wild card. You can't trust me that much."

"I know that during your exploration of the city you picked up a well-tailored suit."

"You were watching me?"

"And you would not have watched me were our roles reversed?"

"Point taken. Okay, so I can dress well."

"And you are very quick. The way you dealt with Catford was most politically astute. I might have found you a crude lumberjack on Helen, but that was a disguise." Gypsy smiled slowly. "But, it does not matter if I trust you or not. My master expresses his wishes and I carry them out. He wants you there, so you will be there."

"Anyone else I know?"

"None of our little family, no. You'll be a guest of the resort for the weekend, then come back here Monday." He nodded slowly. "I'll be fascinated to hear your report on the whole thing. Keep your eyes and ears open."

"I shall."

"One thing, Sam."

"Yes?"

"This access to my boss. It's a onetime thing." His eyes became cold. "If you try to cut me out of things, your plans will live on well after you, and we shall mourn your passing."

═══ 26 ═══

*In war, as in love, we must come into contact before
we can triumph.*

—Napoleon

Contressa, Garnet Coast District
Basalt
Prefecture IV, Republic of the Sphere
9 February 3133

I opted not to let Gypsy's threat color my plans to enjoy
the weekend. I took the time to do a bit more research
into Emblyn's hotel properties and learned he'd been sent
to Basalt to run a string of hotels for an off-world concern.
According to business journal articles, when he arrived he
found things an absolute shambles. The hotels were making
no money and this was because money was being skimmed
all over the place.

The articles put a positive spin on what happened next,
making him into a white knight, but I was looking from a
different perspective. The core of the problem he had to
deal with was that while The Republic was prospering, people didn't need a world like Basalt as a resort. There were
other, more famous places, like Terra, where they could

spend their time. And a lot of their money went to things that improved their own homes and communities, so they had even less inducement to travel to a backwater world to get rained on.

Emblyn realized he couldn't possibly make the hotels make money without significant concessions from the local government. He went to them and basically represented himself as having been sent to Basalt to close the chain down since it was not profitable. He entered into a conspiracy with the government to give him significant tax breaks on the properties if he could put together a local consortium to buy the places and keep them open. He raised the capital he needed, then made the parent corporation an offer to buy the Basalt properties. The parent company sold them off to him, while keeping them affiliated, at the moment, with the chain. This gave him the benefit of some booking services thinking they were part of the chain, so his potential customer stream didn't suffer immediately.

Emblyn started upscaling things, and lobbied the local government to allow him to add casinos to his properties. Emblyn said it would bring a lot of money in from off-world, and it has, but has redistributed even more local wealth. A lot of it ended up in his pockets and three thousand of that was burning a hole in mine.

Emblyn was shrewd enough to know that if he could lower costs, he would boost profits, so he started buying into the various firms that serviced his hotels. Food wholesalers, liquor distributorships, breweries and the like sprang up or profited from his investments. With his direction, they expanded and suddenly became profit centers on their own. Most articles tried to put estimates on his total wealth, but I figured they were off considerably, no matter how generous they were.

Part of me wondered at how the man could want me at his party. Everything I'd said to Gypsy was true: I was a wild card and Emblyn had no way to judge me. For all he knew I could be there and when someone asked how I knew him I could say, "Remember the sewers backing up in Manville? I did that so he can take over the planet."

Clearly he wouldn't have asked for me to attend if he thought I was that stupid, so Gypsy must have given him a good impression of me. Likewise I imagined that he'd not have invited me if I were the sort who would be impressed with three thousand stones. Perhaps the invitation had been tentative, based on Gypsy's assessment of my reaction to the bonus.

I decided I would play things by the rules, but go in cautiously. There was only one place where I would press my luck. I doubted he would notice one way or another, but success would give me a bit more freedom to operate if I needed to do something quickly.

I packed my clothes and caught a hovershuttle up to Contressa. Taking a shuttle isn't very elegant, and the transport company had some really beat-up vehicles. I got put in one of the newer ones, however, while non-Anglos were directed to the older ones, and packed in tightly. While the shuttle didn't cost much, there *was* a surcharge applied to those with almond eyes, and that disturbed me a great deal.

Even the newer shuttle wasn't all that comfortable, but it was half full and let me see more of the planet. Route One followed the eastern shore of the Broad River to the northern delta and Contressa. It skirted the edges of a major rain forest preserve and while I didn't see much more than some brightly colored birds and perhaps some apelike things, just seeing that much deep blue was very pleasant.

When I wasn't reading or staring out the window, I did check out the others on the shuttle. Most were kids traveling home for the weekend from school. I suspected there had been a lot of communications traffic to and from Manville after the sewer backups, with worried parents demanding their children head home for a weekend. Some older couples joined them, and far in the back I saw a young woman wearing a billed cap and big dark glasses—indicating she didn't want to be noticed, but attracting all the more notice for it. She wore very casual clothes, no makeup or jewelry, and was pretty enough that I could imagine her being some model or minor celeb traveling north for the resort opening. I'd probably see her later that night as someone's eye-candy arm-piece.

Whoever she was going to be adorning, he had to be pretty low-rent if he made her travel on the shuttle. I found it pretty easy to imagine her being a single mother who was working hard to support twin daughters. If that was the case, she'd clearly cashed in some first-class air transport ticket for this, so her kids could have new shoes.

Shoes that had been ruined because they'd been floating in sewage.

We arrived in Contressa in just over two hours. I only had one bag to get since I was just up for the weekend and I noticed she was traveling similarly light. She went for her bag, but a large man bodied her aside so he could grab a plasticene crate with some rat-dog-thing in it. As he waddled away cooing at Snookums—yes, the name was painted on the crate—I grabbed her bag and handed it to her.

The protest at my touching her stuff died quickly and she smiled. "Thank you."

"Not a problem. In the future don't get between a man and his snack."

She laughed and it was a pleasing sound. "More true than you know." She gave me a nod and turned to disappear into the crowd, taking advantage of the trough the fat man had plowed through it.

I wandered over to ground transportation and hired a hovertaxi to take me to the resort. The ride took a half hour and ran along the northern coast. It really was prime resort property, with beautiful white sandy beaches and patches of blue jungle matching the water in color. It was true that having wave after wave of clouds pass stripes of darkness over the earth was annoying, but between them I got a great view of the triangle of Basalt's moons. It was all pretty enough that I thought about trying to get Janella to join me here for a vacation.

The Palace resort matched the sand in hue, making it look almost as if it were a castle raised by magic. The main building did not have towers and crenellations, but did have a soaring majesty that evoked power and beauty. The long drive up to the door had been flanked with statues of beautiful men and women of all races and sizes, including Clan Elementals and pilots. The statues were naked, but more along the line of art than anything salacious. Beyond and around them, azure lawns stretched as far as the eye could see, save where they ran to jungle or were dotted with blue topiary cut to the shape of local fauna and mythical creatures.

I checked in easily, was shown to my room and put my

clothes away quickly enough. The room I'd been given was fairly standard for size, but featured some nice amenities. The refreshment center had been fully stocked with Diamond Negro. The beer could have been there because Diamond was an exclusive supplier to the hotel, but I suspected it was because that was the only thing Gypsy had ever seen me drink.

I showered and changed clothes, then took my bonus money and descended to the gambling floor. If the hotel was a temple to money, the casino was the Holy of Holies and I went right to the altar. I didn't have to wait long to get a seat at a poker table, and after three hours walked away with seven grand more than I'd started with. The people I'd skinned were all guests, just like me, and took their losses with good grace. Given that most were wearing big, blocky rings studded with enough gems that I'd have had trouble lifting one, much less buy one with my nest egg, they could afford it.

I retreated to my room and dressed for the evening. The store in Manville had done a great job with the suit. While I was certain there would be people in the room who would recognize it was not custom made, they would know it had a designer label. One could decry such shallow behavior, but it made those folks pretty easy to peg and, subsequently, manipulate.

As I dressed I found myself smiling just imagining what Janella's appearance at a party like this would do. Her beauty and elegance would get her noticed right away, of course. Her being nobility and from Fletcher would have caused a bit of a stir. Her being a Knight of The Republic, however, that would be serious stuff. People would be all over her, wanting to know what The Republic intended for Basalt, for Emblyn and, hopefully, themselves.

And if they knew what I was, well, I'd not be there if anyone knew what I was.

I took the lift to the top floor and actually gasped as I stepped out. The entire ceiling and three of the walls had been made of glass, affording a wonderful view of the night sky. On Basalt that meant we'd be able to see a stunning display of lightning. The clouds were gathering to deliver it, and part of me wondered if Emblyn hadn't managed to arrange things that way.

I joined a line of people snaking past Emblyn at the entryway. An aide standing well back behind him had a noteputer which she consulted as we entered. She subvocalized and an ear-bud microphone transmitted her words to Emblyn, who smiled and greeted everyone by name. He shook hands heartily, asked little personal questions, and laughed at the replies. I took it as a very good sign that no ethnic segregation had been done to the guest list, and Emblyn seemed equally at home with everyone.

He really did look every inch the successful businessman he was purported to be. Unlike Jacob Bannson, Emblyn was tall and slender, with his thick black hair brushed perfectly into place and his deep brown eyes wet with sincerity. As I came up, his smile grew just a bit broader than it had been with the elderly couple before me. "Mr. Donelly, so pleased you could make it."

"I appreciate the invitation, Mr. Emblyn."

"Call me Ring. Everyone does."

"And I'm Sam."

He shook my hand heartily. "I understand you won a little bit of money at poker this afternoon."

"A little bit depending upon who is doing the accounting." I smiled, impressed that his people had been watching me. I'd spend the rest of my stay watching for the watchers, though I knew the casino's security system would make surveillance child's play. That meant I'd also be very careful. "Should I feel guilty that they were your guests?"

"Not at all." He leaned in closely. "They'll just drop more in an effort to reverse their bad luck, so take all you want."

I laughed. "Spoken like the master of ten-percent rake."

He nodded and let me go. "Please, enjoy yourself."

Thus released I moved into the room. A person in hotel livery found me and handed me a small chit. "You will be sitting at table twenty-seven, right over there. The bars are to your right and left, appetizers at the stations. You will be seated in an hour."

"Thank you." I pocketed my chit and wandered to one of the bars. While I waited in line I studied the selection and found they had my favorite Irish whisky. My mouth immediately started to water, but I held back. Emblyn's people had pegged me as a Diamond Negro man, and I didn't want to give them too much to think about. Moreover, anything, no matter how innocent, that could link me back to my old self was to be avoided. For all I knew, someone in here could have spoken once with Victor Steiner-Davion and heard him mention that whisky, and bits would start to be flipped here and there until someone decided there was something interesting to learn about me.

Once I had my beer, in a great big pilsner glass with the Emblyn logo emblazoned on it, I started toward the hors d'oeuvres table. Yes, normally at a party this impressive there would been a small army of servers circulating with silver plates full of these things. Most of them were, in fact, wandering with flutes of champagne. The appetizers, though, all arrayed on twenty-five linear meters of tabletop, made for an exhibition that was as much art as it was food. Things had been color coordinated so the produce from one world resembled the planetary banner, or items from a particular corporation were spread out to look like its logo. The centerpiece, however, was a collection of things that were the picture of the hotel itself, as if shot at dawn from the shoreline. The help could have been carting all that around, but they would have been hauling pieces of a puzzle that no one could have put together.

The display was breathtaking and, I'll admit, I'd just started to drift unconsciously past, trying not to drool on myself. I was not paying attention until I felt a hand on my right elbow. It jerked me back just as a behemoth that, in his evening clothes, looked like the biggest penguin ever seen, slashed right past me and went straight for the hotel. Clutched under his arm was a tiny dog that graced me with a growl as they slipped by.

I turned and looked at my savior. "Thank you."

She smiled, her blue eyes full of fire that matched the sapphire at her throat. "Just returning the favor."

"Pardon?"

"Never get between a man and his snack, remember?"

I blinked. "That was you?"

"Yes, and that was him, too. Perason Quam, the food critic for the Manville *Journal*."

I glanced at the broad back and wavering hips as huge holes appeared in the mural. "That's his name, Quam, not yours?"

"Yes." She frowned very slightly. "You've not been on Basalt long, have you?"

"Not long enough to know him, nope. You, on the other hand . . ." I slowly smiled, buying another second or two for my brain to start working. In the blue, off-the-shoulders gown she wore, she looked much more elegant than she'd been on the shuttle and, *yes*, it came to me. She was far more elegant than she'd been in Tri-Vid reports on the sewer disaster. "You are associated with some of the private shelters that took people in last week. I remember you, but only caught the middle of a report. I didn't get your name."

"So you had no idea who I was on the shuttle?"

"No, just being kind. Would it have made a difference?"

"To some, yes." She offered me her hand. "I'm Bianca Germayne. I'm Count Hector's daughter."

===== 27 =====

Emblyn Palace Resort
Contressa, Garnet Coast
Basalt
Prefecture IV, Republic of the Sphere
9 February 3133

"**H**is *daughter*?"

"She is, depending upon his mood." Quam had waded back through the crowd, little orange greasy stains curling down the valleys of his multiple chins. The little dog held beneath his left arm alternately licked at his face and the edge of the plate on which he had created a sagging pyramid of food. "Forgive my intrusion, I am Quam. How are you, my dear lady? Who is your friend?"

Bianca smiled indulgently. "Perhaps we can find out together. He was on the shuttle with us."

"Oh, the shuttle. I hate it, but Snookums won't fly, so what can I do." He smiled, deepening the crevasses in his flesh. "Besides, the *Journal* need not know what I did with the cash for the fare here."

"No, they don't." Bianca laid a hand on his right arm, the one holding the plate, which engendered a little growl from Snookums. "Thank you, again."

"My pleasure, child." Quam glanced at me. "Your name, sir?"

"Sam Donelly. I'm a special projects consultant." I smiled. I didn't offer Quam my hand because I figured I'd lose a finger or two, either to him or Snookums. Bianca shook my hand, enfolding it in a strong grip. "If I might ask, what did Quam mean about your father's moods?"

Quam rolled his eyes. "Not from around here are you?"

"Be kind, Quam." Bianca smiled softly. "My father rules the planet benignly and well, but holds certain philosophies with which I disagree. He sees The Republic's requirement of community service in exchange for citizenship as a call for everyone to work. He finds those who fall below the poverty line to be malingerers and sociopaths who would suck us all down into a morass. He thinks they were born evil and have failed to rise above their base nature."

Quam swallowed a mouthful that was more than I'd eaten in my last two meals combined. "This angel here, on the other hand, believes in the virtue of mankind, and has dedicated her life to helping the less fortunate. She created the Basalt Foundation, which uses private donations to fund shelters, meal programs and the like—for all people, regardless of their backgrounds. Her father thinks she is coddling criminals, though his mood lightens when her efforts are praised."

Bianca risked a growl from Snookums by patting Quam on the shoulder. "Quam donated his fare to the foundation, and was instrumental in getting restaurants to save leftovers for delivery to the shelters."

"One does what he can, isn't that right, Snookums?" The man planted a kiss on the dog with lips so thick that he obscured half the dog's head.

"It sounds as though you do very good work." I reached into my pocket and withdrew one of the two five-thousand-stone credit chits I'd been given for my winnings. "Please, take this. I'd like to help as well. I saw all those poor people who were rendered homeless because of the sewer flooding."

Quam shifted from foot to foot as if his knickers were bunching up and the dog whimpered in sympathy.

Bianca accepted the chit with wide eyes. "Mr. Donelly, this is quite generous. I really can't . . . I mean, it will help, but are you sure?"

I nodded. "Not me you should thank, but the inferior poker prowess of that man over there, those two there, the woman there and that red-headed man over there."

She followed my finger as I pointed, then she snorted. "This is the first donation they've made to the Foundation. I will take it, then."

"Good. If I win any more, I will continue to donate."

Quam frowned. "You should really join one of the high-stakes games. More money, worse players."

"You know this from experience?"

He shook his head, and his jowls remained shaking long after he'd stopped. "They don't let Snookums in the room with daddy, do they. But I watch, I listen. I *am* a journalist, after all, even if all they value me for is my palate."

I'd walked past the high-stakes room, and the buy-in started at twenty thousand. "Alas, they won't let me in there either."

Quam gave me a long look up and down. "I'll stake you for a hundred thousand. Half of what you win goes to the Foundation."

"And if I lose your money?"

He laughed. "My dear boy, I have little need for money. Any establishment I wish to visit on this planet will give me a meal or three, and a room, and lavish gifts on me in the hopes that I will, if not mention them favorably, at least not mention them scathingly. And there are a whole host of companies that create these dreadful packaged meals who hire me at incredible fees as a consultant, specifically so my conflict of interest will prevent me from telling people that consumption of the plastic containers in which the food arrives would impart more nutrition and more taste than the alleged foodstuffs themselves."

Snookums, having heard that diatribe before, backed it with a chorus of growls.

"You're most kind, then."

A harsh voice growled, "That's the first time that's been said of this tub of bacon drippings."

"Better to be the renderings of a noble animal than an ignoble beast." Quam sniffed and turned away to the buffet table as a tall young man with blond hair and hazel eyes laid a hand on Bianca's shoulder.

The man looked at me with pure contempt dripping from his sneer. "You are dismissed."

The sneer I could have taken, but the high-handed attitude and complete conviction that I was something he'd easily crush under a boot heel got to me. I looked slowly at Bianca. "You would know, my lady, if there is a doctor present at this gathering."

The question surprised her and she blinked distractedly. "I think so. Yes, of course. Why?"

"Because if he does not remove that hand from your shoulder, I will dislocate his elbow in a manner he will find painful and that will require two operations and a year's worth of physical therapy to mend."

The icy tones in my voice froze the sneer on his lips. "Do you have any idea . . ."

Bianca shook her head. "Bernard, Mr. Donelly is new to Basalt. Sam, this is my brother, Bernard."

I looked him up and down and could see the resemblance. He looked different from the book illustrations, with his hair now lighter and without a beard. I said nothing.

Bernard sniffed, and didn't do as good a job at it as Quam had. He let his eyes linger on me for a moment, then looked at his sister. "Father wishes to see you."

"Here? Now?" She stood on her tiptoes to look at where Count Germayne was shaking hands with Emblyn, the two of them smiling as Tri-Vid cameras recorded the event for posterity. Despite the smiles, however, I could see the tension in the tight grip, and the way the smiles stopped at the corners of their mouths. In those eyes there was nothing but pure venom.

Behind the Count in the line stood two more people who bore a family resemblance to Bianca and Bernard. The man was Teyte—a little older, a little taller and a lot stronger than Bernard. The woman, Sarah, I recognized from articles about Emblyn that showed her in his company. In the pictures she had been a blonde, but now wore her hair dark brown. Her brother was still blond, but that hue came from a bottle.

Bianca smiled at me. "If you will excuse me, Sam."

"Of course, m'lady." I bowed my head to her, then just looked up and glared daggers at her brother.

The two of them slipped into the seething mass of people, and Quam again appeared before me, eclipsing the reunion. "There you have it, Sam, the future of Basalt. Bernard will rule after his father, and you've just seen him on his best behavior. I've heard a rumor that when the sewers backed up on the west side, Bernard and Teyte stood on a balcony of the palace and laughed so hard at the plight of the *little people* that they actually soiled themselves. I doubt it is true per se, but not wholly out of character for either of the racist prigs."

I frowned. "I gathered, from Bianca's surprise at her father being here, that this was the last place she'd expect to see him."

"Indeed, but so many of the rich and powerful are here that the Count could not afford not to be seen among them. He and Emblyn had a falling out after our host asked for Sarah's hand in marriage. The Count, who is conservative enough to make the Blakists appear to be the soul of liberal enlightenment, was incensed that a lowly off-world merchantman commoner would think he was worthy of Germayne blood. The pity is that Emblyn really liked the old man, and had cut him in on a number of deals that buoyed the family fortunes for a bit, but now that pipeline has been closed off."

"And yet he is here."

Quam snorted and his dog sneezed. "Of course he is. Emblyn would not stop him. I'm sure no invitation was issued to him, but a suite was reserved all the same. Emblyn does want entrée into the highest echelons of Basalt society. He wants to be seen as an equal, and if his blood does not measure up, his manners can. His sense of philanthropy helps as well, and he donates to the Foundation both to help his image and to tweak the other Germaynes for their niggardly participation in Bianca's enterprise."

I gave the man a sly look. "That's rather astute political analysis for someone who purports to be little more than a food critic."

Quam started to slip back into his character and deny all, then his dark eyes narrowed. He whispered in the dog's ear. "Mr. Sam sees what others do not, Snookums. He will bear watching."

"I hope you do watch, Quam." I smiled. "After all, it's your money I'll be playing with."

The dinner was very good. I was seated at a table for ten, between an actor and a psychic, which was pretty much my definition of hell, especially when the psychic congratulated her on the awards she had won in past lives. As they compared notes on who it was the actress likely had been, I felt myself slipping closer and closer to my next life.

After dinner there were music and dancing. I did manage to get Bianca onto the floor and we moved well together. I would have asked her to dance more, but the night's storms rolled in early. Everything ground to a halt as massive silver spiderwebs of fire raced over the dark clouds and stabbed at the earth. The lightning came so quickly and so bright that it left dark spots before my eyes, and spontaneous applause arose after particularly spectacular strikes.

I smiled. Emblyn, I realized, had hit upon something that all the other promoters had missed. They tried to hide the rain. They thought people would fear the lightning. Emblyn had raised the Palace so people could stand like gods just beneath the clouds and watch the argent bolts torture the planet below. The sense of power it gave one was indescribable.

And, if dwelt upon too long, might convince one that a planet's fate should be put in his hands alone.

As the storm abated, the evening ended. Quam called down to the high-stakes room host and set up a line of credit for me. I left the party and went there, finding a few people I recognized from above already involved in a game. I sat in and watched, playing cautiously for the first few hands. I folded quickly since I'd caught no cards, but it was really too early for me to do much anyway.

As the old poker saying goes, if you can look around the table and you don't see the person who is the pigeon, then you're it. I actually found several pigeons who played as if the money had no value. They were looking for the thrill of Lady Luck kissing the top of their heads as opposed to using those heads to supplement with guile what luck was denying them.

I watched how they bet and what they bet on. There were a couple of abortive attempts at bluffing, but the bluffers backed off when an aggressive raise came back at them. I knew those people could, therefore, be bluffed. And those who raised to counter a bluff could fall hard to a hand that looked horrid based on the cards showing but had some powerful combinations hidden in the down cards.

I started by pulling thirty thousand stones from the line of credit, and dipped as low as twenty-two before I began winning. I won one hand with a bluff that brought me back even. The very next hand I caught a full house, but you couldn't see that in the up cards, so I was aggressively counterbluffed. I kept raising and doubled my stake on that hand alone.

A couple of the players decided to retire for the night, which left seats open for Bernard and Teyte. The table really hadn't needed more pigeons, but we got a brace in them. It didn't hurt that Bernard didn't like me, that Teyte caught that dislike from his cousin, and that the two of them downed liquor shots with the enthusiasm Quam used in scarfing canapés.

The other players at the table saw how the power was shifting and they continued to play. They lost hands to the Germaynes that they'd not have lost to me. I quickly realized they were paying a voluntary luxury tax, since the Germaynes did have power. If they plied their power the way they played their cards, however, it would be squandered fast and uselessly.

What I did to them that night wasn't pretty. Ideally I'd take little pride in leaving two drunks not so much as a stone in their shoes, but it was a joy to fleece the two of them. They'd likely not faced any real competition in forever and kept ordering up racks of chips, signing chits that, if I'd read the reports on the family financing right, were stealing from their own great-grandchildren.

I kept at them until, finally, Emblyn himself came to the room and cut their credit off. He was good about it and they acquiesced. The others at the table got up, happy to be let out of the meat grinder. I gathered all the chips and chits, stacking them neatly, then picked up the deck, ordering cards and shuffling. I kept my face expressionless despite having won enough to buy myself a little distillery where I could make the finest Irish whisky known to humanity.

Emblyn sat down opposite me as the staff cleared the room, and he motioned to me to remain seated. "You realize, Mr. Donelly, that the Germaynes drew half a million stones into this game and it's all sitting there in front of you. It was my money with which they played, and they will never pay it back. That's a lot of money."

"I know. Half a million of your money, three hundred thousand and change of other people's money." I slid five stacks of chits to the middle of the table, then stacked the deck of cards on top of them. "Cut for high card, double or nothing."

Emblyn sat back for a moment, fingers brushing over his chin. "Interesting. A pure gamble offered by a man who doesn't really gamble. You feel safe in offering the bet because you realize I don't gamble either."

"Oh, he who owns the house has the odds in his favor, so it's not gambling. I know that. You like sure things. As do I. The question is, will you take the chance?"

He shook his head. "No. As you said, I don't gamble. Neither do you. So, what I will do is this. I will double that to a million if you cut the deck. If you cut the deck to the three of clubs."

"And if I don't?"

"In four hours there is a DropShip leaving Contressa spaceport. You and your winnings will be on it, never to grace Basalt again."

I thought for a moment, then nodded. I squared the deck there on the stack, then cut and revealed the three of clubs.

"Very good, Mr. Donelly, very good. You stacked the deck. You knew what the bottom card was, so you knew where the three of clubs should be. I like that. I want to know that a man in your position has the foresight and courage to stack the deck in his favor, and then the guts to take the plunge."

"You might mistake me, sir. Could be I thought walking away with my winnings was worth the risk."

"If that's true, there are two fools at this table, and I think the odds of that are highly unlikely." He stood slowly. "Your account will be credited with an extra half a million stones."

"Send it to the Basalt Foundation."

"So, poker isn't the only game you play?"

"Nope." I shook my head. "But every one of them I play to win, and since I'm working for you, I hope you won't mind."

28

Let wealth and commerce, laws and learning die,
But leave us still our old nobility!
                              —John Manners, Duke of Rutland

Emblyn Palace Resort, Garnet Coast
Basalt
Prefecture IV, Republic of the Sphere
10 February 3133

While the junket at the resort was supposed to last until the twelfth, I opted to join Bianca and Quam in leaving on the last shuttle on the tenth. A number of the people I'd skinned asked if they were going to get a chance to win their money back, but I could see they really didn't want me at the table. That was fine with me, as I'd done a bit more damage than I expected to and my encounter with Emblyn had made it clear that I was an employee. While he did have an entrepreneur's appreciation of my skills, in his organization there was only one big dog, and he was it.

And on the scale he worked, I made Snookums look like a wolfhound.

I was content to leave early as I'd attracted a bit more

attention than I wanted to. People were noticing me and knew my name, and it wasn't because I'd given money to the Basalt Foundation. The story of the B&T Poker Express Limited jumping the maglev tracks and crashing at Half-Mil Junction had gotten around. It was better to fade than stick around and give folks an opportunity to form an opinion.

At the terminal in Contressa Quam was determined that Snookums would not travel as baggage. Bianca opted to help him out and took possession of the dog while Quam wrestled with a big basket of food. The shuttle's conductor recognized Bianca and allowed her to bring the dog on, whereas all other pets were relegated to the baggage compartment.

Quam took up the back bench and we nabbed seats one row forward. Snookums, who sat with her master, growled at anyone lingering around waiting to use the bathroom, so we had a fair amount of privacy. This pleased Quam, who opened his basket and set about melding various foodstuffs into combinations which he shared with us and one three-year-old waif who wandered in our direction while his mother slept.

Bianca smiled at me. "I can't thank you enough for the donation. Ring transferred six hundred thousand into the Foundation's account. It's all anonymous, of course, but it was nice of him to match your donation stone for stone."

"Indeed, it was." I nodded slowly and even smiled. Emblyn had given *more* than he needed to, but claimed half as his own generosity. He had to have known I'd find out. I could think of any of a number of explanations for his action, and all sorts of messages he was sending me. It was clear he was testing me, seeing if I would take umbrage at his having laid claim to money I had won. If I were a rash man, it would provoke rash action, but he already knew I wasn't rash. So, he reminded me yet again who was more important.

What he seemed to forget was that it was all his money anyway. The conclusions I drew from that oversight were not a message he wanted to send, I was fairly certain.

I reached a hand inside my coat and brought out a cashier's check for another four hundred fifty thousand stones.

It had been made out to the Foundation as well. "This represents half the winnings I had, plus the eighty thousand I tried to have friend Quam take as interest on his loan."

"Mr. Donelly, Sam, you have given much too much."

"My lady, this is in keeping with my agreement with Quam."

She fixed me with a hard-eyed stare. "Sam, this is a lot of money."

"I have more than enough left over you know." I smiled. "I appreciate your concern, but I am doing well right now. And if I decide to give more, you'll not protest, right?"

"Ahem. I spend my days dealing with people who have unrealistic expectations and ideas about money. You've won what anyone would consider to be a life-changing amount of money. I just want you to be one of the success stories."

"Oh, I'm a survivor."

"Okay, I'll take you at your word. But I won't play cards with you." She softened her expression. "And if there is anything I can do for you . . ."

"You can answer a question."

A hint of fear flashed through her eyes for a moment, then she nodded. "Anything."

"Quam gave me his perspective on the nature of the disagreement between you and your father. Is your father's opinion of people really that harsh?"

Bianca's brows furrowed. "It wasn't always, but it has changed over the years. My uncle Ivan and my mother both used to soften his opinions, but after they died, he relied more on Bernard. You see, my grandfather was a Mech-Warrior who fought for Victor Steiner-Davion, and then threw in with Devlin Stone. He wanted peace so his sons would never have to pilot 'Mechs, and this was good because my father is singularly bad at it. Bernard, on the other hand, is very good. So is Teyte. Growing up in a time of peace, they've harkened back to the Davion warrior tradition from before The Republic—this despite Basalt being blessed with a lot of peace and prosperity over the last three centuries. We weren't entirely without combat—what world has been—but fate has been very good to Basalt. As my father has worked with Bernard to train him to rule in his stead, Bernard's influence has grown steadily."

"I skinned your brother and cousin both. Bernard is not exactly the sort of compassionate ruler I'd want over me."

"He wasn't always like that, and I hope he will get back to being himself. He was a happy child. It was his idea that I start the Basalt Foundation. I like working with the Foundation because there is lots of organization to deal with, and I can make a difference. Coordinating things during a disaster is hectic, but I get things done and it feels great." The rising tone of her voice and the light burning in those blue eyes underscored her words. "Here and there we get to ease some burdens for some people."

"You do it well by all accounts."

"You are too kind. I just want to do better and more." She shrugged. "What is your ambition, Sam?"

"Same as yours, I think. I like the idea of making life better for folks."

"And you do that by robbing them blind at poker?"

I smiled. "Well, sometimes you have to make them look at what they value, and encourage them to take steps to preserve or abandon same. How well you react to adversity reveals the strength of your character. Some folks turn out to be stronger than they think."

"And the others?"

"They're a headstone shy of discovering they've got nothing."

I left Bianca with Quam and returned to the Grand Germayne. I placed a call to the cutout and within two hours of my return I was sitting in a nondescript bar with Gypsy. I filled him in on relevant details of the weekend, then quickly outlined a strike. We organized the operation swiftly that night and then, the next evening, we executed it flawlessly.

The Heights district of Manville was located in the southeast quadrant. It had grown up around the Germayne palace and featured some of the finest homes in the city. Because these homes were built on the sides of hills well above the level of the rivers, water was pumped up to the tops of the hills to reservoirs, then gravity served to provide suitable water pressure to deal with the citizenry's needs.

Our operation consisted of three separate actions. The first involved setting fire to the wooden framing for a seventy-four-thousand-square-decimeter mansion on Beryl Road. While rain had soaked the wood, suitable application of accelerant started a merry blaze that was visible from most of the city. An alarm immediately went out and fire crews from two station houses reported to fight the blaze.

The second stage of the operation, in which I participated directly, involved the blowing of two pumping stations that sent water up to the reservoirs. Bolt cutters got us through the lock holding the gate shut. A code-cutter used some arcane device to pull the lock code from the pump house door, then fed it back and got us inside. We rigged explosives to both the pump, since replacing it would be tough, and the pipe on the downhill side of things.

Once we'd wired our station, the team and I pulled out and blew it. Because it was night, it was possible to see a tiny flash, but even in the news Tri-Vid of the fire coverage, the explosions of the pump houses are barely noticeable. The effect of the explosions, however, aside from requiring the replacement of two relatively expensive pumps, was to have a lot of water gushing around. The water cut through a roadway and gnawed the foundation of another mansion.

Because we couldn't possibly hide the damage to the pump houses, we decided to go for a trifecta and also blew up one of the two firehouses from whence the firefighters had responded. The team that took it out stole a liquefied natural gas hovertruck, drove it through the closed garage door, then detonated it after the crew had gotten clear.

Now *that* explosion showed up very well on a Tri-Vid. It leveled the building and left the wreckage burning brightly. The blackened skeleton of the hovertruck, with the ribs of its skirts looking like cilia on some twisted insect, was impressive. To make the whole thing a bit more complicated, the first fire was drawing enough water out of the fire hydrants that the company fighting the firehouse blaze had a tough time getting suitable pressure.

Because news organizations were putting out reports as fast as they could field rumors, and because the fires could be seen from elsewhere in the city, the media went into high gear. Pundits claimed everything from it being an accident to the work of subversive Clan agents bent on completing the conquest of the Inner Sphere. Newscasters started by being very grave about the goings on, but when the majority of damage was limited to buildings that put no one out of their homes, they grew calmer.

The citizenry had a variety of reactions, all captured and

broadcast live over multiple channels. What played very well was Tri-Vid of rich Heights residents who had low water pressure using buckets to harvest water from their pools. Their panic over not being able to water their flowers, or having to shut off their interior waterfall features pointed up how out of touch they were. While some newsies did note that the lack of fresh water could become a health concern, even they cracked a smile when watching Tri-Vid of a doyen in a sequined gown kneeling at the edge of a pool and drinking alongside her two lapping hounds.

The people in the street felt some vindication as barely a week before they'd been unhomed by a catastrophe that had left the rich untouched and decidedly unsympathetic. Some people did fill up jugs of water and run them up to the Heights in neighborly gestures, but a lot of others just sneered. As one man pointed out, "They're worrying about water on a world where, in another fifteen minutes, it'll be pouring so hard you can't see three meters in front of your face. It's not a desert."

The Germayne government fared very badly, since the Count and many of his Ministers happened to be ensconced at the Emblyn Palace when the disaster struck. Ring immediately jetted back and did what he could to help out. He arrived two hours before the Count, and rumors had it that Hector had waited until someone could hunt Bernard and Teyte down in a Capellan brothel in Contressa and sober them up. One news-wag noted that Bernard had "diddled while his home burned," and everyone who caught the allusion to Nero agreed it was on point.

Bernard just found the word "diddled" entertaining.

The government did point out that the three events were related and clearly were acts of terrorism. Linkage was made with the whole sewer system problem, again citing the blown gates there. The forensics folks did aptly point out that the same explosive was used, and that the placement pointed to professionals, but government critics turned around and suggested that the government was behind the second set of attacks, to bolster the claims they had made about the first, and to elicit sympathy for the rich. The fact that so many of the well-to-do in the government were at the Emblyn Palace *did* make the idea of a government conspiracy sound good.

And, as one commoner put it, "How come we had to clean up stuff, and they're just reduced to drinking their bottled water and their wine? Where's the justice in that?"

Bianca and Emblyn came off as the big winners in the whole aftermath. Emblyn had his own crews come and help make repairs to the pumping stations. He even brought in a pump that was supposed to be used at the Emblyn Palace to make a fountain. Since the Palace's reception had been part of the shake-out month and the place had another six weeks before opening, the sacrifice was not that huge, but the symbol endeared him to many folks.

Bianca won because of the news angle of one of the rich doing things for her beleaguered brethren, especially when they were the ones normally giving to charity. Many were the rich who, upon receipt of a case of bottled water, waxed eloquent on the nature of The Republic, and how charity was so appropriate for the citizenry. They said they would give more and do more, and many even volunteered to help the Foundation do the sweaty work of delivering things to others less fortunate than they—by which they meant those living lower down.

Throughout it all, Bianca was gracious and positive. She credited the hard work of the volunteers and some very generous donations she'd gotten that weekend as the reasons things were going so smoothly. Newsies had a hard time keeping up with her, and she really did appear to be in her element, which brought a smile to my face.

LIT was working better than I expected, primarily because we picked the right targets and had the benefit of timing. Resentment over Bernard's actions and the Count's policies toward the poor had already started things simmering. This just brought it out into the open. The next strike would have to be against an economic target, like JPG. At least, that was the plan.

The problem was that LIT had not counted on having someone like Bernard in the mix on the other side, with a whole cadre of warriors ready to go. It struck me that he was likely to act out in some way. That could heat things up and he was unpredictable enough that I didn't want to leave him alone. If he was an agent of chaos, I wanted to focus him.

There was only one way I could do that.

I headed for the Egg.

29

No man can serve two masters.

—Matthew 6:24

Manville, Capital District
Basalt
Prefecture IV, Republic of the Sphere
12 February 3133

One aspect of my training as a Ghost Knight had to do with observation. That makes sense, of course, since most of the time I was gathering information. That's best done with your mouth shut, just watching folks and listening to the differences between what they tell you, and what they actually do. When you find a disconnect between the two, you know where to start pushing.

More important than all that, though, is self-observation. There are great little tricks to it. For example, you take a normal breath and hold it until your lungs begin to burn for oxygen. The object isn't to see how long you can hold your breath, but just to know how much time passes until you feel that fire. Twenty seconds, thirty, it doesn't matter except as a measure of time.

When I walked into the Egg I stopped where I had before and just stopped breathing. I wanted to see how long it would take before I was noticed and Alba was sent for. I didn't want to appear concerned or anxious, so I wasn't going to look at my watch. I just held my breath and waited for the burn.

Of course, an added benefit of this method of timing was that I didn't have to breathe in there. I thought at first that the whole sewer backup thing might have been the source of the problem, then I recalled that it was only the west side that was affected. A shortage of washing-up water could have explained some of it, too, but we were nowhere near the Heights.

I can't say the tension was palpable, but the nervous stink was. The pilots there were irritated. Worse yet, they were bored. A chance comment could have started a brawl that would have wrecked the place. It wouldn't improve the decor, and I doubted it would do much for the stench.

After a minute and a half Alba arrived from a back room and smiled at me. "I was wondering when you'd be back."

"I was asking about, as you suggested. I've seen the opposition."

She nodded. "Follow me."

I did and she led me through a side door and up some stairs. Down a hallway and to the left we entered a small office that had been supplied with Clan War surplus and likely hadn't been painted since before the Blakist uprising. In fact, the newest item in the place sat on her desk.

It was a small holoprojector and hovering eighteen centimeters high was an image of yours truly, slowly rotating. She followed my gaze, then looked up and smiled. "It was given to me by someone who wants you very dead."

"What's the price?"

"Fifty K."

"I'll beat it."

Alba shook her head, then sat, and waved me to the chair opposite her desk. "Don't bother. I'm a warrior, not a hit man."

I sat. "Has to be Bernie. Teyte would do the job himself."

She smiled carefully. "You're insightful. I can't tell if you know or you're bluffing, but I'll confirm neither."

"But we'll find out soon enough since someone downstairs let the contract issuer know I was here. Actually, you made the call, otherwise I'd just be a body waiting for delivery." I stretched. "I wonder how we could pass the time until they get here."

"Profitably, but not the way I might prefer. We have twenty minutes."

"Not enough time, I agree, so why don't I tell you why I came here."

"Please."

"Since this comes from a security Tri-Vid from the Palace, you know I've met Emblyn. He's taken credit for something I did and, therefore, he is a jerk and has earned my ire. He must pay, and I know exactly how that can be accomplished."

I proceeded to tell Alba all about LIT. I stressed the focus on targets that are a serious capital loss to the owner. Unlike the Cat, the former Lament grasped the philosophy immediately and saw the possibilities behind it. She nodded sagely as I showed how a government couldn't fight it.

Her eyes narrowed. "The one vulnerability here is an ancient one. Hannibal used it against the Romans. He fought on their territory. The only way to make someone like Emblyn stop is to make victory too costly for him. The government has obvious targets to hit, but he does as well—and he has no established constituency. If he were to be hit he might get some initial sympathy, but people will be reminded how rich he is, and that is seldom an endearing trait unless his money is being spent on *you*."

Her gaze flicked to the doorway, giving me a moment's warning. Even as Bernard surged through the door with hands outstretched and fingers clawed, I was up and out of my metal-frame chair. With a snap of my wrist I spun it into his path. He barked his shins on it, stumbled and went down hard.

I whirled and my right leg snapped out in a kick that caught Teyte on the left side of his head. The laces cut his cheek and tore at his earlobe. The kick snapped his head around. He smacked hard into the door jamb, then staggered back. He tripped over Bernard's legs and crashed down. He struck his head on the floor and sprawled there, unconscious and bleeding.

I grabbed Bernie by the collar and dragged him into a

chair. "Sit. Stay, or you and your cousin will be comparing kicks to the head." I righted my chair and pulled it back where I could watch all three of them.

Bernard snarled at Alba. "You bitch, you ambushed us."

Her nostrils flared dismissively. "It was self-defense. You picked a fight with someone who has already kicked your tail, and you just got it kicked again. It's a good thing he did it, too, because if he hadn't, I would have been forced to."

"Do you know who you're talking to?"

"Very well, thank you. And you're talking to the person you've hired to make certain you will inherit your father's throne. Mr. Donelly has just given us the means to fight against your enemy and, curiously enough, to deal with others who might come along. He's told me everything the other side is doing and we have a way to fight it. Judiciously managed, the whole crisis might also prompt your father to step down in your favor, far sooner than you ever expected."

Bernie looked from her to me and back again. "Him? But he's working for Emblyn."

"Which would somehow make me immune to the fact that he's a conceited jerk?" I snorted at him. "Of course, I think the same of you, but you were born to it. He's no better than me, but has airs and that just doesn't go down well. Besides, what I skinned from you is more than he'll ever pay me, and he's probably scheming to get it back from me now."

"That's true. There isn't a credit that's passed through his hands that doesn't have his thumbprint etched on Stone's cheek." Bernard rubbed at his shins. "How is it that we get to Emblyn?"

I held my hands up. "First thing you do is tell me how much you're paying me."

"I've already given you a lot of money."

"And I earned every pebble of it. We're talking *more*. I'll earn it, too."

"You'll get paid." Bernard's sneer returned. "Once I'm running Basalt, you'll get yours."

I glanced at Alba. "You working on promises?"

"No, but I do think the guarantees that have been banked with ComStar have put Lord Germayne here in something of a liquidity crisis." She gave me a nod. "I promise you a quarter of what I've already got against anything he offers you."

"Done."

Bernard stopped rubbing his shins and rubbed his hands together instead. "Tell me, how do we get him?"

"Okay, look, Alba already knows the plans Emblyn's people are working. You can leave the details of all that to her. You don't need to know, and you don't *want* to know. Also, I'm not going to ask you what resources you have or anything like that. I'm just going to suggest things and if you have the stuff you need to make it work, just make it work. If I don't know logistics and timetables, you can't blame me if something screws up. Alba, I have scouted some dead-drops and we'll set up a servicing plan for them. If I hear anything that will interfere with plans I've suggested to you, I'll let you know."

"Good, I was going to suggest that."

Lord Germayne frowned. "Yap, yap, yap, just like some little Kurita mutt. How do I get Emblyn?"

"Here's the whole package. It comes in two parts. First, Emblyn's people have not claimed credit for either the sewers or the fire. They've hesitated because governmental critics are playing up the conspiracy angle and that makes the government look bad. Once some group pops up to claim credit for things, the government's assertions are proved true and the citizens will realize their government is under attack. So, step one, you have people create some sort of anarchist group that issues some manifestos and claims credit for the attacks. You promise more attacks to come in the future."

Bernard's impatience deepened the frown. "I've still not heard what I want to hear."

Alba made a gentle gesture to calm me, and I nodded. "Second step: you have to hit him hard, in a place that will embarrass him. You can't kill innocents, since that pattern has already been established. You want to nail a big target that will cost him a lot of time, money, heartache and prestige."

The man's eyes lit up. "I know the place. Perfect."

"Great, whatever. I'll assume you have the resources to do the job. It's going to be important for you to make sure your little liberation front or whatever you call it takes credit for your action, and comes up with a consistent reason why they hit Emblyn. It will take the shine off him from recent activities *and* will drive him nuts, since he knows your people didn't do the first attacks, but he can't stand up and say anything about it because his only proof is that *he* was behind the original attacks."

The idea of Emblyn being hoist on his own petard clearly thrilled Bernard. "Yes, this will work. Dolehide . . ."

"I'll make it work."

"Give me the details. I want to be driving one of the 'Mechs."

I shook my head adamantly. "No you don't."

"Oh, I do."

I sighed. "If you do that, you completely destroy every possible advantage you could gain here. You have to be held above and apart. Think, you hit a target hard, what will Emblyn do?"

"Hit back."

"Right, just as hard, or harder. And who is going to be the person stepping in to resolve the matter by force of arms? You will, with your handpicked cadre of warriors whom you have brought here at your own expense to guarantee the peace and tranquility of your nation. If you go on this raid and something happens to reveal your presence, you lose everything. You need to be somewhere else, rather conspicuous."

"I need an alibi." He got a feral grin on his face. "Obvious and visible."

"Exactly." I stood. "I'm leaving you two to this. There's a back way out, right, the same way they came in so Neimeyer's people across the street don't have a holo of him?"

Alba nodded, then got up and came around the desk. She stepped over Teyte. "I'll be right back, my lord."

"Fine, I'll be here thinking."

We left him to that arduous task. She guided me down two flights and out through a hole that had been knocked through the basement wall into the storage for a restaurant next door. "Up the stairs, out through the kitchen, and you're clear."

"Good, thanks." I shook her hand. "I hope you can make this work with little interference from him."

"I will." Her hand tightened on mine instead of releasing it. "When Teyte wakes up he's going to want you very dead. He'll hold off because Bernard will see you as useful. Teyte will work against that and when he succeeds—however he succeeds—you *will* be killed."

"Not the first time I've heard that."

Alba gave me a curious smile. "But they run the planet, and they will rat you out to Emblyn. His reach is longer than theirs, and he'll be even more vindictive."

"It's a chance I'll take. It's not easy playing both ends against the middle, but it can be profitable." I nodded a salute. "And, as you know, anyone who fights for anything other than money is a fool."

30

Oderint, dum metuant.
Let them hate, so long as they fear.

—Accius

Emblyn Palace Resort, Garnet Coast
Basalt
Prefecture IV, Republic of the Sphere
15 February 3133

It should come as no surprise that Bernard chose the Palace resort as the target for his strike. I'm fairly certain Alba pointed out that it was also patently obvious, but there were few other places that would create such a splash with so clear a chance of minimizing casualties. Because the resort was not yet open, very few people would be on site at night. With a bit of warning, the building would be empty before a 'Mech assault could bring it down.

What impressed me was how quickly and easily the Germaynes created the Basalt Socialist Union and started it claiming responsibility for some attacks. They claimed the sewers and the fire, and tossed in a couple of other things that the government had taken heat for in the past. I found that very clever in that it cleared the government's plate *and* gave the BSU a longer history, which made it that much more menacing.

Gypsy was immediately thrown into an uproar, since part of our plan had been to claim credit and shape public opinion. I carefully pointed out that we'd still be able to do that, and rather easily. "Look, we both know the Germaynes have issued these statements to bolster their claims and to take the heat off the government. We know we can destroy their claims because we can provide the Constabulary with technical details about the explosives used and a dozen other things that only we would know. We can take back credit *and* expose this as a government effort, if we so choose. Moreover, the government is clearly trying to lay claim to these events so they can use the BSU as a cover to take a poke at Emblyn and get away with it."

Gypsy and I then went through a version of my talk with Bernard and Alba. I let him figure out Bernard's most logical target and we agreed that it had to be the Palace Resort. Because there was a constant stream of transports and the occasional DropShip making short hops into and out of the resort's landing area—bringing in construction material and other bulk items—delivering a light company to the site was relatively easy. We figured that a pair of BattleMechs and ten vehicles commanded by Catford would do the job. Emblyn Holdings Limited had a license for a lance of 'Mechs for weapons evaluation purposes, since one of his small companies did produce munitions. They'd been painted up in gray, with an Emblyn Eagle in black splayed over the chest or flanks. A platoon of infantry came in disguised as workers.

I got frozen out of the whole military operation, and that was okay with me because I had a very fine line I had to walk. I worked mostly on setting up the JPG strikes and helping Elle create the "real" guerrilla movement on Basalt. We chose "Freedom from Want" as our title, and used FfW as a logo. With that name we could justify anything, decry anything as evil, and we'd be set.

We knew that exposing the BSU would be tricky and would have to take place in two steps. Catford, as Emblyn Security, would stop the BSU attack on the resort. An investigation would be launched, likely by Colonel Niemeyer or his northern compatriots. Right after that we'd hit JPG, claim responsibility, and release to the investigators details that proved we were responsible for everything else. We would then be able to disavow the earlier attacks that the BSU had claimed, pointing anyone with two brain cells to rub together that the BSU was a smokescreen to take pressure off the corrupt Germayne regime.

Elle impressed me with how hard she worked. Not only had she collected a bunch of rumors and scandalous stories about the current government, but she'd done the same for Emblyn. The latter we analyzed so we could prepare counters to them, whereas the former pointed out the vices we could expose to embarrass the Germaynes. She was not only thorough in her research, but rather insightful about how to employ what she had discovered.

I left the disinformation campaign to her and prepped to travel north to the resort to witness the battle. How did I know when the raid was going to take place? Well, Bernard had gotten it into his head that he needed an alibi and he was very inspired. He agreed to go on a live, late-night Tri-Vid show hosted by a comedian who had scored a lot of points off Bernard gags even in the short time I'd been on Basalt. Reading between the lines of reports about this appearance, I gathered the host had been a long-time thorn in Bernard's side, so everyone was salivating to watch the encounter.

Before I went north I employed a dead-drop to leave a message for Alba to warn her that something was going on in my camp and that I was afraid they had caught wind of the raid, so she should abort it. I wrote the message out, folded it neatly, put it in an empty beer can—Diamond Negro, just for the record—and dropped it beneath a small bridge in one of the downtown parks. I then proceeded to a corner and drew an X on a lamppost with some chalk, to let her agents know there was a message at the dead-drop.

And, of course, I did this late enough in the day that the message would never be found in time. I made one call after that, then got on the shuttle and made my way to the resort. Eluding security was relatively simple since most of the guards were underpaid locals entranced by the ongoing construction. I took a hovercab to the site, walked in with a small case and said I'd been sent to see the construction supervisor. Once I'd signed in, the rental guard started to escort me, but I told him I knew the way and he let me go.

I entered the resort and made my way to the restaurant. To get there I had to open the lift's control panel and cross two wires, but that did no permanent damage, so my passage went unnoticed. During the subsequent evac search of the building—which followed a fire drill—a guard did appear and ask if anyone was up there. I remained silent and the closest he got to finding me was filching a bottle of Castel Del Lestrade '28 Cabernet/Merlot.

Now, if he'd gone for the Chardonnay, I'd have been found out.

Sipping some of the '24 Chardonnay, I watched as a storm rolled its clouds in above, mirroring the gathering forces below. From that vantage point I could easily imagine myself to be Ares, ancient god of War, delighting as Humanity sought to slay one another. Humanity was far removed from the days of infantry armed with sword and spear, and the type of slaughter that would ensue might not only delight Ares, but would please Hades no end also.

There is nothing natural about modern combat. I watched the BSU forces come in from the east. They brought two 'Mechs, one armored lance of Scimitars, another of Fox Armored Hovercars and a pair of Demon Medium Tanks. The platoon of troopers they brought in rode on the Foxes, but hopped off and formed up into four squads once the vehicles entered the resort property via the construction road through the jungle. Everything had been painted or uniformed in dark browns and greens to make them tougher to see. While I had a set of nightvision goggles with me, I didn't put them on because the jagged flashes of lightning strobed brightly enough for me to watch their approach.

The centerpiece of their force was a *Firestarter*. While the 'Mech was not a big threat in combat, against the building in which I stood, it could do a lot of damage. While I was fairly certain Bernard would have preferred having the Palace pounded into rubble, having it go up as a votive offering to the gods would be spectacular *and* in keeping with the pyromaniacal leanings the BSU had already claimed.

Their other 'Mech was a *Panther*, which could move quickly and sported an extended-range Particle Projector Cannon. That weapon and the pair of short-range-missile launchers in the 'Mech's torso made it formidable in combat, while its jump jets and armor gave it maneuverability and longevity in combat—at least while matched by a comparable 'Mech.

I do have to give Catford credit. While I thought he was an egotistical giant and an intellectual dwarf, he was very good at setting up an ambush and executing it. He'd done a great job anticipating what Germayne would throw at him, and matched their forces almost exactly. He'd culled Gypsy's resources for the best pilots and equipment. That, coupled with the advantage of surprise, gave him a gross advantage. His choice of 'Mechs heightened that advantage. His first shot, targeted and timed perfectly, doomed the BSU effort from the start.

A pair of Condor Multi-Purpose Tanks—hulking tracked vehicles with lots of armor and an LRM launcher in the turret—joined a *Catapult* in launching their full missile payloads at the *Firestarter*. They'd been fed targeting coordinates from one of the construction shacks because they were waiting in the foundation pit for Tower Three. The launches rivaled the lightning, and sixty missiles arced out at their target. Explosions wreathed the humanoid 'Mech, blossoming red and gold. Armor shattered and rained down in semi-molten fragments. Its left arm whirled away in a twisted mass of metal while the *Firestarter* staggered. It sank to its knees, then flopped back, lashed by sheets of rain.

Everything on both sides opened up at that point, with red, green and jagged blue beams slicing through the storm. Some pilots, as always happens, shot at phantoms. The artificial lightning of the Particle Projector Cannons looked anemic compared to nature's wrath, but they carved steaming furrows in armor. The BSU *Panther* coordinated its attack with the Scimitars, choosing one enemy to beset. Their pilots fired fast and accurately, trying to take out Catford's lance of Joust Medium Tanks before they could mow down the infantry with their machine guns.

Turf rooster-tailed high into the air as the Jousts raced forward. Their turrets traversed to cover targets and the large laser each vehicle sported spat out thick beams of green light. The *Panther*'s chest armor boiled away, leaving angry smoking scars, but the pilot kept his 'Mech upright. It shot back with its PPC, and the Scimitars joined in by launching a dozen SRMs at just one of the Jousts.

The BSU strikes savaged the left side of the Joust, peeling the armor back as if it were made of roofing tin. The PPC raked across it and then down. The azure beam sliced through the track, which whipped off like a snake in agony. The Joust spun around to the left, presenting its front armor to its attackers as the three other tanks in the lance raced on.

Another exchange would have likely killed the Joust, but before the *Panther* could attack, the *Catapult* and Condors rained fire down upon it. One moment it was standing there, looking strong and terrible. In the next, fire and smoke surrounded it like a magician about to disappear. As the light evaporated, a transformation had occurred, for in the place of a proud war machine there remained a battered hulk. One arm had been torn completely off, the other snapped at the elbow, and the 'Mech had dropped to one knee. Torso armor had vanished and structural members glowed in a twisted body.

The stricken 'Mech's head nodded forward, then the body slowly sagged in on itself. It looked as if the *Panther*'s corpse might remain frozen in that position, and I had visions of it resting in the Boneyard on Terra. Then fire lit the cockpit; the faceplate blew out as the pilot ejected. He rode his command couch's jet out, but started from a bad angle, so he hit the turf hard and tumbled. The couch came apart and so did he while, behind him, the force of the ejection toppled the *Panther*'s body.

The BSU troops must have known from the first they were in trouble, but they were game. The Scimitars made runs at the Emblyn tanks, unloading their short-range missiles, lighting things up with their lasers, then scurrying like roaches exposed by lightning flashes. By luck or skill, they combined with the Demons to take two more of the tanks out, even though the last Joust's machine guns scythed fire through the BSU infantry, killing all but a handful.

Catford clearly found the Scimitars and their valiant effort a personal affront because he moved his *Jupiter* into the battle when it really wasn't needed. The hundred-ton BattleMech strode into the firefight much as its namesake might have three millennia before. Watching it, I could not help but feel a thrill, for the forces before it would be all but powerless to stop it, and he could kill them at his will.

And killing was what he wanted to do.

The *Jupiter* is a humanoid 'Mech with autocannons in each arm, ER PPCs, and LRM launchers in the torso. When it walks, the ground trembles. It is both wonderful and terrible, the reason Stone wanted 'Mechs restricted, and yet the means he used to destroy the enemies who defied the restriction.

The *Jupiter* turned almost casually toward one of the Scimitars. The PPCs fired, thrusting blue energy spears into the tank's right flank. Armor disintegrated and the chassis glowed white before it melted into molten metal puddles. The turret sagged and collapsed, before the SRM magazine touched off. A gout of fire flipped the turret into the air, where it was lost in the darkness.

The BSU troops began to withdraw, but their effort was too little, too late. Missile barrages struck at fleeing targets. One of the Fox Armored Hovercars simply ceased to exist when the Condors and *Catapult* deigned to notice it. The explosions left a crater where it had been, with its armor and shell reduced to shrapnel.

Of the BSU force, only two of the Foxes got away. Catford would have gone after the escapees, save for the intervention of other forces. The forces that came in were the Garnet Coast district Public Safety Department troopers. They arrived in helicopter and infantry carriers disgorging officers in battle armor. Before I'd left Manville I'd phoned an anonymous tip into Niemeyer's division that something would be going down that night at the Resort. Their intervention meant that surviving BSU troops were rounded up for questioning, which was bound to cause the Germaynes some trouble.

It would also frustrate Catford, since I was fairly certain he'd have wanted to treat them as prisoners of war. I didn't know what his thoughts were on proper interrogation techniques, but I'd heard rumors about Siwek that meant I wanted to keep people out of her hands. I doubted the fighters would have anything useful to offer and I certainly didn't need them giving me up on the off chance they'd seen me at the Egg.

I watched the PSD officers round people up, and saw Catford descend from the *Jupiter*'s cockpit. Some of the PSD emergency medtechs came over to help him, but from his gesticulating I could tell he didn't want them touching him, and he didn't want the PSD on Emblyn property. Someone encased in metal—I would have guessed Niemeyer, but they all looked huge in that power armor— pinned him back against the 'Mech's leg and Catford seemed to settle down.

In the distance a PSD helicopter chased the escaping vehicles for a while, but peeled off when lasers and machine-gun fire threatened it.

I watched a little while longer, then turned away. I'd have given my eyeteeth to see the live feed of Bernard's face when this news flash ran over the Tri-Vid, but I refrained from finding a set and turning it on. After all, I knew I'd see the replay endlessly and, with that thought in my head, I found a bed and slept very happily indeed.

31

I will make thee a terror to thyself, and to all they friends.

— Jeremiah 20:4

Manville, Capital District
Basalt
Prefecture IV, Republic of the Sphere
16 February 3133

Despite the resort not being open, it did have all manner of amenities available to the casual guest. Before I left in the morning, I was able to download all of the news reports on items of interest. The two lead items in almost every journal involved the raid at the Palace and Bernard's performance on live Tri-Vid.

Bernard actually handled himself better than I would have expected. While the host had poked fun at him, and Bernard had shot back with a few jokes that someone had scripted, the talk turned to recent events, and that brought up the whole BSU thing. Bernard had some remarks prepared that were wholly self-serving as far as the government was concerned, and constituted a nationalistic appeal to the citizens' pride. It pretty much amounted to a call for folks to rally around the Germayne government.

"Our world has been a very peaceful one, where we have shaped a harmonic society." Bernard composed his face into a mask of sincerity, which, for the most part, remained in place. "The Federated Suns always found us stalwart and a positive model. The Republic did, at the start, and made us part of their grand experiment because they needed our example. But now, as this experiment is weakening and failing, we need to look to ourselves, for no one from the outside is going to come rescue us. In fact, forces from the outside are here to destroy us.

"Our future is in our hands, and we must grasp it as tightly as we can, defending it mightily. The people committing these acts of terror, we know who they are. You wonder, but you will see among them those you thought were friends. You know who you can trust, you can see it in their open, honest eyes, in the clear voices with which they speak, and in their welcoming openness, not self-segregation. We must all band together to keep our home safe from outside influences that will tear us apart."

His appeal soft-soaped the racist underpinnings of his philosophy, but the clues in his comments could not be missed. He directed his fellow citizens to keep their eyes on foreigners, and from what I'd seen, that meant anyone who didn't have round eyes or who happened to be fluent in the tongue of their ancestors as well as English. His message was as subtle as he was capable of, which told me it had been scripted, and made me wonder, just for a moment, who put those words in his mouth.

If the host noticed Bernard's restraint or slick delivery, he made no comment and went to a station break. In keeping with the show's format, Bernard moved onto a couch as the next guest came out, and the next. Right after some local teen sensation had sung her heart out, the host provided Bernard a chance to comment on the news flash that the BSU had tried to destroy the Emblyn Palace. I could see a vein start twitching in the middle of Bernard's forehead, but he refrained from exploding. In a moment of insight, he channeled his anger into his voice and denounced the BSU and its efforts. "I was just at that facility and I know why they wanted to destroy it. They are bitter people who cannot stand seeing others succeed. Basalt, which has been a peaceful place under my father's guidance, and shall be again, welcomes success. We all work for the common good here, and just as we pulled together for the good of the people of Manville during the recent upsets, so we must unite against the BSU. We cannot let *them* win, and we will not. *I* will not. This is my vow to the true citizens of Basalt."

In seeing the little clip on my noteputer screen as I rode the shuttle south again, I thought he'd done a good job—terrifying though it was. The Contressa and Manville media shared my assessment, but as I read other stories about it, from cities further flung and on other continents, the reviews were scathing. Some pundits suggested that he didn't want the Palace destroyed because that was the only resort he'd not yet been tossed from. The further from Manville the source, the harsher the criticism, and his divisive comments did not go unnoticed. One editorial even suggested that Basaltines might want to look at what BSU was saying, to see if their world had not become stagnant and, in fact, needed a quickening of blood and spirit from outside.

It's always that way in any society were power is centralized. The further one is from the locus of power, the weaker the grip. While the people in the outlying regions might not be disgusted enough to start a revolution, they could be induced to support one. Gypsy had already talked about salting journals and opinion shows in such outlying areas with shills who would accentuate the negative about the Germaynes. A lot of the material Elle had gathered could be leaked out there and would further weaken the Germayne regime.

The stories about the raid were curious. Initially the raiders were identified as BSU, and that identification was tracked down to a nameless official in the government. I don't think it was anyone connected to Bernard, but just some bureaucrat who made a lucky guess, leaked it, and waited for the PSD to confirm it. Journalists in the outlying regions had not picked up the later revisions coming out of Contressa, so the hicks in the sticks spent the early part of the day figuring that the BSU was done for.

Contressa's PSD did provide a box score for the raid.

Both 'Mechs down, both pilots slain. The quartet of Scimitars was destroyed and their crews killed, likewise two Fox Armored Hovercars were destroyed and both Demon medium tanks went down. Most of the infantry had been killed, though three had been hospitalized, one in critical condition. Three other soldiers had been captured and were being interrogated, but it sounded as if they were keeping their mouths shut. I knew Alba was bright enough that they'd not know for whom they were working, so had little to sing about. If they could keep silent for twenty-four hours or so, that would provide enough time for Alba and her people to erase all traces of themselves in Manville.

That actually worked in favor of the plan to turn the tables and supplant the BSU with FfW. The government identification then silence could be built into an embarrassed conspiracy to hide governmental wrongdoing. It would drive Bernard even more nuts, which means he'd be looking at lashing out hard at Emblyn.

Reading fully occupied my time on the return trip. Quam had a great review of a restaurant on the east side, so I made a note to go there. From the terminal in Manville I took a hovercab to the Grand Germayne, went to my room, washed and changed. Just as I was going to leave, there was a knock at the door.

I opened it and found two officers from the PSD, Capital District standing there. "Yes?"

"Mr. Donelly, you're to come with us."

"Colonel Niemeyer too busy to deal with me?"

"We need you to come now, sir." Both of them wore mirrored sunglasses. Their faces and their voices remained expressionless. Young and well muscled, they loomed up and pretty much let me know that saying "No" was not an option.

I went with them. They took me to the lift, then down to the garage, and directed me to a dark, nondescript hovercar. "You'll have to sit in the back. Regulations."

I nodded, ducked my head and started to climb in.

That's when one of them dropped a fist into my left kidney. Pain shot through my body and I couldn't breathe. My legs just went all rubber, then he hit me again. One more shot to the right kidney and I knew I'd be voiding blood for the next couple of days. *If I live that long.*

They grabbed my hands, forced them behind my back and clapped restraints on me. Folding my legs up, they stuffed me into the rear seat foot wells, then slammed the door. Moments later they were in, the engine purred and we were moving.

I would have tried to time how long it was taking us between turns so I could reverse the route, but holding your breath until your lungs burns is tough when you can't breathe. As painful as it was to do, I arched my back and drew a little cool air in. Crunching forward I exhaled and then arched to inhale. Not pretty, not efficient, but effective for the moment.

Oddly enough, despite being able to identify my kidnappers, I didn't fear for my life. If the PSD was going to kill me, it would be Niemeyer himself, and I'd done nothing to give him leave to want me dead. I could see him wanting me roughed up so I'd leave, but murdered when no innocent blood had been shed? It didn't track right for him.

Eventually the vehicle stopped and I was dragged through a loading dock door into a small office complex. The trash strewn around and the scent of sour urine suggested it had been abandoned. Things started looking bad at that point, because it was easy to imagine being shot, left here, and only discovered after the neighbors reported an odd odor and a lot of flies buzzing around.

They hauled me into a room, sat me down in a chair, then I caught a cuff on the back of my head. I flashed back to being on Helen, and looked up, expecting to find Commander Reis there. No such luck.

It was Bernard and he was, ah, rather cross.

"You lying sack of shit, Donelly." He backhanded me, but did it badly and cracked his knuckles on my skull. "You're more treacherous than some Kurita suck-up. You sold us out. You told them where we would be and when."

"How would I do that when I didn't know those things?"

"Well, you set us up. You made me think of the Palace and made me think of being on Tri-Vid." He glanced at my two escorts as he sucked on a skinned knuckle. "Teach him a lesson."

"Sir?"

"Hit him, dammit. Make him hurt."

One yanked me from the chair, slipped his arms through

mine and clasped his hands at the back of my neck. The other pulled on some leather gloves that had lead shot sewed into a pouch on the backs. It would add that much more weight to the punches.

Sure, you're thinking that here I am, a Ghost Knight. I've got lots of training in how to handle a lot of situations. With my martial arts skills I'm lethal with no weapon at all. Getting out of this situation should have been child's play.

And it would have been save that my hands were restrained, a guy who could wrestle a 'Mech to the ground had a lock on me, and my kidneys were burning like cherry-red charcoals. This put me at a severe disadvantage, which grew larger as the PSD officer in front of me tried to permanently lodge my navel in my spinal column.

There was little I could do. I puked on him. I let my bladder go and spat until I was dry. The two PSD guys didn't like the whole bodily fluid thing. Bernard thought it was funny that I'd peed on myself. He took great pains in informing me of this fact, humiliating me, which is why he let them sit me down again.

"I hope you like sitting there like that, Donelly, because that's how you're going to die."

"Sure. Fine. I'll die. That won't save you."

He grabbed a handful of my hair and yanked my head back. "What do you mean?"

"Think about it. Ask Alba. I sent her a message. I told her to abort."

"She didn't get a note."

"It was at the dead-drop. In a can." I turned my head and spat, missing him. "I made the mark. I told you to abort."

"Liar!"

"Fine. Not my fault some eco-freak picks up the can." I raised my head myself. "You sure she didn't get it?"

"She didn't say anything. . . ." His eyes narrowed. "What are you saying?"

"Maybe she didn't. She's a merc. She can be bought. Maybe Emblyn owns her. She knew the details, right? Who else?"

"Me, Teyte, her."

"And her boss. Or your cousin's."

That earned me another slap. "Teyte is not a traitor."

"Fine. One less suspect for you." Bloody saliva dripped to pool between my feet. "She'll say she got it too late. She just picked it up too late."

"She's not a traitor, either."

"Yes, my lord. You have a traitor. You have to smoke him out." I snorted. "You don't, Emblyn hurts you bad."

"How do I find the traitor?"

I straightened up, then looked at the guards. "How much do you trust them?"

Bernard looked up, then waved them out of the room. "How?"

"Tell Alba you're doing a political op. Tell her one plan. Tell her subordinates each another plan. If it is a political op, Emblyn will use me to counter it. I get the details, tell you. You know who leaked it."

He thought for a moment, then nodded. "I can see that working."

"Good. Keep the pressure on Emblyn. More action."

"More disaster. We'll get sold out again."

"No, you have to do what he's doing. He can't cover everything. You went for a big bite and got hurt. So now go for nibbles. So many, so fast, targets chosen at random by teams with no oversight. He can't cover them all. A hundred little cuts will bleed him just as well as one big one." I smiled. "And *then*, when he's scrambling to cover the little ones . . ."

"We go back after the Palace." Bernard started pacing. "Was I wrong about you, Donelly, or are you setting me up again?"

"You know what? I don't care about you or Basalt. Get me out of here and I'm heading off Basalt. If there's a DropShip going this afternoon, I'm on it."

"Oh, no, you're not."

"Why not?"

"You're my man inside Emblyn's organization. You'll deliver the traitor to me."

"Fine, then I'm gone."

"No, Mr. Donelly, nowhere near gone." Bernard gave me a smile that made me nostalgic for Helen. "After the traitor, you'll give me Ring Emblyn himself."

32

He who has the gold makes the rules.
                              —The Golden Rule Rev. 2.0

Manville, Capital District
Basalt
Prefecture IV, Republic of the Sphere
16 February 3133

Bernard called his bullyboys back in and they dragged me down to their hovercar. Given the deterioration of my personal hygiene, they stuffed me in the trunk and drove around for a while, then dumped me in an alley. They took turns kicking me in the stomach, then uncuffed me.

One grabbed a handful of my hair, then slapped me with the other hand. "Be smart. Do what he wants. Next time we're planting you where you'll never be found." He let my hair go then kicked me into a garbage midden.

I passed out at that point and when I came to, I actually thought I was dreaming. I was on my back in a garbage pile that reeked of puked pizza and oranges. A rather large rodent was sitting on my chest and came upright as my eyes opened. It flashed me a grin full of nibbler teeth, which made my belly ache more, and then it spoke.

"So sorry a sight even a nibbler won't bite you."

It took me a moment to marvel at the nibbler speaking about himself in the third person, but then my brain coordinated things and told me the voice was actually coming from above and to my right. The nibbler and I both looked in that direction simultaneously. The rodent scampered off and I wished I could have.

I groaned. "Good evening, Colonel Niemeyer. Out for your constitutional?"

"Nope. Back from the coroner's office, where we're putting BSU corpses together like puzzles. Lots of work, and it's your fault."

I rolled to my right and gained a knee. "My fault? Enable help files, please."

"Come off it, Donelly. I know what's going on." He posted his fists on his hips. "Why do you think I'm here?"

He almost had me on that one, but my head had cleared just enough for my training to click in. Any time someone in authority asks an open-ended question like that—"Do you know why I stopped you?" or "Do you know how fast you were going?"—they're fishing for information they can use against you. The logical answer to his question would be to assume he knew about FfW or BSU and actually had tied me to things. In an effort to avoid trouble, I might spill my guts, which would just put me in deeper with him.

I was about to be sullen and vaguely insulting in my response, but my brain had started running and an idea popped up. "Actually, I think you're here because of an internal PSD investigation into the activities of officers Higgle and Giggle. You know they're working for Bernard Germayne, you're afraid laws are being broken and that the integrity of any investigation you might be doing is compromised because of them. You need to catch them red-handed, however, preferably with Bernard there too, because he has enough influence to be able to protect them and discredit you. How close is that?"

Niemeyer blinked, then crouched down beside me. "I think you're a lot smarter than I give you credit for." He looked me over, then shook his head. "Not that you give that impression in your current state."

"Yeah, well, I fell down the stairs. Into a urinal."

He reached out and turned my face to the side where a

bruise was coming up from Higgle's last slap. "Okay, we're going to have a conversation, and I want to fast forward through all the macho posturing. I know you won't give Bernard up to me. You're not going to turn nibbler. And maybe you have it in the back of your head that you'll get Haggle and Gaggle yourself. Ditch that idea. They'll kill you or you'll kill them, and if you do, I'll kill you. I'll just have to."

"Okay, you've saved yourself twenty minutes. The point you're going for is?"

"My world, my people, I care. So far, aside from the mercs that got splashed up north, all we've had is property damage. That's not Bernard's style. Someone is exerting a lot of influence to keep things on a simmer. I'm glad of that, but that same person has to know things will boil over. He can't control someone like Bernard. No one can."

I narrowed my eyes. "No one? Not even you?"

"I can control him, but I have to be able to put him away."

"And you want me to give him to you, somehow?"

"No, that would be going back to the part of the conversation we skipped. You won't do that. Fine." He slowly stood. "I will get him, one way or another. A smart guy like you might just want to be clear before that happens."

I looked up. "And how would a smart guy like me know when that was going to happen?"

"Same way that someone who called a tip into PSD knew when the assault up north was happening. You're not smart enough to leave Basalt, so I hope you'll be smart enough that you don't get stuck here forever."

Niemeyer didn't offer to give me a hand up, much less a ride back to the Grand Germayne. When I could finally stand I checked myself for injuries. I had lots of bruising on my stomach and chest, but no cracked ribs as nearly as I could tell. I was going to be pretty tender for a while, but could still function.

Once I got to the street, I figured out where I was and made my own way back to the Grand Germayne. I entered through the garage and got to my room unnoticed. For once no one else was waiting for me, so I stripped my clothes off and tossed them into the shower. I let the water run fast and hot, and the steam filling the bathroom felt good. I also liked the fact that it coated the mirror so I didn't have to look at the purple mottling.

I showered carefully, bagged the sopping clothes and called for valet service, then dressed and headed out again. I arrived at the main branch of the public library and stood next to a statue of a stylized lion from the hour to ten past, then wandered down the street to a Javapulse Generator. I got coffee and a scone, getting halfway through both by the time Gypsy showed up.

He was smiling broadly enough that he indulged in a pastry, too. "It was brilliant. We are set to go with the details of publicity and our next move." He glanced at the storefront and I visualized it all fire-blackened and melted.

"When?"

"We launch our campaign tonight, with full coverage tomorrow for the early news cycle."

"Good. What do you need me to do?"

He chewed and then swallowed as he drew his noteputer from his pocket. "We had hit on an angle of directing praise and, hopefully, money to some worthy causes. I have a list. Pick one."

I looked at the list, then frowned. "The Basalt Foundation isn't on here."

"Family ties make it a negative."

"I disagree. She offers such a contrast to the others that she makes them look worse. They have ostracized her, and she is so nice, they look yet more like monsters. Moreover, having her still present means that when an olive branch is extended, there will be someone who can accept it and salve the sensibilities of disaffected portions of the population, especially the off-worlders she's helped. We have to look two steps ahead here, don't we?"

Gypsy slowly nodded. "I'd actually had it on the list, but Elle argued for it to be deleted. It's back on and it's the one we'll use. I like your analysis."

"Good. Do you need me tonight?"

"Why, you have a hot date?"

I winced as I shifted in my chair, then tapped a finger to the slight bruising on my cheek. "Niemeyer's boys wanted to convince me to leave Basalt. I could use a lot of sleep."

"We've got it covered. Sleep well." Gypsy smiled, then

jerked a thumb at the shop. "Me, I'm going back for two more, large and hot. It's going to be a long night."

Manville boasted eight Javapulse Generators scattered about. We hit three outside downtown, then hit the largest in the heart of the city. As seen on some surveillance holos, a hovercar cruised past the place, a thermal detector checked for inhabitants, then a satchel containing high explosives and a detonator sailed through the plate glass. It bounced once or twice as the hovercar sped away, then a vicious gout of fire vomited from the storefront. Debris spread everywhere and out at the Heights' site the fire companies arrived too late to stop a Capellan-owned shoe store next door from burning. Luckily it was empty, too.

Almost immediately FfW made its appearance, claiming credit for our previous strikes. The media messages pointed out that the explosives used in these attacks were from the same lot as had been used previously. FfW denounced the BSU as a government operation, citing the extra strikes BSU had taken credit for. FfW went so far as to claim that the reason the attack against the Palace had gone awry is because FfW, in its quest for freedom for all, had tipped off Emblyn Security. "While we decry the private possession of weapons of war, in a time when the government cannot be trusted, we must be free to make ourselves secure."

The reasons given for attacking JPGs were the usual. They were part of a multiplanetary corporation that generated lots of profits and drew them off-world. While JPG did employ a large number of people, they only offered the Republic-mandated minimums for benefits, and their wages, while competitive within the service industry arena, were barely enough for someone to rise to middle-class status. "Until such capital enterprises realize they have a duty to the community—the *whole* community—their cost of doing business as a bad neighbor will be high and get higher."

I don't know who Gypsy used to speak to JPG officials locally, but by noon on the seventeenth, the remaining JPGs had initiated several schemes to help improve their images. They donated a lot of product to shelters, as well as put out boxes as collection points for all manner of things to be distributed to the less fortunate. By four in the afternoon they announced a strategic alliance with the Basalt Foundation to fund some daycare centers for parents with young children.

That part of the plan actually worked far better than I had expected, and I knew Bernard would begin to react. Alba was all that stood between him and being out of control. I had to debate as to whether or not I wanted to flick that safety switch off. Without her he'd lose a competent planner. While I expected he would begin to model his little attacks after the JPG strikes, that also assumed he wouldn't think he could do things better his way.

It turned out this was a flawed assumption.

I decided that I might not want Alba out of the picture, but having her a bit uncomfortable with Bernard would be good. Using the dead-drop system, I sent her a note saying, "Talked with your boss. He was curious about what you heard from me and when. Be careful." Once I left it and made the mark in the appropriate place, I returned to the park and saw it get picked up.

I smiled. At least she would be warned. Forewarned is forearmed, and in this game, if you weren't forearmed, you would end up dead.

In retrospect, that was a lesson I should have thought a lot more about.

=== 33 ===

Guerillas never win wars, but their adversaries often lose them.

—Charles W. Thayer

Manville, Capital District
Basalt
Prefecture IV, Republic of the Sphere
18 February 3133

My warning to Alba Dolehide resulted in a harvest of unintended consequences, which took my plan, removed all calculation, and let things roll forward at the level of gang warfare. While there were resulting casualties, there were no fatalities, but I had no sense that this would always be the case. In fact, I had a disturbing certainty it would not be, and that things would deteriorate rather quickly.

Though I did not learn about it until later, the message to Alba was delivered, but the courier told Teyte about its content. Teyte immediately assumed that Alba was in league with me, and that both of us were in the employ of Emblyn. Teyte moved to grab her and have her interrogated as I had been, but Alba was one step ahead of him. She'd learned about my meeting with Bernard, looked far enough ahead to see what was going to be coming down, and had already slipped away. With her went a certain amount of knowledge about where a couple of 'Mechs and several vehicles had been stashed, so not only did Bernard lose competent leadership, he also lost a portion of his firepower.

That loss of firepower was a very good thing, because Bernard decided to hit Emblyn all over the place. It struck me that Bernard must have been getting tactical advice from somewhere, because as things progressed his attacks became more tightly focused and, while still doing more damage than was absolutely required, they were stinging Emblyn badly.

In the immediate aftermath of the JPG strikes, Bernard hit four Minute-Meal™ eateries. They were a Republic-wide chain of franchise quick-food restaurants and, here on Basalt, Emblyn owned them. Those attacks mirrored the FfW attacks and, for all intents and purposes, people assumed FfW had done them.

For his next trick, however, Bernard blew up an IceKing warehouse. IceKing was a grocery supply company owned by Emblyn that delivered product to Minute-Meal™ and JPG, as well as a large number of other restaurants. Quam did an article decrying this shadow war spilling over and affecting the culinary genius native to Basalt. In short, he wrote, the destruction of nonnative eateries was fine by him, but when such an attack destroyed a source of good food for all, things were getting out of hand. While the piece did seem to be praising the terrorists, Quam's true point was that the strikes, while they had killed no one yet, were destroying lives. Those people who worked in the shops that had been put out of business were forced to take temporary jobs or go on the dole.

He centered his story around a small family restaurant that had been serving Asian food for three generations, and showed how their business had been destroyed by the attack. Quam used his skills as a writer to point out the absurdity of Bernard and others calling ethnic Kuritans and Capellans off-worlders, His outrage at their treatment was enough to get blood boiling in some sectors, and a number of private donations flowed to the family profiled.

Quam was unique in his writing because he actually took

a stance on the issue. The rest of the newsies focused on rumor and innuendo, ignoring the microeconomic impact to cover instead their projected fears for the future. Articles whined about how unbridled warfare like this could make the Basalt economy grind to a halt. The fact that it had ground to a halt for the affected families was something relegated to the "soft 'n fluffy" parts of media reports.

Gypsy immediately stepped up the FfW's rhetoric, decrying some attacks, usurping others. He also picked a variety of targets for FfW operations. Gypsy was sharp enough to choose targets where he could minimize the sort of impact Quam had complained about. Toward this end he authorized a lot of transportation and vehicle hits. The approaches to a couple of bridges got blown and then repair vehicles were destroyed, maximizing inconvenience for all without putting anyone out of a job.

What it took Bernard some time to figure out was that this new wave of strikes, which came very thick over the next three days, might have hurt Emblyn a little, but they really damaged the government. Officials had been standing up to say that they would protect the citizenry, but all of a sudden attacks were happening all over the place. Because they came off at night, people tended to stay home, which put a damper on most of the nightlife economy. Companies that did not believe the government could protect them took to posting their hours of business very prominently. As one entrepreneur put it, "We can remodel and rebuild, but we don't want to do so after funerals."

The Germayne government immediately authorized overtime for constables and the Public Safety Department. Officials said they'd sent requests for assistance to The Republic's Planetary Legate, Tawanna Thurin. She said she'd forwarded the pleas but had heard nothing back. I doubted the messages sent were anywhere close to reaching Terra, so nothing like Stone's Lament was going to show up to set things to rights. News stories noted that new taxes would have to be levied to pay for the overtime, but that was a black cloud hovering on the horizon.

Society did begin to crack openly under the pressure. Charity, which had spiked when the LIT campaign began, started to tail off as people hoarded things against the uncertainty of the future. There was no way they could know if they would be the next victim, so they weren't donating money and, since they really didn't want to expose themselves to danger, many stopped volunteering their time. Moreover, because the rich in the Heights had been the target of an attack, they resented the terrorists and felt that since, clearly, none of their "own" would be part of such a group, it was war on their class and they sought to retain what they already possessed. The lower classes began to keep to themselves, with each cultural population segregating itself to its own neighborhoods and businesses.

Even Ring Emblyn's charity efforts shrank. He focused on taking care of the people who had worked for him and had been subject to attack. This still played well in the press, but instead of folks thanking him for his generosity, it was folks in his employ thanking him for his "loyalty." While that's not a bad trait, it does draw a line between *us* and *them*, and the *thems* often don't like being on the outside.

About the only person who came out smelling like a rose was Bianca. The Basalt Foundation moved quickly, cutting deals to supply people with everything they needed to survive the sudden loss of their jobs—regardless of cultural heritage. While the absolute numbers were relatively small, every single one of them was a wonderful media filler piece. Smiling faces on folks laden with armsful of clothing, toiletries and treats, singing the praises of Bianca Germayne, played very well, especially when counterpointed against local government officials saying that everyone would have to tighten their belts and pull together until the crisis passed.

Gypsy realized the full import of the attack on me. He already knew I'd betrayed Bernard's plans to him, but that my usefulness as a double agent was limited. We had to assume that, one way or another, Bernard would be keeping tabs on me. My job, then, was to keep out of sight to make him use resources to find me, or become very visible. Gypsy, by having others watch me, would be able to pick up on Bernard's agents, identify them, and set them up for neutralization.

Either strategy would work for Gypsy, but both of them meant I was out of play. It made sense, since I'd been compromised. Gypsy, based on target selections, was keeping with the overall LIT plan, but I hated not being informed about what was going on. Gypsy was, after all, a mercenary. If Emblyn started pressuring him from above and Catford from below, he might decide to kick things into high gear and a lot of things would be laid waste that didn't need to be. In essence, with Alba vanishing from Bernard's camp, and my being ostracized from Emblyn's camp, the folks most likely to apply the brakes were gone.

I opted for the plan that would make me very visible. I had to because going to ground meant I'd have even less of a chance of knowing what was going on. In addition, having me wandering about would give Bernard more to think about, and that might slow him down. It would also keep Niemeyer happy since he didn't have to go digging for me. Lastly, by being visible, it was possible for me to make reports.

The dead-drop I'd used with Alba was not the only one I employed. Prior to coming to Basalt I was given information on a number of dead-drops that The Republic had already established on the world. While it might have seemed unusual for a government to be setting up procedures that allowed their agents to spy on the citizenry, in essence they were just planning ahead for the eventuality that an undercover operation might have to be run some day.

When I reached Basalt I scouted the sites and then made a wrong-number call that activated a run on the notification target. Basically I made a call to someone, asked for Mr. Arkadis, and was told there was no one of that name there. I said, "This must have been his old number." They said, "We've had this number for twenty years." I said, "Oh, my mistake. Happens when you're older than The Republic." Whoever I spoke to would relay that conversation to others, then orders would be given to check a drop target. No one had a clue as to who I was, and I didn't know who they were, and that kept us all safe.

The reports I'd sent back had been pretty basic: just identifying people, trends and so on. I had little time for in-depth analysis, but I did note that both sides seemed to have enough people for a decent shooting war. In my latest report I noted that unless Bernard was able to activate the Basalt Militia, the edge in military strength would go to

Emblyn. The losses sustained at the Palace coupled with Alba's disappearance put Bernard at a severe disadvantage. I would have liked a company of Lament on planet to use to curb him when, not if, push came to shove.

I put that into my last report. I had no idea if any of my reports had even made it off Basalt.

I left the Grand Germayne and made some basic checks to see if I was being followed. I didn't think I was, but aborted my run to the dead-drop. Something didn't feel right, and I wasn't certain if it was external or internal.

Instead of doing my ghostly business, I headed to one of the Basalt Foundation relief centers. It would have been easy to talk myself into believing I was going there to get a feel for the social impact of LIT, but I knew that was a lie. I was playing puppetmaster, and things were going along too well. I didn't have a connection to the people being hurt. It could have been a residual effect of reading Quam's stories, but whatever the cause I did want to see what was going on at the center.

And I wanted to see, firsthand, how Bianca handled the enormous pressure she was under.

I asked for Bianca and was directed to the large commercial kitchen where meals were being prepared for later in the day. The dining hall could seat five hundred at a time, and a schedule on the wall showed they had four seatings spaced forty-five minutes apart. People had already lined up for the first seating, and they looked to be a mix from all cultures and almost all social classes.

As foretold, Bianca was in the kitchen and so was Quam. Even Snookums was there, sitting on a stainless-steel table. He had a little chef's mushroom-cap on his head and growled when he saw me. Quam, who was chopping black mushrooms with a nimble facility flicked a sliver of fungus to the dog, which it snapped out of the air and quieted down.

Bianca smiled. "Sam, what brings you here? Do I see the last of a bruise on your face? What happened?"

I smiled and brushed my fingertips over my cheek. "Walked into a wall." I refrained from opening my shirt, where my chest was still a mess, because I didn't think she'd believe that the wall had retaliated by walking all over me. "They're keeping you very busy, aren't they?"

Quam laughed. "And we thought you capable of seeing more than the obvious, Sam. Aprons are over there, gloves next. Mix these mushrooms into that stuffing, then fill those game hens."

"Yes, Commander." I complied with his order and began to work. Bianca wandered in and out, not so much giving orders as just encouraging people to work together. Quam explained that half the staff were volunteers like me, drawn from the clientele, and the others, who handled most of the cooking, were students at a local culinary school, or apprentices with some of the restaurants that had been put out of business.

I frowned. "If the attacks on IceKing put those places out of business, how is it that the shelter here has food?"

Quam smiled. "Fine restaurants will not serve food that has survived a bomb blast. It still eats fine, but be careful. If you feel any shrapnel in the stuffing, set it aside."

I thought he was kidding, then I noticed a couple of pieces of jagged metal in a small pile on the table. They looked like pieces of nails, which would be in keeping with nail bombs. While such devices were fairly easy to make and therefore quite common, the nails generally indicated something that was meant as an antipersonnel weapon.

Bernard, while using my game plan, was improvising on the means of execution.

"What's the reaction been to your pieces about the FfW hits?"

"They vary from sympathetic outrage, to those who want to know why I'm covering that instead of puking their press release about some new food product into my reports." He glanced up. "You read them. What did you think?"

"Pretty brave." I pointed to the nails. "No telling when someone on the other side might take umbrage and make you a target."

"True, but how can I let that stop me? My job is to write about food and life on Basalt. These strikes are affecting both. Moreover, so many people here are willing to turn a blind eye to things, and yet that is not what our parents and grandparents did in establishing The Republic. If I don't stand up against tyranny the way they did, am I a worthy heir to this life?"

"You clearly think the answer is, 'no.' "

"And you don't?" He brandished the knife. "You can say you don't, but you do, Sam. You'd not have given money to the Foundation if you didn't. You'd not be here helping."

"I gave money because that was our deal, Quam. I'm helping because you have a knife." I shrugged. "And even if you're right, I don't know that it's worth my life."

"I know it's worth mine, but mine is not in jeopardy." The fat man smiled ruefully. "I am Quam. Hard to forget, but easy to dismiss. When the *Journal* decides that with no nightlife there need be no Quam, I will fade. Even though my words should be taken seriously, they aren't and won't be."

"You don't think so?"

He laughed and his jowls quivered. "In this madhouse world? No. The government has made people angry, and likewise Emblyn has made them angry. Now, are the angry people a part of the government striking at enemies, or angry people striking at enemies, or hunks of both? The latter has to be true, because while angry people might protest and even riot, not many can field BattleMechs."

"That's a point the press seems to have missed."

"No, it's a point that the Constabulary has asked the media to back away from. They don't want to start a panic." He waved the knife toward the dining area. "Two weeks ago, two sittings would be almost full. Now we turn people away. There already is a panic."

"More astute observations."

"I'll give you one more to mull while you stuff those birds, Sam. This is going to get a lot worse before it gets better. The 'Mechs that attacked the Palace aren't the last we'll see on Basalt. When the real shooting starts, it will be bad. Instead of feeding people, this place will be turned into a charnel house. And if that doesn't make you lose your appetite, nothing ever will."

34

That which does not kill us makes us stronger.
—Old saying

Or it just leaves us weaker for the next thing that
wants to kill us. And the next thing. And the
next thing.
—Mason Dunne

Manville, Capital District
Basalt
Prefecture IV, Republic of the Sphere
22 February 3133

I stuck around and helped serve the meals I'd prepared. I guess, in part, it was because I was feeling guilty over the trouble I'd instigated. The people who came in were grateful for the food, and many were the offers to help clean up. In fact, the last seating helped clean the room, stacked chairs, and there was no segregation. A cynic might have noted that trouble makes brothers of us all, but I tended to think that some people were able to put aside petty and benign differences to help each other. That was what I would have expected from reading about Basalt, and here I saw it. Bernard might be pushing divisive ideas, but his sister was unifying people.

Once things had been cleaned up, the staff sat down and had leftovers, of which there was not much. I did get a bit of one of the game hens and the stuffing. There was no shrapnel in it, which would have been the only thing that could have marred perfection. Not only could Quam write about food, but he could cook as well.

I looked at him. "You cook so well, why don't you have a restaurant of your own?"

He laughed at me. "Your innocence is refreshing, Sam."

Bianca smiled and got up from our table. "I've heard this lecture before, so I'll go get us some dessert."

Quam waited for her to leave, then interlaced his fingers and settled them over the curve of his middle. "In running a restaurant, one has to give lots of orders, which I can do, and prepare many meals, which I can do. What I cannot do, however, is subject my genius to the know-nothing-but-ready-to-share-their-ignorance customers and critics who will come to my establishment. People who dine out want two things: good food and *different* food. They will hunt down the latter before they settle for the former. I could create a menu of the best dishes ever created on Basalt or in The Republic, and people would still quest after the *new* thinking, quite wrongly, it would be better."

I gave him a smile. "Well, it *could* be better, couldn't it?"

Snookums, seated on a stool beside Quam, growled.

The man hushed the dog. "He's innocent, remember?" Quam regarded me with half-lidded eyes. "On a good day, on the chef's *best* day, perhaps. That is immaterial, however, because there is a second, greater reason to avoid it: I would be bored. Doing the same thing, day in and day out, even allowing for innovation, would kill me. Better to venture in the wilderness seeking that magical meal that approaches the divine than to dish up Olympian fare every day. I mean, Sam, would *you* want that sort of wretched, stable life?"

I hesitated. There were times when the idea of settling down with Janella did strike me as perfect, but more often I liked the challenges of what I did. The hunt, as he described it, was fun, and the victory, better. I had the luxury, perhaps illusory, of believing what I did helped people. Quam could make that same claim and, on a daily basis, he had a stronger case than I did.

I shook my head. "No, I guess not. Still, it would be great to have a place where one could get food this good when I wanted to."

"And it would be fun to create it, but that is a job for others." The fat man dabbed the corners of his mouth with a napkin as Bianca returned. "And each of us must do that to which we are best suited, lest our efforts be wasted."

I won't describe dessert because I don't want to think about it anymore—being as how the chances of tasting something that good again are nil. After dessert, I helped clean up, then took a long walk back to the Grand Germayne. I checked a couple of times to see if I had a tail, but didn't detect anyone. I hoped that any agents Bernard or Gypsy had covering me had enjoyed dinner, at the very least.

As I'd left the building, Bianca and others had said they hoped I'd be back. Part of me wanted to return, but I knew I couldn't afford that luxury. While I might have been able to help there a little, I'd also attract attention to Bianca's operation. Bernard or Emblyn might decide to hit the place just to make a point to me or to just kill me. I didn't want to be responsible for that sort of thing.

Moreover, I reminded myself, I was a Ghost Knight. I had to maintain a certain detachment. If I got too close to things, I would not be able to act in the manner that was vital to dealing with Basalt's problem. I needed to be clear-headed and impartial, so I could play the wolves off against each other and, hopefully, control the damage they were doing. I had to remain cool and aloof, so there would be no more charity work for me.

My other job came first, and if I failed at it, all the meals the Foundation served wouldn't amount to a hill of beans.

At the hotel, the desk clerk caught my eye and handed me a message. It had been sealed in one of the hotel's envelopes. I opened it and saw a simple message: The Bar. E. I refolded it, half wondered why Elle wasn't waiting for me in my room as she had before, and walked into the bar.

I found her at a corner table studiously avoiding the

glances from a group of men at the bar. The guys immediately checked me out and watched. I figured a number of them had made a run at her and had been shot down. They were waiting to see me crash and burn, so without even a word, I slid onto the bench beside her and gave her a huge kiss. A slap would amuse them, fingers in my hair would annoy them—win-win in my book.

Elle returned the kiss, slipping her fingers into my hair, and holding my mouth on hers until, I'm guessing, the groans from the bar had reached a piteous enough note. I gasped, as did she, then she licked her lips and smiled. "I'm happy to see you, too, Sam."

"And you weren't waiting in my room because?"

"Colonel Niemeyer of Public Safety obtained a court order to plant listening devices in there. The order was sealed, of course, but . . ." She bridged her fingers and cracked her knuckles. "I can't cut off the data flow, so you had to be warned."

"I'd actually assumed someone was listening in, so all I do is sing in the shower."

"You might talk in your sleep."

"Good point. Did I on Helen?"

A flicker of annoyance tightened her features. "Let's not talk about Helen, shall we?"

I nodded, then looked at her carefully. "Tell me, then, what else is going on. It's something more urgent, else you'd have left me a note I'd figure out."

Elle lowered her voice and leaned into me, nibbling at my left earlobe as she whispered. "Gypsy has authorized a mission two nights from now. It's at the Hanse Highway and Thirty-ninth Avenue. He wants to hit a communications switching station. It will take communications down for the Heights. Catford didn't like it initially, but he thinks he can make it work with a few hovercars."

I let myself laugh as I thought. I didn't know the city that well, but Hanse Highway had exits every fifth street, so the closest there was Fortieth. That would make getting out difficult if things went bad, since heading east on Thirty-ninth would lead directly into the twisting, hilly warrens of the Heights. Catford was right to not like the situation, and it was rather typical of him to think he could change things to his favor somehow.

I whispered back to her. "Why tell me?"

"I thought you might be able to take a look and give me your thoughts tomorrow night. If the plan can be modified, it should be. Things are going so well, we don't want to lose control now."

I pulled back and looked her in the eyes. "You're risking a lot. If you have to tell Gypsy to abort, you'll need to tell him you told me his plans."

"If we need to abort, he won't care. If we don't, he won't know."

"Fair enough." I thought for a moment, then nodded. "I'll check it out and meet you here for breakfast day after tomorrow."

Elle frowned. "Why so long?"

"To know if the plan is going to work, I need to study the area and that will be a day and night job. Order something filling for me, and lots of coffee, very strong." I gave her another kiss, just for appearances sake. "You were right to bring this to me. No disasters this late in the game."

As I told her, figuring out what sort of plan would work to take the place out would take a lot of work. I got up bright and early the next morning, packed a day bag with some clothes and a pair of nice digital binoculars, then took a hovercab to a rental agency. I procured a Cabochon Hovercar which, I was assured, was the most popular model on the planet because of its safety construction. That meant it was small, boxy, heavy, sluggish, cheap, ugly and unlikely to attract any notice at all. In an accident I'd be protected enough not to die, though the embarrassment of being caught in it might just do the job.

And I did pay extra for insurance. I did that on a whim, but some of Elle's uneasiness had transferred itself to me. I normally am not superstitious in the least, so I hate it when I get "feelings" of impending doom. Still, whenever I do I take appropriate action to combat them, and I can't think of many situations where that has been the wrong thing to do.

I drove around the site, which was Basalt Public Digicom Routing Station No. 8. The brick building rose to two stories for most of its rectangular length. The front had a single story and lots of windows, serving as a store where service could be purchased and bills could be paid. It had a small parking lot in front, and a longer one on the south side. The highway passed in front of it, elevated to twice the height of the building, and Thirty-ninth Avenue paralleled the long north side. A wire fence surrounded the perimeter and cameras mounted on light poles monitored everything, but beyond that I saw almost nothing in the way of security.

In my recon effort I constantly checked to see if I was being watched, but I couldn't detect any surveillance on me. I felt fairly confident that I was clean, but did periodic sweeps in case someone ran across me accidentally and started to follow me. Starting at No. 8, I worked out in a spiral, noting the location of Constabulary precinct houses, fire houses and anything else that looked suspicious—which wasn't much in this mostly Davion section of town. I could have noted any buildings suited to housing BattleMechs— there were certainly a few of them—but their exact locations were not important. The fact that they existed within my search area was not a good sign, but any 'Mechs or troops hidden therein could only be brought into play if the mission failed to get in and out quickly.

I watched throughout the day, pausing only to get lunch and then supper at nearby restaurants where workers from the center ate. I didn't pick up much in the way of gossip. The heaviest shift traffic was during daylight hours. It nearly filled the employee lot, but the second shift appeared to be nothing more than a few security personnel. This boded well for minimizing casualties, and calling in a bomb threat to the plant just prior to the strike might guarantee all security personnel exited the building.

In fact, such a call coming in from FfW folks disguised as bomb removal teams would work really well. They could go in, wire the place, then come back out and say it was badly compromised. It goes up, they light out, and the damage is done without anyone getting hurt. I liked that idea and would certain pass it on through Elle so Gypsy could employ it.

By early evening it became apparent that the site was not quite as badly situated as I had feared. While it was not close enough to the highway to let that be a fast escape route, Thirty-ninth Avenue had such light traffic that heading west into the city would be easy to do. While I did not like Catford as a person, his defense of the Emblyn Palace did show some tactical sense. If he timed the strike for sometime after midnight, things could work.

In fact, Catford had the attack go off at 12:06 A.M.

While I watched.

My mind began to race as a trio of hoverbikes—*military grade* hoverbikes—came screaming up Thirty-ninth, cut south and bumped up over the curb. They came into the smaller parking lot and pointed their lasers at the building. In unison the pilots cut loose, sending coruscating beams of ruby energy into the switching station. The glass windows melted as if they were ice. Things inside the store combusted instantly, but did nothing to stop the beams.

The hoverbikes waggled back and forth, like children squirming. Their beams played side to side, working up and down. I couldn't see how deeply they pierced the structure, but one lanced out through a side wall while the others touched off more fires. Secondary explosions shook the building and one or two alarms that began to wail shut off immediately as some vital equipment melted.

More important than what they were doing, however, was the sudden advent of Public Safety Department agents in Hauberk battle armor. In teams of three they ran from nearby buildings. The heavy armor, painted an urban gray that worked well to camouflage them in the night, gave them bulk and deadliness. Unlike the way such armor appears in Tri-Vids, no lights illuminated the agents' faces. They remained dark and brooding—no less sinister even without the bulk of the LRM launcher packs they would have carried on a battlefield.

As two troop carriers appeared around the corner from Thirty-ninth and began disgorging troops, a voice boomed from one of the power-armor teams. Despite the distortion, I recognized it as Niemeyer's voice. "Stop! Police! You're under arrest. Don't make us . . ."

Even before he could finish, two more hoverbikes raced north on the access road that paralleled the highway. Their forward-mounted Gatling cannons vomited fire and metal, scything through armored troops. One laser lanced scarlet fire through a troop carrier. The vehicle exploded, casting silhouetted figures in grand arcs through the night sky. When they landed, they crumpled and lay still.

Niemeyer's troops returned fire. The unarmored officers had little effect, save to play bullets over the hoverbike hulls. One driver did shy, turning his vehicle, so a small laser beam from one Hauberk armor suit burned into his spine. That hoverbike jetted forward, then crashed into a hovercar parked on the side of the road.

More explosions shook the switching center and part of the building sagged. As the roof collapsed, jets of flame shot out the black scars in the front. Burning debris gushed out, then rained down in a hellish snow. Lasers flashed, burning red and green, bullets flew, striking sparks and spinning men to the street.

Then, from atop the highway, a dozen and a half LRMs arced down and sowed fire over the parking lot. The first hoverbike flew into the air, tumbling end over end. The pilot went one way, bits and pieces another, until the burning hull smashed down. The fans shredded themselves, spitting shrapnel into the air.

The second hoverbike just evaporated while the third went spinning out of control. It plowed into armored troops, which scattered like toys. A second gout of flame from the center washed over that vehicle. The pilot vanished and the hoverbike burned.

The launch of missiles from a *Catapult* had shattered the FfW assault. The 'Mech came running along the highway, closing almost to a range where his missiles would not work. I assume that was because he wasn't going to launch again, but this assumption was misplaced. Fire blossomed in the left shoulder launcher and, at this range, he couldn't miss what he was shooting at.

I hit the accelerator on the Cabochon and whipped the wheel around. The vehicle shot across the battle zone and edged around one of the burning hoverbikes. Turning right, I cut the back fan to drag the rear. Sparks shot from behind me as the hovercar slowed, then I killed the forward fan and ducked my head.

Had one of the LRMs hit me dead on, no matter the Cabochon's safety record, I'd have been clean dead. The explosions playing toward me ripped up reinforced roadway, snapped light poles and blew fencing apart as if it were cheesecloth in a gale. The closest bounced the hovercar a meter in the air, and the landing left an imprint of the steering wheel on my forehead. The shrapnel took the roof off and shattered the windows, but the side panels were enough to deflect a lot. I felt a sting in my legs as some of the safety panels spalled off, but the pain told me my legs were still there, which I counted as a plus.

Most importantly, however, the Cabochon shielded Niemeyer and his crew. The only reason to shoot again was to kill him, and the only person who would want him dead would be Bernard. That put Bernard or his agent in the *Catapult* and *that* started all manner of things running around in my brain.

Niemeyer popped up on the passenger side and, though his face was hidden behind smoked glass, I could almost see his eyes widen when he saw me.

"Get your men in here, we're going *NOW!*"

"No."

"It's your ass that thing wants dead. Leave and your people are safe." I kicked both fans on. "Get in unless you want them to die."

Snarling, he boosted a wounded man into the backseat, piled another on top, then tore the passenger door off the Cabochon. He knelt on the seat as I hit the accelerator and spun the hovercar around. I drove toward the *Catapult*, then under the highway overpass. We emerged going fast, cutting back and forth across lanes. I figured it was an even-odds shot that we'd get a couple of flights of missiles once we were in range, so I hit the first small cross street, and then another.

"If he's going to shoot us, he'll wipe a lot of real estate."

Niemeyer grunted. "Bernard?"

"My guess. In the morning media he'll have saved Public Service operatives from an FfW ambush. Someone sold the FfW to him, and you to him."

"And we were sold to FfW. Set up." His right arm swung and snapped the jagged roof post off. "Next right, then along Fiftieth to the hospital."

"With all speed."

"Yeah, with all speed." A low growl sounded from him. "Just the way my world is going to hell."

35

He who wants to kill a snake must aim for its head.
— Danish saying

Manville, Capital District
Basalt
Prefecture IV, Republic of the Sphere
24 February 3133

We reached the hospital quickly and both of Niemeyer's people were rushed into the trauma center. He should have been looked at first, but he wasn't going to let them drug him until his men were out of danger or while there was a possibility that I might get away. I gave him my word I'd not leave, which he laughed at. He had me join him in a trauma room, where the doctors took care of both our shrapnel wounds.

In the trauma room I looked down at my bloody trouser legs. "See, no running away for me anyway."

He just grunted as they began to peel him out of the armor. His chest plate had been punctured and the armor on the right shoulder had been ripped away. No gashes there, but a licking tongue of flame had clearly toasted him a bit. Interns pulled shrapnel from him and applied sutures, while medtechs slathered unguents on the burns.

Interns similarly worked on me and, like Niemeyer, I passed on anything more than local anesthesia. He didn't want to pass out and I didn't want to become a babbling idiot. While I had enough evidence to have Bernard arrested, and enough circumstantial evidence to have Emblyn picked up, it would have been for minor offenses. The prosecution would have dragged on while the war for Basalt continued. The winner would pardon himself and the loser would likely be executed for minor crimes.

Minor crimes all wrapped up as a treasonous conspiracy.

Aside from grunts and the occasional hiss, Niemeyer and I fell silent. The doctors talked, forceps clicked and shrapnel clanked into metal pans. I pushed all that and the little tugs and pinches away. I needed to gather my thoughts because Niemeyer would be on me hard and fast. I had to figure out what I was going to tell him.

I couldn't tell him the truth. My claims of being a Ghost Knight would be looked upon askance and, with the HPG network down, couldn't be verified by anyone on Basalt. While I could send reports in through local staffers, they would just treat them like agent reports. While mine might be accorded higher priority than others, there would be nothing in their handling to compromise my identity.

Regardless of that, I still didn't have enough evidence to put the principals away. With Bernard willing to kill Niemeyer and his men, arrest became a moot point. There really wasn't an authority on the planet that could stop him, unless it was someone who was going to terminate him. And, if that were to happen, there would be nothing to stop Emblyn from completing his takeover of the world, since all the attacks had left the people's trust of the government in tatters.

Bernard had successfully hit on one point that seemed like a way out of the LIT trap. His appearance at Number 8 to smash the attack—much akin to Reis' antics on Helen— elevated him to the image of a strong, central authority figure with the power to hit back at the enemy. If he were able to capitalize on this political asset, it would make him very strong.

The problem with LIT is that halting such a campaign is like nailing gelatin to a wall. Yes, Bernard did stop one attack, though not until it had done an incredible amount of damage. Not only did it take out Number 8, but it devastated a contingent of Public Safety Department officers. While their deaths would ratchet up the public's concern, and would invest Bernard's calls for vengeance with some power, Bernard could never command enough in the way of troops to put a stop to the FfW attacks. He couldn't have troops everywhere all at once, and absent that, some sites were going to be vulnerable. Without completely subverting the system of civil liberties guaranteed by The Republic, FfW could not be stopped.

I realized that thinking about that was getting ahead of things. In the hovercar with Niemeyer we'd hit on the core understanding of the raid that I needed to sort out. Gypsy had planned the raid and turned it over to Catford to execute. Someone had sold the raid to Niemeyer, though the chances of my learning who that was from him were zero. The same individual might have sold Niemeyer back to Catford, but I doubted that. Catford could have easily had troops in reserve waiting for trouble. If nothing else they could have been used to cut off pursuit or secure an alternate escape route and Catford was cunning enough to deploy forces to do just that.

I already knew that Bernard had people in Public Safety on his payroll, so they clearly sold the operation to him. I wasn't sure if the guys working for Bernard would have expected him to try to assassinate Niemeyer. If they suspected Niemeyer was watching them, they might have. That was really another moot point since Bernard could have had dozens of reasons to want Niemeyer dead, right down to not realizing he was there and just wanting Public Safety bodies to blame on FfW. The idea that killing Public Safety officers might move his agents up in the organization could not be discounted either.

Elle was a wild card in the mix. She'd clearly told me the operation would be going off twenty-four hours later than it did. Gypsy could have moved the timetable up, though Catford likely would have balked at that. Gypsy could have misled her for whatever reason, or she could have lied to me. It didn't make much sense for her to do that, but that fit with the odd nature of the conflict here.

Bernard's escalation of things did make sense—frightening sense. His action, while unilateral, would show FfW to be an enemy of the state in a very direct and threatening way. His military reaction to their effort—as opposed to Niemeyer's law enforcement one—made them into a military threat. Calling up the Basalt Militia and arraying them against FfW could now be easily done. With inside knowledge of what FfW was doing, he could hurt them, giving his forces an advantage if Gypsy decided to stage a military coup.

As I thought it over, it seemed to me inevitable that things would come to some BattleMech slugging match worthy of a Solaris championship. Frankly, that solution would have suited me well, since it would have limited the size of the conflict, confined it to an arena, and would have chosen a winner without ripping apart the lives of a lot of folks.

The problem is that neither Bernard nor Emblyn would abide by the outcome of such a battle. There would be more outbreaks and as folks got desperate, serious damage would be done. So far the attacks had caused a lot of property damage and inconvenienced people, but death had not slopped over into the civilian population. I was not sanguine about that situation continuing. Bernard's willingness to murder Public Safety officers indicated there would be no restraint on his part.

And once he had taken power, I could imagine a lot of civil rights abuses in the name of maintaining security.

This analysis was all well and good, but left me with nowhere to go and nothing to do, short of a wholesale murder spree—which, I will admit, was tempting. I mean, I knew I would never do it, which is why I could entertain the fantasy. Each clank of shrapnel in the dish was another bullet pumped into Bernard and Emblyn. I tossed Teyte, Catford and Siwek into that mix, just because I knew I'd have that many bullets in a clip, with a couple to spare for anyone who twitched one more time.

Niemeyer looked over at me as an intern swathed his body in gauze. "Don't expect that your intervening there will spare you from prosecution."

I frowned. "Look, let's cut to the chase, shall we? You're going to figure I was there as some sort of a spotter for the whole thing, right, which explains in your mind why I was present when things went down. You've seen my files and you know what I'm capable of piloting, so you know if I were going to be there in some capacity, I'd not have been there in a Cabochon. And if I *was* there working for FfW, why would I have rescued *you*? If I wanted to save you and your men, I wouldn't have called in reserves, right? And if I was working for the guy in the 'Mech, I'd not have pulled you out, right?"

His nostrils flared. "So, you just happened to be there? Out for a midnight drive."

"Yeah, insomnia is a horrible thing." I shook my head. "Look, there is no way you can prove I was there for any reason other than circumstance. You investigate, you find out I had lunch in the area, supper, too, but nothing sinister. I was definitely at the wrong place at the wrong time— 'cept I was able to help you out. I don't regret that at all."

His hands tightened on the edge of the treatment table. "So, you're telling me that the ends should justify your means?"

"Nope, just that actions speak louder than words."

Niemeyer snorted. "I'd rather believe you hit the accelerator by accident."

"And I'd rather believe this is all a bad dream, but we both know it isn't." I shrugged. "You can haul me down to headquarters, or break into my hotel room, and grill me. You'll get nothing."

His brows furrowed. "You truly think that second barrage was not an accident?"

"I think of it as a weather forecast: seventy-five-percent chance of treachery, with mixed stupidity. We both know how it will be spun, and how it is being spun now. By noon you'll have him here, visiting survivors, talking to the media, building up a frenzy of activity. We both know it. You'll be lauded as a hero, as will he, and circumstance will toss you together. He'll be legit and your hands will be tied."

"Not as much as you think."

"But more than you'd like." I almost added, "And more than I'd like," but I held back. Sam never would have said that.

"There's a lot of things I don't like, but I have to abide them." The big man shrugged, then exhaled loudly and seemed to shrink a little. He turned his head slightly and regarded me carefully. "You are a material witness. I'll want you to give a statement on what you saw."

"Sure, I'll head down there later today. After the crowds have cleared from the media conferences."

He nodded wearily, then slid off the examining table and stood. "I've got people to check, reports to make."

"I have a question for you. You'll have to trust me with the answer."

His head came back up as wariness tightened his eyes. "And the question is?"

"Insider or anonymous tip?"

"Just like before."

Just like when I had tipped them about the Palace raid. This brought a new player into the mix, someone who wanted FfW to fail. It had to be someone inside the organization, but who? Catford, Gypsy and Elle all had to be candidates. Tactical commanders would have been, too, but they wouldn't have called Public Safety in on themselves. I included Siwek just for the fun of it.

Niemeyer watched me, then nodded. "You going to cause trouble?"

"Probably, but not for you."

"Why? Why not just leave?"

"Did you have someone following me last night?"

"No, but I know where you were. At one of the Basalt Foundations kitchens. You helped out."

"So maybe I'll be helping out. It's a nice world you have here." I gave him a Sam-nonchalant shrug. "I would like to see it remain that way."

Niemeyer hesitated for a moment, then nodded, but said nothing. He shuffled from the trauma room.

An intern slapped a light anesthetic patch on my legs, then gave me a pair of scrub pants since mine had been cut clean off me. I retained the rags in a plastic bag because they held my identification, squawker, noteputer and some money. Wandering out of the hospital, I took one look at the smoking wreck of the Cabochon and hailed a hovercab. A Drac brought his cab over and picked me up.

The trip back to the Grand Germayne did not take that

long, but I managed to use my noteputer to do a bit of work before we arrived. True to my word, I was going to stir up some trouble, and I wanted to have a safety net in place to make sure I could clean up after myself.

About a block and a half from the hotel, an unmarked Public Safety unit hit its lights and siren and the taxi pulled over. I gave a moment's consideration to bolting from the taxi and running, but my legs just weren't going to go along with that plan. Two plainclothes officers—the two on Bernard's payroll—approached with needle pistols drawn and ordered me out of the vehicle. While one of them conducted me back to their hovercar, the other told the taxi driver to get going and that unless he wanted to be associated with "all the other Drac terrorists," he'd just forget the fare.

I snarled back over my shoulder, "Don't be cheap. You're bought and paid for. He works for a living. Pay hi . . ."

The man behind me brought the butt of his gun down on the back of my neck, dropping me to my knees. A shove to the back bounced my face off the vehicle's door, and I slumped to the pavement. My nose hadn't broken, but it was leaking. I could feel the detective winding up for a kick that would drive a kidney up through my throat, but the rear door on the unit opened and two big boots hit the pavement.

"No need for that, Oates. Mr. Donelly is our guest."

I rolled onto my back and looked up at Teyte Germayne. While his voice had been pleasant, his expression was anything but. "Make sure he tips the driver. I'm a big tipper."

Teyte leaned down and smiled coldly. "No, Donelly, you're not a big anything. You're nothing, should have remembered you were nothing, and should not have tried to defy Bernard. If you're lucky, it's a lesson you'll learn from. If not," the man shrugged, "hope that reincarnation is true."

36

As flies to wanton boys, are we to the gods;
They kill us for their sport.

—Shakespeare

Manville, Capital District
Basalt
Prefecture IV, Republic of the Sphere
25 February 3133

Teyte's exposing himself in public as my captor would really seem, on the surface, to be one of those stupid things done by Tri-Vid villains. They capture the hero, place him in a death trap and, before he dies, they tell him everything he needs to know to thwart them when he escapes, as he always does. How much better evil would function if the boss or his chief minion just put a gun to the hero's head and stroked the trigger.

Not only do dead men tell no tales, they really don't often thwart plans.

Teyte clearly saw it all differently. First, from his point of view, he was the hero and I was just a pawn being removed from play. As things developed over the next several days, there never was any question of Teyte's killing me; the questions were when to do it and who would have the privilege. Bernard, I gathered, really wanted to do the job himself but events, as they unfolded, kept him far too busy.

Teyte's presence on the scene was only a minor risk, since he was in the company of legitimate Public Safety officers. While he had no official standing with the department, it mattered not at all. He was a Germayne, and that was really all that counted. While most citizens would have disagreed with the idea that the Germayne cousins could do anything they wanted and get away with it, the Germaynes themselves swam counter to the conventional wisdom. In short, no one had told them they had to abide by the law. While their transgressions in the past might have been forgiven as minor and "youthful indiscretions," treason and the stakes being played for here elevated and intensified things.

My captors allowed me to sit in the hovercar's backseat instead of the trunk this time, though Teyte moved to the front so I'd not bleed on him. En route to the little apartment where they decided to stash me they stopped only once, to smash both my squawker and noteputer and dump them into garbage bins. Destroying those devices was a tactical error, since they could have learned a few things from them, but they wanted to get rid of evidence. They did keep my identification, which, I assumed, they would leave with my body at some point.

A bullet to the back of the head can sometimes make the sort of exit wound that renders quick identification difficult.

From the very start I knew they would kill me and I was wondering why. I mean, there was no reason for them to let me live, but there was even less reason to want me dead. I'd been marginalized in FfW. Short of an all-out war, when Gypsy would sit my butt in a 'Mech, I was pretty much useless. My removal from the FfW command structure would have been a minor inconvenience, and actually would make Catford happy since Siwek would get my command.

It did dawn on me slowly that Bernard had yanked me in, at least in part, because he really wanted to avenge himself for both my interfering at Number 8 and, more importantly, for my having showed I was smarter than he was. I'd brutalized him and Teyte at poker, I'd helped the family's black sheep, and I'd even provided him with the plan that he was using to fight back against Emblyn. As much as Bernard wanted to win the game, he wanted even more to be seen as the architect of it all, and I could expose him rather easily as a treasonous fraud.

Teyte, judging by the fare we had to watch on the Tri-Vid unit, was well versed in the ways of stereotypical villains and heroes. While the apartment I'd been brought to was small, it had been lavishly appointed with a big display unit and a full entertainment package. The Tri-Vid dramas were all old, but full of action and adventure. There were a couple based on Victor Steiner-Davion's trip to the Clan Homeworlds and his slaying of their leader. Teyte did cheer for Victor, which might have been endearing save for the way he sat in his recliner as if it were a 'Mech command couch, moving his hands on the arms as if he was fighting the battles.

They kept me restrained at all times, with a short hobble that stopped me from running. No one bothered to change the bandages on my legs, and I kept waiting to get a whiff of gangrene. My hands were kept cuffed behind the back of a stout wooden chair or to a bedpost when they let me sleep. I always had at least one person other than Teyte watching me, even when I relieved myself.

I pretty much remained quiet during the whole time and caused no trouble. In part this was because I hoped they would let their guard down at some point. They did, to a certain extent, allowing me to do little things like pull out a lock of hair and scatter it around so some forensic investigator could find it and know I'd been there. I even managed to scratch open one of my leg cuts and dab some blood around. I wiped it up quickly, but I knew the application of chemicals and an ultraviolet light would make it show up easily.

Mostly I kept quiet because events going on in the outside world got worse than I'd imagined they could. In between films we watched the local news stations. Count Germayne had activated the Basalt Militia and allowed them to deploy armored troops and vehicles all over the planet, not just down in the Capital District. Reports came in about protests that were put down hard and order being restored. Unless Gypsy had been a lot more active than I imagined, the demonstrations were spontaneous and their repression painted the government in a bad light. A few protesters were killed in one clash on the northern continent, and the government blamed the trouble on FfW, as one would expect.

Bernard did emerge as a hero. No mention was made of his second salvo and how badly it hurt people. The media, looking for a convenient face to put on the government, lionized Bernard, and he took to it like a cat to cream. I could see that this made Teyte a bit uneasy at points, but I suspected he was looking to let Bernard be the stalking horse for trouble. He would play the loyal lieutenant until Bernard stumbled, then he could step in.

This actually wasn't a bad plan. While the media suppressed the stories of antigovernment activity, the public safety folks who wandered in let slip a few things. FfW or copycats were petrol-bombing a variety of targets to make trouble. Nothing was as coordinated or devastating as a real FfW attack, but chaos is chaos and the government lost when too much chaos flared.

To oppose chaos, Bernard imposed more order and, at least in the Capital District, Basalt Militia called up its MechWarriors and authorized patrols. The locals got great imagery of 'Mechs striding through the streets. Their torsos swung left and right, weapon muzzles tracked up and down. It was the first time in decades Basalt had seen such a sight.

Bernard must have hired an image consultant because some of the scenes were silly. I half-expected shots of a 'Mech on the outskirts of town helping tug a stuck hovercar back onto the road or something, but these displays went further. In probably the most ridiculous of all, a pilot emerged from the cockpit of a *Hatchetman* to provide a tourist with directions. She looked great, the tourists thankful, but the whole thing was rather farcical.

Things began a slow escalation and likely would have taken two weeks or more to reach the flashpoint save for an event that was broadcast live. Count Germayne appeared at one of the Basalt Foundation kitchens—doubtless sent there to reap the benefit of association with Bianca, who was quite popular. The Count donned an apron and was on the serving line dishing up soup. He'd hand a bowl to his daughter who would then place it on a patron's tray. People would smile and nod and the Count almost looked as if he was enjoying himself.

Then one young man named Gavin Prin—as Davion a specimen as Bernard or Teyte—produced a small holdout laser and lit the Count up from point-blank range. The red beam burned in halfway between right nipple and breastbone. The Count looked down at the black hole in his apron, then staggered back while the youth shifted for another shot. Bianca interposed herself between the assassin and her father and the man hesitated just long enough for other patrons to tackle him.

The shot put the Count in critical condition in the hospital. I caught flashes of the same folks who had worked on me laboring hard to save his life. Bianca traveled to the hospital and was there, with Quam using his considerable bulk and Snookums' growl to keep the media at a respectful distance. Still, the long shots showed her sobbing, then looking up tearfully as a doctor came to give her the Count's prognosis.

Bernard got nowhere near the hospital. Within fifteen minutes he was live on Tri-Vid, having assumed his father's authority. He looked shaken, so I dismissed any possibility that he had tried to have his father assassinated. He put the planet under martial law, declared the would-be assassin to be an agent of FfW and then dropped a huge bombshell.

He stared right out at the viewers and said, "I have been given secret but incontrovertible evidence that Freedom from Want is funded entirely by Aldrington Emblyn. I have ordered his immediate arrest. He will be tried for treason and attempted murder, in accord with our law, with all penalties allowed to be applied."

Almost immediately the view cut to a live shot of Public Safety officers taking Emblyn into custody. He, too, was shaken, though that quickly flowed into outrage. "I am innocent of any and all charges of treason. All I have ever wanted for Basalt is the best, and you all know I have given it to you. Once everything is sorted out, the people of Basalt will see this for what it is: a purge of those Bernard Germayne hates. Beware, my fellow citizens, for as I am now, soon you shall be, unless you dare to be free."

Teyte, ashen-faced, looked away from the Tri-Vid unit

as Oates' squawker rang. The man unclipped it from his belt and went into the back bedroom to speak in private. Teyte blinked twice and, just for a moment, seemed very vulnerable.

I saw a chance and I took it. "I hope you're certain of Bernard. If he plays this wrong, it all goes away. He can ruin this."

"Shut up!"

I let surprise fit like a mask over my face. "You don't actually think he had his father murdered, do you?"

Teyte shook his head quickly. "No, he couldn't have."

"You better hope not."

"What do you mean by that?"

"Think about it. The only evidence he has that Emblyn is involved in things is me. He doesn't want me able to contradict him: I know too much to be allowed to live." I jerked my head at the back room. "That call. That could be Bernard telling Oates that he has to kill us both, make it look like you came to capture me and I shot you, Oates shot me. It's perfect. He eulogizes you, since he can't eulogize his father quite yet, and he gets rid of a popular rival to power."

"No, he wouldn't do that."

"No?" I shook my head. "Call him. See if he's talking on his squawker."

Teyte took the bait. He pulled his communications device and dialed. "Bernard, this is Teyte. Donelly's saying you had your father attacked and that you're going to kill us because he can't be left alive!" What he said was actually a bit more hysterical than that, and referred to me with a sobriquet that most JumpShippers would hesitate to use.

What he said really didn't matter, however. Bernard spoke and Teyte started nodding. He said, "Yes, yes, of course, never doubted it. Yes, I will. I'll tell him." He then lowered the squawker and smiled calmly in my direction.

"He said to tell you that you were right. You can't be left alive." Teyte slipped his right hand to the small of his back and drew out a squat black needle pistol. They shoot slivers carved from a block of weapons'-grade polymer. My previous comments about exit wounds don't really apply, save that a shot to my chest or throat would kill me, and a postmortem shot to the face would make me look like a bowl full of soggy shredded wheat.

With lots of blood splashed around, just for fun.

He reached over with his left hand to cock the weapon, then the squawker rang. Teyte turned it over, looked at the small screen and got a puzzled expression on his face. "What the . . . ?"

The apartment door crashed inward, half torn from the hinges. A Public Safety officer in Hauberk armor burst into the room. Teyte came around, the pistol tracking the lead target. He snapped off a shot, but the needles just skipped off the armor like toothpicks hurled against a wall. The armored figure's right arm came up. Scarlet bolts of cohesive light burned through the air. The heat flashed against my face, and vaporized both Teyte's chest and bits of the wall behind him. He dropped to the floor with a trio of smoking holes in his chest.

Oates came from the back room, with a pistol in one hand and identification in the other. "Police!" he yelled, but his pistol came up and swept toward me.

Before it could accidentally misfire, Niemeyer raised his right hand and fired from the doorway. The laser bolt sizzled past my head, singeing a bit of hair. The lead officer cut to the back room and pronounced it clear.

The visor on Niemeyer's armor came up. "We're even now, Donelly."

I nodded, stunned. "What are you doing here?"

"Saving your ass."

"Why?"

Niemeyer snorted. "Some people think you're worth saving." He stepped into the room, then waved toward the hall. "You have powerful friends, Donelly."

I looked up and Janella strode into the room.

37

It is a silly little game where nobody wins.

—Thomas Fuller

Manville, Capital District
Basalt
Prefecture IV, Republic of the Sphere
27 February 3133

I looked at her and held my smile back. "Do I know you?"

Lady Janella Lakewood nodded rather regally. "Yes, Sam, you do. Colonel Niemeyer knows we have worked together before."

I nodded. Janella had gone with option one, which was to depict me as an informant who had been useful to her in the past. Niemeyer still wouldn't like me, but he'd trust me a bit more. He'd trust her a whole lot. In many ways this was the best choice of cover, since it minimized my notoriety and let my current files stand. He'd imagine that I worked with Janella to get some of the charges against me reduced to nothing.

One of the Public Safety officers undid my cuffs and I rubbed at my wrists. "Oates, Teyte and another officer nabbed me after I left the hospital. They brought me here and were just holding me until Bernard could squeeze some time into his schedule for making me very dead. Even if you caught the last call and can decrypt it, he'll deny everything."

I looked up. "How did you find me, anyway?"

Niemeyer smiled. "The taxi driver you had is a chronic complainer. He got roughed up resisting arrest once—we wanted to take his taxi out of service to look for evidence and he objected. He's always in and out complaining about something. When they grabbed you, he came immediately to headquarters and started filling forms out. He recognized Teyte and Carlson—the other officer. We got authorization from a magistrate to look for the location data for their squawkers. We narrowed it down to this sector, brought in special equipment and triangulated. We found you."

"What took you so long?"

Janella frowned at me. "We had to find a magistrate who could authorize the squawker monitoring and yet would not spill his guts to the Germaynes." She looked at Niemeyer. "Colonel, I would suggest your report on this incident concerns the wiping out of an FfW cell. There were casualties, with identities withheld, pending notification of next of kin. Sam would be the only person identified as being dead."

The big man frowned. "That will make Bernard think he is safe, which might free him to do more."

I stood, then reached back and supported myself on the chair. "He'll know he hasn't heard from Teyte, and this Carlson will likely let him know he's not heard from Oates. He'll know something is up. He's going to feel pressure no matter what we do."

"Well, Carlson's on ice, so that's not a problem." Niemeyer pointed at Teyte's squawker. "If you want to grab that and turn it off, people will leave messages, which will buy us some time. He won't know Teyte is gone for a bit yet."

I did as he suggested, killing the squawker. "Okay, so this pulls a little bit of pressure off him, but not enough because bigger trouble is going to come rolling down the line and fast. Bernard has Emblyn, and Emblyn isn't going to stand for that."

Niemeyer lifted the helmet from his armor and tucked it under his right arm. "He's limited in what he can do, though. Lawyers will wrangle, but treason isn't an offense that will allow him to get out of jail. He's stuck."

"With him, it's going to be less actually being in jail than it will be his being in Bernard's power. I imagine he'll have his people unleash waves of terror attacks, and the real deal this time. Lots of people will die, and I'd not put it past him to have Catford spring him from jail."

The colonel looked past me toward the apartment's window. In the distance somewhere was the Capital District holding facility. "A battle to get him free would cause so much damage . . ."

"Agreed, so we can't let that happen." I smiled. "We won't."

Janella's eyes narrowed. "What are you thinking, Sam?"

"Colonel, Public Safety arrested Emblyn, so he's nominally in your control, right? You could move him if you thought there was a safety issue, couldn't you?"

The big man slowly nodded. "It would take a little doing, but it could be done."

"Good. We know they'll be coming for him one way or another, so we have to minimize collateral damage. I have an idea about how to do that and, just perhaps, get everyone and everything right where we want it." I glanced at Janella. "Did you bring a ride?"

"Two, and a delivery system."

"Two's not much, but we might let them rip each other up for a bit before we have to intervene."

Niemeyer frowned. "I thought you said you're going to minimize collateral damage. Letting Emblyn's people chew on the militia and Bernard's private corps doesn't sound like it will stop them from laying waste to Basalt."

"Oh, the battle will be sloppy, so we'll just have to get them to fight it in a place where neatness doesn't count." I gave him a smile. "In a tourist book on Basalt I ran across a mention of a place that I think would be perfect: Obsidian Island."

Janella's eyebrows rose questioningly, but Niemeyer just smiled. "Yeah, that will work perfectly. And, you know what? I think I might just be able to help you even the odds."

Obsidian Island is one of those weird, storied places that every world has. They are just tailor-made to be haunted, absent hideous murders being carried out inside or battles fought around them. The place's complete and utter isolation helps, likewise the fact that virtually no one visits and only the bravest of hearts spend the night.

And those who do tell alarming tales of the experience.

Sure, it's likely ninety-nine percent tourist hype, promoted by a service that for five hundred stones would run you out there and, for three times as much, arrange for a night's stay. Not the sort of rates or place that would bring any but the most weird from off-world to visit.

Technically speaking, it's not an island and isn't made of obsidian. Located south and west of Manville, in the heart of a huge rain forest preserve, Obsidian Island is a barren platform of rock in the heart of a small, black-water lake reputed to be the home of monsters. A small curved causeway connects the island to the shore, though the roadway is overgrown with weeds. The shore is also rocky and provides a dark crescent between the lake and the rain forest. While some hearty plants have tried to colonize the rock, their efforts are several centuries shy of success.

The island itself boasts a huge castle made of basalt and trimmed in obsidian. While styled after Terran medieval fortresses, this one has none of the weathering. The two centuries that have passed since its construction have not been especially kind to it, but those who created it meant for it to withstand anything this side of a nuclear blast. Unlike the knights of yore, however, they were not concerned with keeping people out as much as they intended to keep one man in.

Tacitus Germayne is not much mentioned in the histories of Basalt, and really is little more than a footnote in a grand family's history. The second son of the ruling count, he just was never quite right. Stories of petty cruelties were hushed up, payments were made, witnesses suppressed. It's hard to judge what the family was thinking at the time, but realizing that a child of yours has grown into a homicidal sociopath can't be easy to accept. They denied it and, while they got help for him, when that failed they just hired more and more.

Tacitus had developed an unhealthy affection for Gilles de Rais, a French nobleman and friend of Joan of Arc. De Rais, who had a nearly inexhaustible treasury and enough power that governmental forces were unable to stop him, delved into demonology. He murdered countless boys— peasants by and large, so as to escape notice—and it was not until he defied both the Church and the Crown that societal forces combined to crush him.

Tacitus only notched up five victims before he was caught. He was tried and convicted in two cases of murder and in the other three was judged innocent by reason of mental defect. The net result was that he was to be institutionalized until cured, then his consecutive life sentences for the other murders would go into effect. He would never walk free.

His family, however, still loved him and created for him Obsidian Island. They paid for its construction themselves, then ceded it to the government, where it was registered as both a mental institution for the criminally insane and a penitentiary. It is said that Tacitus took to wearing the same sort of clothes Gilles de Rais did: fabulous robes of scarlet and gold. He would only speak ancient French and would use no commercially produced product. He fled into his psychosis completely and died there at the age of 108 after seventy-five years of incarceration.

Niemeyer did a great job of convincing Bernard's people that moving Emblyn to Obsidian Island—which technically was still a prison—was just the thing to do. Not only did it isolate him from communications, but his imprisonment there would cast him as the new Tacitus. This would be particularly damning in the court of public opinion, or so Bernard's people were led to conclude. Niemeyer added that the lack of distractions would make it easier for his people to fend off attackers, provided, of course, they weren't coming in 'Mechs.

He was told, in no uncertain terms, that would not be a problem.

Bernard immediately deployed a mixed company of Basalt Militia and a light lance of his private security troops to the Obsidian Island area. This was a tactical error, since he knew that FfW commanded a much larger force. To a certain extent, however, it was forced on him, because if he pulled all his resources from Manville, FfW would have a field day tearing the city apart and he'd be left looking like a fool.

Things got coordinated pretty well so that FfW wouldn't hit too early. Niemeyer announced that, "for his safety," Aldrington Emblyn would be moved to Obsidian Island very soon. He further avowed that media would be allowed to cover the transfer, but on a pool feed basis. The media fought over who would actually be the pool reporters, and backed things up by positioning themselves all over the area of the jail to catch things. That just turned the jail into a chaotic arena where no commander would want to put troops.

The transfer occurred on the twenty-ninth, which meant Catford and Bernard had two days to plan their attacks and marshal their forces. Niemeyer stationed the best of his troops in the fortress, but aside from mounting some short-range missile launchers on the battlements, they and their Hauberk armor would be toys against what was coming. Janella and I were set to go in the 'Mechs she'd brought—including my new ride, Ghost. I thought it was rather appropriate to be in a 'Mech with that name at that place. When the time came, the Leopard-class DropShip would drop us into the fray.

The reason she'd come to Basalt ready for war was because of some back-checking done against the message sent to recruit Sam. Republic researchers had uncovered a lot of messages going out, and load factors for ships traveling to Basalt spiked when compared to those leaving, both in sheer numbers and pilot demographics. When warriors are coming in and families are going away, trouble is brewing. She actually got my first couple of reports in a bunch when she reached Fletcher, which is why she went to Niemeyer when she arrived.

The only complication to the plan to minimize collateral damage came when Bernard decided that Gavin Prin, the youth who had shot his father, should likewise be sent there. It actually was a smart move on Bernard's part, because it strengthened the linkage between the young man and Emblyn. Any rescue attempt on Emblyn would seem like one for Prin. Prin actually had no connection to Emblyn. He'd lived in Manville for a while after dropping out of the university. Earlier on the day when he'd shot the Count, he'd been informed that his father had been killed in a riot-suppression action up north, so he struck out while angry. While that story was known at the time, Bernard's spokespeople spun it into a tale of evil where Emblyn had used the tragedy to twist the young man into a monster.

Gypsy and Catford waited until the afternoon of the thirtieth to strike. The FfW forces came in two groups, with my command being given over to Siwek, as expected. That wing, made up of a heavy 'Mech lance and two wings of light and medium vehicles came in from the west, then angled down sharply to the south, while Catford's force had started from the south, then turned almost due west. It sported two lances of 'Mechs, one heavy, the other light, with vehicles to round out the company. This gave FfW half again as many 'Mechs and far more vehicles.

Bernard had invited disaster, and he was going to get it in huge handfuls. The FfW made no attempt to hide what they were doing: little drones that Niemeyer flew from Obsidian Island were able to track the heat signatures coming in. He relayed the information to Bernard and to us, back in Manville. Bernard seemed unconcerned, which made him as mad as Tacitus in my book.

Janella glanced through the holographic projection in the *Valiant*'s main cabin. "Time to target from here is twenty minutes. We'll have clearance to leave as soon as we request it."

I flipped the display over to a tactical map that calculated the time to contact between the forces. "The eastern force will arrive first and engage, then the northern force will hit the Militia flank. Forty minutes to contact. We leave in fifteen?"

"Twenty, I think. Catford will want to go at it immediately, but if they don't start shooting right away, we aren't going to be able to tip the balance."

"This isn't going to be pretty, and it isn't going to take long." I sighed. "I just hope we can tip the balance, because the alternative is having the whole thing come crashing down on us."

She reached through the holograph and stroked my hand. "I know, lover, so we'll just have to be especially good. We might not be able to trip the giant up but, with any luck and a good push, we can determine where he lands when he falls."

38

He who bears the brand of Cain shall rule the earth.
                                        —George Bernard Shaw

Obsidian Island, Blacklake District
Basalt
Prefecture IV, Republic of the Sphere
2 March 3133

The battle started while we were en route, but Niemeyer's drone and Tri-Vid-cam feeds gave us more of the battle than we really wanted. I kept the image from Obsidian Island on my secondary monitor, then channeled the feeds from drones to my auxiliary monitors. Once I'd done all my system checks on Ghost, I flipped the Obsidian Island view onto my holographic combat display. Despite my being tucked away in the DropShip's hold, I felt as if I was in the middle of the fight.

Unlike Teyte, however, I did not let my hands stray to the targeting joysticks. I'd have more than enough work for them soon, and pulling a trigger in the hold was not a good idea.

Bernard had arrayed his forces somewhat poorly. From Obsidian Island we had the Basalt Militia company on the left, then a small gap and Bernard along with his mercenaries. They stood with their backs to the lake, which was not a tactical disadvantage by any means, but the gap between the two units could be exploited. Only a hundred meters separated them, but that was enough for an enemy wedge to split them. Once that was done, so were they.

The Militia had one of the two largest forces entering the battle, though two of their 'Mechs were modified ForestryMechs that were grossly underarmored and undergunned. A *Panther* and a *Centurion* rounded out their 'Mech lance, but both of those machines were antiques. Such a force was certainly a sign of the times—resources were in short supply and improvisation was the order of the day. The other two lances they supplied consisted of vehicles. The Shandra Scout Vehicles made up their northern flank, and were fast enough to be tough targets to hit. Four Demons made up the center of their position and would be nasty in the fight. If their love for their homeworld made up for their lack of combat experience, they could be key to the battle's resolution.

The Militia would face Siwek's force, which had been arrayed rather oddly. The two lances of vehicles—mixed Scimitars and Condors—formed the right and center of her front respectively. This placed her duo of 'Mechs—her *Ryoken II* and a *Pack Hunter*—closest to Catford's formation and left the vehicles to harry the Militia from the north. Her 'Mechs were positioned to drive into that gap and against Militia troops, a move that would likely demoralize them and could even spark a retreat. A pair of SM1 Tank Destroyers backed her 'Mechs with serious firepower.

Catford let his vehicle lance take up his left wing. He'd chosen four JES Tactical Missile Carriers, which bristled with SRM launchers. In close combat, the quick hovercraft could be devastating. Given that they'd skirmish with Bernard's lance of Scimitars, there would be a lot of carnage at the south end of the battlefield.

Catford's 'Mech lance would make up the center of the FfW line once it joined up with Siwek's force. In addition to his *Jupiter* and the *Catapult* from the Palace, he added a *Black Hawk* and an *Arbalest*. His 'Mech lance was the heaviest in the battle, and well suited to blasting enemies at range, or wading right into things—which I had no doubt he would do.

Bernard's 'Mech lance did not boast as much power, but could still be very effective. He piloted his *Catapult*, and also had an *Arbalest* to help with long-range missile attacks. A *Legionnaire* and a *Hatchetman* made up in accuracy what they lacked in firepower. Whether or not that would turn the battle's tide, I didn't want to hazard a guess, but the way the forces were arrayed, the FfW troops had the edge and, I expected, would win the day if fate or other forces did not intervene to ruin things.

Janella's voice came in over the neurohelmet's speakers. "I want us dropped to the north, so we can support the Militia."

I agreed. "Check. We take the vehicles and roll up the 'Mech flank."

"You're reading my mind."

I smiled. "I just hope doing it is as easy as thinking it." She did not reply, but the two of us knew it wouldn't be. One very real possibility was that we dropped into the fight and both sides blasted us. Bernard had showed no compunction against shooting up Niemeyer's people, and he'd be even less well disposed against us. We were dropping into a situation that could get very bad, very quickly.

But, then, we really had no alternative.

On the big display, with five minutes yet to target, the first of the hovertanks that had come in from the north assembled to attack the Militia. Over on the far right, Catford's Missile Carriers emerged onto the plain. The Jessies arrayed themselves in a screen before pulling back to form the left flank. Then, like warriors emerging from the forest, the 'Mechs began appearing. Some looked very human, like the *Jupiter* and *Arbalest*—and strode forth as if they were hunters returning from an expedition. Others, like the *Catapult* in Catford's force, emerged like mechanical beasts preparing to invade the battlefield.

Bernard's combined force turned its fury on Catford's battalion. Clouds of long-range missiles arced across the battlefield. The targeting choices almost seemed planned out well as salvos pounded the *Catapult* and *Arbalest*, which had long-range fire capabilities. Why he didn't go after Catford I couldn't imagine. I thought at the time it might have been some misplaced sense of honor, but subsequent events proved that assumption wrong on several grounds.

Vehicles from all sides came in fast to harry and nip at the flanks. They launched missiles and fired lasers. Their attacks shattered some armor, bubbled it up in other places. One of the Militia's Scout Cars fell victim to a coordinated assault by Siwek's Condors. It exploded spectacularly. One burning wheel flew and bounced over the battlefield in an omen of what awaited the combatants. On that side of the field, however, only the Militia advanced. Bernard held his troops back, even his Scimitars, letting Catford's troops draw closer for reasons I could not fathom.

The scene in my cockpit shifted as *Valiant*'s pilot gave us a direct feed from his nose cameras. We swept over Obsidian Island, passing just beyond Bernard's right flank. Flights of missiles launched from both sides, scarring the air with vapor trails, then wreathing 'Mechs with fire. Catford's 'Mechs had moved out ahead of the FfW line. Siwek's 'Mechs and SM1s were slow to deploy. Her vehicles continued the attacks on the Militia, wreaking yet more havoc. Siwek's hovertanks weathered the counterattacks and continued to close to point-blank range, where their fire would be murderous.

The view shifted to other cameras on the DropShip as we came about. A tone sounded through the cockpit, quickly followed by staccato piping. When those trilled sounds ended . . .

The drop bay snapped open and Ghost slipped into the air. My holoview shifted to that supplied by the *Mad Cat III*'s own sensors, and a timer in the lower right corner counted down until landfall. I braced myself in the command couch and at five seconds I hit the landing rockets. They roared beneath the cockpit and slowed my descent just enough that, when I hit, the jolt merely loosened teeth in my head, but didn't rattle them free.

"Down and full green." I hit a button on the left joystick, jettisoning the landing rockets, then turned left and pointed myself at the battle. My display lit up with dozens of targets as Janella's *Tundra Wolf* stalked up on my right. Our 'Mechs were resplendent in the red and gold of Republic armed forces, and there wasn't a combatant down there that didn't realize that the banner and silver star at the *Tundra Wolf*'s throat meant a Knight of The Republic had just entered the battle.

Our intent had been to lay into the vehicles attacking the Basalt Militia. During our drop, they'd closed and unleashed another attack, which had crushed two more of the Shandras. One burned where it stood, a blackened skeleton, while the other cartwheeled back into the lake to disappear in a cloud of steam. A concentrated set of salvos from Catford's 'Mechs and I was fairly certain the Militia's inexperienced pilots would break, leaving Bernard and us to be overwhelmed by FfW's superior numbers.

Before we could begin to even the odds, however, the tide of battle shifted dramatically and I learned why Bernard had not gone directly after Catford. It was, instead, his intention to torture the man. Catford, who likely saw the battle of Obsidian Island as his return to glory, got to watch his dreams evaporate.

Driving further south and hooking back to the west, Captain Isabel Siwek brought her command lance around and unloaded everything they had into Catford's 'Mech lance. The bird-legged *Catapult* just crumpled like a toy hit with a sledgehammer. One of the SM1s blasted the *Arbalest* with the autocannon, blowing its chest apart. The humanoid 'Mech staggered backward, then crashed into the trees. A small, resilient sapling snapped upward through its missing chest and wavered there for a second before bursting into flame.

Bernard had bought Siwek and her company of 'Mechs with a hefty bribe. As her treachery became manifest, Bernard's mercenaries launched more missiles at Catford's command. They concentrated on the heavier of the remaining two 'Mechs. Missile explosions rippled over the *Jupiter* but could not bring it to bay.

"Lead, which is it? Cat or the Rat?"

"Save the Militia."

"As ordered, lead." The command made sense, as the Militia troops were the only innocents in the battle. I dropped the gold crosshairs on the *Black Hawk*, got a pulsing dot in the heart of them to indicate a lock, then tightened up on two triggers. Ghost rocked back and down as forty missiles arced skyward, then converged on the 'Mech.

Waves of heat washed over me, and watching the damage done sent a chill through me.

The missiles sowed fire all over and around the *Black Hawk*, pulverizing armor. It fell in a ferro-ceramic blizzard around the 'Mech's feet, in some cases sloughing off in whole sheets. The humanoid engine of war wavered for a moment as the smoke cleared. The pilot fought to keep the machine in balance, but the sudden loss of tons of armor and the battering it had taken left him unable to control it. It pitched forward, smashing down on a knee and then its hands.

Janella used lasers and LRMs to further savage the 'Mech. Missiles shattered yet more armor, then the ruby needles of her medium lasers stabbed into the myomer muscles providing the 'Mech's strength. The corded fibers in the left arm parted with a snap, flicking little gobbets of artificial tissue into the air. The *Black Hawk*'s left arm crumpled, plowing its shoulder and head into the ground. Her attack left it struggling vainly to rise again.

Though clearly surprised by Isabel Siwek's treachery, Catford reacted swiftly and brutally. He spun his *Jupiter* with an agility I'd not expected and extended both of his 'Mech's arms toward Siwek's *Ryoken II*. The pair of PPCs mounted on the left forearm crackled with artificial lightning. Their jagged cerulean beams slashed the squat 'Mech. One seared an ugly scar up through the left side of the body while the other danced lightning over the cockpit itself. Melting armor gushed in a torrent down to the ground, where it bubbled and smoked.

The quartet of autocannons on the *Jupiter*'s left forearm likewise proved terrifyingly efficient. Two chewed their way into the armor on the left arm and right thigh, leaving stippled trails of granulated armor behind. The other two, however, blasted into the cockpit, obliterating the canopy. Whether it was the hail of glass ripping her to shreds, or the heavy slugs pulping her human remains, Isabel Siwek died as ugly as the treachery she'd been a party to.

Bernard's mercenaries again launched on Catford's command. Missile fire pounded his *Jupiter*, but he didn't go down. The Militia blasted back at the incoming vehicles in Siwek's command. While they showed little coordination in their attack, fortune smiled and their attacks knocked out several of the hovertanks while they only lost one Demon Medium Tank.

With Siwek down, her company could have buckled, but being professionals they held it together and began to maneuver cautiously to close with their former allies. Catford's *Jupiter* exploded a Condor, but took some laser and autocannon fire in return, then another salvo or two of missiles.

Janella's *Tundra Wolf* laced a Scimitar's right flank with laser fire. The green and red beams turned armor molten and opened a fiery hole into the crew compartment. That hovertank slew around to the side before both fans died. Its burning hulk marked a point past which none of Siwek's other vehicles advanced.

This was good for the Militia, but not so good for us. The remaining Scimitar and three Condors began to maneuver to focus on us. I used more missiles to rake one of the Condor tanks. I got lucky and popped the left tread off the tank, which created more of a driving hazard for the others than any serious damage. As one spun to the left to avoid the stricken tank, it plowed into the downed *Black Hawk*'s right arm. Neither of them benefited from the collision. The Condor remained operational, but the one I'd hit slammed into it from behind, wedging it in place.

Bernard Germayne might not have been the most politically savvy guy, but as a tactician he had some talent. The battle hinged on finishing Catford's force as fast as possible before he had to deal with us. We were a wild card and, for the moment, we were being played in his favor. With Catford gone, he'd have his company, Siwek's company and the remains of the Militia, against which the two of us could not possibly stand. Killing a Knight of The Republic could have repercussions, there was no doubt about it, but if he was in firm control of the planet, the chances of retribution coming swiftly given the current crisis were negligible.

His *Catapult* launched two more salvos that laced Catford's *Jupiter* with explosions. Armor shards whirled away, shattering further on the hard ground. The *Jupiter* seemed to hunch down, like an old man beneath a pounding rain, then rose up again, but did not turn to face Bernard. I don't know if, in that moment, Catford realized he was not going to walk away from this fight, or chose to die in it to avoid the humiliation of being trapped and beaten. I might even give him the benefit of the doubt and suggest he decided to save some of his people. He sent his *Jupiter* into the midst of Siwek's company, blazing away with the autocannons and PPCs, laying about with his right arm, smashing the *Pack Hunter*.

He did make inroads into their formation, but he never made it all the way through their murderous return fire. With its armor in tatters and right arm melted beyond recognition, the *Jupiter* fell forward. Fire vomited from the cockpit as the command couch ejection system ignited. The rockets that should have boosted him high into the air instead smashed him into the stone crescent around Blacklake.

With Catford's death, the FfW left wing stopped its battle against Bernard's Scimitars. The three remaining Jessies swiveled their SRM launchers skyward in surrender, and clearly some intense negotiation went on. When the launchers came back down and the vehicles oriented northward, I figured the negotiations had ended in Bernard's favor.

Bernard's mercenaries and the remains of the FfW fighters turned toward us.

Janella's voice came through strongly and loudly over the radio. "Lord Bernard Germayne, I am Lady Janella Lakewood, Knight of The Republic of the Sphere. You and your people are to power down immediately. You are under arrest for conspiracy to murder a Republic citizen."

Arrogance filled Bernard's reply. "I control Basalt. Your Republic is powerless. Your charges have no validity here. You have no authority here. You are not wanted here. Leave my planet."

"Lord Germayne, I ask you again to surrender, for the consequences of your refusal will be most dire." Janella kept her voice even, but a little bit of an edge crept in. "Surrender, if not for yourself, then for your people. They need not die for your foolishness."

"Your arrogance is unbelievable, woman." I could see the sneer on Bernard's face as he said that. "A hundred thousand C-bills to the one who kills her."

In saying that, he gave Janella no choice.

She employed Colonel Niemeyer's surprise.

39

*Of all the nasty surprises to be had, stumbling into
a trap of your own making has to be the worst.*
—Anonymous, quoted posthumously

Obsidian Island, Blacklake District
Basalt
Prefecture IV, Republic of the Sphere
2 March 3133

Bernard Germayne had managed to make for himself two
enemies, one old and one rather new. The old one, Colonel
Niemeyer, disliked Bernard as much as he loved Basalt. I'd
seen his love for the world in the first visit he paid me. It
never occurred to me that he'd have treated anyone else
less harshly than he had me when he became aware of their
presence, and he had not. He'd even kept tabs on us as
best his resources allowed.

Which reacquainted him with Bernard's newest enemy.
Alba Dolehide really had not appreciated Bernard's lack of
trust in her, so she ran—right to Niemeyer. She'd correctly
guessed that Niemeyer could hide her until things cooled
off. She wanted to see Bernard brought down—both for

personal reasons and because it was no mystery to her what sort of lousy ruler he'd make.

As a brake on him she'd even absconded with the location of a mixed lance of Bernard's toys. Once the confrontation had been set for Obsidian Island, Niemeyer rounded up a group of pilots to man those machines and they were brought to a point in the jungle just west of the killing field. Since Niemeyer's people were handling perimeter security, all reports of contacts in that direction were edited out of data sent to Bernard.

Short-range missiles shot from Obsidian Island, corkscrewing into their targets. Their detonations blasted craters in armor, but dropped no 'Mechs. Niemeyer's people directed their fire at Bernard's mercenaries and the remnants of the FfW, leaving the Militia untouched. Once they'd launched their missiles, they hunkered down to let pilots waste munitions and hot light on the ancient fortress.

The long-range shots from Alba's lance likewise pounded the mercenaries, but with far more effect. She piloted an *Arbalest* and its missile salvo crunched the aft armor of a *Legionnaire*. The missiles opened its back and the autocannon ammo in the right side of its chest cooked off. The resulting explosion tossed the humanoid 'Mech to the right, where it clipped the mercenary *Arbalest* standing next to it.

Bernard and his people faced some tough choices. While Bernard didn't fear attacking a Republic Knight, others in his command were more thoughtful, and yet others utterly mindless. The eager but stupid pilot in the *Hatchetman* launched his 'Mech into the air on jump jets. With the club upraised, he clearly intended to strike a swift blow and earn the bounty on Janella's head.

Calmly and coldly, Janella backed the *Tundra Wolf* and brought the right arm up. The quartet of medium lasers snapped red light at the flying 'Mech. All but one struck it in the right elbow, vaporizing the last of its armor and burning into the joint. Titanium bones glowed red on their way to white, then became fluid. The forearm and club sailed away and the 'Mech, unbalanced, came down hard on the left leg. The hip joint snapped, driving the thigh up into the torso. The left arm flailed, as did the smoking stump of the right, then the 'Mech fell back. It smashed into the ground, shaking it, and shaking the confidence of those who thought the bounty would be easily won.

The warriors who had been in Siwek's command hesitated before entering the fight. Catford's Jessies did come forward, clearly anxious to win Bernard's favor. With Alba's people behind Bernard's position the tactical situation balanced out the forces arrayed against us. It should have been an even fight.

What unbalanced it, however, was the Basalt Militia. As the commander said afterward, Janella and I had come into the fight and defended his people and planet. Bernard might have wanted to dispute his arrest, but ordering the murder of a Republic Knight wasn't the way to do that. Being forced to choose sides, they chose for us and laid down a pattern of fire that drove the venturesome Jessies back.

All these actions happened in the course of five seconds, and I watched them with the same distance I'd watched Tri-Vid dramas while Teyte's prisoner. I was in the combat, no doubt about it, but I was still detached from it. I knew that was how I had to be as a Ghost Knight.

I also realized it was wrong.

My mind flashed to the kitchen where I'd helped serve meals. Quam had said it would become a charnel house, but I saw another vision. I saw it as a prison compound, with Bernard's enemies, wasted and filthy, warehoused until the whim struck him to kill them. He would do that without question, and with his leadership, others on Basalt would follow him. His poison would infect them and this beautiful world would die.

Detachment and distance indeed *had* been my stock in trade, but that was during a time when The Republic had been strong and able to deal with problems like this in a benign manner. My job was to investigate and seek solutions others could implement. The problem now was that Bernard was a force that was accelerating entropy, and the only way to counter that was to inject more energy into the system.

My energy.

I discovered that Bernard had made himself a third enemy: ME.

I brought my crosshairs around and dropped them on the outline of Bernard's *Catapult*. Without a second's hesitation I launched two flights of missiles at him, and he returned the favor. Both of our attacks hit solidly. Heat from the missile launchings flooded my cockpit, then his missiles poured down over me. Ghost shook as if in an earthquake and the explosions sounded as if I were in the heart of a Basalt thunderstorm. Light flashed, shrapnel pinged. Alarms went off in my cockpit and the outline of my 'Mech on the primary monitor went from green to yellow as armor was reduced to dust.

My *Mad Cat III* staggered, but I managed to keep it on its feet despite a feeling of dizziness and sweat burning into my eyes. Though my 'Mech massed less than the *Catapult*, I could hit harder. My only weakness was that Ghost was a bit more fragile than Bernard's 'Mech. As the smoke cleared around me, I cut to the left, moving perilously close to Siwek's old command.

Another barrage from Alba's lance nibbled at the rear of Bernard's mercenary formation. Her troops emerged from the rain forest and were angling toward the last of Siwek's command, but kept their fire on Bernard's mercs. The implications were clear: they didn't have to get dead if they didn't want to. The Militia ripping into their former comrades gave everyone a pretty good indication of the locals' dislike for them.

Bernard fired at me again, but as we were both moving, half his missiles missed and the rest just ground armor away. I retaliated by hitting him with some lasers that burned away the last of the armor over his left thigh. Another chunk of damage there and he'd go down.

Easier said than done, however. He was already moving east, toward Siwek's company, doubtless exhorting them to enter the fight. With his 'Mech moving that fast, the chances of me getting a specific enough target lock to take that leg out were slim. Each step carried him further from me, but if I pursued, I would trade movement for range in targeting trouble.

Janella's voice crackled over the speakers. "Be aware, helping Bernard Germayne will subject you to arrest by The Republic as well. You can never hide. He cannot save you."

I keyed my microphone. "Not only that: he's broke. You'll never get what he promised you."

I must say that is the nice thing about mercenaries: they are loyal to themselves and have a fine grasp of microeconomics. The two SM1s swiveled their turrets and shot, but not at Bernard. Their autocannon fire gnawed through two of the Jessies. The rest of Siwek's old command focused on Bernard's mercs as well, making them into an "Oh God why me?" sandwich against Alba's force and the Militia.

Bernard flew on toward the rain forest, seeking escape. I punched two buttons on my communications console and tightbeamed a message to him. "Has Germayne blood turned yellow, Bernie? Is it that you're stupid enough to think that if you run away, you'll live to fight another day? Teyte didn't—I saw to that—and I'll do you, too."

I'm not sure if it was just the words, or his recognizing my voice, but sparks flared from beneath his 'Mech's feet as he brought it around to face me. The LRM launchers on the 'Mech's shoulders spat fire. His anger might have made him foolish, but it also focused him. Though my antimissile system whined and picked off a few projectiles, Bernard's salvos still smashed unerringly into Ghost, ripping the right arm clean off.

The blasts staggered the 'Mech. I slipped to the left— was knocked to that side, truth be told. Sweat and a bit of blood from my bitten tongue filled my mouth. Struggling with the controls, I kept the *Cat* upright, then shifted the left foot forward and raked my crosshairs over his 'Mech. Bernie, in what he saw as a moment of triumph, stood there, tall, imposing—his 'Mech mirroring his posture at our first meeting.

The gold dot on my crosshairs burned bright.

My missiles streaked out on smoky ropes linking me with him. He had no defense, but even the best would not have blunted my attack. His momentary motionlessness, his arrogance, gave me a better target than he really wanted. The missiles leaped from the *Cat*, then dipped down for a second before all arrowed in at his *Catapult*.

Bernard's 'Mech had lost all the armor from the left thigh. While not all my missiles struck that target, out of forty enough did reach it. Explosions clawed their way through the myomer muscles. They chopped at ferro-titanium bones, knocking great chips from them while other blasts just twisted and warped them. The *Catapult*, which massed sixty-five tons, shifted to the left as the ravaged bone screamed and parted. The shin fell back and the 'Mech crashed left.

It landed hard on a missile rack, which exploded and almost managed to pitch the 'Mech back upright. I could almost feel Bernard's spirit soaring for a second. In his mind, I was certain, he felt victory in his grasp.

He clung to it the way a drowning man clings to a life preserver.

It did no good. The *Catapult* crashed back down and Bernard's plans crashed with it.

And as smoke shrouded his ruined 'Mech, I smiled.

With the final shots they fired, Siwek's company became a mercenary unit led by Kim Knutson—the *Pack Hunter*'s pilot. They called themselves Knutson's Rangers and accepted a hundred-thousand-stone reward for holding Bernard's troops off—which I paid out of the monies I'd earned at Emblyn's casino. I believe their intention was to try to get off Basalt with their rides and offer their services as mercenaries in what they saw as coming troubles. Janella pointed out that this simply was not going to happen since they had been involved in actions to overthrow the legitimate government.

The government of Basalt came up with a plan that traded ten years of community service in return for full pardons. The Rangers and their equipment were drafted into the Basalt Militia, strengthening it greatly. Even before their service would be finished, those who were not Republic citizens would have earned the right to become citizens. While this was appreciated by many, it wasn't by one or two who believed The Republic would not last that long.

The plan and the general amnesty that moved toward reconciliation was crafted by the planet's new leadership. Count Hector did recover from his wound, but would never be the robust man he had been before. He had a change of heart, which many put down to rumors that he'd actually died in the hospital and had been revived. Others assumed that learning of his son's treachery had wounded him more deeply.

I put it down to the fact that while Bernard was off trying

to supplant his father, Bianca had been there at her father's side. The media reports would have had everyone believe that anyone Bianca had ever helped had turned around and sent messages and flowers, or made donations in her father's name. The outpouring of concern for how she felt was tremendous and, for once, the media couldn't blow it all out of proportion.

Bianca, at her father's request, assumed leadership of Basalt and immediately set about using her network of friends to calm fears, organize relief efforts and expand the sorts of things she was already doing. The people rallied around her and the peace that Basalt had known again descended on the planet.

Public Safety personnel did manage to nab Gypsy and, with just a little pressure, he began to sing loud and long about his affairs both on Basalt and elsewhere. Republic analysts are still poring over the transcripts of his interviews, pulling out tidbits. If even a tenth of what he reports is accurate, the burgeoning political storms on the horizon really could rend The Republic. Some people have dismissed his claims as clearly fanciful, but based on what I saw on Helen and Basalt, I fear he could tell us even more, all of it true.

His testimony was enough to convict Aldrington Emblyn of multiple counts of treason. Share prices of Ring's corporation collapsed abruptly, which caused something of a disaster for those people who had invested in it. Bianca's Basalt Foundation organized a relief effort there, funded by large donations by two savvy individuals who had shorted a vast amount of Emblyn stock. On the way back to the hotel from the hospital, I'd shorted a million shares and suggested to Quam that he do the same. He shorted two million: "When I get advice *that* good, I employ it twice."

Jacob Bannson swept in and snapped up Emblyn's holdings at fire-sale prices. He guaranteed jobs would continue and that he would find a way to let the entire Inner Sphere know what a stunning resort destination Basalt was. It was a quick and brilliant move on his part, for not only did it save Basalt's economy and let him expand into a market he'd not previously had, but everyone on Basalt thought nothing but the best of him. He'd bought a lot of loyalty, and I was afraid of how he might go about spending it.

My concerns stemmed from the fact that I was pretty sure Bannson had been the instigator behind everything. Isabel Siwek's files showed she'd been given a million stones to come over to Bernard's side, and Bernard didn't have that sort of money. Someone had bought him a present. I was fairly certain that someone was Elle, who had vanished. She'd set me up to be killed or arrested on the night of the raid on Number 8: if I'd not died there, Gypsy could have figured her leak to me became my leak to Bernard, so he'd have had me killed. Since I was a moderating influence and once I was out of the picture things escalated sharply, it struck me that she was playing both ends against the middle, and Bannson certainly did well in that middle.

My speculations about Bannson never made it into the media, primarily because the chronicler of all things treasonous and evil held himself to very high journalistic standards. Armed with exclusive interviews from a Republic Knight, Colonel Niemeyer, Kim Knutson, Countess Bianca Germayne and a shadowy insider who laid bare the entire covert war for control of Basalt, Quam vaulted from lifestyle commentary and restaurant reviews to investigative journalism at its finest. His stories, which were well written and delivered even better when he hosted a documentary series, elevated him to a position of respect that he never would have imagined he would know.

The other nice thing about working with Quam is that we were able to kill Sam Donelly and leave him dead. Bernard's conviction on charges of treason far overshadowed the auxiliary charge of conspiracy to murder Sam. Someday I'll go back to Obsidian Island and visit him. He'll have lots of time on his hands. I wonder if he'll want to play cards?

All is well, they say, that ends well, and the war for Basalt did end well. Casualties were minimized and damage done likewise. Still, there was some unfinished business that needed taking care of. Though I could only watch on Tri-Vid from a bar on Helen, I did smile as newly minted Republic Knight-Errant Nicodemus Niemeyer and his aide, Alba Dolehide—seconded to duty with him after her recall to and reinstatement in Stone's Lament—arrested Ichabod Reis.

When Gypsy started singing, the events on Helen had become very clear. Reis had hired Gypsy to organize a small terrorist group so the citizenry would back Reis' getting more power. In the jittery days after the HPG net went down, the plan worked perfectly.

Andy Harness turned on his barstool, jerked a thumb at the Tri-Vid projection, and smiled. "Could you believe that, Sam? He finally got what was coming to him. There he was, thinking he was invincible, and they got him. Shows there's some justice in the universe, after all."

"That there is." I wanted to tell him that Niemeyer's next task was to find him, interview him, and present him a lump sum representing all the pension he'd been robbed of, but that wasn't my place. I'd told Niemeyer to take holos. I wanted to see the look on Andy's face, but it was time for Sam Donelly to fully fade away.

I tossed a ten-stone note on the bar and pointed to Andy's mug. "Keep it coming and cold until this is gone." I slid from my stool and slapped him on the back. "Be good, Andy. Have a good life."

He looked up at me. "Don't say it like that, Sam, geez. Makes it sound as if I'll never see you again, as if you're dead or something."

"*In vino veritas*, and beer, profundity." I smiled and backed toward the door. "I *am* dead, Andy. You won't see me again."

"I'll see you again, Sam." The man hoisted his refilled mug in a salute. "You'll be around. You don't look like a ghost to me."

No, my friend, I don't, which is exactly why I am one.

DEEP-SPACE INTRIGUE AND ACTION FROM
BATTLETECH ®

LETHAL HERITAGE by Michael A. Stackpole.
Who are the Clans? One Inner Sphere warrior, Phelan Kell of the
mercenary group Kell Hounds, finds out the hard way—as their
prisoner and protégé. (453832)

BLOOD LEGACY by Michael A. Stackpole.
Jaime Wolf brought all the key leaders of the Inner Sphere together at his base
on Outreach in an attempt to put to rest old blood feuds and power struggles. For
only if all the Successor States unite their forces do they have any hope of
defeating this invasion by warriors equipped with BattleMechs far superior to
their own. (453840)

LOST DESTINY by Michael A. Stackpole.
As the Clans' BattleMech warriors continue their inward drive, with Terra itself as
their true goal, can Comstar mobilize the Inner Sphere's last defenses—or will
their own internal political warfare provide the final death blow to the empire
they are sworn to protect? (453859)

To order call: 1-800-788-6262

Don't miss out on any of the deep-space adventure
of the Bestselling **BATTLETECH**® Series.

To order call: 1-800-788-6262